LX 8/21

5/2021
McGRAW HOUSE LIBRARY

THE
MOST
INTANGIBLE
THING

ALSO BY
CLY BOEHS

BACK THEN

THE MOST INTANGIBLE THING

WE ARE WHAT WE TELL.
AND OUR RELATIONSHIPS TELL ALL.

CLY BOEHS

CRITICALLY-ACCLAIMED AUTHOR OF *BACK THEN*

LIFFEY PRESS

an imprint of
OGHMA CREATIVE MEDIA

OGHMA
CREATIVE MEDIA

Liffey Press
An imprint of Oghma Creative Media, Inc.
2401 Beth Lane, Bentonville, Arkansas 72701

Copyright © 2019 by Cly Boehs

We are a strong supporter of copyright. Copyright represents creativity, diversity, and free speech, and provides the very foundation from which culture is built. We appreciate you buying the authorized edition of this book and for complying with applicable copyright laws by not reproducing, scanning, or distributing any part of it in any form without permission. Thank you for supporting our writers and allowing us to continue publishing their books.

Library of Congress Cataloging-in-Publication Data

Names: Boehs, Cly, author.
Title: The Most Intangible Thing/Cly Boehs
Description: First Edition | Bentonville: Liffey, 2019
Identifiers: LCCN: 2019942398 | ISBN: 978-1-63373-530-9 (hardcover) | ISBN: 978-1-63373-531-6 (trade paperback) | ISBN: 978-1-63373-532-3 (eBook)
Subjects: | BISAC: FICTION/Literary | FICTION/Psychological | FICTION/Short Stories (single author) | FICTION/LGBT/General
LC record available at: https://lccn.loc.gov/2019942398

Liffey Press trade paperback edition September, 2019

Cover Design by Casey Cown
Interior Design by Erin Ladd
Editing by Gordon Bonnet

This book is a work of fiction. Any references to historical events, real people, or real places are used fictitiously. Other names, characters, places, and events are products of the author's imagination, and any resemblance to actual events or places or person, living or dead, is entirely coincidental.

To Gordon Bonnet
writing buddy, dear friend and faithful muse

Thanks so much for your enthusiasm, encouragement, wisdom and insight
and for all those lively critiques that have
helped me to hope and grow

ACKNOWLEDGEMENTS

My heartfelt thanks to Casey Cowan and Gordon Bonnet of Oghma Creative Media for all of their work, support and commitment to the publication of this book. Special thanks to Casey Cowan for his masterful design and a cover that I love. And to Gordon Bonnet for his careful editing and help in finding the best form for these stories and who has always encouraged and inspired me even when I resist and who swears every obstacle can be gone through, jumped over or flung out of the way. And he is always right, bless him! He's a joy to work with and a cherished friend.

Enormous gratitude to:

My parents, Frank Eugene Boehs and Viola Becker Boehs whose trust in my creative endeavors was boundless. They became the rock solid foundation for my efforts, especially in the later years of their lives.

Franki Jean Boehs Dennison, my sister and loving friend, for her unfaltering being-there, for her love and support through all my frustrations, vents and joys of the writing life. Her friendship means everything to me.

Nancy Osborn, my confidant and dearest friend, for helping me keep the faith, for all the long talk therapy-exchanges and shared cultural events, trips, adventures. We are living an enormous and wonderful friendship. It's my life support. Thanks with all my heart.

Shade Gomez for our grand journey together, of growth and madness, laughter and sorrows. You were a man of so many answers and connections. You touched me deeply with your knowledge, wit and reliance. Your critiques, advice and encouragement of my work are treasured beyond expression.

Judith Pratt, my friend and drama coach, for her theater workshop where I discovered Roberta who has stayed with me all through the years and whose voice has become stronger and stronger as we've grown older together.

Special thanks to my writing friends of Oghmaniacs and the Quillies. Your home base for continual information, enthusiasm, open and trusting discussion and support is valued greatly.

Heartfelt thanks to Elizabeth Wavle-Brown, Emily Rhodes Johnson, Joan and Ed Ormondroyd, Bob and Cara Franchi, the Sheavlys, June Wolfman, Shirley Brown, Anne Furman, Jae Sullivan, Tonia Saxon and John Levine, Zee Zahava, Marjorie Clay, and to Marcelle Lapow Toor, always.

CONTENTS

The Most Intangible Thing *3*

Living in the Country with the Neighbors and Maurice Sendak *49*

Francis *113*

Revival *157*

White Horses of the Apocalypse *167*

The Sign *177*

How to Defrost the Refrigerator *181*

The Flirting *215*

Roberta *221*

THE MOST INTANGIBLE THING

THE MOST INTANGIBLE THING

1.

The interview went well enough but now I'm stuck with the aftermath—a seventeen-minute CD I can't stop watching.

Karen Long-Lee and I are seated at a great faux mahogany table, across from each other faux Charlie Rose interview style. Long-Lee has one of the most widely viewed programs in the area, something close to Terry Gross's *Fresh Air*.

"What do you write?"

"Subtext that matters, when I'm at my best."

"Would you explain what you mean by 'meaningful subtext'?"

Both smiling. At each other. At the camera.

"I think of subtext as the underlying meanings of just about everything that makes up a story. It's hidden, of course. Deeply hidden, when I'm at my best."

Light laughter.

"Can you give us an example?"

"Well, let me see." I had something already in mind, of course. I was in an interview on WYRS, Syracuse, to sell my book, after all. "In my story, 'Snittering to Roscoe'—"

"Your piece in *The New Yorker*…"

"Yes. 'Snittering's' storyline, its plot, and characters are about four young Americans who admire and imitate some English celebrities. Unfortunately they end up getting their admired celebs' *endings* instead of their *livings* as they had hoped."

"Wouldn't we all like to have Elton John's living!" More laughter. I'm wondering why women laugh so much. Nerves, I'm thinking. That's it for me. For them, probably a cue card, but we all lean toward trying-to-please. "So you're saying that the subtext is about the message? The meaning of the story?"

"It is, but it's implied meaning from the sum of the parts. Well, if you're at your best."

Again, light smiles, laughter. I continue.

"Writers use various devices to symbolize, evoke or demonstrate what we want to get over, and we do this in small ways that add up to an overall effect which becomes the theme or message or meaning of the story. Where characters are placed both literally and figuratively in a scene can indicate dominance, insecurity, arrogance and so forth. What characters say, think, how they act can demonstrate a generalized atmosphere of intent. It's all in what's implied in both the characterization and the action, *what's underneath.*"

"Can you give us an example of what you consider to be strong subtext?"

"Yes. I consider Don DeLillo to be one of the best contemporary writers at subtext. In his short story, 'The Starveling,' for example, he creates a man who spends his life going to the movies. This man notices a woman and begins following her, but he doesn't know why. He calls her 'The Starveling' because of his own projections onto her. He interprets her in light of his own life, although he perceives his interpretations as arising from his observations about her rather than his own needs and desires. In Jungian terms, she's his shadow, even as he's shadowing her. He knows he's making up a story about her, but he thinks initially, at least, that the story is based on observable information, on some kind of truth. Slowly he begins to realize that he is the one that is starving, of life, of love. The darkness of the theater, his *scripted* thoughts about her and his relationship with her, these figuratively mirror the made-up movie-stories he's watching in the dark theater and the drama in his own mind. This story has more going on, of course, but for me it is so much subtext that by the end of the first read, I was exhausted, feeling as depleted as the main character was shown ultimately to be. Subtext, when it's well done, is not just *read*, but *sensed, felt*."

"So the subtext is what was going on underneath, in this case, the woman he's following as his shadow and his need to follow her for reasons not always known to him."

"Yes, well stated."

"Can you give us an example in your own work?"

"Okay. In 'Snittering,' I wanted a generalized feeling of excitement, one that permeated each of the characters at the same time that I wanted a feeling of anxiety and foreboding of imminent danger, individually mirrored from the life of some unfortunate celebrity. The manner, the style and techniques that I used to produce this is the subtext of the story."

"One character actually dies in an automobile accident as Lady Di did, doesn't she?"

"Yes, but I wanted to produce similar insecurities and strengths in that character as in Diana, hopefully hidden such that there isn't a one-on-one parallel, but which leads my character to a similar tragic end, not so much in the accident itself but in the tragedy of her life and Diana's. In Diana's case, that tragedy was in the ending of love with the Prince, and that she didn't have the opportunity to regenerate, recreate herself, her life, with another Prince. The accident truncated that opportunity as it does in the life of the character imitating her in my story."

"How does the title relate to your hidden theme? What does 'Snittering' mean? And what is 'to Roscoe'? Will talking about this give the ending of your story away? But I guess you're telling us that the ending is about ending, in the ultimate sense—so what's to give away, right?"

Light laughter.

"True enough. Snitter is a village in England, Northumberland, and Roscoe is a famous diner in a village by that name in upstate New York. Snittering is a spin on the idiom Englishing, meaning imitation of the English by the non-English who admire them. In my story these young Americans from upstate New York 'English' their way toward disastrous results."

"It's often said, that 'reinventing ourselves is an American pastime.' What's so disastrous about that?"

"For the characters in my story, it's because they aren't living who they really are. Like DeLillo's man in the movie theater, they're young men and women, throwing their lives away. Englishing represents the desire these characters have to *be* someone else. In most of their cases they aren't able to see—though hopefully the readers do—that they're *afraid* to be themselves and that's because they're terrified of the ordinariness of their everyday lives."

"Are you talking about self-acceptance?"

"Well, yes, but also not being afraid to grow, to self-develop, rather than morphing that into becoming somebody else, especially somebody they find so much more stimulating and exciting than they feel they ever could be. Alas, we can't get away from ourselves whether we live in Snitter, Northumberland, or Roscoe, New York. And we certainly can't exchange one for the other."

"Interesting. It's a little like the wish the genie grants. One should think the wish out clearly because there is follow-through."

"Perhaps, yes. But it's more about learning to know what is implicit in our desires."

"Isn't that called therapy?"

Laughter.

Long-Lee glances at the clock. "Before we run out of time—this is so interesting, time's just flying." She leans toward me. "There are so many questions to ask you. Tell us about your writing process."

"Groan."

Light laughter.

"Routine, really. Every day at it, right after my shower and coffee. Like a banker, like the banker T.S. Eliot—that's when I'm at my best."

Smiles.

"He *was* a banker, wasn't he?"

"Actually a bank clerk and only for a short time. He and Paul Gauguin…" I pause. "…which isn't exactly true either—in his youth Gauguin was a stockbroker, so the parallels break down completely. So much for banking and the arts."

Laughter.

"But I do like to think about my writing process like that. Going to work, doing my job."

"To take something to the bank."

More smiles.

"Something like that. But 'the work' is craft and the learning of craft boils down to 'the work schedule.'"

"Demystifying the creative?"

"Perhaps, some, a bit. I'm not afraid of the mysterious side of what I'm calling 'the work,' but it feels false to make it into some inspirational experience that requires odd and unusual nourishment to be sustained."

"In other words, writing is *a lot* of work?"

"Exactly."

A pause. Genuine tone. Clue for taking my reply seriously. "Where do your ideas come from?"

"You mean, do I have special invocations to the muse?"

"Exactly."

"No, not really. I'd have to say, mostly reading. I have a basket with clippings and such, as well as ideas that arise from someone saying something that sticks and won't go away. Since this often happens with family and friends at a table over dinner or at a snack bar, I've labeled my basket the clips-bits-and-bites bag. When I need a new idea, I clip, bit and bite it!"

We smile over the label. I don't tell her that bagging-for-ideas has grown very old and tiring and isn't working anymore.

"How did 'Snittering to Roscoe' come about? We should remind the viewers that 'Snittering to Roscoe' is the title story for your new collection just out by HarperCollins—the subtext for our discussion today!"

Laughter.

I think to myself, last story in the collection, last story written for some time, but I say, "The more complete storyline for 'Snittering' came about through a flash, oddly, in the shower, getting ready to begin my day of writing. But I'd read an article on Princess Diana just before bedtime the night before. And on a side page was an advertisement for Holiday Inns all over England. One in

Northumberland, in a village called Snitter. For some reason it resonated. So the story idea came partly from my old method and partly from something new."

"'Resonated' sounds dangerously close to 'inspired' to me!"

"Perhaps, but it's not a one-to-one printout, as though 'being inspired' is how one gets started. You do need that spark, that emotional interest, something little that can mushroom into something big and it does have to be pretty big to carry you through the long haul."

"Are you talking about passion?"

"Or lots of drive and, well, urges. I think of passion in writing as the steady desire to want to know, to find out, to discover."

"Do you write from an outline?"

"I don't. But whether a writer does or not, there's always the will of the beast. In other words, the story's idea should carry you on its back, not the other way around. If a story I'm working on wants to run away, I hold on to the reins and let it run as fast and hard as it wants to. Anyway, I find that if I try to force-fit characters and or actions into a preconceived structure or idea the story too often falls dead in the water."

"You were saying that your clips-bits-and-bites basket is how you find your ideas. But you also referred to this as your 'old method,' I believe, and you hinted at 'something new.' Where is your writing coming from now?"

"I don't know."

"I don't understand."

"I'm not sure I do either." I decide to bite the bullet. "The old pluck-from-the-basket isn't lighting the creative fire as steadily as before. I've never been without something to say and I know I'll find something again. It's a bit like a singer having a cold, maybe. I know it will pass."

"Well, this may sound pretty obvious, but do you ever just consider what you like, or for that matter, what you don't like, something that strikes you viscerally and write about that?"

"Never." I feel a chilly anger arise. I'm not certain from where but it's very much there, filling my chest like wind in a dark cave. "First, creative people on the whole have a lot of interests, passions if you will, so deciding and sticking to one might be difficult—a little like reading several books at once. It can be done but then there's a question about involvement and follow-through. Is each book getting the full attention it deserves? Writing is even more challenging this way. It demands deep attention and commitment. Secondly, remaining balanced in the writing is always a challenge. If I chose a subject at the visceral level, the writing almost certainly will suffer with over-involvement, lack of discipline and objectivity. Passion is one thing, indulgence is another. No, I'm certain something will arise soon. I've some stirring. Well—and here's another writer's challenge—*patience!*"

"Well said." Long-Lee leans back and smiles. "How do writers nurse themselves, when they need it?"

"Many have used alcohol and drugs, but if writer's biographies are any indication, this usually ends both the writer's career and life. It's important to stay alert to one's fears, I think."

"You mean in the writing."

"Yes. Writer's block, idea block, is fear taking root in one's work. It may not be about the work itself. It might be some blockage in one's life, actually, one's own person. As therapeutic as it may sound, the only way out is to recognize the fears and confront them."

"Sound advice." A beat, then, "Are you telling us you're presently afraid to write?"

"No, writing, to me, is ideas. It's a matter of finding the right one. I'm saying that I don't know where my *ideas* are going to come from next."

Mercifully, our time was up. I gave my thanks all around after the cameras turned their attention to the next show, and I was out of there.

That was a week ago, and I'd watched the CD the station gave me at least a dozen times and each time, I paused and replayed over and over the portion of the interview which began where Long-Lee asked, *Where is your writing coming from now?* Even when I wasn't playing the interview, the question hummed, hummed constantly, underneath:

Where is your writing coming from now?
I don't know.
I don't understand.

I don't either…but fears need to be recognized and confronted.
Are you telling us you're presently afraid to write?
No, writing is ideas. I'm saying that I don't know where my ideas are going to come from next.
I didn't say, "I don't know where my *next ideas* are coming from," did I?
I said: I don't know where my ideas are coming from next.
I think now: Is there a difference?
I think there is.

In the first instance, it's about sequence, the order of ideas—there is one idea, then the next and the next and so forth. It's just a matter of the next one popping up.

In the second instance, there's an implication of the unknown, parallel to, "what *happens* next," and then by implication, "what happens *to me* next."

Where do your ideas come from now?
They come from whatever happens next.
What happens to me next.

Are you afraid to write?

On the couch, a week after the interview, watching the CD for the last time, I hear a voice deep in that dark interior cave whispering, "Yes."

2.

Years ago, I ran onto a Michael Crawford cartoon while leafing through *The New Yorker* in the dentist's office—this was long before I had published my "Snittering" story in the magazine. The cartoon showed a man sitting at a desk typing in the shower, which was going full blast. The caption read: "Earl gets his best ideas in the shower." It was hilarious, of course, because all writers have heard this adage since the day they began writing but know if it were true, we'd all look like prunes. When the secretary left the room, I'd torn the cartoon noiselessly from the magazine, had it rather extravagantly framed—after all it was only a copy from the magazine—and hung it on the wall over my computer in my writing study. I looked at it a lot these days. I was getting desperate for an idea that carried some weight.

I hadn't mentioned the cartoon during my interview on WYRS, which was now six months ago, because, quite frankly, I hadn't thought of it. I'd told Karen Long-Lee, that "Snittering"'s storyline had been somewhat developed during a morning shower. Now I was glad I hadn't brought the cartoon up because no ideas had started flowing, in or out of the shower.

If I remembered correctly, the interview CD was located somewhere between an album of comedic performances by Victor Borge and some grade-C documentaries on severe storms from the weather channel.

Then one morning foaming away with my Coast bar, eyes tightly closed, a tiny image appeared as clear in my mind as if it had been shown by PowerPoint against the shower stall's back wall. I saw, or I should say, I *imaged* myself in my Honda Civic driving toward Ithaca, nine miles south, to my part-time job at Ithaca College as an instructor to undergrads in creative writing. I opened my eyes as this image widened much like the cinematic technique that starts out a pinpoint of light and becomes within moments "the scene" filling the entire viewing field. An audio book was on, William Patton telling a James Lee Burke story of Dave Robicheaux, Clete Purcell and the whole New Iberia, Louisiana constabulary. Just as Dave and Clete were spitting at each other over Clete's inability to once again see, his out-of-control aggressive behavior, my car began floating over into the lane of the on-coming traffic.

White knuckled, I jerked the wheel to the right and just short of a head-on collision with a green Volvo, I jolted back to the shower, soap no longer in hand, somewhere below, slipping and sliding like an eel around my feet, a bruise swelling on the side of my left forearm where I'd righted myself by slamming against the shower wall, willing myself not to fall. A thought flitted across my mind that this was the sort of experience one has in a dream, waking up just before the bullet pierces the skin, the closet door is opened by the serial killer, the airplane hits the mountain wall.

Shaken, I cut my shower short and patted myself dry with slow deliberation. Hands trembling, I dressed, downed only coffee—I couldn't stomach anything else—and drove carefully to work, finding a parking place with unusual ease.

After work, I drove home without incident, in fact, there were fewer cars than usual on the road after five. The commute was a breeze. I chalked up the shower experience to a vivid imagination because, I reasoned, my head had been still half-tied to the pillow.

But then the following Saturday morning while showering, this time with gel, thinking at the drug store that the disorienting experience might've been in the Coast bar—some unknown allergic response to chemicals, who knew?—I felt a slight shift in my peripheral field, then an alteration in my vision so quick and with such force that the entire stall went askew sending the shower halter with shampoo, soap bottle and bar banging into my feet. When the stall again righted itself, just as I started to pull the curtain back, out of the grey mist of plastic sheeting, a shaman, the Odin of the Tarot and Runes, in slow motion moved toward me, wearing a cow's skull, the headdress of death and destruction. He held up a short staff, an extension of a bony finger, and the walls burst into flames, streaming brilliant heat to the sink, toilet, floor, ceiling, window where it stopped and restructured itself into cascading luminosity from the glass, down the curtain, to a triangle of light on the vinyl floor.

When I reclaimed my normal senses, I was clinging to the shower bar like a recovering survivor of a train wreck. By the time I had towel in hand, I stood on the bath mat. With bended knees, I lowered myself onto the toilet seat and began to cry. What was happening to me? Was I having seizures, the precursors for an aneurysm? Were these hallucinations? If so, emanating from where? Triggered by what? They didn't feel, or even look, like hallucinations—as though I knew the character of hallucinations. I'd never had one that I remembered, not even in my heavy pot-smoking youth. Did hallucinatory experiences even have generalized or archetypal characteristics such as shamanic images? I had no idea. I'd seen the Peter Fonda movie *Easy Rider* way back when and if that was any testimony to such, I was guessing they did.

I'd had two such visions now within days of each other. My calling them "visions" seemed less frightening and possibly more accurate in many ways than "hallucinations." They were vivid in the way of visions. They passed for reality, with their intense quality of imaging, despite the presence of a shaman with other-worldly power. The figure *had moved* toward me naturally, not as in a dream or some bizarre time frame, but had done so as in a movie that I might be watching, only without the psychical distancing that comes with realizing one is sitting in a theater observing a happening on a flat screen. My visions, however, had a life span of only a few moments but those moments were like, as Horatio would say upon first seeing Hamlet's father's ghost, "most like" the reality of him, so like in fact, it "harrowed one with fear and wonder." But in other ways, the notion of hallucinations seemed to fit more comfortably. Visions were often grandiose in a biblical sense. They were burning bushes, clouds that spoke—sometimes through thunder, wind and rain—and angels with six eyes, wings and feet. It was preposterous to give even the slightest credence to God attempting to talk to me through such means. I was a rationalist, an avowed rationalist. That was ridiculous!

I rose on weak but sturdy legs, patted myself dry and willed myself to walk naked toward the hall and my bedroom without looking at the shower stall. Once in my terrycloth robe, I toweled my hair and cursed myself for not bringing the hairdryer from the bathroom into the bedroom with me. On the one hand, I couldn't allow myself to be intimated by a shower stall. On the other, I couldn't bring myself to walk back into the bathroom and retrieve it from the cabinet near the shower. I felt fine now. But what had happened to me? Was happening to me? I was thankful today was one of my days off from the college.

Padding my way toward the stairs, I decided to forgo the blow job and make coffee and toast. I smiled at my dirty little joke, hopped down the stairs, flipped two multigrain slices into the toaster and hit the start button on the coffee maker. I set out a plate, cloth napkin and utensils. I would order my life into normalcy through sheer everyday ritual and routine, if nothing else. What was it again I'd said to Karen Long-Lee? The answer came back to me verbatim. "Routine," I'd said about my writing process. "Routine, really. Every day at it, right after my shower and coffee. Like a banker." So this morning, after coffee and toast with a half hour of NPR news, I beat a path upstairs to dress, and back downstairs, I enter my writing studio with purpose. Sitting in front of Microsoft Word, I willed one sentence to appear from my fingers, shaped perfectly over the keys like a pianist ready for Chopin. After one hour of starts and stops, I hit the discard button and raced to my journal folder and wrote a lament for yet another day of no useable work.

One week later, there were two half-pages of junk in the recycle bin. Everything else written had no life at all and had been deleted forever.

3.

Showering was fast becoming a problem. There hadn't been an incident in a while, but I was watchful, anticipating another episode at each and every stepping into the stall. I had tried feigning courage by disrobing straight out of bed, hitting the bedroom and hallway floors in a speed-walk, turning like a race driver into the bathroom and jumping into the shower, with recklessness and as much abandon as the space would allow. That hadn't gone so well with the water still cold and the chances for slipping greater than I wanted to take. But since nothing had happened while doing this, it was tempting to see it as a possible approach.

After three such tries, I determined after a couple of slips that the chance of accident was too high. If I was going to allow slippage, I reasoned, I might as well see the vision that went with it! But not wanting any more bruising if I could avoid it, I attempted to nonchalantly, almost seductively, advance toward the shower by way of the lavatory, first turning on the shower water, letting it flow while I brushed my teeth, telling myself—and the shower?—that I could then decide how I wanted to bathe. More often than not, I went into the stall, stood there waiting, the idea being that the minute the shift began to occur, I could extricate myself in time to stop the imaging. I found out soon enough that this failed utterly.

My premonition of the imaging returning had been founded on some kind of truth, because the "scenes," as I now thought of them, came back with even more vividness and intensity. I had driven a motorcycle at top speed off a cliff near Bixby Creek Bridge on Highway One, Big Sur; fallen into a vat of snakes during a rattlesnake round-up in Okeene, Oklahoma; and hung onto a railing in the Bat Cave in Carlsbad Caverns, New Mexico while the winged creatures swooped and swirled overhead, several dive-bombing toward my head before I fell back into ordinary life in the shower stall. In all of these, no other humans were around. I only knew the location of the event by the highway and sightseeing signs that blurred an indication of the broadening vista of my visions as I sped past. It was all beginning to feel very much like I was cloning scenes from a psychedelic trip or taking an out-of-body vacation through the shadow life of the American Landscape.

My reasoning dictated that these were all coming from some mental file, much like those on my computer labeled, My Pictures, My Videos, My Media. But this theory fell apart when I reflected that I had never been to any of these places or sought them out for online viewing. The nearest I'd ever come to a shaman of the stature in my vision was through articles I'd read on shamanism in *National Geographic* and *Natural History* and a stop at the American Indian reconstruction site in Anadarko, Oklahoma. *This was the source for a shamanic bony finger pointed toward my heart?* Or was it the November I took a trip to visit my brother in San Diego and dipped down to Tijuana for Mexican cocktails at a tourist bar during The Day of the Dead festival? What brought on a rattlesnake's venom racing through my veins while two other reptiles were shaking their warnings of more to follow? The shaker percussions used during one free lesson of the Bachata in the Latin Studio for Beginner's in Boston, Massachusetts where I was attending a creative writing course on scholarship?

Since these hallucinatory visions didn't happen each time I showered, it was difficult not to be tempted to give it a shot when the shower-passes came close to five, six days. Mornings could go by without anything occurring and then two events would happen straight in a row. And the visions could come, anytime, day or night. I'd tried that one. The visions were not tied to time but seem to be tied to my shower stall.

The last had sent me to my bedroom, literally shivering from a nude downhill ski at Vail that seemed endless until the shower stall smashed into my head and arms. I lifted the phone to call my doctor for an appointment. When the receptionist answered, I said "wrong number, sorry," and hung up. I didn't have the strength, the sheer perseverance it would take to explain and sort through Dr. Shires's interpretation of my visionary storylines. The question came to mind, used so many times in mysteries, where the storyteller finds talking to the police riskier than enduring the life-threatening situation. *What would these hallucinatory descriptions sound like*? In my case, three things would doubtlessly occur: a thorough examination by Shires of whether or not I was abusively using drugs or alcohol and then a thorough series of tests to see if my brain was malfunctioning or had a tumor. If these proved unproductive, she would recommend seeing a psychiatrist. What other options could there be? Since these visionary happenings were occurring only in my shower, there wasn't much credence in brain malfunction or damage.

Anyway, online researching revealed the cost of a mere CAT scan with contrast was around fifteen hundred dollars and an MRI started at twenty-five hundred. Part-time-employment at the college didn't include health care benefits. I couldn't afford that on thirty thousand a year. I knew from personal experience that stress could cause a plethora of maladies, but was hallucinations one of them? Could a fear of showering—I didn't think I felt this but still if some underlying trauma was surfacing—correlate somehow with stress to produce what was happening to me? Dr. Shires already had me on anti-anxiety medication from the sheer pressure of the writing life. What did I think she and her recommended specialists could do for me in my price range? Give me a stronger Xanax especially balanced for visions in showers?

I'd waffled for days between sponging in the lavatory and doing nothing at all, that is, with water and soap. On work days, I doused myself with a musk oil from the local alternative market labeled, "Forbidden Fruits," at once so cliché and citrus-y, I threw it into my cart without looking back. It reddened my eyes and upset my stomach for the first day or two, not to mention the stares from people who knew I was eco-friendly beyond reason about scented anything but food. But it was covering my increasingly dreadful situation.

I had consciously changed my diet, one with lower sodium intake, and I'd stopped visiting the fitness center in the hopes of cutting down on sweat. I was finding less interest in much of anything. Where once I had to mindfully resist watching television while eating and work at jamming errands between the writing and research, I was now going days without grocery shopping and cooking or taking care of situations not handled well by phone. The tube was comatose except for reflections migrating on its surface from the bay windows. I was eating steamed vegetables straight out of the bag with a pat of butter thrown in, a few mozzarella strips and hunks from a baguette on the side. A cooked meal was two strips of turkey bacon with two scrambled eggs thrown over them or poached fish on toast on a plastic plate. I was feeling homeless, increasingly like a bag-lady in my own house. The major difference being that I changed my clothing two, sometimes three, times a day. The flow of water was constant—from the washer, not the shower. I washed my hair in the kitchen sink using the side spray. I went out only to teach, keep office hours, and hold a few consultations with students—which I tried to jam on my teaching days.

Today was the second day of "forgetting about it," which was how I'd come to view my shower-passes. It was also the third cycle of such passing—the first and second had ended a five day semi-dry-spell with a trip to the YWCA pool as a guest of an acquaintance from the neighborhood. I had put off approaching Christine Glockman for the favor because I knew it opened the door to drop-by klatches that just weren't my cup of tea. I thought if I collected on her countless invitations for a companionable swim, I wouldn't have to invade her home for a shower, thereby signaling her to reciprocate the invasion with get-togethers. I might even join the Y in order to permanently bypass my own at-home showers. But the Y was on the other side of town, across the lake, a good two or more hours out of my day by the time I counted the swim. When I caught myself in such thoughts I realized I was becoming irrational, downright dotty about what was happening to me.

The fourth cycle of non-showering was broken by my asking a secretary in the Humanities Department, where my writing courses were based, if I could use her shower at home. The excuse I gave Marcilla was that my bathroom was in repair, and it looked now like the replacement of piping from copper to PVC was going to take longer than the workers thought. I might have to steal a couple of evenings in her stall, would she mind? Desperation was driving me to face her shower stall with downright curiosity. I wanted to know if these cerebral events of mine would transfer themselves to another venue. Marcilla's shower was a temporary solution but it was also a test, especially if I showered at her place more than once. The visions were coming more frequently but they still were not everyday occurrences. If they happened in her shower, I'd know it was me. If they didn't happen there, I still wouldn't know whether it my shower or me or both, but I'd know I'd given this my best effort to find out. Until their occurrence became more predictable, I was at a loss as to what else to do in order to figure out what they were. I wasn't sure which was more terrifying—to remain not knowing when or where they might occur or to know they would happen with regularity when I showered.

I hadn't visited Marcilla in her home before, since our socializing outside of our on-the-job encounters had been at an across-town diner on the cutting edge of deep-fried road kill. Marcilla was born and raised on grits and gravy in St. Louis, Missouri. Her idea of music was talking your way through love and loss in a tumble toss of word-rhythm at full tilt which I found hard to listen to for longer than a couple of songs—which actually was giving this music a fair chance since these songs could go on for what seems like fifteen, twenty minutes apiece. She had her iPod hooked up with KATZ 100.3fm, the beat out of St. Louis streaming through her head half the time. Once in her house, I saw that streaming hit maximal volume through ceiling-to-in-wall speakers parading throughout the house. All this was a bit over-the-top for me, but I found her humor infectious.

I wasn't wrong when I hoped she just might be my raft after forty days and forty nights of paddling in shark-infested ocean, which had actually been my last hallucinatory vision—a deep-water submersion with a host of predatory fish, glistening in a slithering, silver stream toward me with jaws open, teeth within inches of my naked flesh before I found myself lying flat on my back in the bottom of my shower stall being pummeled by what I at first thought was the perfect storm before I recognized the shower nozzle facing down at me out of the steaming clouds. The rubber mats I'd thought to put at the bottom of the stall saved me from more bruising than I already had from the fall. My body was looking like the punching bag of an abusive significant other or the outcome of a too high dosage of Coumadin. If I continued to shower in my stall, I might need a helmet.

Marcilla's bathroom was the antithesis of mine. In a room about the size of my pantry, she had stapled what she told me later were six thousand plastic flowers, mainly black-eyed Susans and sunflowers. As I walked around the room studying them much as I would paintings on the walls of a museum, I realized that they were all different, no two were the same. On a ledge surrounding the room were dozens of miniature vases. One I turned over was from war-occupied Japan. The whole bathroom scene lightened my spirits—what could possibly be more out of the ordinary than this— and I stepped into her shower with a hopefulness I hadn't felt in far too long. Towel and washcloth had been carefully laid on the lavatory by the stall. Everything had a wonderful order to it. I picked up the Dove bar and, holding my breath, I began what used to be my morning ritual at home. Three minutes into the shower, I knew I was free. I had no idea how I knew, but I did. Whatever was happening to me in my shower at home was not going to happen to me here.

As Marcilla and I were enjoying her scrambled eggs with white gravy, fried blood-and-pig's head sausage, dinner rolls slathered in butter and hot mush in bowls sprinkled with brown sugar, I asked her where she got so many plastic flowers. She said she had collected them from Hobby Huts and other craft stores from her travels all over the country. It took her over a decade, and, at the time she started collecting them, she lived in a rented apartment, but she knew when she bought her first home, she would do what she ended up doing with them. When I asked her to marry me, she nearly fell out of her kitchen chair with laughter. A creeping, shivering thought darted in and out of my mind all during breakfast. I didn't want to go home. I wanted to crawl into her bed, form a fetal position and never leave the warmth of the quilted blankets I'd seen there as I'd walked past toward the kitchen.

4.

Things were falling out of routine faster than I could count them. My computer crashed from some kind of malicious threat. The computer geek who took the hard drive with him to his shop said that this was "better than a virus," explaining that "m-threats" meant that I'd have my files back in order within a week, but for a price tag almost exactly the earnings I made for "Snittering" at *The New Yorker*. The bright spot was that it was a relief to not sit in front of Microsoft Word, festering.

And then the washer went on the blink, taking the Sears Maintenance guy a good part of a day to replace the drive shaft and pulley belt for reasons he said he corrected in the struts that had either been misaligned from its manufacture or thrown out of alignment from its shaking free of its support on an uneven basement floor. In either case, the warranty had long since expired and without a renewed maintenance contract it was either another six hundred dollars for a new machine or paying half that for the repair. Since the repair ultimately came to four hundred and seventeen dollars, I was left to stew over the difference. New York had only two months until spring and severe weather season. I almost prayed for a tornado to hit my house and force me into a new shower stall, which was a solution I'd considered until the washer went on the blink and threw my budget against the wall.

The next imaging event came after a night of drinking at an Irish pub in Ithaca. Things had not been going well. Writing wasn't happening at all, and there were stirrings at the college that with reduced state funding, lay-offs for part-time lecturers were inevitable. Rumors spun around that we were to know who would stay and who would go by mid-May, only two months away. Marcilla was the head of the rumor mill, so I got a special heads-up. Since she sat in on many of the budget and policy meetings as note-taker, we knew she was good for the rumors we were getting.

It didn't take much to knock me out of my socks at the bar. I ordered sloe gin fizzes—my last count was only three—until the bartender leaned toward me in confidence, saying, "These fizzes are called 'slow' for a reason." I knew how they worked, as if the two kinds of gins in them weren't enough, they were mixed with maple syrup that pushed the already glycemic level to high-octane. The fizz drinker was absolutely fine as long as she didn't venture from her bar stool. The minute her foot hit the floor, her body would follow, as mine predictably did. On the floor I thought, but didn't say, that at least something in my life was predictable.

The bartender shook his head while he lifted me to a chair at a table, poured me a black coffee and pushed the beer nuts in front of me. When he came back half an hour later and he saw that my eyes could follow his swaying finger in front of my face, he called and paid for my taxi because he knew that although I wasn't a regular, he saw me enough to know I was good for the tab. I knew I'd suffer the next morning, but since I had two days before Tuesday and work, I could purge with less guilt.

Arriving home via taxi too drunk to think twice, I marched upstairs and into the shower fully dressed, justifying this as both defiance to the forces sending these misfortunes my way—I did see *everything* happening to me now as emanating from the shower—and a courageous act, built around the rationale that I could retreat as fast as possible fully dressed should another vision begin occurring. What that would get me, I wasn't sure—but whatever it was, at least I wouldn't be nude. Later, I realized that climbing into the shower clothed or otherwise was actually a mental seduction. I was being lulled into that sense of security the mind invents when it can't tolerate any more stress. It was either that or my mind knowing its own mind better than I knew it. What followed was something of a miracle, a real honest-to-goodness breakthrough.

Starting my shower, I noticed I had picked up the Dove bar—the one I'd purchased after my Marcilla showers, hoping her light-heartedness would literally rub off on me—and was about to put it down on the sleeve of my sweater, when I suddenly became aware of how absurd my life had become. I couldn't articulate any of what was happening to anybody with a straight face anymore. I stood there, water pouring over me, and I started to laugh. All at once, I realized that I had nowhere else to go, no other means coming to mind, no other way to be but this—where I was, as I was. I laughed so hard I threw the bar in the air like a cap at a graduation, stepped out of the shower with a confidence I had no right to have, and began tugging off my soggy clothing. And this wasn't the easiest thing in the world to do because laughing and undressing are two pretty much exclusive acts. Once naked, I started singing, partly made-up Marcilla songs, "You took my life, you Dumbledore, and threw it on bathroom floor" and partly of the You-Are-My-Sunshine and Oh-My-Darlin'-Clementine sort. In the shower, naked, gurgling under the water, swinging side to side in a steady sway, totally disregarding slipping and falling, I had an epiphany. On a Jenny Holzer LED sign, words scrolled past my consciousness as clearly as a reading at Times Square or, for that matter, my shower stall wall.

Write….the….fears….that…happen.

As the message rolled out of my mind's eye, I got out of the shower, dried myself off, stepped over the towel and my clothes where I'd let them fall and walked downstairs to my writing study. I dropped into my computer chair and started clicking out a list of words. I must have worked several hours, because when I stopped, I was shivering, naked with a lap blanket I kept on the back of the chair thrown over my shoulders. I laid myself down to bed in just such swaddling clothes and fell into deep sleep that lasted the rest of the night.

—

In first morning light, wide-awake, dressed, coffee-and multi-toasted, I clicked past the screen saver to the still bright open page of Microsoft Word:

Head-on collision
Shaman
Ocean with sharks
Motorcycle off Big Sur cliff
Rattlesnake roundup
Bat cave
Skiing downhill in the nude

In a column on the other half of the page, I'd written:

Heights
Flying
High winds
Stage fright

Speed
Snakes
Bats
Deep water, the ocean
Monsters in pursuit

Next to Heights, Flying, High winds, Deep water--the ocean, and Monster, I'd put asterisks which referred to the label at the bottom of the page, "Uncontrollable forces." Next to Speed and Stage fright, I'd put crosses which referred to "Controllable acts." A small circle designated Snakes and Bats as "Natural phenomena." Then I'd drawn crisscross lines leading from the incidents in the shower and those I'd listed as my fears.

There was a space down the page, a list of two, separated from the others:

Knowing my future
Dying

I stared at these last two entries, not remembering at all having written them. Curious about my categories and comparisons to the visions I'd had so far, I googled Top Fears and clicked the site labeled, *Snakes Top List of Americans' Fears*.

The following litany was depicted in a graph with descending percentages:

Snakes
Public speaking
Heights
Being closed in a small space

I laughed out loud, there was my shower stall, wasn't it?
The list continued:

Spiders and insects
Needles and getting shots

Mice
Flying on an airplane
Dogs
Thunder and lightning
Crowds
Going to the doctor
The dark

I clicked on other sites and found some with more psychological results, including the fears of failure, intimacy, being alone, abandonment, change, engulfment, God, falling, and dying. I spent some time reading the analysis of these fears. Some were visceral—those we are born with such as falling and dying. Others, still close to these, were abandonment and commitment emanating from a basic human need to belong, even to survive, especially as in infants and children, though the degree to which we need these was debated by the experts. Most of our fears seem to be cultural or learned from our families. Some are personal, from experience or, as some psychologists argued, are foundational to personality, which is a concept most hotly debated as to whether these are an amalgam innate or learned or a combination of both.

I wasn't sure why all this had such a pull on me, but I couldn't stop reading. I spent the greatest part of the day researching the analysis of what I considered my major fears. It was interesting to me that my list changed somewhat as I read but the central issues surrounding my list of fears remained the same—I was afraid of losing control above anything else, even above anything to do with relationships and personal growth. My fears, like with most other people, were on the level of need for perceived survival.

Staring at the list of hallucinatory visions I'd had in the shower, I tried to make sense of them. Collision, Shaman, Ocean with sharks…. As I began to analyze them, I realized that they encompassed far more than I had at first thought. I'd been so enthralled with *why* they were happening that I hadn't thought to sit down and take a look at what they might *mean*. Not the meaning of why they were happening but the meaning that they held for me personally.

I knew they weren't dreams. If somebody had asked me to articulate the difference between what I was experiencing and my definition of dreaming, I wasn't sure I could. As I remembered, Neil Gaiman had Fat Charles saying in *The Anansi Boys* something like—one way you can know something is a dream is that you're somewhere that you've never been in real life. If I accepted this, then my happenings were indeed dreams. But it didn't make sense that I was dreaming for only a few moments in my shower stall before I woke back up to reality. I knew now I was having real-live "black-outs" that weren't black, but images-as-happenings, which were visions, because I was trying to tell myself something. I was coming closer to acknowledging that I knew or sensed something I was finding hard to accept. But now I had the tyrannosaurs by their tails and even though they were still slapping me against the shower wall, I was getting closer to figuring out what the monsters were. I was showing myself my fears and was requesting, no, I was requiring that I confront them. And I was coming into an understanding of how I might do that.

My first thought was to do what my scrolling shower message had told me to do—write my fears, which made sense. After all, I was a writer. So I began writing about them in journal entries but as I worked with this, I naturally fell into the language, context and structure of fiction. What was it Karen Long-Lee had asked? *Have you ever thought of writing about something that strikes you viscerally?* I had been so quick to dismiss that idea, giving all kind of rationale for my dismissal. *Why was I afraid to write from my gut? My heart instead of my head?* I had told her and the audience out there: *Writing is ideas.*

I clicked out of my journal file and into Microsoft Word. I typed the first sentence that came to mind: "When she died in the head-on collision, just before her consciousness left her, she knew there was an afterlife."

5.

I had actually won—not earned—my place in *The New Yorker*. Each year the magazine reserves an issue to the fiction of writers of promise. There's a massive selection process and I was the odd one to push up through the cracks. Most of the recipients were more published than I, but I had a strong agent with lots of networking clout. She had agented several writers who went on to at least respectable publishing fame, in Europe if not presently in the States, where agents talked a lot about post-commercialism—translation for "no more marketing of fiction in mainstream magazines." I had made the second-tier literary journals and *The Sun*, and I'd used my position at the college to garner a few articles on creative writing and the future of fiction in respectable magazines. My literary agent, Tonia Hollenbeck, knew the trails to follow that lead to the open doors, but the doors were closing faster than she could open them. Recently she'd become unrelenting in her push toward what she drawled out—she was originally from Austin, Texas—in capital letters as *"The Reviews,"* and her notion of an acceptable review was one that had been established prior to the late sixties and early seventies when the surge in publishing literary journals had begun.

All the great fiction markets open a decade ago were gone—*The Atlantic, The Saturday Evening Post, Cosmopolitan, Redbook* no longer published fiction in each issue. The only magazines with any stature still publishing short stories regularly were *The New Yorker* and *Harper's*. Editors were giving in to pressures from the top to fill dragging magazine sales with subjects more catchy and sexy, following the trends of reality and talk shows on television and radio. In Tonia's view, the older reviews were now the keys to the inner sanctum of the publishing houses, which in turn were the keys turning the locks to *Harper's* and more of *The New Yorker*, which in turn opened the revolving doors to the paying outlets in the larger world of books, audios, DVDs and e-media of the publishing houses.

I'd made it to *Ploughshares, Nimrod, Glimmer Train Stories*, and *The Iowa Review*, the one review to my credit—though it was founded in 1970, sniff, sniff—and all of these were before the "Snittering" story and the collection that followed. She had called in a favor to get the book out at HarperCollins. Selling well depended on my dove-tailing quickly. The stories of mine out there were publishing-thin—in other words, they had been recycled to the point of smelling like the left-overs from Marcilla and my Across-the-Street-Diner.

So when I lifted the phone and told Tonia Hollenbeck that I had two long stories ready for her perusal, one on death and the afterlife, the other on a relationship gone vicious through engulfment issues, I held out the phone away from my ear during her tongue-clicking on the other end of the line. What came next was a southern version of a Prada queen's explicative: "Well, well, well, where in the world did these come from *all of a sudden*?" And then she hooted at her joke on me.

"You wouldn't believe it if I told you," I countered.

"You didn't plagiarize them, did you?"

"Not unless you want me to give my showers a footnote."

She snorted, then in a sing-songy voice, "Earl gets his best ideas in the shower?"

I nearly dropped the phone. "You know that cartoon?"

"Hell yes, girl. Where have you been? Half my people have that hanging in their writing areas or on the wall of their bathrooms." She laughed deliciously again. "Not two feet from the shower stall, probably."

A strange feeling came over me. Disappointment? Dismay? Fright?

The recognition didn't take long in coming. It was a feeling of emptiness, *of something being taken from me.*

Four days later Hollenbeck called to tell me that the hereafter-story had made *The Mississippi Review* and the smothering-smoldering marriage piece had made *Harper's*. I was slowly arriving, which rhymed with surviving. In the secure files of my desktop, rough drafts of two others were in tow, one already long enough for a novella. It had the title, "The Shaman's Prediction," a mystery but one with a twist on fortune-telling and predestination. The other was lighter fare, a motorcycle ride straight out of *Harold and Maude*. Sales on *Snittering* had increased by 37% at Barnes and Noble and Amazon. My *Snittering* collection sat on a display stand facing the front door when I walked into Barnes and Noble. I wasn't recognizable to anybody but the sales manager—for the book—and the clerks behind the coffee bar—for my version of cappuccino. I found that comforting. Who would recognize Phil Roth or John Updike if they walked into the B&N in Ithaca, New York? J. K. Rowling, maybe, but these literary giants had their own crowds to trawl after them.

That night I stopped in at the Irish Pub and paid Kelly-the-bartender what I owed him plus a hearty tip when I shook his hand after a couple of whiskeys. I'd pulled money out of savings to do it. What most people don't realize is that even at the top, journal and magazine publishing doesn't earn writer's much of a living. I received just over five thousand dollars for my story in *The New Yorker* and most top literary journals pay from three to five hundred dollars a story. This is before the agent's sales percentage fee, which includes marketing expenses. My advance on the *Snittering* collection paid my mortgage for two and a half months. The percentage of publisher's receipts—my royalty terms were net receipts—were still pending. It made these new story publications imperative for me. An Edie Falco's quote I'd read somewhere, sometime stayed ever present in my mind. Even after *The Sopranos*'s success and fame, she said, she knew she could easily be back at waitressing for a living. It's always there—making *the living*.

At home, I fell into bed, properly attired in my lime-colored pajamas with white piping around the collar and sleeves. I gave not another thought to showering or writing.

—

This morning, I was curious about both, but I lacked courage, the old twist of fate coming back in the wringing of my hands and the batting of my head against the old writer's block. I ran my thinking through the Long-Lee interview, seeking the question I needed to ask in order to know what to do next. Anything I found there I'd used already, and I was terrified of discovering that well was dry. Many of the shower visions had netted a story. I was cutting and pasting my way through the others, including a novella that I'd told Tonia I'd have shortly. I was finding once again that I couldn't get past what was already on the page. Nothing was moving forward.

So I took the day to fumble my way around errands, some useful, some not—ink cartridges for the printer, wine and fresh fish for supper, a new sweater to replace the one I'd ruined in the shower. In the supermarket, the cart half-full of carefully selected items for meals for the week, my hand stopped on the frozen vegetables. I put them in the cart only after I decided to take the club-sized package instead of the steamers I'd eaten slathered with butter in my bag-lady days.

At home I put everything away, cooked and ate dinner and was seated on the couch watching Clint Eastwood in one of his old cheroot-chewing roles as a western gunslinger when I knew what I had to do. I went to the wall in my study, took down the Crawford cartoon, and threw it in the trash. It stayed there for an hour before I scrounged my way through cucumber and carrot peelings to bring it out, wipe it dry, clean its frame thoroughly with Windex, and put it back on the wall. It rested there again, gleaming in its place, one it had held for over a decade. I slipped out of my clothes, went into the bathroom and turned on the shower. I stood on the mat looking at the stall, wondering. I couldn't concentrate on much of anything. There didn't seem to be any steady thought gaining ground in my mind at all. I didn't feel fear or curiosity. I strangely didn't feel much of anything unless it was emotional exhaustion.

I stepped into the shower, turned to soak my hair before I reached for my shampoo. And then, a small almost imperceptible sound, like the distant cracking of ice, began to break through the spewing noise of the flowing water from the shower nozzle. By the time it reached the height of its crescendo, and for my mind to take it in, the shower stall and I were falling without obstruction down into the darkness of my writing study on the main floor below.

6.

A neighbor heard the crash, used the key I'd given her for emergencies to enter the house, and called 911.

I was in the hospital for two-and-a-half months—intensive care for the first ten days and various physical and occupational therapies for eighteen months. Every doctor and specialist who saw me said that it was a miracle I was alive. Several told me I was the *luckiest person alive*. A few even told me it was the hand of God. Most of the nurses pursed their lips or clicked their tongues, shook their heads or snorted a kind of approval while they poked, prodded and gathered me up for movement here and there. I thought for a while that gurneys were chaise lounges since they took me in and out of both real and false sunlight—x-ray and MRI rooms and, of course, to and from the glare of OR with the seven surgeries I endured, minor to major ones.

The fractures and breaks collectively on my legs were eleven—six to the fibulae and five to the tibiae. My left femur sustained a hairline fracture. My knees were intact but my ankles were shattered since I landed standing up. I lost one and three-quarters inches in height upon impact because two vertebrae collapsed. My left clavicle was broken and the right side of my pelvis was fractured. I escaped traction by the skin of my teeth—one young doctor, trailed by three medical students, actually said this to me through a perfectly orthodontic smile. Of all the pain, the spine and pelvis injuries were the greatest, at times unbearable.

My primary orthopedist, Dr. Kathleen McPherson, was conservative with the morphine, using Demerol injections during post-surgery recovery but weaning me off it earlier than most—or so I was told my Marcilla from her online investigations. For months, some for over a year, I lived on various dosages of either Vicodin, Lorcet or Dilaudin, then tapered down to Percocet and aspirin. Once at home with weekly visits from a homecare health aide, the advice I received from Dr. McPherson was to stop taking aspirin when my ears started ringing. McPherson did not tell me I would never walk again, but she did say that walking would be a different sort of ambulation in my life from now on.

I literally learned to walk again, making every-other-day trips by Capability van to the rehab center and with daily exercises supported by an aide at home. It took sixteen months before I walked alone without any support other than a cane and three more months before I walked without a notable limp, the cane coming out for support when the weather turned cold or damp—which I hated—just like the song says. My physical therapist was a retired female army drill sergeant. To Helen McCrutchin, not walking was never an option. The first time I stood up from my wheelchair she did not reach for me or give me support. When I looked up into her face, though, her eyes were shining with tears.

I had no family. I was an only child with abandonment coming at the age of twenty—both parents killed instantly in an odd train accident in Barcelona, Spain. The conductor was drunk, as these stories go, and a civil action by Americans on a cruise, stopping for a two-night stay in Barcelona and on that sightseeing train, had solicited me to sign along with them, which I did even though my parents were traveling independent of their cruise. The action was in remission, as my lawyer liked to say, suffering from a malady that only international law can propagate and massive amounts of litigation can cure.

Just as I was entering my homebound stage of recovery, my job at I.C. suspended—though the college had taken the unprecedented step to offer me at least partial healthcare benefits upon future contractual signings—the civil action was resolved. I was awarded enough after litigation fees to defray much of my share of these astronomically-mounting medical costs. If I had been writing a novel about this, such machinations would have been the ultimate *deus ex machina*. But I was learning—the slow learner I am—that in life these sudden changes in direction can indeed happen unreasonably and inexplicably to the level of fiction. With everything in place, I settled back in my writing chair for the long, long trailer ride toward uphill recovery.

Insurance was paying, slowly, but they were paying. Part of the charges for the remodeling of the bathroom were mine since it was a complete make-over. Now my bathroom vied with Marcilla's in its own way—Mediterranean tiles on the walls with commissioned murals of dolphins at play overhead. The insurance agent looked downright disgusted with having to go through the argument about whether this would be covered in my policy. I paid.

The project foreman stared at me when I said, "No shower, not of any kind." His repartee was in place for the installation of a luxury steam shower by Aquapeutics, complete with hand-held spray. But I wasn't to be swayed. It seems the workman—my contractor told me of the old shower install—was an inexperienced, handyman special from probably the late 1970s, early '80s, given the date of the stall. The idiot or idiots had not added the additional cross studs to hold the weight of the shower which may have passed except for insufficient planning for seepage. It was only a matter of time before the entire stall gave way because of rot. The attachment to the wall just hadn't been enough to carry the load over time.

After I'd given him the abbreviated storyline of my accident, he understood my reluctance to have a shower reinstalled, but he couldn't quite fathom why I wouldn't at least put in a hand-held side spray fastened to a pole attached to the shower curtain ring around the tub. When I told him the curtain wouldn't be necessary either, it really threw him into total project-planner consternation. But he finally came around, finding me a vintage clawfoot tub from an old hotel demolition in Rochester, paying under a thousand for it. Of course the transport of the item to my house was another matter. But if I took the old tiles from the hotel as well, he could arrange the shipping of everything for under three hundred. Of the tiles, he added to seal the deal on the phone, "Hand-painted ones from Italy." I borrowed more money. Maybe the bank felt sorry for me, too.

Marcilla became my project advocate, actually my advocate at the hospital and with home help as well. She carried in the groceries, did a lot of cooking and baking and house cleaning, along with bringing me almost daily reports of the construction process through my drug-induced haze. She loved ordering everybody around and was gathering the courage, she told me, to ask the project foreman out to dinner. I told her he sounded wonderful on the phone, but I cautioned against taking him to the Across-the-Street Diner, and we hooted. Even as drugged out as I was, I remembered to give her explicit instructions that no plastic flowers of any kind were to be attached anywhere in my new bathroom.

When I finally made it back home, she had iPhoned a gallery of pictures—the bath was upstairs after all—that she showed me, indicating in the final shoot of the lot, one small vase of plastic sunflowers on the back of the toilet.

7.

Some time ago I ran onto another *New Yorker* cartoon by Lee Lorenz, this time from my own subscription, of course. In this one, a writer is at his computer keyboard, clicking away furiously as an angel hovers behind his back about to pull the computer's plug out of the wall. Of course it struck me as hilarious upon sight because of the many times I'd lost my earlier writings due to the surges and blackouts we often had in the village where I lived. Since the creation of auto-recovery this wasn't a problem anymore, but as my visions seemed to have faded away with the accident, the cartoon had taken on a new dimension.

Most of us don't handle fate well, if we give it thought at all beyond our mortal state when a friend or pet dies, at least not until we are old or have some trauma that brings us to it. And writing interruptus is a temporary condition of the writing life, much like catching a cold—hadn't I said that in interview?—or clogged drains needing attention. Oddly now, into recovery in both body and mind, I was writing at break-neck speed, like the Lorenz cartoon guy at the keyboard. In fact, I was busy on my current novel when the phone rang.

"Hello, my dear." It was Agent Tonia Hollenbeck. "How are you?"

"I'm alive," I answered, deadpan.

"You said that the last time I called." She laughed.

"Yeah, well, nothing's changed."

Pause.

"Got something for me?"

"Yes."

"You do?" A beat, then, "I mean, glad to hear it. Whatcha got?"

"Tonia, what do I do best?"

She laughed hoarsely. The woman sucked cigarettes like a vacuum sweeper—this at ten dollars a pack. I listened to her smoke.

"You make up stories with lotsa subtext."

I had her well-trained. We had each other well-trained. I was writing even though I was still on drugs at regular intervals.

"I used to and I still do."

"Talk to me, girlfriend."

"A woman dies in a deprivation tank…"

"Oh God," Tonia groaned. "Not another hereafter story. I mean, I can't complain, death and dying have done very well for you recently, but do you want to repeat yourself?"

"Of course not. Authors who repeat themselves can't win the Pulitzer." I paused. "No wait, didn't Roth, Updike and Mailer all win, and they repeated themselves like Rabbits—sorry! Let me start again. I can't repeat myself. It makes the writing boring, for me, forget my readers and those writers who got away with it."

"So…"

I interrupted her. "It takes her a long time to die."

"A lingering death. About as exciting as dying in a deprivation tank."

"Death is the last excitement."

"You're scaring me." Tonia sounded serious. "But I'll listen. How can death in a deprivation tank be the great excitement? You can't do much in such a tank can you?" Pause. "Don't you just lie there….well, I guess that's what you do when you're dead…but…"

"There's a wicked magician running the show."

"Like Oz?"

"A little like the Wizard but more like the CIA."

Another pause, longer this time. "So how long is it?"

"As long as it takes."

"Oh, you're still working on it." Real disappointment.

"No, it's…"

"Don't be coy. C'mon. Well, okay, let me reframe my part of the conversation. When will I get this, whatever it is? Sounds like a thriller and unless you've become John Banville, oops, Benjamin Black, or William Faulkner…."

"It is as good as Banville-aka-Black, believe me. Faulkner's mysteries I leave to you and God to judge—in that order. I might add, though, at this point in my career, these undoubtedly are interchangeable. I'll send it to you as soon as I'm out of the tank."

Tonia Hollenbeck was laughing as she hung up.

Eighteen months later, *Tanked* didn't win the Pulitzer, but it did win the National Book Award primarily because it took on the underworld of torture, deprivation and human rights of the CIA and global secret police networks in the name of bargained and negotiated peace. A December interview with my old Karen "Scoop" Long-Lee, who had moved from WYRS Syracuse to WLS

Chicago, was scheduled after the awards presentation in November. That interview was cancelled, however, by the nasty little angel hovering behind my back who pulled the plug on my writing life, well, and pretty much on my life, period.

8.

I wasn't sure when the fatigue, tremors in my legs and spasms from my spinal injury would stop. The drugs brought relief, but their side effects—sleeplessness, upset stomach, dry mouth, itching, and swings between constipation and diarrhea—made me hard to live with. Though there weren't a lot of folks around, except Marcilla and my home healthcare nurses, aides and a few friends from the college drifting by. I was either euphoric or depressed and I never figured out which, when, or where. I floated in and out of myself, watching from the sidelines or so far inside it felt as though the siren's call was becoming more shrill and nasty, tinnitus hissing and ringing in my ears, begging me to give into the everlasting fall from life—screw the hereafter.

Had it all been premonition? Had the shower visions and the acknowledged fears all been about my end being near, as the monks carrying such signs in cartoons tell us? Was this what I was trying to tell myself—to give in and up to fate and let the fall take me, in or out of the shower? Or was the premonition more practical—that mysterious interior knowing that was informing me that the shower stall wasn't right and if I continued using it as I'd always done, it was out to get me through self-induced madness? Was this the Shaman's Prediction, and I didn't know that his skeletonal finger pointed to my heart-- my life—in order to warn me of this imminent danger? He appeared on the shower curtain as I was *leaving* the stall. Was that significant? Even if it was, what did it signify? That danger was out there, only God knows where? Was that the message for all the other hallucinatory visions—a phantasmagoria of fears to convey some message of vague imminent danger?

I had two separate talk therapies—one for the trauma I had endured, the other for support during my withdrawal from painkillers. This latter therapy was totally no-nonsense, consisting mainly of how-to group sessions in which various techniques and strategies were offered for support during the weaning-off period. It was in the private therapy sessions with the trauma therapist assigned to me from the mental health clinic that I began to talk and tell. At first she seemed puzzled, if not confused, as to whether my descriptions came from actual visionary events before the accident or from the trauma and all the drugs I was taking because of it. The more I told her, the more I could see the growing skepticism on her face even as she sought to accept my view of this dream-world reality. In the end, after months and months of analysis in relation to everything from my original family script, my parents' traumatic death and my own near-death experience, she came to believe that these all converged into what I labeled "the crème-de-la-crème of stresses" that gave rise to my present *necessary* state-of-mind. I had gone a little mad, she thought, so that I hadn't gone totally mad. She pointed out that the writing life was no help, with my ambitious aims and push from the Hollenbeck behind. There was, after all, the constant threat of the boot.

Dr. Claire Rosenberg cited precedence—much like a lawyer on *Law and Order*—for my stress-induced hallucinations. In patients diagnosed with Charles Bonnet Syndrome, for example, very complex, vivid hallucinations can last over several days. She wasn't certain about the sporadic nature of my visions and their seemingly expansive visual development, but she said she was open to the character of them *for me* since there was, in the professional literature, such a wide range of causes for such events, in many cases, causes that remained unknown.

Dr. Rosenberg and I parted with me having far more questions than answers popping around in my head. Therapy, I knew now, if I'd ever doubted it before, was a heady mind game. I left that "talking art" with an understanding that my emotions churned, boiled, simmered and finally rested on what I was thinking. After all, what else was there? The body did what the mind told it to do. I reasoned that if I cut off my head, there wouldn't be much to feel!

With this in mind, I sometimes humorously, sometimes frantically, searched online for a cartoon of decapitation. I found lots of funny ones about last thoughts at the guillotine and many more of sufferings on the rack, but those lines I already knew by heart since I felt I'd recently done some form of both.

I was hoping for a reminder that my thoughts made my reality which seemed to be the message of the Law of Attraction people, a camp far from my usual ground. Stay positive, positively real, and the outcome will arise that I was wishing for.

At times, I was in extreme fogginess and stupor, even during trauma therapy, but oddly, it wasn't until I was released from the hospital, with homecare nurses in part-time attendance, that I began to gain some clarity of mind and spirit. But when the tapering off of drugs began, what had kept me going in the writing life, what had actually enabled me to produce *Tanked*, was taken from me. My talisman had been the incidents in the shower, however ghastly that turned out to be. I'd used it to produce some stories that found publication, even unexpected success. My new drug-charms, once again as ghastly as they also were, were working. Or I should say, were keeping me working.

With the latest Dr. McPherson visit, since I was becoming more ambulatory, the good orthopedic doctor started reducing the dosage of Percocet. As withdrawal from this final medication increased, the clarity and calm I'd felt right after release from the hospital decreased, and the hallucinations began again—very different in content, though still vivid—only this time greatly shortened so that I knew they weren't the same kind of experiences as I'd had before. The most telling characteristic was that they took place everywhere and anytime, lasting only seconds. After a while, I grew to accept them, through sheer exhaustion, as drug withdrawal symptoms.

One Saturday, though, alone and sitting in the support chair in my newly installed bathtub, I had a sudden interior swelling of images as though I'd never left my old shower stall. It was as though once in the tub, delirium had just been waiting in the wings to carry me away. After all I'd been through I didn't even think to respond with disappointment. I just did the most expedient thing automatically—I called 911 before collapsing to the floor in hysterics, images racing through me like those old-time cinematic illustrations of madness.

Back in the hospital, I was told by a doctor in a calm but sympathetic voice, that my mentation was seriously compromised by either the drugs, their withdrawal, or by infection, maybe all three. He was highly suspect of the wound around the pins of my left ankle which had been hurting, pain that I'd grown accustomed to ignoring. In the past few days I had noticed that the ankle had taken on a new ugly hue which hadn't yet appeared when I'd had my last visit with Dr. McPherson. After blood work and a day in the hospital—walking was becoming torment—it was discovered that there was indeed an infection located in the bone of my left foot, a wound not healing, it was surmised, because of too much time at my computer, writing with too little of the rehab exercises I was supposed to be doing. What was regarded as a hard-to-heal area around the pins in the ankle bone had actually begun to ulcerate, suppuration hidden until the wound began to weep. I had carried a low-grade fever which hadn't concerned my doctors as I had wounds that were still healing. Three months of hyper-antibiotics therapy brought this new infection under control after the area was cleaned and pins reinserted—yet another surgery.

In and out of drug-induced sleep or euphoric trance, much of drug rehab down the tubes, I began to see calmer images when partially awake, perhaps like those a person sees coming out of the deep stillness of a dream. In the steno pads Marcilla brought to me I started writing these images down in words that first came to mind, following the imaging with a sort of hand-eye coordination. My left arm had been the one damaged, so with the help of the rehab techies, I was able to write on the pads held in place with clips and jury-rigged braces attached to my tilted over-the-bed tray. It wasn't the first or last time I would be grateful—to whom I wasn't certain, but grateful nonetheless—for being right-handed.

Once I'd written a word-referent to an image on the pad, other words would form, like memory traces or involuntary echoes, which I would write down as they came. It was a slow process since I couldn't write as fast as I was imaging, but in time, using a kind of invented short-hand, the process became easier. Stream-of-consciousness in the beginning, these words filled quad-ruled pages in columns. After filling several books—thousands of words in oddly-shaped columns, some so tightly rendered they were hardly decipherable, others sprawling like worms attempting to escape from the page—I began writing from a place of abandon. The reflexive nature of the activity sometimes carried me away into a trance-like state, at other times it left me exhausted—much like a person who struggles to move under the constraints of paralysis. But I found that each time I attempted to force my conscious mind to write in any way, I was unable to continue. Only feeling-states seemed to propel the words forward.

My morning routine fell into a steady line—tea following breakfast from my tray, then my usual hospital ritual of vital signs, sponge bath, medications. After a short meditation, I'd ask the nurse to pull my writing table to me. McCrutchin, my sergeant-at-arms physical therapist, had taught me well. The body likes routine. I was learning on my own, however, that my mind craved the new, while my soul demanded transcendence. My definition of soul was more like a sense of my whole state-of-being-as-is than some internal divine entity having the potential for eternal life. This morning, without realizing my soul was in control, I allowed my eyes to follow the columns not vertically but horizontally and whole vistas began to appear, distilled images as in haiku—boots, float, mud, room, sea—rest, anxious, voices, repose, hue—surly, imposter, careless, tree, shape—shadows, fall, lawn, dream, rose. On and on it went, column after column but there was a humming underneath, the first excitement I'd felt since the accident-inspired stories had run their course. Something was taking shape in all of this I didn't understand but wanted to figure out, no, that wasn't quite the nature of it. I was on a search for the hidden images I was beginning to *feel*. These feeling-states associated with the image-words were what brought me the satisfaction I had in the past sought for in the completion of a story.

Over several weeks, continuing after my hospital release at home, I began to form two, three words that I put together in a group. Writing across, I'd look at a page and attach my vision to a word in this column or that one. Resisting the urge to form conscious images or ideas, I'd drag down, as with computer-like cursor, but in long-hand, the attached word into the mix until an image-feeling-state would arise—some small vision I sensed in my gut.

rain-clear-dust
trip-branch-ice

I filled two steno pads like this, not going back to see what was there, just continuing forward, to the next and the next and the next image-feeling-state.

I was determined to not allow my interior critic to corrupt the rhythm of the words forming on the page.

Several days later, alone in the early morning sun after being wheeled to the hospital atrium, I heard a cacophony of poems—some longer, some shorter—but an entire orchestra of sound and voice wheeling in my head—noisy, without order, unrestrained. In time these found a rhythm, pace, and form that were three syllables-a-line on three lines.

By the time I left the hospital, I'd composed over a hundred variously formatted haiku. Once home, I began reading everything I could find on the art, its history and development in Japan, then in the English-speaking world and even globally. I ordered books online and used a mobile library service to get what I needed for research. As I began to gather information, I realized that my earlier writing world was fast retreating. Despite Hollenbeck's beckoning voice calls and email messages, I continued on in silence until she fell silent. As the writing began to flow, I started working at my physical therapy, spending hours in the rehab gym and my living room with its treadmill, stationary bike and exercise balls of various sizes.

Many of the great haiku masters from Japan had been wanderers, as had philosophers and writers from the States and Europe. I was getting in touch with that elusive, hard-to reach communication between thinking, feeling and walking. In the spring, when I was able to get around on steadier legs, even before my ankles had fully healed—first with a walker, then with an array of quad and single-support canes—I began walking outside. It was agonizing slow work, simply going around the block, my cell in my pocket with its speed-dials for 911 and Marcilla. Then I began slowly clocking the minutes, twenty, thirty, forty-five, and on to an hour. I knew if I kept track of the distance, I'd get discouraged. But walking daily, increasing slowly up to two and three hours in a single outing, was making me strong in more than just body. The burden of what I'd come to think of as "the great ordeal" was lifting.

McPherson wasn't altogether pleased with what she saw as distance walking too far too fast, but McCrutchin—her name had become a constant source of amusement--asked me when I was entering the Paralympic Games. When she questioned what was compelling me to walk like this, I told her the distance was unimportant, I needed the challenge. Of course, it wasn't the whole truth of it. The challenge had become non-competitive, even to me, but I wanted to, not just find, but experience what I was seeking.

At home writing my haiku, I continued the search:

away from home
a stalled
commitment

darkened cave
stormy coast
fright then flight

moon on edge
cliff hanging
waterfall

These weren't Bashō, Buson, or Shiki. Not even the revisionist Japanese-American Yasuda. I knew I was still lost to art and life, but I was compelled to move, to create. I was becoming physically athletic and mentally robust. My heart had grown steady, my blood pressure perfect, the panic was gone. McPherson was silent, except for an occasional, "Well, I'll be damned." McCrutchin let me believe it was all my doing, but she insisted I carry her home number on speed dial. I knew what she meant to me. I had to have special shoes and inserts made from molds of my feet. Pain from pressure in my legs, pelvis, and especially my feet were constant. Sometimes I laid in my bed gritting my teeth, tears running down my face, while I watched old movies on TMC or re-read *The Heart of Haiku* by Jane Hirshfield with aspirin-induced ringing in my ears.

One day in Barnes and Noble, limping with my support cane, I ran across Rebecca Solnit's book on the history of walking, *Wanderlust*. I read it in three days and for weeks afterward I kept returning to the chapter on pilgrimages. On the third line, first paragraph, she had written, "...*walking in search of something intangible*." It became a mantra. I began to walk. Walk, write, walk, write—the thinking accompanying the walking, the non-thinking accompanying the writing.

I had problems controlling my head which told me to go farther, faster. My body told me to go slow and steady, increasing with a sense of healing, not with the principle I'd learned from fitness training—no pain, no gain. That pain ultimately made my decisions. In time, as the pain subsided, the walking expanded. As the walking expanded, the haiku grew, both finding a steady flow. The form became hypnotic, as natural as iambic pentameter, my foot step, my heartbeat. I walked in all kinds of weather except temperatures at freezing and below or when the streets and roads were glazed with snow or ice. It was a solitary act, like writing. When somebody attempted to stop me to talk or ask for directions or interrupt me at all, I nodded my head, saying, "I'm sorry." One older man began passing me with a smile, waving and saying, "I'm sorry," before I did. It became our greeting. But there were regulars who couldn't let me slide past. A couple had even sat down next to me at Gimme! Coffee and asked if I wanted a companion. "Walking buddies," they said, "make the time go faster." No, I told them. I need my own pace.

"Oh, you're in training," they said.

"That it?" they asked.

Truth was I didn't want companionship. If I was seeking comfort, it was the comfort of routine—at least that's what I told myself for a while. But I knew I was growing increasingly restless for that which was eluding me. I was the greyhound with the rabbit in front of its nose. I just wasn't in the race for time or money anymore. In fact, I wasn't in a race at all. I thought of myself as *waiting* forward.

9.

My job at the college resumed as soon as I could walk around the block without a nurse or aide and I could drive. I had full classes which I taught at first in circles so I wouldn't have to be on my feet any more than necessary. As I grew stronger I kept the circles, larger classes two and three rows deep, doing a round robin every week from front to middle to back and up front again in the hopes nobody would feel left out of that prized inner circle closest to the teacher. I held discussion groups, smaller classes and office visits online part of the time, even gave assignments and short lectures through Skype. My life was once more full of people, the inter-collegial life of teaching. Writing was on hold except for the daily journaling I did in long-hand and a small amount of professional publishing, reviews mainly on the internet. And the haiku.

Tonia Hollenbeck hadn't contacted me, but knowing her as I did, I figured she was getting antsy, if not angry, about having something from me to market. I had sent her a small book containing an abbreviated interpretation of my accident and subsequent path into haiku, a small annotated history of the art and then some of my poems built around my 3-3-3 structure. I called it *The Pulsating Heart*. When I hadn't heard from her in over a month, I called her.

She was oddly lukewarm, almost distant, as though she was distracted. I heard background talk and the fluttering of papers. I thought I heard a shredder going, but didn't have the energy to wade through the almost certain lecture about her desire for "something more substantial," from me which seemed the most likely explanation for her distance. I assumed she was either not finding a placement for my book or not attempting to find one because it wasn't up to her standards. It seemed strange that with the National Book Award my name couldn't sell a small book of poetry, even stranger that she wasn't contacting me about this one as it had been some time since we'd corresponded. I had gone silent on her for a while during recovery, and I was busy on the job and walking daily for longer periods of time, so I let pushing Hollenbeck for an answer slide. Now I wanted to know.

She informed me that she was moving. So it really was about her and not me or the book. She had to be out of her loft within the month, she said. I was wondering where this was going because she'd moved from Austin to Palo Alto when I was a client, and there hadn't been any loss of continuity in her agency service. Most of our talking was by phone or email, and I usually sent her my manuscripts by attachment, special courier or snail mail. But she threw me a curve. She was giving up the business for marriage and life abroad. As she related her story I felt like I was caught in an episode of *The Golden Girls* with Blanche Devereaux. With great animation, she told me she and her fiancé were taking a year to go sailing in his yacht down the Côte du Languedoc—here I laughed as she worked her grade-school way through the French—and the Costa Brava, Spain.

"He wants to go down to the Costa Dorada, Benidorm, and then Alicante where he often stays at the Ponderosa Hotel. Can you imagine?" She laughed outrageously. "I wanted to tell him the TV ranch was in the Sierra Nevada, but, hell, the characters acted like Texans, didn't they? Well okay, without the accent it's true, but I decided to not get into it with him. And a six hundred thousand acre-ranch? Sounds like Texas to me! Anyway, he loves anything Texan." I guess he does, I thought as I tried to picture Tonia Hollenbeck in ropers with rhinestones and a girlie-styled Stetson—was there even such a thing? I had only seen her three times, twice on book tours near her California residence, and in New York City for my National Book Award presentation, but it was enough for me to have to work at imagining her as a decked-out Texan woman even though she was originally from Austin. The accent was what had captured the French guy, I reasoned. I didn't have the heart to interrupt her so I let her spin on, "He promises that we will be spending unlimited time in the Balearic Islands, primarily Majorca. Not so bad, huh?"

I wanted to ask how this came about, but the story would be as outlandish as what she was already telling me. And anyway, I was reeling over the impact this was having on my life. But I gathered myself enough to ask if this change meant a total abandonment of her agency life?

She laughed. "Which life was that?"

"The one I've pinned my hopes on." As soon as I said it, I knew it was false, even a lie. The comment belonged to another life for her and for me. In that instant I realized what I needed to do. "Tonia, I'm sorry, I'm thrilled for you. I don't know where that comment came from. Maybe it's apprehension about my future. Hell, I don't know. But in all fairness, I've been attempting to gain the courage to call you and announce something close to the same thing—mine, of course, without the Frenchman, his resources, and what has to be that gargantuan ship of his."

There was a long pause. She became serious. "I'm sorry for not getting in touch. I've just been in a maelstrom since I decided to marry this man… situation." She laughed again. "I've been remiss in informing you, but I passed your manuscript to the woman who bought my business, Terri Contento. Crazy name, but she's not. She's great, you'll love her, she'll work hard for you. I assure you she's really, really good for it…"

Suddenly I also knew what was next for me without vision or hallucination—perhaps with an epiphany, a life-sized insight taking shape. "Tonia, I just need to have the manuscript returned. I'm sitting this one out."

"Are you sure you want to do that? It's a fine little book, really it is." She waited and when I didn't respond to this, she said quietly, "I can do that easily for you. You've got to be tired."

"Exhausted. And I'm back at work with a full teaching load. I'm not for certain how much longer this will last."

"You don't mean you're giving up the teaching…." She paused, a light coming on. "Not the writing!" She sounded troubled all at once.

"Maybe. At least as you and I've known it."

"Oh honey…" she began.

"Tonia…." How could I explain my current life in two hundred and fifty words or less? "I'm fine…this is fine…" I felt suddenly wordless. Anything coming to mind was clichéd. "I'm not sure what's going to ultimately happen but let me just say, I'm sure about the next step." I finally got this out in one sentence.

I reassured her some more, wished her well, vowed to stay in touch and hung up. The phone had barely disconnected before I called the Humanities Department at the college and asked for an appointment to see the chairman.

10.

After spring graduation my college teaching life was behind me. It wasn't easy—involving contractual disputes and settlements—but in the end I came out without too many embattlement scars. I had to pay back some of the medical imbursements and reach a few agreements about transitioning in the new instructor and giving up curricula designs. It was easy enough to do. Resigning hadn't been as difficult as I thought it might be. Afterward I felt weightless, though remarkably steady. "Falling Back on the Wings of Life" became the title of a visual journal of haiku I started with illustrations in watercolor. I simply filled the pages one by one with no purpose beyond filling them.

With the coming of autumn, I had the urge to touch everything I owned. After a walk and bath, I'd put on fresh clothes and sit down in the room I was working on, carrying each item to my lap or feet and sitting with it.

I did this room by room, beginning with the writing study, lifting and carrying books and magazines from shelves. I looked at each one carefully deciding whether to keep it in my life or let it go. Day by day, hour by hour, I looked at and through my possessions. The books and magazine articles called this de-cluttering. I wasn't sure what I called it. It felt as though I was cleansing, purifying, the way that priests do before entering the inner sanctum, the way shamans do before entering caves where they sit alone and wait until their souls fly away from them to gain power. I knew I was preparing myself for some transition or new direction. Looking back, some of my searching had felt like clothes shopping, trying on garments to see what fit and felt like "me." Now it was more like cleaning out the closet to see what I couldn't live without.

In the end I kept very little because when I stopped with one room, before I moved on to the next, I went back through it again, and again, then again. I was obsessed with the notion that everything should be fresh, nothing should remain on shelves, in cabinets, standing around gathering dust from the past or turning to mold waiting on a future. I needed everything to be as if it were just born, alive and squirming in my hands. If any item didn't give me that feeling of aliveness, I turned my back on it. The trash was overloaded each week and I made many trips to the garbage center. Everything else went into recycling at the curb or was given away through free recycling online. People arrived and carried away my life, almost daily, pieces at a time.

Marcilla came and went, not helping me much, bringing food and chatter, sitting across in a chair eating a lot of Mango Häagen Dazs, telling me it was protein and fruit. She finally expressed dismay over what she felt she was observing. She suggested carefully, pleadingly, that I might be calling death to my door. Was this what I was preparing for? Was she watching an impending suicide?

I told her, "It's the opposite. In birds and snakes, spiders and insects this is called molting. We humans just do it a little at a time, losing dead cells constantly, becoming other people. We just don't realize it. When we do it intentionally with our possessions, we notice it because it's materiality, external to us. But our bodies take care of us moment by moment, invisibly. We just don't pay that kind of attention, don't take the time to see it happening."

One afternoon, she put her half-eaten pint of ice cream down and waited until I looked directly at her. She was crying. "Why do I feel like I'm losing you? And after all of this…this immense amount of work in order for you to get your life back. Hollenbeck's disappearance isn't the end of your known world, you know."

I reassured her that it wasn't Hollenbeck, that she, Marcilla, was now representing another way of creating and being. I wasn't attempting to get *that life* back anymore. I wanted a new one, but I was still the old me and she was right there beside me. I didn't know if this was totally true. I honestly didn't know what was calling me forward, propelling my life into another state of being. I told her, "In snakes, one sign of molting is that their eyes turn cloudy. Evidently the cap that covers the eye is loosened up in order to be shed with the skin. I like this metaphor, and the whole idea that these creatures find rough surfaces to rub against. You're my rough surface, Marcilla. I need you to help me shed."

But my vision had cleared. Each morning as I slipped into my bath, an ocean of possibilities floated out and over me. I listened and waited for that call sailors hear beyond the railing of ships at sea. I reasoned that if Orpheus could be saved from destruction by his creations, perhaps so could I. Or as in the contest Hera, the queen of heaven, instigated between the Sirens and Muses, perhaps my muse would win. I lifted my feet above the water and marveled at how they had healed, only small indented scars on both sides of each ankle told the tale of my shipwreck and rescue. I wiggled my toes and laughed at the forming image of a mermaid's tail which I brought down on the water with a mighty slap.

LIVING IN THE COUNTRY WITH THE NEIGHBORS AND MAURICE SENDAK

We were six around the table in a local bar where we'd taken to gathering after our book club meeting, which had disintegrated into more of a social club with each monthly get-together. All of us were still working—our club had met on Thursday evenings for a couple of years—so it became harder and harder, the longer we met, to read the literary selections every thirty days. The majority picked what we read, all fiction, works we hadn't gotten around to because we didn't have the time and knew we never would without a pressing reason—recent works, just not current, such as Nicole Krauss's *Man Walks Into Room* and *The Great House*; Ha Jin's *Trash*; Don DeLillo's *Underworld*; Thomas Pynchon's *Gravity's Rainbow*—really old but four of us hadn't read it. Forget about the classics. Dostoyevsky or Proust after work and supper most nights instead of *Law and Order* or even re-runs of *The Sopranos*? It wasn't going to happen. The week-ends were sacrosanct to us all, reserved for our personal lives.

It was a most unlikely bunch—a librarian, a computer designer, a professor of epistemology and ethics, an antique dealer, a therapist, and me, a retired art teacher with a job at the local district part-time—one of everything. But after the first five, six months we hit an amicable stride and our discussions were lively and on the whole stimulating. We were generally well-read, filled with curiosity and argumentation about, well, you name it. "Taking issue" got to be a hilarious interjection, as in: "I take issue with that." Lots of laughter. Also, the more pejorative "disconnect," as in: "There's a disconnect here, people," meaning there was a difference between what someone thought the author intended and other readers' interpretation of those intentions. Lots of groans on this one. We spent a fair amount of time discussing if we could even get to the authors' intentions, how relevant those intentions were in any given passage, and whether our analysis and interpretation of the narrative was valid or whether validity could even be established—and if so, on what grounds. The professor of philosophy in the group—who we called Prof—forever weighed discussion down with his "deconstruction," "exegesis," and "premises, propositions, and justifiable conclusions." But we had a healthy respect for each other, a love of humor, laughter and talk, so any imbalance was usually restored rather quickly. Periodically expounding on this or that had to be set to rules, which in time would unravel, and we would again build another matrix for discussion. All in all, though, it was a gathering we didn't want to abandon, but after a year or so we found our rationale sagging as a reading group. We finally admitted that we didn't want to read together so much as talk together; hence, our drift more and more to the nearby Irish pub, Heather on the Hill-- the owner was Heather McKeon--for libations and, well, *talk*.

Our socializing wasn't the usual day-to-day chatting about our jobs, our personal lives, or even about divulging some remarkable incident that happened to any of us since our last get-together. Without any prompting we seemed to do during our social hour what we found hard as a book club. Somebody would begin a story with an interesting discussion topic and anybody who related to it told a story of his or her own having to do with that topic and we were off and running—at the mouths, at least—digging to find the essence or truth of the stories we were exchanging.

Tonight the storytelling was begun by therapist Stella—whom we called Ella. Even though she now lived in town, she told us about her life in the country and asked whether we thought living there would change our perspective about nature, especially if we moved there as city-dwellers, and—most importantly to her—why folks who thought of themselves as city-dwellers would decide to take on the country at all. How many had lived in the country at one time or another in our lives, she wanted to know? Interestingly, even though all but Gloria were now living in the city or in some village within ten-to-twenty minutes' drive from it, each had lived in the country at one time or other or stayed with farmer-relatives over extended periods of time as children or young adults. Three told their stories, each telling beginnings with another round of drinks. By the time my turn came around, twilight was seeping through the blinds and coffee and sandwiches were ordered so that listeners could stay awake and attend to what I had to say. And I needed the coffee to help me keep the tale going at a goodly pace. I was the last to speak as the other two said they'd spent a couple of meetings telling their stories of family dynamics and moral decisions surrounding the illness and deaths of their parents and wanted to opt out of this round.

Everybody knew I'd lived in the country before they'd met me two years ago and knew I'd lived in the village outside the city for the past three but few knew I'd lived in the country just six months shy of thirteen years. When I told them this, they expressed surprise.

"Don't I seem like the country type?" As far as I was concerned my appearance was a dead giveaway. I lived in flannel or cotton over-shirts, tees, jeans and hiking boots most of the time and thought I had the complexion of an avid outdoor walker.

"Not so much that," Gloria, the antique dealer, offered. "It's just a long time to live there and then leave. Most folks who live in the country that long stay in the country unless they move out of the area."

"Or get too old for it," Ella chimed in.

"It is a lot of work," Katherine added. "All of us are now living in town, which says *something*. Well, except for Gloria, who still looks pretty lively to me." I wondered if librarians had a special attraction to outdoorsy appearance and attitude. Katherine was on the petite side with a braid slung over a shoulder and the pallor of somebody who rarely left the stacks—stereotypic but nonetheless true.

"Here, here." Gloria raised her cup.

"How long was each of you there?" I asked. A fast count revealed that most had stayed no more than three to five years.

"Well, that shoots my theory to pieces," Gloria said. "I just want to add that the country makes me feel younger each day. I feel as though I'm participating in forces greater than those that move my little working world. I don't think the city can do that, at least not for me. I spent my childhood in New York City, as you all know, and the energy doesn't hum the same."

"So maybe we all march to a different hummer?" Katherine offered. We laughed and raised our cups to her and Gloria and humming. Everybody went back to sandwiches and coffee for a bit.

"I find the length of your stays in the country fascinating," I told them. "Because it took Katie and me three, four years to get settled, which is actually what my story is about. I think I'm aiming toward answering Ella's question about why city-dwellers would take on the country and whether it changed my attitude about nature.

"I'm not sure while Katie and I lived together…let's see, I was on my own after the eighth year of our living in the country." I stopped and thought for a minute. "It actually was eight and a half years," I said, wondering why I felt the need to get that time so accurate. "Anyhow, I'm not sure we—I—ever truly settled into country living. I had many adventures out there, some usual, some extraordinary, some strange and others, I guess you could say, were just downright enlightening but…"

"Enlightening?" Prof interrupted with a slight cast of sarcasm.

"I think so, yeah," I said, attempting to think through what this meant to me. "You know, when something happens that seems very ordinary but when you reflect on it later, it goes far beyond what had been revealed to you at the time and that reflection changes your perception and the meaning of what's happened. I had quite a few of those insights out in the country that I don't think could have happened, at least not in the same way, in the city."

I sighed. All at once, this felt heavier than I'd intended when I started, but I trudged on. "We'd moved to the country for the quiet. I wanted to write full-time after I retired, which was coming up soon. I thought the country would be a less distracting environment. Katie had a job at City College, which was only five, six minutes' drive from the country house we ended up buying. But we discovered very quickly that unless you were fortunate enough to purchase property during one of the recessions or inherited some real land or money from deceased parents or you caught a foreclosure advantage of a special sort, you wouldn't have enough acreage to keep the noise at bay. In our neck of the woods, there weren't any noise ordinances, which was the main reason most of our neighbors raised chickens with roosters that crowed at daybreak, hunted anything non-human that moved—in and out of season, and at all hours—repaired heavy-duty trucks at a New York registered auto shop at the top of our driveway and raced motorcycles in the summer and snowmobiles in the winter around a track that came within two hundred yards of our dining and living room sliding glass doors."

"In the *country*? That's crazy!" This from Prof who had only spent a month in the country as a kid during summer breaks from school. "You'd think. And that's exactly what we did think before we got a view from the reality side of country living. This biker and his mama-wife who owned the truck repair garage and sponsored the motorcycle and snowmobile club also had weekly gatherings of a dozen to twenty friends who raced—in this case 'weekly' means both Saturday and Sunday—and afterwards participated in outdoor barbeques or indoor country music fests, the guitars and twangy voices live and on record seeping through their doors and windows or blasting from the deck into our meadow, front yard and house."

"You lived out there *how* long?" Ella asked.

"Yeah, well, perhaps too long, as you'll see, but twelve-and-a-half years to be exact."

"You put up with this for twelve…"

Gloria interrupted Ella by telling her to let me finish what I'd started, that she'd probably get a better answer through my story. They both raised their cups as a sign for me to go on.

I raised mine and continued. "Katie and I—I should tell you who don't know that I got the property in the divorce settlement—we'd seen our house on a flier in an alternative grocery market's bulletin board. The guy selling the place told us when we called that he'd tried to make the sale himself but found the whole procedure daunting so he'd finally put the place on the market through a local real estate agent. We got the owner's number from one of those tear-off slips at the bottom of his personally-designed-and-printed flier that he told us he hadn't bothered to take down figuring that the more notices out and about, the better. I thought that was against real estate agency rules but didn't alert him to that fact. When we got the house description from his real estate agent—this was some years before notices were widely used online—we had to laugh at what we read. It was described as 'funky Dutch' with three bedrooms, two baths, and an open area for dining.

"But when we went to look at the place, we were wowed. We passed a meadow swaying lazily in the sun, a pond teeming with life, and caught a view of woods that cast a shadowy canopy over the house on an increasingly warm sunny day. Maples, poplars, and elms shaded the back porch and the upstairs terrace. It looked downright poetically bucolic. But once inside, we discovered much of the house was unfinished, including the floors which were actually sub-flooring without any coverings—I'm talking about no-nothin' of any kind, except slivers. There were actually tin can lids nailed over knotholes, and both up-and-downstairs spaces were totally open without partitions for rooms with the exception of the baths. And the baths! The one upstairs could hardly be described as such. The door practically hit the toilet when we opened it to take a look, and in order for the bathtub to fit, it'd been placed on a platform two steps up from the flooring, even with, and almost touching, the lavatory. I kid you not. There was room to walk in, turn to the toilet or take the steps up to the bath or stand to wash your hands with your butt practically out the door!

"The entire house looked as though it had been thrown together with items from a developers' garage sale. All of the doors and windows were of different size and style, as were the hinges, handles, knobs and such. 'Funky' we understood right away. But what was 'Dutch' about all this, we weren't certain, unless it was the quasi-gambrel roof. There weren't any dormer windows or colonial features of any kind. In later years, we would sometimes call our house 'Dutch,' as in Dutch needs a paint job again or Dutch could use a partition off the kitchen for a pantry. We thought this particularly hilarious since we both were politically left of liberal, and Ronald Reagan's nickname was Dutch."

Ella interrupted again, declaring that "the Gimp" was also Dutch's other nickname, which was apropos of what, none of us was sure, unless she was insinuating that our house was on its last legs. Prof, clarifying every detail as he so often did, came to the rescue, in this case by pointing out that "the Gimp" was the name of James Cagney's gangster character in *Love Me or Leave Me*—Martin "Moe the Gimp" Snyder—while Reagan's nickname was "the Gipper." Oh, oh, oh, sure, sure, sure, they all howled, while I sat there wondering how the heck the Prof remembered this kind of trivia among his arguments for the foundation of knowledge and morality. Soon everybody's attention wandered back to me and my story, so I started a new paragraph.

"The house was heated by wood—it had an old Vermont Casing stove—with a small propane back-up, which Katie and I thought was interesting, even charming. We should have been tested for competency of purchase! After we'd moved in, we were stunned by how huge the wide-open areas both upstairs and downstairs were. Our possessions looked tiny in the enormous spaces. But we got to work on it right away. We had the living room carpeted, the subflooring oil-based painted—I did that because of Katie's allergies—and then we spread large area rugs throughout. We divided the rooms by new and used furniture and the house began to take on the appearance and feel of warmth and familiarity we'd hoped for. An inside-outside atmosphere was created by the four large sliding glass windows. We could sit and watch life in the meadows and pond and on the back side of the house, the woods. So we began to settle into country life, or I should say, what we *thought* was country life.

"Several questionable features had slipped our attention when we bought the house. One was the enormously long driveway. The house sat down from the road almost a quarter of a mile. We actually thought this an advantage since it seemed the road we were to live on had a fair amount of traffic, and we would be removed from it by our low, sloping drive. But when the blizzard of '93 hit—remember that one? Well, you can just imagine."

A couple of listeners slapped the table and made some agreeing noises. Gloria had to slide in a few comments about how this storm had pushed her country living almost to the limit and how she went about getting her rural mojo back. When I won the floor again, I elaborated, "Well, when the storm unloaded on our driveway, we were snow bound for two and a-half days, while we waited for a backhoe to dig us out."

"The county can do that work for you, you know," Gloria instructed, as though I were still living there and could use this information for future blizzards.

"Forget the county public workers on this one—at least, not where we lived. They had their hands full getting the main roads cleared for people to get to and from town and the highways. The fellow who dug us out came plowing down our drive at twilight with headlights swinging back and forth like a miner's hat, depositing the snow to the left and right sides of the meadow until he reached our house. For this bail-out, we were charged one hundred eighty-seven dollars—an exorbitant rate at the time for about an hour of work. Hourly minimum wage was four dollars and sixty-one cents. I looked it up, because I'd been so outraged with his charge, the price tag indelibly stamped on my brain, but what're you gonna do? He left a path of snow up to the windows of our car and just wide enough for passage. The spring thaw left our dirt drive a soggy mess which had to be dug out, several tons of mud carried away, and then resurfaced with gravel, setting us back a couple thousand. We hired the neighbor and his dump truck for the hauling in and out of the old and new gravel. This was before we confronted him about his level of noise in our little valley."

"Noise can be a problem, I grant you that." Gloria looked contrite, as though she'd been the one who'd convinced us to take up country life.

"I'll get to that, but first, there was another aspect of country living we hadn't counted on—the amount of insects. To the right of the huge upstairs open space, a storage area under the eaves contained a wasp's nest big enough to handle a few generations of buzzing insects, and they weren't just in our storage area but hosting in our house everywhere and of every kind and description.

"We had somehow missed during the purchasing process much of what we consciously began taking in after we started settling into the house. We saw *some* of it before we bought the place, of course—we weren't totally stupid—but it didn't strike us as anything that couldn't be changed easily by a little cleaner and paint. All houses need work, we told ourselves. We were to find out from our neighbor when he helped with our driveway that the former owner, who had been characterized by our real estate agent as a 'free spirit,' had left all four of the downstairs sliding glass doors open for summer ventilation and access for his dogs and cats to run in and out at will. He hadn't mowed any of the meadow down for a yard, let alone a lawn, so every crevice and cranny of the house had cobwebs, small insect nests, or left-over remains of their having been there at one time or another. Fly specks made upper parts of the rooms seem like randomly-stenciled designs. Listen, I'm all for free-spiriting but usually my generosity in this direction is if-and-only-if I don't have to do the wipe-up!

"Since the outside of the house was made of thinly-stained, rough-hewn timbers, we were invaded by droning carpenter bees that bore perfect holes into the sides of our house every spring. We felt after living there several years that the Du-Right Pest Control guy was a friend—the same for the chimney sweep and the fellow who cleaned our septic tank each summer. It took a good two years to establish decent front and side yards with definite boundaries and a path leading from the back porch to the wood pile and on into the trees."

"Did you have termites? Sounds like a perfect habitat for them, with the rough timber on the outside of the house," Doug-the-techie asked.

"Well, that's another issue. Supposedly, the house had been treated. I say supposedly because we never saw anything in writing....Yeah, I know, I know. And as most of you do know, infestation can go on for years because the outside wood may not show any signs of termites being there. I noticed trails—what I later learned were called tubes—along the foundation but, hell, I didn't know what I was looking at. And I saw some winged insects in the early spring in places, but I took them to be ants, and since we didn't have an ant problem inside—wonders of all wonders—I just assumed the tubes were connected to the weeds and wild grass growth that had been around the house for so long. Hey, it'd go away in time, right? Well, no. Several applications of termiticides later by the Du Right guy—and no, his name wasn't Dudley, it was Frank Something-or-other. Anyway, the problem got under control but I don't think was ever fully cured. It passed inspection when I sold the place, thank God Almighty." I drank some coffee and waited. After a small silence, I went on.

"We hadn't known anything about how to heat by wood. So we ran short the first winter and overdid our purchase on the second, which turned into 'a chunk of change,' as we complained to every friend who would listen. The stacking took weeks, especially since we both worked and had to stack after suppertime and on week-ends. The Vermont Casing was a remarkably efficient stove despite its years, but the heat was uneven. It was either, as the song goes, too hot or too cold, according to whether the flames were waxing or waning, and the heat didn't penetrate upstairs until we had floor registers installed and small fans at strategic places to suck the warmth upstairs and to circulate it around the open space. The small bathroom was icy cold all winter and a sauna during July and August."

"I hate heating by wood." Gloria shook her head. "I simply don't do it anymore. I had propane installed."

"I hear you. We should have taken the wood stove out and left the propane, but that meant a whole redo upstairs and, well, I won't get into it. You know how that goes."

Gloria rubbed her fingers together in the familiar gesture for money.

"I have to say the home place did have its advantages. The house sat on eleven acres of land with a huge front meadow and a pond, which attracted all sorts of birds including a brief morning visit once by a white egret, rarely seen as far north as New York, and bullfrogs which serenaded us to sleep all summer long. I purchased bird, wildlife, and wild grass-and-flower field guides and delighted in learning the common and scientific names for all that surrounded us daily throughout the seasons.

"And, God, was there ever wildlife! No end, really. We once had to hire a pest control outfit to come and remove a raccoon and her babies from our crawl space. The window-vent had fallen out without our noticing, and the creature had taken advantage of the hidden and dry shelter to have her babies. All three were taken by the Wildlife Haven and Conservation Service which reassured us that the animals would be safely relocated, despite an increasing epidemic of rabies in our area. I thought of my father's remark as he cleaned out my younger sister's pet mice cage once when she was on vacation with a friend from school. 'My God,' he said, 'we set traps constantly for these rodents in our farm house when I was growing up, and now I'm cleaning out their house and laying down new flooring for them!' Having my sister's love for animals of every kind, I didn't want to hear anything from the pest control guy but relocation for our discovered raccoon and her newborn family."

"We had a problem with wild dogs," Gloria interjected. "They run in packs, believe it or not, just like wolves. And I'm not talking about wolves, coyotes and the like. I mean *wild dogs*. I guess I should more accurately call them feral. Dogs that people drop off in the country, some that are born on the streets or in the country. They're social animals so they form packs and go through garbage or attack farm animals in groups. In some areas it has reached epidemic proportions, especially in metro areas where they present a huge danger to the public and various delivery services."

"Did a pack attack you or something?" Ella asked.

"No, we saw them at night rushing around the outside fences of our animal sheds and yard. We had chickens and goats when we first moved to the country. Everett called the pest control people, and they maintained watches for several weeks. Evidently the dogs moved on. I understand that on reservations this is an enormous problem, but I read somewhere that vet programs are in place now to neuter these animals. There are even sanctuary programs that take some and turn them into loving domestic pets which are adopted. It's a huge problem worldwide, really."

"I've seen ads about abandoned pets. People think they're saving their animals from killing shelters when they drop them off in the country. But in some places there're shoot-and-kill policies, which are slowly being replaced. But humane societies, vet services, and pest control agencies don't want to deal with it because it's so huge. They're overwhelmed."

"Hell, c'mon, it's money," Ella said, disgusted, leaning back in her chair. "These kinds of programs seem superfluous unless the public is educated."

"And the politicians," Doug added.

"And the politicians," Gloria echoed.

A silence fell over the group. We all had pets and the reality was hard to contemplate. So I picked up my story, to change the subject if nothing else.

"We were smart enough to take a few twilight drives past the place, and on one of these a small cloud of dust and a distant rumble caught our attention out in the field too near the house we were considering buying. But the biker came into the neighbor's yard at cruising speed, and we thought we spotted a muffler on the engine. So we put in a purchase offer, deciding they weren't into anything too outrageous. But we went out there several times later and realized that our judgement had been overshadowed by our desire for an affordable country home. Three years later, we were still talking about why we didn't follow our instincts and find some legal way out of this potentially unpleasant state of affairs, even if it meant forfeiting the purchase offer deposit. But we didn't, so in that third year of our ongoing discussion about the noise, we called the neighbors for a council.

"'I moved out here to race my bikes with friends,' the neighbor told us, once seated in a relaxed manner in our dining room, shoveling in the baked treats we'd offered with coffee, his wife by his side. 'I love racing. It's why I live in the country.' His wife smiled and waited, both of their tattoos flashing aggressively from their bare upper arms. 'Harley,' said one, 'Love,' said the other."

"Tell me his name was Harley! C'mon. It was, wasn't it?" Doug smiled and slugged down more coffee.

"That would've been a perfect mama-touch, Doug, and the 'Love' tattoo on her arm was probably just that, for him, not the bike. But alas, no. 'Twas just the name of their bikes. Anyway, I asked him if there was some kind of compromise we could reach. I explained that we couldn't have friends over for dinner on any week-end afternoon or evening without their motorcycles or snowmobiles raising such a ruckus that it, literally, shook our house past any decent level for conversation or pleasant atmosphere for an enjoyable meal.

"When he seemed cemented to his claim of no-holds-barred-country-noise-rights, I asked him if he liked opera. He just stared at me before asking, 'What does that have to do with anything?' He knew what was coming. I was certain he was just playing dumb."

"Arias on the terrace, right?" Doug interjected again.

"You betcha," I grinned back at him and the group. "So I said, 'I have two Pioneer 9 speakers with the capacity for rather ear-damaging volume that I can put out on my front deck aimed directly at your house and play arias of major sopranos and countertenors at full blast anytime night or day. Since, as you say, there are no laws governing noise in our fair country neighborhood, why not?'"

My colleagues clapped their hands, did some whistling and high-fiving like teens used to do, and had Heather refill their cups while I went on.

"He didn't think the other neighbors would take to that very well. I told him that his motorcycling, trucking, and snowmobiling didn't seem to bother them, so why not opera?"

"Didn't the neighbors complain? I mean, about the motorcycle noise?" Ella asked. I looked up to see four puzzled faces. Only Gloria knew.

"They were too far away to care, right?" she offered, with disgust.

"That's about it, yeah. I had already tried to petition the noise issue with them—at least with the neighbors nearby—without success and knew that the distance between the properties did made the difference. Nobody up the road in either direction could hear much of his truck repair, let alone their motorcycle racing down the hill further away from the road. They knew what the situation was but were removed from it, so didn't personally want to 'make trouble with the neighbors.'"

"Well, shit!" Gloria hit the table. "So much for community. Friggin' cowards."

"True enough, but his wife surprised us. She said that they were attempting to find land to rent where they could race and promised to keep up the search until they found something suitable, which they eventually did. And they were gracious enough to allow one day on the weekend with no racing until their move to the other tracks."

"Fuckin' big of them," Prof added, his swearing surprising me. It occurred to me that he had some hidden talents he hadn't made visible yet.

"After their move to the rented racing land, silence was hardly restored as there was still a generous amount of heavy truck engine noise from his repair shop but because it was at the top of our drive, it at least wasn't causing the doors and windows in our house to clatter, and there wasn't much noise after sunset. During the final years of my living in the house alone, things became relatively quiet, in fact far too quiet."

I asked my friends if I should stop and continue next time, because I had a bit more to tell or did they want me to stop altogether which was fine by me, but they all insisted that I continue. Prof asked if I was going to get to the point of my story anytime soon. He was quick to add that he wasn't rushing me—really and honestly—but even though it wasn't exactly late, he needed to be home at a reasonable hour to help his wife with one of their sick sons, since she hadn't had much sleep in the last two days and nights. We all glanced at the clock. I was surprised by my irritation over his comment. *My story's point?* Had he sat there bored out of his mind—and how many others as well?—while I went on and on about what I thought was an answer to Ella's question about why any of us now living in the city might want to live in the country.

"You know," I said, attempting to sound agreeable to answering his question. "I don't think that's what storytellers actually do, even the really great ones." The professor stopped picking up his iPhone and getting ready to stand.

"You don't think storytellers—writers, film-makers—have a point to their stories?" He seemed flummoxed.

"I do. But I think they do it in a round-about way." I waited a minute. *I thought that's what I was doing*, passed through my mind, but I let it slide. Instead I offered, "Maurice Sendak is one of my favorite writers and he…"

"The kiddie-book guy?" the professor interrupted.

This time my anger was quick, but, again, I held it in check. "Once at a book signing of his, a woman called Sendak just that and he told an interviewer later that he wanted to kill her. I don't think he told his accuser that but I understand his wanting to." I grinned at Prof with what I hoped was a steady, genial attitude. "And I'm not saying I want to do you in for that thought either." Somebody whispered a "whew" and scattered, mock laughter followed. "But Sendak stated more than once that he wrote *books*, and *people* were the ones calling them 'children's books,' which has a lot to do with what I'm getting at, maybe." I didn't wait for the Prof's argument. "Sendak talked about what he called 'the story within the story,' which is what he said was his intention for *anybody* reading his books but especially the kids who did. It was important to him to not condescend to children. He wrote to them with honesty about their passions, even the ugly things, things that scared them. That's why they loved him. He thought it was the adults who were actually afraid, 'seeking safety from their own monsters,' is how he put it."

"The Wild Things," somebody added while I was looking down into my cup. It sounded like Katherine.

"Yeah, exactly that." I looked up at her, then back at Prof. "Moyer interviewed Sendak on his program sometime in the early 2000s, I think it was. On *Now with Bill Moyers*. I actually saw that interview and in it Moyers related to Sendak a time when he'd talked with Joseph Campbell about Sendak's work. Campbell had told Moyers that one of the great moments in literature for him was the scene in *Where the Wild Things Are* when Max first sees the monsters who try to scare him with their eyes, teeth and claws. But Max stares them down and tells them to 'be still,' and in that moment the fear is reversed. The monsters become afraid of Max and make him King of the Wild Things. Campbell told Moyers that it was only when we confront our demons that we become the king of ourselves and perhaps even of the world. So Campbell recognized that Sendak's 'story within the story' was for us all, not just for kids."

I saw that the professor was getting antsy to respond, but I held up my hand so that I could continue with the thought I wanted to complete about all this before I lost the courage to confront him with it.

"There's something else that Sendak brought out in that interview. He said he was an observer of both nature and art and implied that this was also true for everything that happened to him. It was his job as an author, though he didn't call it that. He believed there was a connection between his observations and his readers' perceptions of them, which was the point or truth or message or outcome—whatever you want to call it—of his story. I like his idea that the communication of 'the story within the story,' between the teller and listener, is the truth of what is being told. And when I say 'truth,' I know it sounds very abstract, and monumental, and beyond our everyday experience so as to seem almost ungraspable. But I also think that's the point Sendak was making. He mentioned his special connection to Mozart and Melville. The truth of his listening and reading them was ineffable, close to mysterious and beyond comprehension, but which, he claimed, carried a deep affinity with him, nonetheless."

Prof had either decided to give up or hear me out because he remained silent, tapping his iPhone gently on the table while looking down in what I took to be reflective thought.

"And, I'm not sure of this, but it seems to me, that in oral storytelling, especially the kind where you make up the story as you go, the teller can't be sure *when* that connection is reached, because, if it's a good telling, both the listener and perceiver are guiding the truth of the story to its conclusion. The listener participates in the creative act so is part of the point of it. Perhaps that's been reached now in my story. If so, you'll have to tell me, because from my side, I feel that my story hasn't come to its point, or what I'm calling 'its truth,' yet. I'd like to say that my story can be shortened to fit some deadline or timetable, but I can't. I literally cannot and be true to what I'm telling. Stories have a life of their own. They are more delicate than we imagine. The one I'm telling you now holds a portion of my life in its hands."

I hadn't meant to say that. It was far graver than I intended, and maybe twice as corny. But I was stunned by the realization that this was true, very true. Perhaps that's why I'd been so unsparing, uncompromising in my response to Prof. My story was leading me, not the other way around, and if what I suspected was true, my listeners were part of that. And what was pushing me forward was more than listener curiosity, though that was what it felt like during the telling. We both needed to know something that was inherently hidden but important in where my story was going. So the telling was rapidly jumping beyond a little journalistic piece about the difficulties of living in the country and facing the neighbors and their noise. I'd lost something important out there that my listeners were connecting with. I'd lost Katie, but more than even that, I'd lost something I couldn't yet name, perhaps didn't even recognize as lost until now. But I'd gained something as well, this I knew. Though that knowledge had arisen out of a frightening darkness, an awareness I'd learned as though I'd been lost in the forest and had found my way out again.

I noticed that suddenly the table of faces became very still. And then, everybody turned, almost in unison, and looked at the professor, who immediately apologized. I felt awful. I hadn't intended to slam him, though I'd known what I was doing as I did it. But I didn't seem to be able to help myself. I knew now that the book club was indispensable. Reading and writing were crucial to me. In a most particular way, since my move from the country to the village, reading and writing had become the center of my life in a way I'd never anticipated. I related to what Sendak had intended to do in his stories.

And these friends who loved to read, and a few who also wrote, had become an integral part of what was now my life.

"No," I told the Prof. "I'm sorry for not regarding your feelings more. I wasn't aiming this at you and your personal deadline which you need to keep and as soon as possible. It just seemed like the right moment to explain to you, to you all, what I believe reading and storytelling in our group is about for me. You keep me on my toes in the exchange between our life experiences and the stories we all tell. I feel the need to re-examine often what I think storytelling is, why I love to listen to other people's stories and tell my own. We are all storytellers. It's how we define and live our lives, every day, all the time." I stopped and sighed. "But enough. I've had the floor too long. I apologize. Let's stop for tonight. It's right that you asked, Prof. Life runs parallel to any story that's ever being told. I think my voice is giving out anyway."

After a bit of a pause, Gloria lifted her cup again, turned it over to show it was completely empty and said, "Hear, hear." Everyone applauded or slapped the table lightly and began gathering themselves to leave. The professor raised his hand to me with a smile. "Until next month, then." He rapidly headed for the door. We all were quick to follow.

When we met for our next monthly discussion, we didn't even make a pretense of going to the library space where we'd been meeting for the past two years. After a few scattered telephone calls, we had decided to get together at a table reserved for us at Heather on the Hill. Once we had our libations and were settled in, Prof said he'd been thinking a lot the past month about my views of storytelling, especially about our observations about experience, our perceptions of those, and the nature of truth in all of that. He asked me if I knew the work of Walter Fisher. I shook my head and nobody in the group seemed to know who he was talking about either, except Ella who told the Prof that she knew Fisher was a communication expert who'd been mentioned at some conference she'd attended in California a few years ago.

"Well, Fisher is professor emeritus of Annenberg School of Communication at the University of Southern California," the Prof said. We all groaned in unison. "Okay, okay." Prof smiled and hang-dogged his head, then added enthusiastically, "But he's a big deal right now. He's credited with formulating what's known as the 'narrative paradigm.' This is antithesis to the rationalist, empiricist, and behaviorist paradigms which have been and still are normally used in philosophy and psychology to describe human experience."

Gloria sunk into her wine glass and Doug shook the ice in his empty scotch glass loudly. The Prof ignored them both and continued as though he was in his class getting points across for an upcoming exam.

"Fisher believes that all communication of our experiences is articulated in stories which are influenced and shaped by not only our individual character but by culture and history. It's his view that we make sense of our world by telling stories to others. He emphasizes that this doesn't disavow the use of logic and reasoning powers. We use good reasons for the basis of our stories, which he calls 'narrative rationality.' I won't go into all that his paradigm encompasses and explains, of course—my God, it could fill the Grand Canyon—but this view of storytelling is interesting to me because it's a new way of describing how we invent our world and ourselves. Most rational models are based on deductive reasoning, the notion that our minds grasp truths *before* observation. It's easy to see how religions are built around this idea. Evidence isn't required for faith—truth comes *a priori* or *before* any observed evidence. And of course the empiricists—all scientists, your doctor and such, even your therapist if she's worth her salt--" Prof paused and pointed to Ella, who grinned at him. "These folks all use inductive reasoning, case studies, research of various kinds as evidence *a posteriori* or *after* observation as the foundation of what they know as truth. They will tell you—well, probably not directly because they, let's say your doctor, will posit what they're telling you as fact—but they know that the evidence they're depending on is really only true *for now*. I had a great philosophy teacher once tell me *a posteriori* meant that truth-as-fact is held in a three-ring binder, and any page can be replaced when another truer one comes along that's based on better evidence."

"So truth is relative?" Gloria asked. I tried to read her face, but she seemed to be inquiring without prejudice.

"For the empiricist, yes, and, well, I'm using 'truth' very loosely here, you understand. I'm not speaking from an epistemological point-of-view. I'm saying that it's the foundation upon which we take action until something proven to be more solid comes along. The behaviorist model is empiricist in that they believe we learn—know things—through how we interact with our environment which is, to them, an observation of our and others' actions. Cognitive learning theory states that there's first a mental change rather than a behavioral one when we interact with external events that determine how we experience the world." He looked around the group. "So that's basically my initial lecture to Philosophy 101 and many of you probably know all this, but I figure if I have to bore my students to death with it, it's only fair I introduce it out here in the real world once in a while."

"Hear, hear," Gloria said and called for another drink. "So this lecture is in lieu of...."

"I guess I wanted to add my two cents to what Ronnie told us last time about storytelling, especially about truth in storytelling. I got to thinking about it this past week, and I agree with her notions, and with Walter Fisher, that we make sense of our experience through the stories we tell others, and ourselves too, and the truth comes from what we and our listeners perceive as so from those stories. How many times have you heard someone say, after you've told them something, 'Yes, I believe that's true?' Or not, of course."

"That's what talk therapy is all about," Ella added. "And it works. Well, it's worked since Freud, and before that, really. I've personally seen it work over and over with children and adults. We don't think about talk in therapy as storytelling probably, because the word 'story' has the connation of 'deception' attached to it. To 'tell a story' is a phrase that can mean 'lying.'" She cleared her throat. "But I'd like to throw in my small change to all this, if I may. It sometimes takes a lot of talking to get to the deeper story, the one hidden underneath—Sendak's 'story within the story,' that Ronnie talked about. We have some paradigms in my discipline, as well—we like to call them methods, but, hey, six of one. And a well-known strategy, especially since Freud, for therapists getting at the truth of the client's underlying story is through an investigation of images, symbols, and metaphors. Through therapeutic investigation, the therapist and client can separate out the…well, let's take metaphors, for example, separate out the surface stories from the deeper metaphors that we-in-the-business call 'root metaphors.' Surface stories can be very convoluted and complicated. It isn't just that they hide the deeper ones, though they can do that, but they are also the conduits, the channels, for them, and they're vitally connected to them."

"So you're saying it's Maurice Sendak's 'stories within the stories,' but it goes deeper than that?" I asked. "I'm getting the idea that root metaphors store the deeper meanings of the inside stories, which in turn can be the truth of the telling. Am I on the right track here?"

"Well, yes and no." Ella hesitated. "But like Prof's necessary simplification of the narrative paradigm, in psychology, concepts and structures such as the 'root metaphor' also have a number of dimensions. They're different from what's called 'metaphoric thinking' in that they encompass a greater part of our reality and experience. They're actually the narratives, symbols, and images, *und so weiter*, that shape the interpretation of our reality and our perceptions of the world. Some psychologists call them 'myths' and others, 'basic metaphors.' They incorporate cultural as well as personal worldview. Another way of thinking about this is that they're based on existential questions about life—not always, of course, but they often are. For this reason, I like to call them 'deep metaphors.'

"Let's see. To give you an idea, when I was a teen…okay, you can stop laughing now. Yes, I can remember back that far. Anyway, *back then*, I thought girls who had long hair were 'hair flingers.'" Ella throws her hand back across her short curly hair as though she's flipping long locks over her shoulder. Gloria snorts and we laugh. "That was a kind of root metaphor for a basic belief I held about girls and their cultural acceptance of who they were. In other words, 'a hair flinger' was a young woman who was conventional, fit in the social box and wasn't able to create her own identity. Yeah, all that! She certainly was the opposite of what I wanted to be. I held that belief a long time. In all honesty, I still do, as prejudiced as that view is about women. But that's an example of a root metaphor. It informs how I view the world of women. It goes beyond the deeper meaning of any singular story I tell myself about my gender. It's an all pervasive way of looking at who I am and how I fit into my gender identity."

We sat thoughtfully with this idea in silence.

"You can see why they're used a lot in dream interpretation. A lot of psychologists and therapists, including me, believe that metaphors permeate our thoughts and expressions in *all* of our communications, not just dreams and the arts and such. Some believe our means of grasping reality is based on metaphoric thinking all the time. But manifest and latent content are important because they're a way of talking about the separation between what are the masked, often even distorted, stories of dreams that consciousness remembers upon awaking and the latent, deeply metaphoric, content that Freud believed were the wishes, urges and thoughts that the conscious mind wants to hide. So for me, in storytelling—in or out of therapy—it's not that the surface stories are false. It's just that they aren't the deeper stories that can take us to the greater truths, those beliefs undergirding our whole view of reality and the world. There's also this. Our stories don't just *hide* deeper latent desires and motives, they act as a guide to them. It's what therapists are trying to get at all the time with their clients."

"Sounds to me it's a little like Virgil taking Dante into the fiery pit!" I interjected.

"Very like that." Ella is serious but smiling. "But all latent stories and deep metaphors aren't ugly, corrupt, and immoral. The hellhole of our minds, so to speak. Perhaps this is where our idea that to view experiences in our lives *realistically* has come to mean to see them in a harsh light, to see the worst side of things, you know, to bring out the hidden ugly stuff from underneath. Sometimes, though, they're just wishes, desires for pleasure, a more fulfilling life, or even what's bringing us happiness in the here and now. It can be something that we find hard to confront because it feels selfish, indulgent, whatever." Ella stopped and tapped the air with her finger. "You know, confronting those personal demons Campbell talked about in Sendak's *Where the Wild Things Are*. Our stories can be a way to inform ourselves of what we're happy about or what we'd like to change or even what we're afraid of deep, deep down, and if we become aware of their messages, they can give us courage to take action, make changes or appreciate more fully what we have."

"So how does this figure in Ronnie's living-in-the-country story?" Gloria asked.

"I'd say she went to the country for peace and quiet and found nothing but noise and lots of work, beginning with the whole make-over of the house and then all the nastiness with the neighbor. Quiet doesn't just mean an atmosphere without noise. It also can mean wanting more restorative time from our jobs, to be able to focus, not to be distracted, and feel like you have to be taking care of something all the time. At least that's my view of her surface story, a story that seems to be leading toward something deeper that she's getting to."

"How much is your hourly rate again?" I asked, and we all laughed. Doug shouted that he wanted an appointment tomorrow.

I raised my wine glass. "I can't get you an hour with Ella, she'll have to do that, but this one's on me." I turned to Prof and winked. "See what you started. Now we'll have debriefings after every story that's told, or maybe I should say, we'll *deconstruct* the story's language to get at what it's hiding."

"We're a cagey bunch to begin with and after a few drinks, who knows what will surface?" Gloria said. "Isn't there a truth serum? Maybe we should add a couple of drops of that in our brews."

"But there's also the business of how long it will take to get to all our truths. Our legal beverage tabs could get expensive to say nothing of the speeding tickets we might toll up on the way home." Doug grinned at Gloria, and they clinked glasses.

"I'm not having my stories subjected to analysis," I complained. "My last therapy I didn't go back when my wings got too close to the fire. No more inferno diving for me, thank you very much!"

Heather McKeon came out of the shadows to our table and asked if we planned on making our group a standard monthly gathering in her pub—she'd welcome that, she told us—but if so, why didn't we take the banquet room where it's quieter without the television and the rowdies coming back from their ballgames? We asked her the price, and she waved a hand in the air. I had to smile. She looked a little like Ella's hair flinger.

"Keep it quiet," she whispered conspiratorially. "If there's a wedding reception or some big event, I'll simply move you to the smaller room which is only an extension for the overflow of the larger receptions." We all agreed enthusiastically to take her up on her offer. "You more than pay for it with your rounds." She nodded toward our empty glasses as she set them on a tray. We told her we needed to start with our coffee and sandwiches soon or we'd be floating out into the parking lot and that wouldn't be good for her business. But we ordered one more round along with our suppers. After Heather walked away with the tray and her order pad, silence descended for some time.

Finally, Prof ventured, "How about calling ourselves the Narrative Paradigmers?" We mock-gagged and tapped spoons on the table, then threw group names around for a while before finally giving up. Our drinks were served, everybody vowing that these were the last for the night before eats. Once we'd settled down, the group told me to commence with my story.

"Before I start with my story again, I want to say—given especially what Ella's just told us—that I think the story of my living in the country isn't so much about why I moved there—which I'll call Part 1—but why I decided to leave. So here's Part 2." I added quickly, "I didn't prepare what I'm going to tell you tonight, so I'm just going on with the telling until I've reached the end or you hit me over the head and make me stop."

"You know, Walter Fisher stated in his paradigm that the narrative rationality of our stories require that they have coherence and fidelity." Prof grinned.

"What?" Doug was the retired creator of Innovative Computer Designs which included video games with storylines, so he knew as much about narrative rationality as any of us, but he showed exaggerated befuddlement over Prof's remark. Doug looked at me, crossed his eyes, hung out his tongue and asked, "What'd he say, what'd he say?"

"I read Miss Marple stories as a kid," I told him. "I know good reasons in a story when I hear them. Watch me sashay into this one." I formed a gun with my hand and shot Prof between the eyes.

"One of the best *reasons* for living in the country for me," I began, and there were a few hoots here and there, "was being able to walk without having constant traffic around. The cars and pick-ups that frequented our road and those that intersected with it were at a minimum during the day. The heaviest traffic was early morning and late afternoon-early evening, the commuters going and coming back from work, which actually didn't leave me a whole lot of safe times for being out there. The weekends were the best, especially early morning or afternoon when the traffic was at a minimum, and I was pretty much alone on the road. But regardless of the volume, the traffic moved fast. Most of my neighbors' attitudes toward speed limits were like those for noise ordinances—it just wasn't in keeping with their idea of country living. On the hills, small as they were, I was especially watchful, walking always facing the traffic unless I was coming to a curve in the road, which I approached with the traffic so drivers coming at me on the right side weren't surprised by my sudden appearance in their windshields.

"I'd like to tell you that I did a lot of serious hiking, seeking out trails in the state forest near where we lived, but I was a chicken about being alone in the woods, even with pepper spray in my pocket. I'd read reports of a few encounters with small brown bears and foxes in the local newspaper but these were mainly sightings rather than any aggressive wildlife behavior. It was the other hikers on the trails that concerned me. Quite a few showed up when I made my way into the forest shortly after we'd moved to the country. Maybe I was overly cautious—perhaps being a woman without self-defense training had something to do with it—but too many guys looking like mountain-men with scruffy beards, no backpacks, and smelling of sweat from twenty yards away didn't aid reassurance. After a couple of strange encounters I stopped hiking in the woods.

"Once I gave directions to a guy who looked like he never left the trails! He wanted to know where, quote, 'a nearby stream' was, but then stood unyielding and motionless in the path as I attempted to walk around him after I'd told him I didn't know and another who asked some inane question about where the trail was leading, who, after I answered him, started walking ahead of me but then slowed down to near stopping until I turned around and exited the woods at the first available opportunity. From then on, I elected to stick to the main roads and suffer the dust from approaching and receding vehicles.

"I'd also like to tell you that I was a serious enough walker to desire someday to take treks through the Cotswolds, Umbria, the Mont Blanc district in Italy, the Costa Rica's rainforest or the famous El Camino de Santiago—yeah, I'd looked them all up. El Camino's the one that sounded the most intriguing to me. You may have heard of it, the five hundred mile pilgrimage through northern Spain from the Pyrenees on the French border to the Cathedral in Compostela, Spain, some ninety kilometers from the Atlantic Ocean?" Only Katherine had heard of El Camino.

"It's been taken by monks and pilgrims from the Middle Ages until the present-day," she stated with authority, a guide from her research. "Thousands have made the walk in thirty days or less which is impressive—anyway, to me it is." She stopped abruptly and flushed as though she were stealing my thunder. I asked her several questions which she answered quickly—on the uncomfortable side—so I went back to my narrative.

"While I lived in the country, I had a map of El Camino taped to my kitchen cabinets where I could see it to inspire me to get out and walk, but I knew it was highly unlikely that I'd ever walk every day from eleven to fifteen miles to make the pilgrimage in a month or even a month-and-a half. Shirley MacLaine did it in twenty-nine days—I think that's what I figured out from her book about her trek—which means she had to've walked an average of seventeen miles a day, and that, mind you, would be without any days off. Each day off means you have to make up those seventeen miles over the long haul to reach the cathedral somewhere within a month. I moved a push pin along the course on my map for a while but it didn't take long before I saw how my two to four miles a day didn't get me very far, very fast."

Doug said, "Why the hell would anybody put themselves through such misery?" He drank from his glass with gusto, smacking it down on the table. I knew there was plenty of libations along this route, but I didn't bother to go into that with him. I'd read all about the drunks on the Camino.

"It's a pilgrimage. For most people who do it—from the accounts I've read, anyway. It's a spiritual quest to them."

"Medieval monks did it in sandals or even barefoot," Katherine added, shyly.

"Ouch," Ella said, and gave Katherine a little nudge.

"Well, you see why I preferred to make these trips vicariously," I retorted. "I read probably a dozen books on El Camino--even bought a few--and sent away for brochures from three companies who sponsored walking vacations all over the world. It's thrilling to read about people testing the extremes, searching for limits to their physical and mental stamina and endurance. But I was honest enough to realize that I'd rather sit with a good book and let others do that kind of walking—extreme sports, spiritual quest or whatever you wanna call it. So my walking career was confined to the common roads and byways and the common folk I met along the way.

"After my split with my ex, I was left with a spaniel mutt we had acquired from the SPCA pet project in the newspaper. Her name was Jilly Jean. She came to us with a wonderful story, which I'll save for another time. But Jilly and I had found in our treks a comfortable, amicable walking companionship. I took her out with me every walk I could, regardless of weather or season, and she waited patiently every afternoon by the back door until I'd show up for our hour or two together in the great outdoors.

"One very warm late afternoon on a walk with Jilly, I saw a slightly stooped-over woman through the hot haze, walking across the road, her hand up to her head as though she was sheltering herself from blows. She walked with a cane which she carefully hung from her arm as she opened the mailbox door and peered inside. I watched as she reached in, pulled out what appeared to be several envelopes, retrieved the newspaper from its plastic post, pivoted with tiny steps in an arch, slipped the cane back to her right hand after she placed the mail carefully in her left, and began her trek back to her driveway. Then she spotted me, stopping in the middle of the road. 'Dear Lord, no,' I thought. 'Keep going.' But she stayed there unyielding, watching me approach. With still some distance between us, I picked up the sound of a drifting motor. 'Jilly, come,' I snapped at my dog's leash, picking up my pace.

"'Hello,' she called out, her hand making a visor across her forehead, shielding her eyes. I started to tell her to watch out for the car when I realized the distant drone was actually an airplane overhead. I thought to walk to her so that I could guide her to safety, but something held me back.

"'That you, Mildred?' she asked, calling out loudly in my direction. 'I don't see so well.' Then *very* loudly, 'I say, is that you Millie?' I was taken back because my Aunt Milly had been on my mind since I'd talked to her last week after many years of silence. I caught her and my Uncle Andrew at Dad's when I gave him my weekly call. They rarely visited him but had decided to see him for a few days. Now this old woman's calling me Milly seemed a strange and amazing coincidence. 'Hey, who are you?' she yelled at me.

"'I'm a neighbor up the road,' I called back.

"'What neighbor?' she demanded suspiciously.

"Jilly Jean stood waiting, squatting on her haunches, ready to run at the slightest notice. Her ears and head slipped down when the old woman talked.

"'I live up the road on Fairfield,' I yelled back, feeling a little odd at that distance—me yelling my head off in the middle of the road toward this woman who was half deaf and blind.

"'Oh, that's nice.' She advanced a few steps toward the other side of the road. 'We're so glad that you moved into that house. We were all wondering when you would.'

"I waited, not exactly knowing how to respond to that. She stopped after those few steps to say, 'How long has it been now?'

"I felt nervous about telling her it had been over eight years. But time is so different for the very old. I remembered my eighty-nine year old landlady, Bernice, on the south side of Elmira when I first moved into her upstairs apartment saying to me, 'I don't tell people my real age anymore. They just treat you differently when they find out you're so old. One day I got up and decided to lop a few years off. So in January when I had my birthday, I began telling everybody I was 86 instead of 89, and it made me feel ever so wonderful. I'm thinking of lopping off another three years my next birthday.'

"'Why don't you just lop off ten or twelve while you're at it?' I asked her.

"'Oh, no,' she said, 'you can't do that, because you can't live up to the appearance, and then they will know you're lying.'"

The group had their chuckle.

"I looked at the old woman in the road and said, 'I've lived there several summers now.' That seemed vague enough without out-and-out telling a fib. I had seen her once when I was seeking signatures for the noise petition against my neighbor, but she wouldn't've remembered me. It was years ago. She had said no to the petition and practically closed the door in my face. She seemed distracted at the time and I assumed I interrupted whatever she was doing.

"Thank goodness she walked again toward the shoulder of the road and her yard. She nodded her head, staring at the ground. 'Quite right.' Such was her approval of my moving into her community.

"I grinned, knowing she couldn't see me. Then she stopped just short of the grass. 'What's your name, did you say?'

"Oh boy, I thought. Here goes. 'Rhodanna,' I said loudly, distinctly.

"'How's that?' I did hear a car this time, but she'd stepped onto the grass on the shoulder of the road. Her legs bowed under her, giving her the look a little like a lop-sided lawn chair on uneven ground.

"'Rhodanna,' I yelled, louder. Good god, I've taught the deaf and the blind, I thought, and shouting never helps. And why the hell didn't I just tell her my name was Ronnie, though that doesn't always solve the name comprehension problem, especially with someone from her generation. I walked closer to her, Jilly in tow, so she and I wouldn't have to shout, and we'd all be safely past the traffic.

"'Oh!' She put her hand on her cane as though she was going to continue, then she waited, squinting up at me from grayish yellow eyes. 'How do you spell that?'

"'R-h-o-d-a-n-n-a,' I replied in a normal tone.

"'Different,' she said. 'I have a different name too. Mert. ul.'

"'Mert. ul,' I repeated, getting the connection, but there was a long wait between syllables. I asked, 'And how do you spell that?'

"She smiled broadly. 'Why M-y-r-t-l-e.' She spelled slowly and added, 'Like the ground cover.' She waited for my light to come on and some sound of reassurance.

"When I gave it, she went on, 'It's appro. Pree. ut,' and I caught that she was swallowing shallowly every other syllable. 'I like to gar. Den, you see.'

"Jilly lay down, softly panting, as though we were going to stay for hours. I started to jerk on her leash to move on but waited when Myrtle spoke again.

"'Normally,' she said, between her own pants, 'I'd be working out in my garden but this May I broke my arm. And then when that got better, I fell and hurt my back. That happened Friday. Today is my first day up.'

"I started to say I was sorry, but she yelled out as though I was on the other side of the road by the mailbox, 'You gar. Den?' Jilly's ears went down but she didn't sit up or stand in preparation for fleeing.

"'Well, I'd like to, but we've had a lot to do on the house.'

"'Oh, my, yes,' she intoned, looking toward the approaching car. 'And everything is so expensive.'

"I thought again of my landlady in Elmira. When I first had moved in and told her the screens were broken in my bedroom windows upstairs, she said softly, 'How can that be? Ray put those in just before he died.' When she didn't go on, I asked, 'And when was that?'"

"'Oh, let me see now. About twenty-six years, I guess.'"

Again, there were scattered chuckles from the group.

"As the car went around Myrtle and me, it turned slowly into the drive. She said, 'my son' as though she were introducing him. He gave me a cautious look from his window as he passed and then twirled his finger in the air. I wasn't sure whether he was saying 'howdy' in a rodeo kind of way or trying to let me know his mother was not quite right in the head.

"As the car crept up the drive, leaving a soft trail of dust floating over us, Myrtle said, 'I am very, very lucky to have my son watch over me.'

"'Does he live with you?' I asked, hoping that he did. She seemed far too fragile, physically and mentally, to be on her own.

"'Oh, my, my, yes. He gets me everything I need.' She stopped and looked around in my direction. 'Sometimes....' She trailed off, and I didn't think she would go on, but she gathered her thoughts and said, 'It would be nice to leave, to just pick up and go. Away. To leave...leave it all behind. But....' She took her cane in her hand and began the turn to walk away from me again. 'But I'd miss my garden, you see.' She whispered this, barely audible, and seemingly not said to much of anybody.

"'Take care of yourself,' I called out to her back as she walked toward her son and her house. 'When I walk by again soon, maybe you'll be outside. If I see you, I'll stop.'

"'Oh,' she said, turning a few steps around on her flat feet, staring out my way. 'That would be so lovely. Please do.'

"As I walked up the hill with Jilly toward my drive, I remembered Landlady

Bernice calling me one day after I'd lived in the apartment only a couple of months, her voice a whisper on the line. 'I hope I'm not disturbing you, and if you can't stay on the phone, please say so, but would you mind having a little conversation with me today? I'm feeling kind of strange and I think it's because I haven't talked to anyone in two days.'"

"Oh," Katherine sighed. "What a sweet story, Ronnie."

Heather delivered our supper with coffee while several took advantage of the break and raced to the restrooms. Those left at the table asked me questions about what I'd told them so far. Altogether, it took at least half an hour before I continued with my story while we were eating.

"One early autumn day, in the middle of an Indian summer we hadn't seen in years, a torrential rain pounded the meadow and pond and turned the driveway into two rivulets that became deep enough to harden into ruts by the next summer. So I was shocked when I saw a small white Datsun slowly swaying its way toward the parking area just off the back porch. I remember wondering, 'Didn't they stop manufacturing this car years ago?' and thinking that I'd seen this very car in the neighborhood before—who wouldn't remember a rusted tin can on wheels at least twenty years older than any other cars on the road? A lot of cars passed me regularly while I was out walking, but I couldn't place this one, and it left me feeling a little uneasy.

"The man who met me on the porch was slight, his mid-section disproportionately large, swollen beyond the size of the rest of him. It made his head appear slung back from his body and rather small. His skin sagged under his arms and chin. He looked older than his years, I was sure of it. I guessed him in his late fifties. Thank God he had on trousers, rather than shorts, for any number of reasons, of course, but especially because I didn't want to view the legs holding up this strangely-formed body. Perhaps that seems unkind, but the overall impression I had of this fellow was one of hayseed-ed leftovers from a farm in No Man's Land during the depression who might be deciding to make me his next income, though I couldn't for the life of me think of who he'd know to call to get the ransom money. The police wouldn't pay a dime for the likes of me, I was sure of it. The more I looked at him, though, the more uneasy I got. His hair was matted against his head in a ring running around the back from ear to ear. I noticed when he turned and pointed through the open screens of the porch to the woods that the matted ring had an almost perfect worn-down circle of fluff revealing a yellow-white scalp—much like you'd find on an infant who lies squirming around a lot in its crib. He was holding a straw hat in his hand and a zippered Bible trapped in a sweaty armpit. His worn-out shoes had been polished to a crackled sheen and were double-tied with long laces hanging off to each side. Traces of a scantly hairy torso showed through his soggy shirt in spots.

"He looked like a character straight out of a Faulkner novel. My vision was of Jewel Bundren in *As I Lay Dying*. You know, a man full of nervous tension with an underbelly of meanness, but perhaps I'm characterizing him this way now because I was to learn more about him that resembled Jewel later. Especially how Jewel treated his horse, remember that?—a terrible confusion between jealous rage and excitement over life in a creature that fought back. But this man was older than Jewel by at least thirty, forty years. I expected some sort of odor to drift from him but there was enough cedar and pine in the damp air to cover any vapors he might've been giving off.

"The cloudy aura around him sent my intuition on danger-alert. The only times anyone had come down my drive in all these years was the police to ask if my property had been disturbed after a number of break-ins in the area, and once a couple had lost directions and thought the long drive was one described to them by friends on Fairfield Road throwing a birthday party. That this man had shown up on my porch during a rain storm was not just a little unsettling. To this very day I don't know why I didn't just go inside and wait until he left, unless I figured he'd be back until I answered my door. Believe me, he had that kind of appearance. I knew he was selling something."

"You know, at times like this, it helps to show your cell phone, just so they know..." Doug interjected.

I interrupt him. "This was before cell phones, Doug, at least Kate and I didn't have them. In fact, I think I still had only phones with cords in our house. I was living alone at the time."

Doug looked at me like he couldn't quite place me in time. I shrugged and continued while he stared at me as though I was living on a completely different planet than the rest of humanity.

"So I said to this guy on my porch, 'Whatever you're selling, I'm not interested.' I immediately held up a hand to stop him, but he continued to point toward the dark path leading to the woods, now almost indiscernible through the sheets of fog and rain.

"'Nice place,' he said barely audible above the pounding of the rain on the vinyl roof. His words came out a low, sinister hiss. Pull-ace-ssss. When he faced me directly, his eyes were tiny and dark, shining with either a curiosity or humor only he knew. He looked at the back door of my house with a slight nod. When I didn't invite him in, he seemed to look around for a chair. Finding none, he cleared his throat, put on his straw hat and for a moment, I thought he was going to leave without another word. But he pulled the Bible from his armpit, unzipped it, letting its pages fall open before I could protest or simply turn and go into the house. I was a bit mesmerized to tell you the truth. He pulled out a folded paper or brochure and held it out to me after he unfolded it with a couple of flips in the air. *Awake!* He was a Jehovah Witness. I sighed.

"'No,' I said firmly. I started to add that I didn't accept religious solicitations but couldn't form the words in time.

"'Take it,' he said in an exaggeratedly gentle voice but with a piercing stare. I tell you the whole feel of this guy was just plain creepy. He had a weird combination of aggression and restraint. He added, 'You need to know what this says. It's later than you think.' His tone was slightly menacing. A litany of cartoons from *The New Yorker* came flooding to mind of men in monk's robes carrying 'The End is Near!' signs. If the atmosphere hadn't been so tense, I would've laughed.

"'You need to go now,' I said firmly, giving him total eye contact as hard as that was. 'I'm going back into my house and I would like for you to leave.' I resisted looking toward my door.

"He stood unmoving, turning in place enough to look out toward the rain and beyond to his car. When he turned back to me, he asked, 'You don't want to know The Truth?' I knew he was capitalizing the last two words. Jehovah Witnesses do that in all their literature. I also knew the Bible he held was their own translation, that they don't believe in the Holy Trinity, that they believe God's Kingdom's a literal government in heaven ruled since the outbreak of

World War I by Jesus Christ and 144,000 Christians who were and are going to be taken from the earth, and that some of these Holy Spirit-Anointed ones are still among us. I knew their belief is that this Kingdom is the instrument through which God accomplishes His will, transforming the world with the help of his Witnesses into a paradise which will be free from sickness and death. They also believe the Kingdom Hall down the road is where Witnesses gather to plan evangelical strategies and keep their members on the straight and narrow so that they can be doing Jehovah's bidding properly." I had sputtered this all in a rush, as though reading from a brochure. It must have appeared to my listening friends that this information sat in my head like a file ready to be pulled at the slightest provocation.

"How the heck do you know all this stuff?" Doug asked. "They come to my door too, but I usually just tell them, like the Mormon lads, that I have my own religion—which I don't—but once they find out you're an atheist, they never leave you alone. I close the door on them. I've never encouraged them by taking their literature, let alone reading it."

"I'm a curious person about why people believe what they do, I guess," I said. "I understand I can't know even half the beliefs out there and certainly not many in detail, but if I don't know at least something about those that fall under my nose I feel like I'm no better than these single-minded people who think everybody should believe as they do. It doesn't take a rocket scientist to know why they knock on our doors, but why they're so convinced that their message is the one true religion interests me. Call it looking for the evidence of their *believing*, not their beliefs. I feel like I have to know what those are in order to figure out what's up with them. I mean, why do any of us believe what we do? Sometimes we do it without much thought, just pick up notions handed down to us or from here and there as we live our lives—through experience, mostly, probably. But we do base our beliefs on *something*. I'm curious about what that is and why. Maybe some of my reasons are even self-satisfying. I want to compare what he believes with what I believe and see what the difference is and try to reason out that." I stopped and thought about what I'd just said for a minute.

"I've read enough Jehovah Witness literature to understand that this man before me believed he was a chosen witness sent by his god, Jehovah, to speak The Truth to me—who to his mind was undoubtedly a morally corrupt person under Satan's influence—and that unless I believed as he did I was going to die when Satan and his followers are destroyed at Armageddon, commonly known as 'the end of times,' though these believers don't call it that because they believe Armageddon will be *Jehovah's Day* when a New System of Things will be put in place."

"That's disturbing as hell to me," Prof said.

"It certainly felt that way on my porch. But you know, you can't stop people believing what they do, and they'll believe it on the flimsiest of evidence. Sometimes really nothing at all. We all do it. We like to call it The Truth more than we admit—*our* Truth, of course. I'm amazed how many of my beliefs are based on just plain expediency, you know, the fact that they make my life simpler. I'm not talking just about religious ideas here, of course. If you really start examining why you believe what you do, I think most of us justify our beliefs in one vacuous way or another—with religion we call it faith—but most of the time our reasons are really prejudicial, just plain preference without a helluva lot of examination."

"We're back to root metaphors?"

"Yeah, perhaps we are. But the larger question for me in this story is where do these root metaphors come from? Or call them preferences if you like. Deep ones, but still preferences. It's a bag of worms that Ella can squirm around in with us if she wants to, but for now let me tell you, this particular man, in the rain, out there in the country alone, standing on my porch believing I was Satan's child, I wasn't any too comfortable. I've talked to Jehovah Witnesses and the Mormon messengers who've come to my door before, actually quite a few of them, and I've never felt uncomfortable in the least. It was this guy. All at once that warning about trusting your gut kicked in. So I started backing toward the door. I was watching his face for clues so when he reached out his hand, I jumped a little, thinking he was going to try and stop me, but then I noticed he was still holding the limp *Awake!*. It was an awkward moment because I hesitated to turn my back on him but also didn't want to take the literature and invite discussion or his misinterpretation of my action. Backing up all the way to my door—which was some distance away—just struck me as downright ridiculous. He wasn't the King or Queen of England, for heaven's sakes! And then something happened inside me. I can't explain it but a great, sudden weariness came over me. The enormity of his claim—the arrogance of his belief in knowing *The Truth*—shot down any precaution and better judgment I might have had earlier. I was still cautious but I couldn't stop myself from telling him what I was thinking.

"I said, 'You haven't a clue what you're talking about, how big the truth really is.' I wanted to tell him that for me that meant it was everything and nothing, but I knew that would throw him into total confusion. He just stood there, inert, like a statue with an icy blank stare, his Bible still split open in his hand. I went on without regard for anything he might be feeling—I mean, who knew? 'That book couldn't begin to contain the truth. The truth is so very, very *enormous*. To know it, to even claim to know it, what it actually entails, is simply ridiculous.' I was amazed with the smallness of what he was doing there on my porch with something so overwhelmingly huge.

"Prof, you know what this feels like, surely, lecturing on notions of this sort to young people who are just beginning to reflect on this kind of thing." I looked at the professor, who was listening intently. He nodded but didn't say anything. "Whole systems of thought have been devoted to the foundation and criteria for knowledge, concepts such as justified true belief, common sense, knowledge, correlation theories and such. There've been centuries of philosophical investigations about if and how we can know a thing is true, even if it's a viable inquiry.

"I was just overcome by his total lack of curiosity. I'm sure his claim would have been that his sources—you know, sacred text or whatever they were—were valid because in his view the authors of the Bible and the Watchtower Society's interpreters of the Scriptures were all guided by a divine revelation which couldn't be wrong. He was the perceiver of a truth *a priori*, a truth that was given to him by Jehovah and Jehovah wouldn't lie to him. The sources of the Bible's message were channelers, representatives of Jehovah's perfection.

"This simply astonishes me, this total commitment to such a circular claim. I can't recall exactly what I said to this man but it was something like, 'Worlds have been created and destroyed because of *the truth*. Libraries have been built and filled with it and also burned down in its name. Wars have been fought, won, and lost because of 'the truth.' I threw up my hands. 'Do you ever think that maybe all you're doing is…is playing in some kind of *football game*, not between God and Satan but between your belief and everybody else's?' But, of course, to him it *was* a football game between God and Satan because 'everybody else' to him were people listening to the Devil.

"As he was listening to what I was saying, as he took it in, he began to look startled, as though I was hitting him with a very large, heavy stick. His blank stare was gone. But after his initial shock, his face began to rearrange itself for argument. He quickly took on the glow of anger. His face became flushed, his mouth opened, and he breathed hotly, saying, 'It's…this is a battle for *lives*, real people, not any *game*! And the battle *is* between Satan and God. There's going to be *Jehovah's Day*!' He was breathing so hard I thought he might pass out or throw up! 'These…these—' he hit his Bible with his open hand as though he were slapping me, 'are the words of Jehovah, the one, true God!' He started flipping through the pages, forward, then back, the thin paper crackling in the air. He looked up, laying his hand finally over the open Bible like so many televangelists do, like they're holding it together even as they pray over it. I've watched Jimmy Swaggart do it more times than I can count.…"

"You actually *watch* Swaggart *preach*?" Prof was beside himself.

"Sure, how am I going to talk with anybody about the man if I don't know what he says and does? Believe me, I don't look forward to his regularly scheduled shows! By the way, do you know he's Jerry Lee Lewis's cousin?"

"Makes sense," Prof mumbled. "But who wants to waste their time even *thinking* about Swaggart, let alone *talking* about him." This could, maybe should, have shut down my tirade, but I was on a roll.

"Oh, I don't know. He does come up now and again, looks like." I grinned because I knew this was unfair. I'm the one who'd introduced Swaggart into the narrative. "Anyway the next thing this guy on my porch said to me was exactly what I knew he would, 'This word has been given to us by Jehovah through His inspired witnesses. They were guided by His will. The Scriptures weren't written by a bunch of men who just sat down and wrote down their own ideas. They were guided by Jehovah's purpose.'

"'And you know this how?' I asked him.

"'By this.' He held the Bible high in the air by one hand waving it about as though chasing flies the way cows do with their tails.

"'So you use the Bible to prove the Bible?' I asked.

"'Well, yes. Because it says so,' he said. Then he realized the circular logic of this argument, so he added hastily, 'And I've *experienced* it as true.'

"'Our conversation is now at an end,' I said straightforwardly. I could see that he thought I meant for him to leave, as I'd told him to do before. But when I didn't move he just stood there, I guessed waiting to be dismissed again. 'What I mean to say,' I told him, 'is that we're at an impasse because the foundation for your beliefs is not an unchallengeable source to me so we can't go on with our discussion. I don't accept the Bible as a sacred text from Jehovah—as you call your god. You can stand there and quote from it until your tongue turns purple and nothing is going to change this for me. And as far as your experience of its truth is concerned, I've had no such experience so I have no way of knowing if your experience is valid.'"

The professor couldn't remain out of the discussion. It was as though he were on the porch with me and Jehovah-man. "You wouldn't have a way of *knowing* if his experience is true, even if you *thought* you'd had the same experience as he described. Personal experiences are without validation unless there are common references, and how are you going to validate those? We accept them as being the same out of what Hume called 'custom'—and we now call 'habit'—and what Wittgenstein believed was part of the language game. We validate them through context--something we agree upon--and that's exactly what this man and others like him are doing. Only they claim divine declaration or intervention instead of agreed-upon context."

I nodded in agreement. "Well, this man and I weren't having an epistemological debate, Prof, as well you know. For him it was one of faith, or as you say, conclusions drawn from believed divine intervention. What I did know was that what I'd just stated wasn't true for him, you know, that he could witness until his tongue turned purple and I wasn't going to change my mind. Because he believed that his truth was so powerful that when The Truth was told to me just right or told enough or at the right moment, The Truth would reveal itself to me. That was his job as a Witness. The battle of Armageddon was being waged right there on my porch. It was a battle from which he couldn't retreat. He was a soldier in Jehovah's army as he just admitted. Never mind serving in the country's military because he wouldn't. No patriotism or national flags for him! But Armageddon, the war to end all wars? Oh yeah! And this belief in truth's ability to persuade would be why he and his fellow believers would come knocking again and again at my door and yours. Evidently, he felt, though, that this visit wasn't the right moment for me to open to The Truth. And, of course, there's always the hardened souls who are so bound to Satan, that they cannot see the light anymore. Isn't this the ninth circle of Dante's Inferno, the circle before the very center of Hell where Satan dwells?"

Katherine said, "Yes. Those consigned to the ninth circle of hell have committed treachery, especially of God's love, so they are bound in ice, never to feel the warmth of God's Sun."

Doug looked at her with wide-eyed wonder. "It's a conspiracy. All these encyclopedic nuts around me!" Then he apologized for breaking my story and motioned for me to go on as he bit into the last of his sandwich, shaking his head and gathering crumbs with his index finger from his plate.

"So he folded the *Awake!*, put it in the center of the Bible's open pages, and zipped The Good Book closed. Maybe he was just clocking in the hours as a Pioneer—that's a Witness who does this field ministry for ninety hours a month. That's an average of three hours a day, ladies and gentlemen!"

Several members of our group expressed amazement. They had no idea about such a commitment. Questions came fast—does such time spent actually work, what do the witnesses get out of it, and so forth. When the chatter calmed down, Prof asked how I got 'the creep' off my porch.

"'So what happens now?' I asked the Jehovah's Witness, curious as to what he'd say.

"His lips were a thin hard line. 'Unless you accept Jesus Christ and believe in Jehovah's approaching Kingdom, when Jesus Christ rules over the New System of Things, you will be destroyed with Satan and all of his followers.' The rain beat a gentle, steady rhythm on the roof. He looked out at the woods and then back at me. 'I want you to stay away from my mother,' he said abruptly.

"At first I wasn't sure I'd caught what he'd said. Inanely, I thought he might mean the Virgin Mary. When I finally grasped what he might be saying to me, I couldn't make sense of it. 'Do I know your mother?' I asked him.

"'I know you do,' he said, and instantly it dawned on me that the car turning into Myrtle's drive was the white Datsun sitting now in my driveway. I hadn't recognized him as he'd been a blur as he passed his mother and me those weeks ago when he turned into his driveway, making the rodeo-wave as he did. And just as quickly I realized that he was her guardian coming to protect her from me. What had she said to me? 'My son...I'm so very, very lucky that he watches over me. He gets me everything I need.'

"'I don't see your mother,' I stated flatly to him.

"'She told me you intended to drop by. That's not a good idea.'

"'And why's that?'

"'She isn't capable of understanding when she's being fooled,' he said.

"'I assure you,' I said, 'I've spoken to your mother once. Actually, it was the time you saw me talking with her. It was only in passing and I told her I'd talk with her again *if* she was out in her garden, *if* I saw her there the next time I was out walking. I have no intention of tricking her into anything.'

"'I don't want you giving her false hopes,' he said. 'She doesn't understand the difference between reality and the fantasies in her head. When people give her hopes, she thinks they're real.'

"'What sort of false hopes do you think I gave her or might give her? All I told her was that I'd stop and say hello.'

"'Hellos never stay hellos,' he said, hands folded in front of him, his Bible now clenched tight under his arm.

"'I have no hidden agendas, believe me. Hello *is* hello sometimes.' I'm sure he couldn't hear the famous Freudian echo in this as 'a cigar is sometimes just a cigar.'

"'During talks, something said in passing can take on great significance. It does with my mother. She remembers and magnifies the smallest suggestions.

You said something to her that gave her the idea that you supported her notion of leaving. Do you have any idea how dangerous that is?' He appeared sincerely concerned for her.

"I can't tell you why," I told my reading-listening group, "I'll never know why, probably—other than my curiosity to know what people think and believe about such circumstances as these—but I asked him, in a tone I thought was very sympathetic to his distress, 'Why do you think she's trying to get away….' I got that far and his stare could have turn ice to stone. He took a step forward, very close, almost into my intimate space. I stepped back.

"His voice was strained. He was having trouble controlling his outrage. Through tight lips he said, 'She has lived her life within the Kingdom and she has kept to the faith all these years. Now that she is vulnerable, Satan is attempting to play tricks on her. I am *not* going to allow it—not from anybody, no matter what it costs.' He stepped back. His outburst seemed to have an oddly calming effect on him but he was still breathing loudly through his mouth. He continued, 'This may sound trivial to you but she's my mother. There isn't anything I wouldn't do to save her from peril.' He breathed carefully for a moment, then shuddered, lowering his shoulders and relaxing a little. 'She will be there with me, by my side, when the New System of Things comes into being.'

"Now it was my turn to stare. I was beyond fear. I was into some kind of amazement. It wasn't a conversation I could ever have imagined—if this exchange could even be called that. His declaration was so outside the realm of any rationality I was capable of entertaining—narrative rationality or otherwise." I nodded at Prof. "I could only stand before him transfixed. Nothing I could say was going to make any sense to him within his dimensions of reality. Most of the time when we judge people like this, it's on our own grounds—I mean, how else? We think they are living within some reasonable range of our own sense of what's actually going on, what's real. In this moment, his world seemed totally beyond the boundaries of anything I could reason or think possible. His kind of faith wasn't a leap I could make, not even for discussion. It was grounded on nonsense to me. So since I couldn't find anything to say, I said nothing.

"I had no idea how my silence would affect him. I knew it could throw him into a rage as he could read it as obstinacy. He could see it as my unwillingness to acknowledge what he'd just told me and dishonor it by speaking again with his mother. Or my standing in silence could actually calm him, perhaps his seeing it as resignation, my willingness to accept what he'd just said to me as, at least, *his* true belief and honor that by keeping away from Myrtle. Evidently he chose to believe the latter because he said, 'Okay then,' as though this was the end of it all. 'I'll be leaving you for this day.'

"I stopped him from leaving by saying, 'No, *every* day. You will not return *any* day. *Ever*. You've made your request. Now I'm making mine. Don't come back.'

"He nodded his head slightly and moved toward the porch door where he turned around and said astonishingly, 'I know the sheriff. He attends our Kingdom Hall.' He didn't add another word, just walked directly down the steps and across the parking area to his car. Jilly had sat this whole time inside the sliding back doors watching with ears up and eyes darting back and forth from him to me. When I stepped inside, she immediately jumped up and down and ran in circles, thinking we were going out for our daily walk. But I went to the sliding glass door in the living room where I could watch the Datsun pull onto Fairfield Road and turn in the direction of his and Myrtle's house."

"Jesus." Ella breathed in and then out, an audible release of breath which was followed from the others.

"I have to tell you, I was visibly shaken. I sat a long time on the couch, long enough for Jilly to lie down at my feet and sigh. An hour passed, could have been two, before I looked down at her and asked if she'd like to go outside. She was up bounding for the door where her leash and collar hung on a hook next to the coat tree. I was glad to see the rain had stopped, and the sun was attempting to peek through some clouds. When we got to the top of the drive—feet, hair, and fur soggy from the atmosphere—I turned right toward the intersection with a road that led in the opposite direction from this man and his mother. I wasn't sure what I would do about the rising conflict in my mind over what had just happened."

"Sounds pretty damn straightforward to me," Ella said. A couple of heads at the table nodded. "He wanted to control you pretty much as he was controlling his mother. This is a spooky guy, you're right about that. Were you afraid of him? For the future, I mean?" Ella always had personal safety as her first concern.

"It's an interesting question. At the time I was and I found myself more and more keeping away from that side of Fairfield Road. I only went in their direction when I knew he would be at work, at least I assumed he had some job as he drove past Myrtle and me into their drive around the usual commuting time for most folks coming home from work. From that day forward, I only went past their house when the weather was such that I knew Myrtle wouldn't be in her garden or walking to get her mail. But for a while, well, I wasn't exactly terrified, but I was concerned about whether I'd see her and what I'd do if I did."

"Did it happen? Seeing her, I mean?" Gloria asked.

"Well, of course it did. It was a loaded situation, right? It wasn't going to go away so easily, though the motorcycle and truck noise at the head of the drive had, hadn't it, once I confronted it?

"But it made me mad that this man had put me in a frame of mind such that I was afraid to walk where I wanted. Ella's right. He wanted to control me because he saw me as a threat to his mother and himself. I was the outside world knocking at their door that had the power, in his mind, I guess, to change things as they were for them. His notion of that power annoyed the hell out of me, a power that he had twisted into reverse, using it to frighten *me* away from *them*. So slowly I began every now and then walking in the direction of their house which by the way sat back considerably from the road with some trees to hide it from view.

"Come late Autumn, I felt sure that Myrtle had probably winterized her garden and was staying indoors. It wasn't cold yet, but we had some nippy days, and she was, if not frail, certainly not hearty enough to be out any length of time in the chill.

"The day I saw her again, she was walking back across the road, just like before, only this time it was in the morning before the mail was delivered, which was usually sometime in the afternoon. Belatedly, I noticed with a sigh that her red flag was up on her mailbox, so evidently she had taken something to the box to be mailed. When she saw me—by the way, this was several weeks after the incident on my porch with her son—she stopped in the middle of the road like we were doing a rerun of what we'd done earlier. I felt a huge wave of déjà vu. I thought of Bernice, again, standing on her porch ready to take the steps down, one at a time, in order to begin her daily walk to the corner and back, her portable oxygen tank slung over her shoulder like a large purse. 'We have to keep going,' she'd said to me when I asked her if I could give her a hand down the steps, 'as long as we can, don't you think?'

"'That you, Roe-donnie?' Myrtle called out. I couldn't help but smile over her mangling of my name, but was grateful that she had the presence of mind to remember me as who I was and not Mildred, whom she'd mistaken me for when I met her. But I also felt very ambivalent about what to do next. Jilly Jean was pulling at her leash as though reaching out toward Myrtle until she evidently realized it was the woman I'd stopped to talk to before, the one that brought her ears down—I mean, do dogs remember like this? Maybe she initially recognized Myrtle as somebody else, but who, I wondered? I decided that I'd acknowledge Myrtle's greeting and then tell her I was in a rush.

"'Yes,' I said, 'It's Rhodanna....You can call me Ronnie, if it's easier.' As I walked in her direction, Jilly halted her progress to near stopping.

"'That would be nice.' Myrtle sounded relieved. 'And you can call me Myrt. Everybody does.' She went on quickly walking to the grass as though aware of my concern for her. 'I want to apologize to you for not inviting you the other day to see my garden, Ronnie.' Myrtle was very coherent and I didn't notice any sign of her former strained swallowing in the middle of words. But I did notice that she remembered weeks ago as only 'the other day.' 'Nothing much is blooming anymore, of course, but there's still a lot of *green*,' she said, laughing a little. 'Come…'

"'I'm sorry,' I told her as I continued walking slowly in her direction but still on the opposite side of the road. 'I'm in a bit of a rush today as I've…'

"Myrtle looked around toward her house and then quickly back at me. 'My son's spoken with you, hasn't he? No, no, I won't put you in a position of having to deny it, because he told me as much. He said that he wondered why you'd be interested in an old woman like me. It's his way, you see. He protects me from what he thinks are bad influences. He's afraid I'll leave and go live with relations up in New Hampshire. They have a much larger Kingdom Hall, and I'd be able to have ever so many more friends my age.' She didn't take her eyes off of me. The difference in her attitude, her ability to converse so much more easily was short of amazing. 'It's very hard to convince him that I'm perfectly capable of making my own decisions.' She paused a moment, then said, 'Joshua's a good boy. He means well.' How many mothers have said this down through the centuries, I wondered? Probably Nero's before he had her killed."

Katherine, ever the librarian, interrupted. "Actually, Agrippa spoke ill of her son and by Roman standards, therefore, duly earned her fate."

Gloria did her 'Hear, hears' to the Agrippas of this world. Doug snorted, others smiled. I toasted Katherine, laughed and went on with my story.

"Myrt added this about her son, 'It's his earnestness to do the right thing by me which I appreciate in the end.' I felt like I was beginning to pick up some of her son's craziness in her—an overzealousness to protect him as he had done with her. Myrtle wasn't appearing so much the victim to me anymore."

"Right." Ella tapped the air with her finger, then to the side of her head.

"I stood for a moment in the road then decided to cross over and at least speak with her openly. I wondered why she was so different today from when I'd seen her before. She seemed to be reading my mind when she continued. 'My doctor has put me on some new medication and I'm feeling so much better. Can you tell? I'm not sure how long it will last, but while it does I feel like making hay while the sun shines.' She giggled, pulled a hankie out of her dress pocket, and wiped her eyes under her glasses. 'My, my, it feels hot this morning, but it's probably the side effects of the medication—my hands still feel cold.' She turned as though to leave just as I was about to her side. 'I won't keep you then, Ronnie. I understand you're in a hurry. It was wonderful to see you again. Hopefully you'll have time soon to stop by and see my garden, at least how I've landscaped it. I would love that.'

"I thanked her, wished her well with her new medication, and Jilly and I went our way down her side of the road. Evidently she watched us for a long time because when we turned onto Knowles Hill to make the four-mile loop toward home, Myrtle was still standing there, her hand shielding her eyes as she'd done when I'd first seen her. I didn't look back again before I walked down the hill and out of her sight."

"What I wouldn't give to spend some time with those two, together or apart, in therapy," Ella said. "Interesting if nothing else."

"Yeah, the dynamic felt almost incestuous, definitely a kind of weird intimacy. They each told me the weaknesses of the other and then hastily covered up what they'd said as though through guilt. It made me feel uncomfortable. I felt caught in the middle with these two."

"Well, yes, and my guess is that they both were doing it unintentionally 'on purpose,' if you know what I mean?" When I shook my head, she explained. "They were setting up a kind of collusion where you, or somebody like you, was needed by both of them—each on his or her own terms—in order for each to feel as though they had a good connection with each other. See what I mean?"

"That's actually what it felt like. I got the feeling that when they were together they probably nipped at each other, but when they were talking to me, and others, no doubt, they demonstrated a kind of protectiveness toward each other, even devotion, at least by him for her."

"Puts you in a crappy spot," Ella said. "As long as you fed into the illusions they were fostering with you, things went well, I imagine. But the minute you showed any resistance to their mutual protection, they would come at you like dogs, and I don't mean nipping like they do with each other. It's the syndrome of the naughty child that parents both need to punish in order to be viewed as good parents to each other."

"Well, I got that plenty already from him, remember? When I resisted him, the little I did, about what he wanted from me concerning his mother, he became threatening. And that only increased as we went along. After this encounter with her, the only way I could figure out that he knew I'd spoken with her was that she must have told him. Why would she do that? To get closer to him by making me the bad guy? Or to nip at him and use it to argue for more freedom—even strengthening her desire of going to New Hampshire?"

"Maybe both," Ella said.

"Oh my god," Gloria said, a light coming on. "He did something, didn't he? What did he do to you?" She reached over and squeezed my hand.

"Well, it was scary as hell. One afternoon, not too long after this second encounter with Myrt, Jilly and I were walking toward the bend in the road on Knowles Hill when I realized that we didn't have time to get to the side of the road flowing with traffic, so I walked over to face the oncoming car at the bend and waited. I saw a cloud of dust as it approached the curve, coming at an ungodly speed, like they all drove out there in the country, all hell bent for leather. My view of the car was obstructed by the trees so I didn't make out it was the Datsun until it was bearing down on us. Joshua--I knew Myrtle's son's name by now—almost lost control of the car in the turn, but he straightened it out some thirty, forty yards away so I had a decent view of him behind the wheel. But not for long, because at the speed he was going, I only had a very short time to react. The Datsun came straight for us without slowing in the slightest. Jilly absolutely freaked, and in doing so, she probably saved our lives. She dove for the ditch, and because I had wrapped the loop of her leash around my wrist several times to hold her in place, I went head over heels down into the ditch with her. The Datsun swerved at the last minute toward the center of the road so it didn't end up down there with us. I noticed it fishtailed awhile before getting into the right lane again. I got bruised up plenty and had some road rash from skittering across the shoulder gravel before I hit the ditch. Jilly was absolutely traumatized. I held her at the side of the road until she stopped trembling. Let me tell you, she practically ran all the way home, and it was days before I could coax her beyond the backyard. She would go on a brief walk into the back woods along the path I'd made with the mower, but that's all for several weeks after this incident."

"Did you turn him in, call the police?" Gloria wanted to know.

"It's the sheriff's office for anything beyond the city limits and, remember, he said he knew the sheriff."

"Even so…"

"I did call a close friend and she insisted I let the sheriff's department know. But I was afraid of reprisals, to be truthful. And it was impossible to prove it was anything but an accident with me approaching the bend in what he could claim as the traffic's blind spot. It would be hard to refute that he'd simply lost control of the car momentarily. Ultimately, I didn't do anything. It's one of those things where you even convince yourself that it wasn't quite what you thought—you know it wasn't really him and the Datsun, and it wasn't that close, and Jilly just freaked from the approaching noise. But I knew. I wasn't sure he was actually trying to hit us so much as scare the bejesus out of us, but the incident did something to me. I would never have gone on Slater at that time of the day if I'd thought he ever drove that route home." I looked around the table of faces. "Slater is the road running adjacent to Fairfield. Anyway, I tried to be mad about it but I couldn't feel anything but fear. I felt like I was swimming with the sharks."

"No wonder the country didn't seem like such a great place to live anymore," Gloria said. "It makes me mad that this nutcase ruined it for you. And, of course, that's what he intended."

"Oh, but that wasn't the end of it."

"Jesus," Gloria mumbled.

"About two weeks later, I saw Myrt standing on the corner of Slater and Fairfield by the intersection stop sign. At first, I thought she might be thumbing a ride and really was leaving, you know, I mean intending to leave for New Hampshire or some such. This thought came to mind because there was something strange about her appearance. She was disheveled, even more than I'd seen her when she was out-of-it initially. And she seemed to be watching me closely when I turned the corner which was even stranger still. She began waving me down frantically, and when I slowed and stopped, she rushed to my window. She needed a ride home, she said. She had gone out for a walk, feeling absolutely fine and had ventured out further than she should have. She couldn't imagine how she could make it home. Her son normally came up Slater on his way home from work, so she was waiting for him. She said that since her son hadn't shown up, she was hoping someone she recognized would come along. She looked totally distraught. What was I to do? I told her that, of course, I'd take her home. Once she was seated in the car, I did tell her that I'd had strong and definite messages from her son that he disliked my even talking with her."

"'Nonsense,' she said, pushing her hair back from her face, a slick sheen on her flushed skin. It was chilly out there, and she was sweating. It concerned me.

"When she didn't go on, I said, 'It isn't nonsense, Myrt. It's the truth. He doesn't want…'

"'No,' she interrupted me, 'I mean to say that it's all a bunch of *his* nonsense and you aren't to be troubled by it.'" She seemed to be gaining some of her composure again. But I thought of the incident with her son on the bend in the road. I had no intention of telling her about this and possibly starting a series of denials, but I wasn't quite certain whether to turn into her drive or not. When we got there, I slowed to make the turn and hoped she'd tell me to stop at the top of her drive and let her walk the rest of the way to the house. But, of course, she didn't. And even though she had recovered somewhat, she still didn't look any too great. I wondered how long she'd actually been standing there. So I drove her to the porch steps and idled the car, thinking I'd walk around to help her out and then be gone.

"'Oh you must come in. I insist upon it.' She gathered her purse and opened the car door. 'I *insist*,' she said. 'Come, come on in.' She smiled and waved her hand toward the house. 'I mean it.'

"Against my better judgment, I turned off the car and followed her inside."

"For Christ's sakes, why?" Gloria asked.

"Well, hell, why do we do any of these things we look back on and wonder 'why'? Thinking about it later, I reasoned that I was worried about her physical condition. I wanted to make sure she was okay before I left for home."

Gloria grunted, but others nodded their heads in understanding.

"Her house was quite unexpectedly tidy and cheerful. I don't know what I thought it would look like. I hadn't really given this any thought at all, because, believe me, I wasn't thinking about ever being inside their home. But given her frailness and his rather shoddy appearance, I didn't expect what I was taking in. Curtains were pulled back from a multitude of glistening windows overlooking the backyard. I could see where a profusion of plants had been on both sides with a stone walk that led to a small fountain with a brick pathway around it which, in turn, converged and led beyond to an attractive fence guarding the vegetable garden from the deer. When I looked around the kitchen, there were fine antique plates leaning on moldings on cabinet shelves around the room and the table had been set with two china plates and cups, forks and spoons on cloth napkins to the side. I would have assumed that the place settings were waiting for dinner with Joshua when he came home, except for the cake in the center of the table.

"'Are you expecting company, Myrtle? I really mustn't stay…' I began, but she didn't let me finish.

"'Oh no, dear, I was hoping you could have a cup of tea with me.'"

"Oh my god," Gloria said. "She planned all this for you. That's just too friggin' *bizarre!*"

"Yeah, she had. I knew it for certain when she said, 'You look like a chocolate cake kind of person.' I didn't know if she'd intended to come to my house and invite me for tea, and perhaps had gone to the top of my drive and seen that my car was gone, whereupon she decided to stand by the stop sign and wait for me to come home or what. My mind was awhirl. Had she then made up a story in order to get me into her house? I would never have thought she had the presence of mind to plan out such a thing. But there it was, a plan of some sort had been put into place.

"And it's one of those things you just intuit. I suddenly *knew* what she'd done, even if I didn't know how! Later I surmised that she probably didn't know my last name—I don't have it on my mailbox—so she couldn't find me in the telephone book. I use initials instead of my first name, anyway, so it was probably just an innocent desire to have me over. But standing and waiting for me at the corner and giving me the made-up story? Well, it creeped me out. When she saw that I was thinking about retreating back through the door, she said, 'I feel so awful about you getting in the middle of all this with my leaving and Joshua. He's just upset, you see. He doesn't mean anything bad. He wants me to be secure and happy and to him that means he has to take his father's place.'

"I'd never heard either of them mention the husband and father, and I'd wondered about that, but given what had transpired between Joshua and me, I didn't think I was in a position to ask and actually—well, how often had I seen either of them, really? Certainly not enough for the subject to have come up, but I had wondered, of course. She answered my unspoken question quickly. 'He died suddenly of a heart attack, and it left Joshua a mess. He's not recovered, because he and his father were never close and in the months before Alfred passed, they'd started becoming the father and son that they should've been years and years before. Since Al's death, Joshua has been overly protective, not just of me, but of everything. At the Kingdom Hall, he's become one of the most active in the Field Ministries. On his job, which he's work at for over thirty years, he's beginning to have problems, because he can't keep just to his own work, he's crossing lines with other managers, and it's going to get himself fired or into forced retirement if he doesn't stop.'

"I asked her, 'What does he do? Not to the managers. I mean what kind of work does he do?' I took a seat at the table. I wanted to eat Marie Antoinette's cake and head for home—with my head in place—before the executioner showed up at the door. But I wasn't at all sure that I was safe now, in any case, because Myrtle had shown before that she couldn't be trusted when her son was involved. Why had I agreed to come inside, and why was I sitting at this table participating in their *ménage à trois*? Was I self-destructive? Did I have a cat's curiosity that was going to get me killed? I wasn't so certain anymore that it couldn't literally come to pass." I nodded at Gloria, who'd asked why I'd gone inside. "Stupid," I said to her.

"You mean, you felt that unsafe?" Ella asked.

"I did, especially sitting at that table, caught in something more sinister than a casual decision to simply help this old woman out. All at once, it occurred to me that this sort of entrapment kept recurring. I was feeling more and more like the fly in the spider's web. I'm not talking just about with these two—though that was my most immediate concern, believe me. But, I mean, I started seeing a larger picture here which included how Kate and I got taken into the whole country living situation. It was as though there was a blind spot in my vision, and I didn't know it was there until I got caught by it in some way, then saw what had happened in hindsight."

"Well, that's kinda how life flows a good deal of the time, Ronnie. It's not like we all haven't been caught up like this at one time or another." Ella's reality fix was intended to let me down gently, I knew, but it wasn't absolving me, at least in this moment, of my sin of poor insight.

"Maybe so, but it was as though this was just the last straw. I probably was throwing the baby out with the bathwater, but it was where I was at the time. I wanted to get up from the table and simply start running out of her house—and away from mine—and down the road until I was out of the country forever." I shrugged, drank coffee and waited, saying finally, with a sigh, "But I didn't, of course."

"How did you get out of this one?" Gloria asked, not wanting to take sides in the country living dispute, but encourage me on with my story.

"Myrtle served up the cake and put tea in our cups and cream and sugar on the table. 'He's a locksmith and works for a security company downtown,' she said in answer to my question about what her son did for a living. Oh lovely, I thought. 'He's very good at what he does,' she went on. 'Especially in emergencies.' I was listening but eating rapidly, indecently shoveling in mouthfuls to relieve the tension and be done with all this, although I didn't see how I was going to leave as long as she was eating, and she was taking infinitely small bites between her talking. 'I've told him that if he wasn't a Witness for Jehovah, he could easily be a robber, preferably of banks.' She laughed at her own joke. 'He's a regular Houdini. I tell you, he's amazing. He can find his way in and out of any lock. If he's ever in jail, they won't be able to hold him there. 'Course, now he's more a manager than an actual locksmith, but he still is the one who goes when the others can't make the…well, doors open, so to speak!' She laughed again, this time behind her napkin. She'd told this jocular pun at the Hall often, I was sure. I kept checking the time and glancing at the door when she was looking at her plate. I thought of Jilly waiting patiently at home. She was going to be my excuse out of there, after the cake.

"Myrtle told me she'd contacted her sister Milly's people in New Hampshire and they were searching for an assisted living situation for her there. As soon as they found one, she was moving, she said. Her only problem was getting her hands back on her money, her inheritance from her husband. When she wasn't herself, before the new medication, she had given her son power of attorney, and he'd moved the money into an account in both of their names. She could still sign for money and get it out and into her checking account, but then Joshua had put the larger share into a savings account which she now didn't have access to."

"This poor woman," Gloria said. "Isn't there some kind of service that could help her out, resources through the Department of Aging or some such?"

"She was feistier than I would ever have thought. She said she had a bit of hidden resources, not enough to move and establish a new place to live, but, behind Joshua's back, she had consulted 'a woman attorney,' is what she called her, who was looking into the legalities of her getting her husband's inheritance out of savings so that she could move. This had presented a very hard dilemma at home for her, she said, because she had never isolated herself from non-Witnesses the way many members of the Kingdom do, are encouraged to do. She had even thought of leaving the Watchtower Society but all her relatives up in New Hampshire were members, and she didn't want the shunning that came with being disfellowshipped. She loved her sister's children and their kids and wanted to remain close to them. She'd been disciplined by the elders several times over the years for her liberal attitude but nothing much had really come of it.

"This was far more information that I had asked for or ever wanted to know. I was her new confidant, and it was unsettling. I kept one ear cocked toward the driveway, and thought I was constantly hearing the slamming of a car door, but it was only four in the afternoon. I had an hour to get myself out of this house into the safety of my own. When she still had a half slice of cake on her plate, I told her that I'd enjoyed our talk, that the cake was delicious, but I needed to get home to my dog. Jilly had been in the house much of the afternoon, I explained. She was old and would be needing attention by now.

Myrtle put down her fork and said she was pleased that I'd been willing to spend time with her, that she felt more comfortable now that she had told me her backstory. I grinned at her but didn't ask from where, in heaven's name, she knew this term. *But what was the matter with me?* Evidently, Myrtle and her son's religion seemed so insular to me that I'd made the erroneous assumption that they didn't live in my world at all. As Myrtle walked me to the door, she reached out and pulled me to her for a hug. I was downright shocked. 'Please don't hesitate to talk to me anytime, including coming into my home. Joshua will understand. I'll talk to him…'

"Shit," Gloria spat out before thinking. "I mean, you've got to be kidding."

"Well, you can imagine how *this* hit me. 'I'd rather you didn't do that,' I said, glad for the opportunity to tell her this. 'I think we might be borrowing trouble that doesn't need to be...well, borrowed.'

"Myrtle smiled, but said sternly, 'I must tell you, my son and I don't keep secrets. He may be strong in his beliefs, but he has my best interest at heart.'

"'I'm sure that's true, Myrtle. But...'

"'Oh now,' she interrupted me like she didn't want to hear any resistance that might impugn her relationship with her son. "I can see you're of a suspicious nature where people like us are concerned. You don't need to be. Our ways may seem peculiar, but we have only the best intentions. We're Jehovah's *Witnesses*, so there's no cause for alarm.'"

"Now there's a heart-plunging dagger if I've ever seen one," Ella said. "Let's count the stab wounds. First plunge—you have a suspicious nature. Second plunge—you're a bigot singling out 'people like them.' And the third plunge—you're especially suspicious toward Jehovah's Witnesses who really are folks with good hearts and therefore don't deserve any of what you're dishing out. Do you feel just a little wounded?"

"Nothing like what was to come."

"Oh god, please," Gloria said. "There's more? I don't know if *my* heart can take it. What did he do? What? You're still alive, so at least, he didn't kill you."

"I swear, before this was over, I did almost die of fright," I told her. "But that afternoon, I got out of their house ASAP, but I knew I'd jumped from the frying pan into the fiery pit. I was in a hellhole, and without Virgil as my guide, I didn't know how I was going to get out of it. I kept waiting for the unexpected to happen, but, it didn't, at least, not for several weeks. I thought through all of the possibilities of how she might use my visit to her advantage or against him."

"Or both," Ella added quickly.

"My mind hummed with all those possibilities. Perhaps, she had just taken my advice in deference to me and not told him I'd been there or told him gently, but more likely she'd used it to threaten him in some way in order to leave. Maybe she made a deal with him, you know, if he started behaving himself, she wouldn't leave him. I knew there were probably many other options, but, when nothing was forthcoming, I finally gave up my ruminations and settled back into my routine of country life.

"And as more time passed and nothing happened, I got lazy, unwatchful."

"Oh shit." Gloria was no longer trying to hide her astonishment, nor watch her language, as if she ever had.

"Oh yeah. One night I came home from a theater rehearsal late. I'd joined a group who did local performances, and we had three, four hour rehearsals when a show was coming up, usually in the evening as many of the members worked. Well, you've heard me talk about this. Anyway, I'd written a one-act play being performed soon and was helping with the set so when I finally made it home, Jilly had been in the house from noon until suppertime. She bounded onto the porch the minute I slid the door back and headed for the edge of the yard. It was just before sunset so I grabbed her collar and leash and ran after her, deciding to come down from the rehearsal by our taking a walk into the woods together. The air was perfect. It was a wonderful day, one of the last before the hard freeze of the season. Jilly romped in the leaves like a puppy, turning in circles with joy. I wasn't certain how long I'd been out there when she suddenly decided to run after a squirrel or woodchuck or a rabbit and like a shot she disappeared into the deeper woods. It took at least twenty minutes to locate and collar her, snap the leash on and head back to the house. It was now well into twilight and long dark shadows swallowed the house from view until we were almost on the porch. In my haste to run after Jilly, I hadn't turned on the outdoor light.

"The minute I walked into the house I knew we weren't alone. Jilly oddly didn't give the slightest indication that another person was in the room with us. She ran directly to her water bowl in the bathroom and started lapping noisily as I flipped on the light. So much for watchdog!

"He sat on the couch, his legs spread out in front of him, the ottoman pushed off to the side. His hat had been pulled down over his face. He looked like a member of the family who'd dropped by, found me not at home and decided to take a snooze while waiting. In fact, that's what he'd done. He pulled off his hat but didn't stand. He eased back up on the couch and set the hat next to him.

"'What are you doing in my house?' I asked.

"'I was waiting for you, of course,' he said casually. He said 'a-courssse' with that hiss again. 'I figured since you had been in my house, it seemed only fair for me to be in yours.' I really thought he was going to say 'yourn,' like one of Faulkner's characters."

"Weren't you out of your mind?" Of course, it was Gloria again. She had the reputation of country living at stake. "Where was his car? Oh, he walked down."

I nodded. "I was not so much afraid as I was furious, trying to smother it with a scornful glare. 'I was *invited* into your house. You were not invited into mine. Please leave.'

"'Oh now,' he sighed making no attempt to get up. 'You seem to always be telling me to leave.'

"'You will or I will call the sheriff. I really don't give a damn if he's your friend. You have come into my house without permission.'

"'Oh now,' he repeated in his lazy voice, 'the door was unlocked which seemed as good as an invitation. Since you've been sociable with my mother, I felt it totally appropriate for me to give you a call. I was out taking a walk, and I saw your car in the drive so knew you were home.'

"I walked to the telephone.

"'287-2344,' he chimed. 'Ask for Dave. Tell him Joshua sent you. He's the undersheriff but it's the same thing.'

I stood with my hand on the telephone. Jilly came and stood by me, then sat looking at the stranger in our house. I wondered if she recognized him from before.

"'Dog gonna bite my head off?' he asked good-naturedly. I thought he was going to call her to him, but he didn't. 'Look, I just want to talk to you. My mother had her say. I'd like to have mine. Just a minute or two, and I'll be gone.'

"'I told you not to come back, and you agreed to that.' I brought my hand out of my pocket, holding the pepper spray I always took with me when outdoors, especially in the days with rabid animals around.

"'I recall that agreement was based on the proposition that you would not see my mother again,' he replied, ignoring the pepper spray. 'You did see her. Not just once, but twice, and the second time was a social call. My being here seems a fair exchange.'

"'What kind of exchange would you call the one you made with Jilly and me on Slater Road? Was that fair?'"

"I was truly surprised when he didn't attempt to deny his actions. 'Pedestrians are to face oncoming traffic except on a curve or bend in the road that obstructs the view of the driver in a vehicle.' This is a direct quote from the driver's manual put out by the Department of Motor Vehicles. In any case, it's a safety practice for walkers to step off the road if they can't make it to the opposite side in time. I had an obstructed view of where you and your dog were. You almost caused me to have an accident.' He assumed his former casual stretch on the couch, playing with his hat, lifting it and setting it back down, looking at it and not at me. 'Little lady, there is a very simple solution to our dilemma.' He swung his head around and squinted at me as though he were in the midday sun. The motion was reptilian, snake-like, a slithery con-artist getting ready to strike.

"I didn't want to acknowledge his problem as *our* dilemma, but I needed to get him out of my house with as little disturbance as possible. I walked Jilly to the sofa chair opposite where he was sitting. 'I'm all ears,' I said, sitting down, Jilly at my feet.

"If he had told me that he wanted us to bind and gag his mother and leave her in his attic I wouldn't have been more surprised by what fell out of his mouth.

"'You need to move,' he said. There were hoots, hollers and expletives all around the table. "Holy shit" rose above all the others. When everybody calmed down, I went on.

"'How's that again?' I asked him. But I'd heard. I needed time to recover from shock. I couldn't help it, but I started smiling and then laughing a little. He stood up, clearly annoyed. Jilly stood up as well. I didn't know what she would do if I gave her a command. I had not trained her for attack, and I wasn't sure but that she'd turn tail and run if he became menacing. She certainly headed for the ditch before but that wasn't concerning a threat on a level she could handle.

"Joshua said with disdain, 'None of this happened until you came to live out here with us.' There was that phrase again, 'with us.' He was seeing me as the outsider in their world, and in his case, the foreign element upsetting his order of things. So I wasn't so wrong after all, viewing them as living in a more insular world, despite Myrtle's attempt to convince me otherwise.

"'What do you see that I've done?' I asked him.

"'We didn't, haven't and won't consort with non-Witness neighbors. We live our lives apart from non-believers. Mother was getting along just fine until you began socializing with her. She doesn't need you. She has the members of our congregation to socialize with.'

"I stood up. I wanted him to leave any time now. 'That isn't what she indicated to me, Joshua.'

"When I used his name, his first name, he was visibly shaken. A shudder began in his head, chest and arms and traveled down his body. But he gained his composure rapidly and said, 'I don't care what she's told you. She goes off like this sometimes, but she always comes back home to Jehovah. Down deep, she wants what she's always wanted, her family and her life at the Kingdom Hall.'

"I don't know what came over me, but I couldn't hold back the truth any longer as it had come to me. I told him, 'Part of her family lives in New Hampshire, and she wanted to be with them long before I came on the scene. She told me that. I think what's happening here is that *your* family is falling apart, and you don't know how to hold it together—it's getting away from you. Your mother is showing you that she no longer wants to stay in the life she's been living, so you're doing whatever you can to keep it as it was.' What had it been he'd said to me? 'I will protect her regardless of what it costs.' He'd said it on the porch that rainy day, a day that seemed eons ago. Now I was becoming more enraged than afraid of this insufferable man.

"'You know nothing about us. *Nothing*.' He stepped toward me and Jilly growled—that answered my question about my dog and her willingness to protect me. He stepped back and stood with his hands by his sides, glancing at Jilly, and then at me, holding my gaze.

"Before he could say anything more, I said, 'You know, you're right. I really don't know you or your mother. And it's none of my business. I don't want it to be my business. I didn't make it my business. Your mother and you need to work out whatever disagreements you have between you. I want out of this picture. Now and completely!'

"It was obvious he didn't know what to do next. So I went on, 'You know what? I'm done with your business. I never asked to be a part of it. I was *invited* in, if that's what you want to call it. Your mother initiated all of it—the invitation to her garden, the invitation into her…*your* home. She initiated what she decided to tell me.'

"'And what did she tell you?'

"'Go ask her.'

"'She told me.'

"'So why ask me then? Is this some kind of test, to see if I'd lie to you about your mother?' I waved him toward the door. I didn't want to make another evaluative statement."

"Good for you," Ella said. "That's the ticket out of there. Only describe, don't interpret or evaluate. First rule of disengagement."

"Took me long enough to figure it out, but I did. When I no longer engaged, he couldn't sucker me into his arguments. So ultimately he left. He stood there in front of me with a strange smirk on his face, and when I didn't react, he opened the door, and walked out without closing it behind him."

"And was that the end of it?"

"Pretty much, yeah. I did tell him I wasn't moving, but I wouldn't be talking with his mother. I think I actually said 'his *damn* mother!'"

"So that was that?" Gloria asked. The look on her face was searching, one that I took to be hopeful that I would answer in the affirmative, though the storytelling element seemed to be lurking in there somewhere, possibly hoping the tale would go on.

"When Myrtle saw me the next spring while she was in her front garden, she came down the drive and attempted to start up a conversation. She hadn't moved, I noted. I told her I didn't want a friendship with her, as harsh as that might seem. I wished her well and asked her not to get in touch with me. Then I walked down the shoulder of the road and out of her sight. She looked sad as I spoke to her, and I felt rude, but it wasn't worth the disturbance, and I didn't trust how it all was coming down on me. For a little while I went through the worst possible scripts in my head—that Myrtle would lie to him about my stopping and talking to her, which was the big one rattling around in my brain, and then, of course, I mulled over his possibly seeking retaliation simply because I'd stopped and spoken to her at all. But evidently she was telling the truth when she said that she and her son didn't keep secrets. She must have told him what I said about not wanting a friendship."

"Did you ever learn if Myrtle left for New Hampshire," Gloria asked.

"Nope, I didn't. I didn't see her after I told her I didn't want to start a friendship with her. I stayed out there in the country a little while longer, I can't remember exactly how long after this, but as my life grew more and more withdrawn when I was home, I decided country living had run its course. In my solitude, I lost that intensity that keeps things looking fresh and appealing. Jilly Jean died of what amounted to doggie Alzheimer's. It came on fast. She would walk in circles in the house and outside, stopping long enough in the yard to do her job, and then I'd carry her back in the house. I came home one evening to find her lying very still and cold in a niche between the kitchen cabinet and stove that she'd walked into and evidently couldn't figure out how to get out of. I didn't bury her on the land. My vet came and got her, and I had her cremated. She still sits in a box on a shelf in my study.

"The motorcycling couple at the head of the drive separated, selling the house to a family with one daughter in her early teens. Overnight the trucking business disappeared from the neighborhood. I came home every evening my last long winter in the country, sitting alone in my house, realizing that I was fast turning into a recluse. I put the house on the market with the same agent Kate and I'd purchased it from. It took the entire summer and over thirty showings to sell it. But I've never looked back, not once have I regretted my move to the village.

"I've learned that all things have a life span, a time when we can give our attention to that important thing before us that we present ourselves with or we are presented with by fate, whatever your point of view. That focus in our lives can be short, medium or long term. In any case, mine in the country was over. It was time to move on."

"So what do you think is the root or deep metaphor underlying Myrtle's story and Joshua's?" Ella asked. "This isn't some kind of psychological test, by the way. I've got my own idea, but I'd like to know what you and everybody else might think."

"I don't know about deep metaphors," I replied. "I don't know enough about that to say, maybe, but about Sendak's notion of a 'story within the story' and what the Prof was telling us about Fisher's 'narrative paradigms,' I've got some ideas, especially about the mother-son relationship I encountered.

"With Joshua, for me, it was about his character, which was the crux of his story, his possessiveness of his mother. If I hadn't disengaged, as you put it, during that last scene in my house, I'm not sure what he would have done. I think he was capable of great violence. On the one hand that violence could've come fast and furious from sudden eruption, but I sensed he was capable of a kind of stalking violence, as well. He had a sinister way about him. Insidious. I thought about how deceptive he had been by showing up on my porch attempting to witness to his religious beliefs as a means of getting in the door—he literally wanted me to open my door and let him in, and then he finally did come in that door, didn't he? So perhaps there's a deeper metaphor in this after all. He wanted to get inside my house, where I lived, controlling his mother through controlling me."

"In psychological drawings, the house is often interpreted as 'the container,' shallowly stated, of the drawer's life, even his or her unconscious mind," Ella interjected. "When you invite somebody into your house, you are opening your life up to them, in a sense. Both Joshua and his mother felt that, even if not fully aware of it. Myrt was opening their door or, at least, her life to you, and he was desperately trying to slam it shut."

"I've wondered," I replied, "what would have happened if I'd shown interest in his Jehovah Witness material and asked him to witness to me, especially if I'd invited him in."

"It's an interesting question," the Prof said. "Though that might not have totally solved the problem for him, unless he saw that this was going to be enough to keep his mother from leaving—your being a newfound friend of hers, and you could only be that in his mind, if you were a Witness. So perhaps he wanted to try to win you over to that first, and if you did embrace his religion, then see if that would be enough to work for him with his mom."

I nodded. "He also attempted to run Jilly and me off the road."

"*His* road," Ella said. "He wanted to get you off his path, out of his way. There's another related metaphor for you."

"And then his scary hiding in wait in my house."

"A kind of hide-and-seek?" Ella speculated. "Several possibilities, don't you think?"

"I don't get the seeking part, unless he was seeking to scare me, which, I guess, worked, didn't it? Two of these incidents, though, showed him capable of executing planned violence. The deeper metaphor of his actions was to run me—the intruder or outsider—away from his destined purpose, which is a path, a road. Everything he *said* to me was to get rid of me as well, so I guess that was his story, if you can call it a story. When I agreed with him at his last visit, he went away and didn't return."

"Oh, I think you can say he had a story. You just told it, didn't you?" Ella said.

I smiled at her. "I guess you could say that I did."

"His is a classic oedipal story to me," the Prof offered. "He never resolved the oedipal complex, as I see it. He was just bonding with his father when the old man died, so he stayed bonded to his mother and in competition with anybody who showed signs of taking her away from him."

"Freud had a lewd mind," Gloria said. "I don't buy all this sexual fantasy stuff, at least not as the foundation for our social development. This guy, Joshua, just seems needy to me, because he's antisocial and he wants a nurturing companionship in his life. He doesn't know how to feel comfortable alone, because that's what he feels all the time—terrified of losing his mom, being by himself. She's the last of his family. He's already lost his dad. She's old and sick. He's intensified his religion, because it gives him a community, something to belong to, even with his family *eternally*, if you want to push the analogy. And the members of the Hall will be a family for him when she's gone. I think his story is about family, a sense of belonging, not possession on some sexual level."

Doug piped up and said, "The important question for me is why he never married. Fifty years old, and he's still living with his mother? You know what they say about that."

"Yeah, well," Gloria came back. "Society has lots of sayings about a lot of things, and they aren't necessarily true. Most of society's practices are in place to perpetuate society, the status quo. Our culture constantly makes us feel like something's wrong with you if you enjoy living and being alone. You have to couple or you're twisted—and by God, it better be the right coupling! Either that or you need to get yourself to a monastery or nunnery. This whole damn society is sex-obsessed."

Doug said, "What else is there?" and hung out his tongue and crossed his eyes again. Gloria gave him a little slap.

"What about Myrt's story?" Ella asked.

"She's hung up on him as much as he is on her, seems to me," I said. "Her story seems to me to be all about why her son behaved toward me the way he did, and why he doesn't want her to leave. I almost said, 'leave home,' not in Joshua's religious sense but 'home,' as our original family, as Gloria is suggesting. I think that's what Myrtle wanted to do. Her son took her husband's place when he died, but now she wants to 'grow up' in her old age and form other relationships. Whether that's based in some kind of psychosexual development, I can't say."

"But it is a little like a lover who finds a fresh, more stimulating relationship, don't you think? She's looking to the future, and he's caught in the past," the Prof says.

"You really are into the Freud junk, aren't you?" Gloria says to the Prof, a little offended.

"It's one description that makes sense to me, of her and his behavior, yes." The Prof conceding that there were other descriptions out there which seemed to settle Gloria's ruffled feathers.

When we grew silent, Ella said, "I think their stories are about the same thing—bonding but in the sense of being *bound* to protecting each other. Think about the word 'bound' for a minute." She raised a finger and pulled out her iPhone and moved her finger on the keyboard. "The most common sense usage is one of being tied as with a rope or being chained, and in a broader sense, meaning to restrain or restrict, confine something or somebody." She read a bit more and said, "In this sense, even books are bound, which means holding all the pages together. So holding their lives together with each other seems to be in there." She glanced a bit at the text, and then closed her phone and put it back in her purse. "You know, while I'm talking about this, I'm thinking about the saying, 'It's bound to happen,' which means it's certain, sure—we bind ourselves to what's going on in such a way that we feel we know what's going to happen, can be sure about that, secure."

"Wow," Katherine, the librarian, said. It's the first we had heard from her in a good long while. "That's pretty amazing, Ella!"

"Thanks, but I have to tell you I'm really interested in metaphoric thinking and root, deep metaphors in particular. The idea has been used in a number of ways, but lately it's being used a lot in dream theory and interpretation, as I said earlier. But I'm working on a series of articles on deep metaphors in therapeutic storytelling. Jungian psychologists have their archetypes, of course, and universal symbolism has been around forever, but I'm interested in how our everyday metaphoric expressions and language, especially in the form of deep metaphors, can be used to unpack stories in the way we just did." She looked at me and asked, "If you had to characterize your story, what would you say the 'story within the story' would be, I mean about what you've told us about country living for you? And from there, could you find an essential, deep metaphor in all of this, you think?"

"As I've been telling this story, I've been giving this some thought," I replied. "In arts theory—I'm thinking the visual arts and writing in particular—there's a concept called the 'one and the many.' It's a notion found in other disciplines as well, of course. In the study of the arts, though, it usually boils down to the idea of a theme and its variations. If I reflect on my story in this light, I think it's about being alone and being together and the forms this idea took in the various stories I told within this framework.

"Katie and I moved out of city life into the country to be alone together, creating a nest if you will. That's what all that work on the house was about—having a place where we nested together. I was very tied to that, bound to it, if you will, for a long time, even after she was gone and I was alone, a little like Joshua to his mother, maybe. When Katie and I were still together, our neighbors didn't allow us that alone time together that we'd been seeking, and I, in particular, had a hard time adjusting to our being alone together with these neighbors as they were. When that got resolved, and Katie left, I then met this couple who entered my quiet, alone life with their own problems about togetherness and being alone.

"When I first started telling this story I thought it was going to be a little adventure about my life in the country. Now, I realize I've been telling myself a deeper story within it. I guess, I'm learning, with all your help, of course, how stories do exactly what we set out for them to do—to tell us something we want to know about ourselves, our community, our world. And just as in dreams, we find what we need to know sometimes too scary to do that telling directly, so we hide this message from our conscious minds in symbols, images and metaphors. If we don't take the time to pay attention to what we're doing, we never decipher those hidden stories so they....well, stay deeply hidden. *Underneath*."

"*Where the Wild Things Are*," Katherine said and sighed. "I've loved that childhood story all my life. And that's the truth."

FRANCIS

No man is an Iland, *intire of it selfe;*
every man is a peece of the Continent,
a part of the maine;....
Any mans death *diminishes me, because I am*
involved in Mankinde; *And therefore*
never send to know for whom
the bell *tolls; It tolls for* thee.

John Donne

(The famous lines quoted in their entirety in Ernest Hemingway's
For Whom the Bell Tolls)

"**A**re you into poetry?"
"A little."
"Do you know William Blake?"
I almost say "not intimately," but I know the cliché could hurt his feelings. "Of course," I reply.
"Do you know Johnny Depp?"
"The actor? Of course."

"Well, Depp was William Blake in a movie, and he didn't know it."

"Depp didn't know he was Blake?" He stares at me. "Or Depp didn't know he was in a movie?" I wait, hoping he'll take to my joke. He stares at me nonstop. Nothing moves. I continue, pushing it. "Or the character didn't know he was Blake or in a movie?"

He hesitates, his hand in the air, finger pointing out toward someplace over my shoulder. I think it's too much for him, so he chooses to respond to what he can immediately grasp. "The character, the character didn't know it. Depp probably had his director tell him who Blake was." His condescension is clear. He thinking so loud it's almost spoken: *You're such an idiot!*

"You're Francis, aren't you?" I've never met the guy or talked with him, but I've seen him around, constantly. Everybody in town knows who he is. I'm simply making sure.

"Yes, I am." He wants to go on. I interrupted his flow. He's panting now to catch up with himself.

"Okay, so Depp's character didn't know he was Blake," I clarify.

"Right. Right. The *character* didn't know it. Well, he knew he was William Blake but not *the* William Blake. And…and there was a statue of Blake, of Blake right across the river." His hand shoots out across the counter and baked goods case where the river is. He hesitates, eyes glistening, mouth half lost in his soft, blond, curly beard, a mouth hugely grinning now from an insider's knowledge of what's coming next. "And he was right next to this great English poet, with his name, the *same name*, and he didn't know it." He's excited, laughter in his voice, hand slapping his leg. He's all smiles, rocking toes to heels. "And the best part, of course, is that, that there's…there's this *clue* right across the river, a dead giveaway, and he doesn't see it. Get it."

At first, I think he wants to know if I'm following what he's telling me, but he's not asking a question. "What's the movie?"

"Jim Jarmusch. You know. Tonto." But he doesn't want to mess with me anymore, because a man is approaching undoubtedly from the music festival that hits our town every July. One of the best festivals in the nation, a host of magazines tells us. As though we don't know from the tens of thousands of people, half dressed in madras, that flood the fairgrounds for four days and nights, blasting jumbled music in the air beyond sleep. Until I moved here, I didn't know madras still existed. It does. Tons of it in booths lining the main street from the festival grounds to the grocery and drug stores on the outskirts of town, on the outskirts to avoid village taxes.

The man, wearing a grimy beige t-shirt and dirty black shorts, a guitar slung on his back, approaches the baked goods counter. "Do you know dum-dee-dee-dum-dee-dee-dum, dum, dum?" Francis sings at him the first notes of the theme song from *The Lone Ranger* television show of the fifties and sixties. The guitar man points to a large oatmeal cookie with raisins. He doesn't look at Francis.

Francis is silent, stares at the clerk. He waits and listens. The crinkle of an opening brown bag, the slide of a tray, the reach of a plastic glove for the oatmeal cookie with raisins. "Do you know Beethoven?" Francis finally asks the man who's still ignoring him.

The man turns away from the clerk and stares at Francis, sizing him up. "Of course," the man says, looking down at his cookie, passing a bill to the clerk, the register drawer yawning open.

"Bye, Francis." I wave and walk toward the door, sun shooting heat at eye level against the glass.

"Oh, oh," Francis calls from behind me.

I don't turn around, but smile at him as I keep walking. Enough of Francis this morning. But at the door, I do call out to him, "An early morning greeting with you, Francis, is a literary excursion." I have no way of knowing the true meaning of what I've just said.

———

At home, I place the package with scone on the table and walk to my computer in the library. I Google "johnny depp william blake," and wait. Several other searchers have beat me to this inquiry. I double click on "johnny depp william blake movie," the Wikipedia site. To the right, seven photos of Depp pop up, one the poster for *Dead Man*. In a sidebar, movie info is given in bold details:

Circumstances transform a mild-mannered accountant (Johnny Depp) into a notorious Old West gunslinger.

Release date: May 10, 1996 (USA)
Director: Jim Jarmusch
Cinematography: Robby Müller
Box office: 1.038 million USD

I take the time to read the plot summary. *Tonto?* Where is Tonto in this? Was Francis simply spinning off the Old West gunslinger role played by Depp? On a hunch, I Google "johnny depp movies," and there it is, *The Lone Ranger* starring Johnny Depp as Tonto. I laugh out loud. I decide to move on to "Beethoven." I Google "where did the theme music for *The Lone Ranger* come from?" The first site claims outright that *The Lone Ranger* theme is not written by Mozart, evidently as many must think. Beethoven, Mozart. Hmmm. The second declares it to be the overture to the opera, *William Tell,* by Gioachino Rossini, as most true Lone Ranger fans must know. Francis knows his movies, though he's a bit jumbled on his directors and music. I grin. But a probable hit. Definitely a probable hit.

Later in the evening, I am writing at my computer when a question seizes me out of the blue, totally unrelated to what I'm keyboarding. I could have smacked myself on my forehead, but instead I Google, "Did Rossini know Beethoven?" I have no idea what the birth and death dates of either of these composers are, or if Beethoven had ever written an opera. Not that this has much to do with my Francis inquiry, as ridiculously offhand as it is, but it might be a source of the two composers connecting, and hence, Francis connecting, or derailing his musical theme fact, however one wants to look at it.

When the sites come up and I open the one with the most promise, I declare out loud, "Well, well, well, wonders never cease." The two composers did meet, five years before the deaf-and-ailing Beethoven died, when he was fifty-one, and the young Rossini was thirty. Rossini had premiered his successful *The Barber of Seville* two years earlier. In a note to him, Beethoven advised the young composer to continue to write only *opera buffa* because for Gioachino to do otherwise would "do violence to (Rossini's) nature." Somewhat condescending, in the guise of a compliment. But Beethoven was known for his cantankerous nature and aggressively snide remarks.

For some unfathomable reason, I can't leave it at this. I search for Beethoven's operas. He had written only one, *Fidelio*, over which he labored for a decade. The production was in Vienna in 1805, and it met with dismal success—the opera house seats mainly empty, the audience only Beethoven's friends and a few outsiders, soldiers, mainly, who'd probably straggled in. It was held at the Theater an der Wien where his third symphony, *Eroica*, had been first performed in public only months before to mixed reviews. Perhaps Vienna had had enough of Beethoven by the time *Fidelio* came around. Beethoven's work was intertwined with politics and, with Bonaparte's emergence as a self-imposed emperor, the composer had reacted negatively, supposedly tearing up the first page of the symphony that he'd originally written for Bonaparte. Oh well, so much for that. I was now feeling too much like a rolling stone gathering moss. These Francis inquiries could easily slow down my writing and not lead toward any meaningful conclusions. I shut down the Google search and went back to my work.

—

Two days later, I round the corner toward Baker-on-the-Run for my three-mornings-a-week scone. All organic. All whole grain. All beige food with fiber the color of roasted psyllium. Townies call this fast-carry-out bakery, "The Runs," with justification. Francis is sitting on an outside bench below the bakery's large glass window swilling coffee from a paper cup.

"Are you into music?" I ask.

"Of course." He has the jitters. One leg hangs over the knee of the other, swinging jerkily. He eyes me with merriment but an edgy suspicion is circling the clear-blue irises. "I don't go to the festival. I don't have the money." Francis has worked for years as a handyman in our community. He's worked occasionally for my neighbors. Two years ago, before his retirement, he built a chicken fence for the woman who lives next door which took him well over a year. In all fairness, the fence was masonry—she wanted her flowers on the other side of it to catch the morning sun—and Francis required perfect alignment of the stones. He's a diligent worker. Everyone in the 'hood notes that without hesitation. In the case of the masonry fence, he worked under a plastic tent through the seriously blustery months of December and January, the jury-rigged siding of his little shelter flapping noisily against the sluicing gales of forty-five knots or more, a ship anchored by small boulders at the corners, let loose occasionally by the nor'easter that came through that winter. Francis's skin is the color of Missouri shale all year round from the blistering sun and chafing wind he endures. I say he's in retirement now, but it's really a quasi-respite from his once regularly scheduled work, his doing odd jobs for extra cash. So his usual ruddy complexion is a sandy pink these days.

"Know Rossini?" I look at him as directly as he does me. For a minute.

His eyes jump from me to the street where cars are moving bumper to bumper to work in the nearby city some ten miles south of us. "He wrote operas." He speaks in a whisper, sets his cup down to his side and crosses his arms over his thin chest. He sighs.

"That he did. Dum, dee, dum, deeee," I sing slowly and dramatically the first notes of "Tanti affetti." He stops studying the cars and looks straight into my eyes again.

"Joyce DiDonato del Lago."

I am laughing. From surprise but also delight. My Dum-DiDonato singing was hardly recognizable to me.

"What?" His eyes twinkled at my laughter.

"You're a cruel and malicious librarian."

He simply stares at me, mouth totally hidden in his beard. Finally he sings, "Dum-dum-dum-dum."

"Beethoven." I say. Did he just make the Rossini-Beethoven connection from my DiDonato clue?

He looks at me with piercingly clear blues and says nothing. Sensing an unexpected entrance into his more physical world, he looks to his right. A young woman with scattered day-glo hair in a knit-tight macro-mini and knee-high sandy-leather boots is approaching The Runs. "Gotta go." He grins, standing, then steps away from me, leaving his paper cup on the bench, holding the door open for Ms. Day-Glo. I don't bother following them inside. I shimmy back down the block to a heady *La Donna del Lago* and into the Roasted Cup Café, grab a homemade breakfast bar and a large colored decaf before driving back home with one hand on the steering wheel, slurping from the cup held up to my lips by the other.

Saturday morning, I approach Baker-on-the-Run at a brisk walk. Francis is sitting on the bench by the plate glass window. He's looking in my direction. Waiting for me? Walking toward him, he stretches out his hand and waves for me to sit next to him, slapping the bench lightly, palm down. I sit. He drinks from his paper coffee cup. I'm not there to him. Not yet.

Slowly he turns to look at me, with that piercing stare only he can sustain, despite what his body is doing. He pokes around inside a pocket of his vest and with wadded-up fingers, he shakes his fist in front of me. When I open my hand, he drops a small but heavy key into it.

"What's this?"

"Yours, to have and to hold." I think of the wedding vows but that can't be his aim. Can't be.

I shake my head and turn the key over several times with the fingers of my left hand. It has a beautifully sculpted bow, just large enough to fit between my thumb and index finger. I start to tell him that I don't understand when he abruptly rises from the bench, looks at me straightaway and says, "Hemingway." He turns and takes half-dozen steps to the swing-lid trash can, dumps his paper cup and moseys down the sidewalk away from me.

"Francis!" I call after him, but he keeps walking until just before he rounds the corner onto Congress Street, where he stops and sings out, without turning around, "Give a little whistle." It crosses my mind that he's getting even with me for exiting in a similar fashion just days before in the bakery.

"Dum, da, dum-dee, dum-dum. Jiminy Cricket," I sing out. But he can't hear me. He's gone.

The key has a short looped string knotted through the lacey bow. It is a truncated skeleton key. Beautifully crafted. The shaft ends in a bit with two small notches on each side. I'm stumped. At home, I hang it from an empty hook on the key holder in my entry parlor.

—

Sunday morning, getting ready to rise out of bed, still in a hypnagogic state, a clear thought emerges. *Francis Scott Key!* I grunt, slide back into the mattress and fitful sleep. I don't wake up until noon, dreaming of firecrackers and a birthday cake with thirteen candles in a circle poking out of coconut frosting. I jerk out of my dream when the cake catches fire. Less than an hour later, I sit with a homemade French-pressed, strongly-creamed hazelnut decaf and settle into writing at my monitor. I dream strangely. I'm used to it as I take Atenolol for my atrial fibrillation which can induce bizarre dreaming. Over the keyboard, I grin at how I've put "Francis" together with "key" to make the strange Early American reference in my semi-awakened state and subsequent dream.

—

Monday morning I sprint to the bakery. The bench is empty, except for what appears to be a napkin fluttering on the seat in the breeze. I slow to a stop and glance at a thin, lined piece of notebook paper, with torn-out spiral slots running along the top, held in place by a small rock. Reaching down, I pull it free of its mooring. In shaky hand is printed, dum-dee-dum. dum. dum. dum. I know immediately the first six notes to the National Anthem. I'm actually beginning to attune to this guy's rhythm. What a concept! I'm slightly shaken, remembering my dream.

Inside, the clerk sees I'm holding the lined piece of paper. He looks as though he's about to say something, but I ask before he gets to it, "Have you seen Francis this morning?"

"No, ma'am, he…" He stares out toward the window. I look around as though Francis is hiding somewhere in the aisles, although he's never done this before. It's not his kind of joke. "Is the paper from the bench?" He asks, nodding at the note I'm holding between my fingers.

I nod in reply.

"Do you have a key Francis gave you?"

I nod again, and wonder why I don't ask him what business is it of his, but it's clear he knows the right person retrieving the note from the bench is the one who's supposed to have Francis's key.

"This is for you," he says, walking back through the doors into the bakery, coming out again with what appears to be a case of some sort. A heavy case, with a brass handle, the lid specifically shaped to fit the contours of whatever's inside. He carries it out from behind the counter and places it at my feet. It's an old piece, an antique, with a carefully-selected grained and varnished veneer.

"What is it?"

"I dunno. Francis told Sheila it was yours, 'to have and to hold.'"

"Sheila?" I echo inanely, as though I don't know he's referring to the other clerk in the bakery.

"Yes, ma'am. He left it here sometime yesterday. 'For the lady with the key,' he told her. 'And the note.' That's what she told me to say to whoever had the note and key."

"You don't know what it is?"

"No ma'am. Without the key we couldn't look."

He gazes up expectantly. I shrug. I didn't bring the key with me. Why would I? But I don't tell him. Then I do.

"I'll get the key and bring my car." He nods and gives me change for the scone I buy. I drop the change in the tip jar.

———

Back in twenty minutes, I look around for Francis. Evidently he intends for me to have this adventure of his on my own. I show the clerk the key. He waits again. This time without the shrug. So I stoop down, insert the key and turn the bow in the lock. The top pops open. I lift the shaped lid off of an old manual sewing machine, one with a porcelain handle in place of the usual foot peddle underneath a stand. "Vesta" in gold letters is scripted on the face of the black arm with richly decorated floral designs across and down the elbow to the bed plate. *A sewing machine?*

The clerk clears his throat. "You haven't heard, have you?"

"What?" My heart takes a couple of irregular beats.

"Francis died Saturday night. Heart. He had a bad heart, they say."

I stand utterly straight. Still. "Francis?"

"Yes. Saturday night or early Sunday morning, I guess it was. I heard the sirens."

When did he write the note? Put it under the rock? He left me on the bench Saturday morning. I watched him walk around the corner and disappear. Did he come back Saturday afternoon? If so, by yesterday somebody would have taken the note, surely.

"When did he leave the machine?" I ask.

"I don't know. I wasn't here."

I nod. Tears blur my vision. I don't wipe them from my cheeks. The clerk carries the case out to my car for me. I tip him four bucks, but he shakes his head. He leaves me alone at the curb clutching the car door handle. I stare down at the note and four bills with George Washington's picture on them pinched tightly in the fingers of my other hand.

In the shower, I feel my skin keenly when I rub it with the washrag. I use no soap. I want to thresh myself to the middle, scrape to the core, find the essential blade that's sticking there. Raw consciousness stands on end. I wash. I dry. Ten minutes later, I am naked in my house, staring at the hand-cranking machine on the dining room table. *To have and to hold. From this day forward. For better or worse.* Mendelssohn's Wedding March pronounces an approaching marriage in my head. Dum, Dum, Dum, Dum, Dum, Dum...Dum, dum, dee, dum, dum, dum, dum...*What the hell?* I go to my bedroom and dress hastily, throwing on underwear, an over-sized t-shirt and baggy shorts. I return to my computer and

Google, "wedding vows." A long litany of sites emerge with various histories of pledges between the betrothed from medieval Catholic times to the present. This search isn't ringing true.

Francis was into movies, opera, authors. What was the last thing he said to me? "Hemingway." I Google, "Hemingway," and spend over an hour flirting with any synchronicity I can find between Hemingway, wedding vows and sewing machines. Nothing shows up that I can put together. But that doesn't mean it isn't there. Hemingway was married four times, but what the hell does that have to do with what I'm looking for? As though I know where I was even aiming. I give up, do my writing for the day, and take a lunch break at one. I jog to the library, deliberately keeping my eyes ahead of me as I pass the bakery on the other side of the street, especially the bench. At the library, I flip through the *Finger Lakes Sentinel* and *The Local Press* for an obituary. He's not there. Surely he had family somewhere. I ask for the head librarian. I get the director, who's one and the same. It's a small town.

"He came here often," she said in answer to my questions. "He spent some time at the computer, read the newspaper. He checked out materials occasionally. He did have a card. But he mostly read books in the lounge." She juts her chin out toward the reading area where three plush sofas and two tables with straight-back chairs around them sit vacant in the mid-morning light from windows and florescent from overhead. "About once a week he took out the limit of five music CDs. He loved movies. I honestly believe he saw all of those in our collection at least once. He would take the two loans allowed every other day, regular as the clock. And he used interlibrary loan for those he wanted we didn't have."

I glance at the Windsor Schoolhouse pendulum clock hanging and swaying behind her shoulder, on the wall to the left of the large plate glass overlooking her office. Francis is no longer a part of my time, our time, anymore. "What did he read, listen to last?" I don't know why I ask. It's not likely to lead to any answers, but I have to try. Now I'm googling out loud, for godssakes.

"I'm sorry," she says close to a whisper as though admonishing me to whisper as well. "I can't tell you that. Privacy, you understand?"

"Of course." I feel very small, as though I've attempted to steal a precious toy from a child.

She must see my dismay, because she half-turns and waves at the computer on the counter. "We don't even keep records of what you check out of the library, once you return your items."

"Of course." I remember this now.

"We'll miss him." She continues to talk about Francis and his connection to the library. Seems he helped with the book sale, the shelving of returned items, putting the month-old copies of newspapers and magazines in their storage shelves, even mowed the lawn occasionally and did small repairs without pay. "We did compensate for any substantial work he did for us, of course," she clarifies. Suddenly, she appears exhausted after her explanation. I thank her and start to walk away, but she calls after me in a whispered tone. I walk back to the check-out counter. "I think a lot of people thought he was homeless, that he hung out here because he had no place to go, but, it wasn't true. He lived in a modest home, but one very well-kept. Alone, of course. So, to my mind, well, I think he was lonely. He loved to learn, is how I'd put it, but it was more than this. He had a drinking problem, I understand, at least he did years ago. He talked to me about this quite openly once in the library, and I had heard it through village hearsay, so I don't think it was private information. But he had put that behind him, and he threw his energies into his work, then once retired, spent his time here, among people, reading as much as he could."

She smiles, just she and I in a tiny conspiratorial conversation. "He drove us a little crazy at times, in his attempts to share, you know, what he was learning, but, it never truly got to me the way it did to some of the others. He was so full of good-natured loveliness." Her smile never wavers. Her eyes are bright with remembrance. When I thank her, she goes back to her desk behind the glass and begins typing on her keyboard, no longer looking my way. What a remarkable obituary: "He was so full of good-natured loveliness."

When another question occurs to me, I wave at her a little frantically. I start to go behind the check-out counter to rap on her office glass, but get her attention. She comes out of her office and once again approaches the check-out counter. "Are there going to be services? An obituary?" I notice my voice is high-pitched, too near desperation. But libraries are hubs of local information, aren't they? Some of which she has just provided me.

"I haven't heard a thing," she says calmly. "I'd just keep looking in the local papers, if you're interested. Other than this, I don't know what to tell you."

At home once more, I call the hospital and after a couple of passes, I'm told by the head of emergency that Francis Keyton was DOA, and was taken directly to the medical examiner's office. When I call this office for verification, I'm told by some lame-voiced receptionist, following several of my questions, that nobody has claimed the body of Francis Keyton, that the medical examiner has made the identification himself, primarily from the papers in Keyton's wallet as Francis had a long expired driver's license and a county library card. But, of course, official verification will ultimately come through a legal process, she recites in a nasal tone, which includes fingerprint cards and other identifying data sent to the appropriate state and national divisions, including the National Unclaimed Persons Data System if nobody comes forward within the allotted time.

I open my mouth to ask another question, but she continues on, as though reading from a cue sheet in front of her. An adult service worker becomes involved, she says, in a search for a will, advanced directive, next of kin and such. I finally interrupt to ask when interment will take place. She hesitates for a moment, then I'm told that all bodies, unless under some criminal inquiry, are buried as close to within seven days of death as possible. She asks in a mesmerizingly monotonous tone if I am next of kin. When I say no, she hangs up before I can inquire further. She gave me too much information, over-reaching HIPAA privacy policy. Nobody had called about Francis Keyton, so, to her mind, nobody was likely to. But somebody had, so she assumed I was a relative, probably a distant one. Oh well, her carelessness was my gain.

I go back to my computer and verify, through more searches, that the county is responsible for the disposal of all "unclaimed dead bodies," which they are called now. Seems the term "john doe" is only used in old noir films anymore. If Francis's next of kin is not located, he will undoubtedly be given to some school or institution for anatomical study—if his body is accepted for that placement and it would appear a great percentage of them are. Then he will be cremated—it's cheaper than direct burial—and be interred in a local cemetery, through a regional funeral company that has donated a potter's lot to the county. *Just like Mozart*, I think with a shudder, remembering how I had turned away from the screen when Mozart's body had been dumped from a cart into a mass pauper's grave in the movie *Amadeus*. Of course, Francis will be in an urn-of-sorts, but still.

I find out online that the cost of processing Francis's body and burial will cost the county around seven hundred dollars. After more searches, sources reveal that the lot for unclaimed bodies in our county is through the Shelville Funeral Home, up the road ten miles north of where Francis had lived and worked. I also discover that the county is responsible for locating his family if at all possible, which can take months, years, often never. Even if families of the unclaimed are located, those long removed from them, as Francis appears to have been, often don't want to be associated with the deceased.

I count. Francis died early in the morning on Sunday, and it is now Monday afternoon. I've five days to get something moving if I don't want to see his cadaver used for medical research. That's providing none of his family steps forward to claim his body.

I call the medical examiner's office again and get the same nasal-toned receptionist. There seems to be only one. She's icy cold until she hears what I have to say. Ten minutes later, I'm talking to the Shelville Funeral home receptionist who puts a seven hundred dollar credit on my Citibank Card, but I now know the exact location of Francis's burial with assurances that this will keep Francis's body from being carted off to some university or medical school for dissection.

With the large donation for cremation, I simply cannot see committing to the purchase of a lot and appropriate funeral rites. So Francis will meet his fate in the crematorium, and I will take possession of his urn to save him from my own residual images of *Amadeus* and *The Tale of Two Cities*. All of this, of course, is conditional, she reminds me pleasantly but emphatically, on the grounds that Francis is not claimed by "his people" within the legally specified time. Friends can legally claim the body in this county, but I have an affidavit and other forms to sign, verifying that I am the friend of Francis Keyton and the circumstances of that friendship, plus other specific interview question to answer, mainly, I think as I listen carefully, to cover the funeral home and county authorities' behinds. So a trip to the funeral home office will be necessary shortly, she declares. I assure her that I will be there within the next couple of days. In the meantime, I'll study on what exactly I'm going to put in notarized writing about who I was and am to Francis, including how and why.

When I ask for the full name of Francis Keyton, the receptionist pauses but informs me that the name they have is simply Francis Keyton, with no middle initial, but with the last name spelling as "K-e-y-t-o-n," not the more conventional spelling of "K-e-a-t-o-n," like the movie star, Michael Keaton who played Batman. I thank her and hang up. She has to be wondering why someone who doesn't know the deceased's full name is paying for his cremation. It's a thought that hasn't skipped my mind either. And now, I will have Francis-in-a-Box to dispose of myself, together with a mind full of multiple choices as to where that will be. Unless…well, unless, I give "have and to hold" a completely unexpected meaning from the one Francis was probably trying to convey, whatever in the hell that was. But so help me God, I simply cannot not see him tucked away for eternity on one of my library shelves. And then, I wonder what Francis thought of the scene in *The Evening Star* when Aurora Greenway aka Shirley MacLaine opened an urn holding the ashes of her housekeeper and good friend, Rosie Dunlop, allowing the wind to carry them aloft while Jack Nicholson drove a convertible down the beach at full speed? I also wonder how many people have tried this solution to this disposal problem since the movie was released in 1996? As for me, I don't wonder, I *know*, I'd be arrested if I tried it along the shoreline of one of the Finger Lakes. Although, I frown at an image of me digging a hole in my backyard just past the compost pile, late at night, under heavily clouded skies.

—

Waiting until dark, fully clothed in black—was Jodi Foster in black when she went to the Your-Self Storage to follow up on a lead Hannibal Lecter had given her concerning the serial killer, Buffalo Bill, in *Silence of the Lambs*?—I drive past the address I've located for his house from the telephone book. Seems Francis Keyton wasn't all secrets. I'd driven past his place during the day and though it was located on a road leading out of town, isolated by half a dozen trees at the head of the drive, it had a mailbox with its number fully visible as I'd passed. Why I'm doing this, God only knows. I seem to not be able to stop the compulsion to follow the flow of information that's leading me along a path of unlimited and uncharted destination. As a kid, I remember my mother listening to a soap opera called *Whispering Streets*. Its weekday episodes were based on some story involving a minor character or event within the story that aired the day before who becomes the main character in that day's episode—the clerk who waited on that episode's main character at a clothing boutique, the mailman who tipped his hat to the main character receiving a letter he handed her in that day's story, a woman who yelled at a cab driver who didn't slow down at an intersection, a barber who had cut the main character's hair for the past twenty years without revealing anything about himself until this day, in this episode. It feels as though I'm playing in *Whispering Streets*, acting out an array of characters as I'm being jerked along from one part of Francis's life story to the next. And I'm not sure why I'm in this story at all, except I'm in it now, so I simply have to know more. I stop the car, hiding it behind the trees up the drive. I note the garage and glance inside to see Francis's beat-up Ford pick-up there as though he's in his bed for the night.

It isn't that difficult getting into his house, despite that both front and back doors are not only locked but sealed with warnings that have been heavy-duty stapled across the crack between the door and door frame. All of the windows are securely fastened, with the exception of one along the foundation that opens to the basement, hidden by a large azalea bush. The window has a crack that has yielded to framing decay, the glass partially fallen inward, which the authorities must have missed or the crack had given way after the seals had been issued.

Crouching down, I slide behind the bush and with gloved hands, reach inside, unfastening the sash lock, carefully pushing the unstable frame inward. The opening is just wide enough to allow me to twist and wiggle my way through once I remove the glass so I don't get stabbed or cut. I haven't brought any tools with me. I know, beyond doubt, that what I'm doing, even without them, is illegal, a bona fide charge of breaking-and-entering, a charge, if upheld, brings with it prison, not simply jail, time. But in my view, it will go much worse for me if I'm caught inside with hammer, wonder bar and pliers. Without them, I can always argue that my entering isn't a premeditated burglary, that I'm simply searching, as Francis's friend, for the answer to why this man gave me his sewing machine without explanation shortly before his death. Not a lie, but hardly a convincing reason to be in his sealed house without permission, dressed in black and gloves.

In all fairness to my intelligence, I've finally put the clues together of Francis Scott Key, the "Star Spangled Banner," and the sewing of the American flag, especially the one credited to Betsy Ross. My dream had gathered that neatly for me, preceding Francis's gift of his sewing machine. But if caught in his house, I'm not about to tell the police this, and I'm certainly not about to add that I'm satisfied with my answer because I intuitively know that there's more. But if I don't tell it, questions and all, the facts stand out there all by themselves without any reference to anything except Early American history. In other words, how does all this connect to Francis, most particularly as it pertained to Hemingway and Francis, and, most importantly, what the hell was he trying to tell me by it?

His basement is small but jammed packed with an enormous amount of stuff. On hand-made shelves carefully held together by solid two-by-fours, Francis has placed most of his tools and materials in plastic containers with large Avery labels, identified with black permanent marker. I zoom my penlight around, and discover that the basement from floor to ceiling is a warehouse of collected equipment, machinery and household goods.

Large items are neatly stored in rows against the back wall, having been driven or placed in backwards, ready for retrieval and revving to life. The largest one is an old Toro Snapper rider mower with most of the red and black paint peeled away, still standing with the last mown grass clinging to its blade well. Behind this, various equipment has been hung on a long pegboard, tools and appliances for yard and home—weed-whackers—three of these, both powered by electricity and gasoline—sanders—two types—electric-variable to hand-held drills, levelers of various sizes and kinds, measuring sticks, rods and angles—a pegboard filled with implements stretching across the entire length of the basement foundation. Items that couldn't be hung, such as miter boxes and table clamps, are in open door wooden bins which are bracketed to shelves held together with cement blocks. It is as though I've walked into a builder's dream catalog, although many of the items are second-hand, worn or outdated.

In a way, I'm not surprised at the organization of his belongings. One of the first things I observed about Francis was his immaculate dress, at times, down to semi-military-regulated creases in his trousers and shirts. Did he iron these or have them laundered? It made me wonder if he'd served in the military in some capacity. It could explain this highly ordered array before me, but what of his anxious nature, and, at times, confused and disintegrated thoughts patterns, the odd disconnects, the overly exaggerated gestures while talking, the sometimes glazed stare, a little vacant and detached manner, the shifting of weight from heel-to-toe, the slight sway from side-to-side? But that too could be explained as residue anxiety from active duty, PTSD and/or AA recovery. The organization of ordinary things in his life could have brought him a sense of security. Even his work clothes, I realized now that I thought on it, were chinos, sometimes khaki-colored trail pants with side pockets, and loosely fitting but unwrinkled shirts. I don't remember ever seeing him in a t-shirt. His moustache and beard were always trimmed at the same length. He drank lots of coffee, which was a habit of AA folks, but he didn't smoke, which, more times than not, went with that rehab territory. I am surprised at how much I have unknowingly taken in about the guy. But this basement of his is a wonder, if not a total surprise. It's the sheer amount of his possessions and the careful management and their arrangement that commands my attention and earns my respect.

If Francis had been in the military, what of the potter's grave? Surely, the military takes care of their own, including their burials, should their families not be located. But that's only if the military can find their people. Francis may have been deliberately "lost," from family, former friends and his contacts in the service. The authorities could have located his birth certificate and other legal documents, but that doesn't mean they know where he is. And for all I know, I suddenly realize, Francis Keyton may not be his actual name. But he owned a house; at least I thought he did. Didn't that entail certifying your identity through birth records or some such? Or did tax returns suffice? And his original driver's license had to have been verified by a birth certificate on file with the state. I was sure of it. Could these be falsified? Surely the lender's lawyer demanded some kind of certifiable identification from the buyer of a house.

But perhaps I was jumping the gun on this. What was it the librarian had said? Did she say he *owned* his home? I don't think she did. I think she said he *lived* in a well-kept house. My head is swimming, and my earlier confidence is fading. This all is getting out of hand, becoming outright silly. What difference does it make? Why am I getting myself involved in a state-of-affairs that might land me some place I not only don't want to go but can end up being seriously appalling when I get there? I sigh. Well, I'm in it now, I remind myself once again. Francis will be sitting on my mantel sometime soon, and I feel like I need to know what the hell to do with him. My closing thought is that I have no idea who this man I've attached myself to really was, or why he attached himself to me in the way that he did—surely he was trying to guide me toward *something*. Otherwise, who the hell gives somebody a sewing machine and says things like 'Hemingway,' 'give a little whistle' and 'to have and to hold'? But I still knew so little about him, really. Anyway, not anything of substance. False identity can be obtained, and I was finding out that the man I had recently met as Francis Keyton was much more complicated than I'd dreamed, and, I suspect was very, very clever at that.

I look at the basement windows and realize he has smeared all the panes with opaque, dirty-colored paint, which I hadn't noticed upon entry, taking it for grime. Even the lightbulbs dangling on long loosely braided wires are covered with the same intentional camouflage. I walk carefully along a path leading through the maze of stacked plastic crates and containers. Pointing my penlight down, keeping it close to my leg, I ascend the stairs to find that the basement door leading into the kitchen is surprisingly unlocked. *This is going to make my burglary so much easier*, I muse.

I step into an array of containers and labelled boxes on shelves that make the basement appear abandoned. Every available wall space around the cabinets is filled from linoleum to ceiling with neatly arranged tongue-and-groove drawers with antique clear-glass knobs that when pulled allow the drawer to slide out with ease. Everything imaginable is in these containers, many having been carefully designed with interior labelled dividers, so that what is in one bin will not spill into adjacent ones. I'm reminded of the five-and-dime stores I frequented as a child where glass compartments held all the notions for every household need—sewing, fastening, hanging, adhering—buttons, nails, staples, screws, bolts, brads of every kind and description.

It appears in Francis's living space all the shelves at eye-level are designated for his most frequently used items—thread, wire, twine, rubber bands, even rags and steel wool. His reasoning seems to have been to keep upstairs everything that he would need for daily living purposes and protect from basement moisture those items that could rust or rot. I had noted an industrial-strength dehumidifier in the middle of the basement's cement floor, no longer running as somebody must have turned off the electricity. I reach over and flick on the kitchen light switch, discovering that I've guessed correctly. But after I've done this, I realize how risky such a thoughtless action has been. A neighbor or somebody passing by could have caught the light, had it come on, investigated or called the police.

The lack of electricity prompts me, though, to open the refrigerator which I find has been emptied, and, surprisingly, cleaned. Pictures of Francis in various outdoor situations are affixed to the doors and sides of the fridge by colored circular magnets or in clear magnetized frames. Studying these pictures for a while, I note that they are all exclusively of *him*—not another single soul found in any of them. I attempt to find some correlation between their placement, his age in the photos—some were taken when he was very young—and the colored magnetic discs he's used to hold them in place. I can't find any consistent pattern, but that don't mean there isn't one, and if there is, what could it add to what I need to know? It's becoming more and more obvious to me that I'm searching too hard for connections everywhere in everything. But I find it strange that no family members are here. Only him as a young boy, as a teen, and one snapshot taken in his twenties, perhaps. At least, it's of a Francis who's clean-shaven but barely discernible in the over-exposed light. Altogether a dozen pictures. How tremendously odd. It's as though he's wiped out everybody in his world but himself.

I move around the kitchen, opening cabinet doors. Each shelf is completely filled with packed and canned goods of various types, usually a number of preferred kinds and brands. I find nothing perishable. Everything is either canned foods or freezer-bagged items, such as crackers and chips, with small stickers on top and sides that declare their dates of expiration. I am amazed that every space on these shelves are filled completely, as though Francis immediately replaced any items he used with another one of the same kind. I'm curious as to whether he rotated these according to their expiration dates, and only a cursory examination proves my theory correct. There is a psychological label for this behavioral proclivity—*horror vacui*, from the Latin for "fear of empty space." Art historians have pointed to ancient Egyptian funerary and tomb art, as well as Celtic and Outsider art as some of the finest examples of this use of space. Hoarders may have a similar motivation, but, often, with less satisfying consequences. Their *horror vacui* ultimately buries them, sometimes literally, and turns their compulsions to deathtraps from which some escape only by requesting help.

As I move through the house, I am overwhelmed by the exaggerated organization of Francis's material life. There is one central path leading through each of the five rooms—kitchen, dining room, living room, one small bedroom and bathroom. Narrower lanes cut the floor-to-ceiling central shelf areas, except the bathroom, into quadrants, lanes passable only if walked through sideways, drawers and bins on the shelves facing outward for easy access, although those nearer the ceiling, past reachable distance, need ladders. I spot one in a corner of each room. Francis was a skinny, tall man so he probably could've maneuvered around these lanes easily. Which made me wonder if he'd ever had anybody visiting him in his home. Surely the neighbors came calling, if for no other reason than out of curiosity, although the outside of the house gave no indication as to what the interior was like. I certainly hadn't been invited into many of my neighbor's houses nor them into mine. So even though Francis was an outgoing, somewhat gregarious guy, it was entirely possibly that few, if any, had seen the inside of his home. The librarian's statement again came back to me: "He lived in a modest home, but one very well-kept." She, without doubt, was referring to the appearance of the outside of his house and yard or her statement would have been descriptively somewhat different. Vast amounts of stuff don't usually register as "well-kept" despite their organization.

In actuality, he puts me to shame when it comes to ordering his usable items and space. It is true that the only bed is a twin mattress on the floor in the bedroom and the only places to sit are the one chair at the kitchen table and a recliner placed directly across from the nineteen-inch plasma television set. Francis wasn't likely to go to the cinema, but he did watch his movies in theater-style in his living room. Obviously, he wasn't open to receiving company. But the tape across the front and back door was now obviously warranted. One glimpse of what was inside this house could bring looters in droves.

After a couple of hours of going thoroughly through each room, accessing what I am seeing, I decide to sit down for a few minutes before I make my exit back the way I'd come, through the basement window behind the bush. This break-in hasn't been a completely futile attempt to find something of value, but what I've discovered is more clearly how Francis's mind worked and how he lived rather than anything leading to the connections I'm looking for. What those are exactly, I'm not sure, but if they are here, I'm not seeing them.

I follow a path to the kitchen and pull out the one chair at the table, where handled carriers are placed in dead center, holding various spices, salt and pepper shakers, and a sugar dispenser. To the side is a full napkin holder, one of the old-fashioned types found in diners even today. But before sitting down, I try the faucet and find the water still running. Sliding a glass out of a cabinet shelf, I fill it, after running water in the sink for a few minutes, and drink it down slowly while I sit in the faded light from the streetlamp flickering through the heavily paint-smeared window.

What have I learned about Francis from his house? He was unwaveringly meticulous, to the point of obsession. On the television program, *Buried Alive*, he would be comfortably labelled, "an organized hoarder." But most of the hoarders on the show have a desire to keep things that do not seem intrinsically valuable in their lives. Those who hoard garden tools and swizzle sticks are often not gardeners or drinkers. Everything in Francis's house seems to be task-oriented, so he had purpose in mind and stuck closely to that purpose. And thinking on this, I realize that he put items together for their use to him concerning those tasks—needles and straight pins weren't placed in bins with tacks or brads. They were with threads, zippers and hem liners. Did he sew? No doubt he did and probably has another sewing machine or two stashed in bins that I'd missed. Who can see all the stuff, especially at first visit? On the pegboard to the back of sewing bins filled with hundreds of spools of thread, hung scissors, rulers and underneath in marked containers, were neatly folded fabrics of every texture, weave and color. With all the space taken up in his house with so much stuff, where did he do his tasks? If he sewed, it had to have been at this kitchen table. There are no other empty horizontal spaces in the house.

I get up and go back through the rooms studying his method of organization once more. When tasks called for the use of similar items such as scissors, rulers, hammers, there are extras at each consigned task area, while specialty items such as cutters are placed with various types and gauges of wires and nowhere else. There was definitely a method to his collecting madness, if one could call it that. I'm not always catching the relationship he formed with some items—such as a shrimp deveiner hanging next to a very large Phillips-head screwdriver and a ball peen hammer, or, in another case, an engine head gasket next to a jar of petroleum jelly and an owner's manual for a chest freezer in an archival plastic sleeve—but after looking at what I can make out in the dim light, I know there's some logic to their connection, if only known to him.

His material organization is quite like his verbal cues to me. I simply need to spend some real time finding their patterns and connections.

I push back the chair under the table and stand surveying the whole house before me. My eyes have grown used to the small penlight and darkness surrounding it, so that I can see in the partial dark now without difficulty. My sense of smell has become more sensitive as well. The house has a deeply scented odor, mostly emanating from the untreated pine Francis has used to make most of the shelves upstairs, though I've concluded that even though the same or similar wood has been used, they have not been built at the same time. He has constructed his fortress over a number of years, allowing it to grow with the accumulation of his possessions. It strikes me how much time he's had to take to shift and shuffle this storehouse of goods over those years.

I stand in the silence of this dead man's home and wonder at the ordinariness of our lives, lives we attempt to make otherwise, most of the time without realizing. Freud was right about the hidden world of the unconscious. The libido pushes through so much more than our dreams. It governs most of our waking moments. What hidden desires made this man give expression to his life in this way? And then too, what conscious events had fastened themselves to those desires to produce a controlled and sheltered life like this one? I suddenly want to know this person, truly know him, but that's impossible. I never will. It sends a shiver through me. It's impossible, of course, to *know* anybody, not really. Hell, it's impossible to prove that my own consciousness even exists.

But it doesn't stop me from trying. Isn't that one of the most interesting aspects of living, our wanting to understand, to connect, to be with other living beings, some in a deeply meaningful way? On what grounds and with what definitions did I use for the term, "meaningful?" I assume so much of this, especially from social structuring and mores. Was Francis defying this—whether intentionally or not—with his self-imposed definitions of "shelter" and "society?" If I accept the librarian's observations of Francis, my conclusion is that he was a man who had his life in order at home such that he felt safe to reach out to others in the world. However frightened he must have been, his loneliness had been greater, pushing him to overcome his fears.

But what the hell was I doing with all of this information, even if it all was so? Had I come to get my money's worth, having paid for his burial? What connection was I attempting to form with Francis when I'd actually had only three recent encounters with him, a man who'd left me a sewing machine, and, what I was taking to be, a few spoken clues about something I didn't have a reasonable guess at truly understanding?

Before leaving his house, I rinse out my glass, *his* glass I'd drunk from, dry it on my t-shirt, then replace it where I'd found it. I prepare to exit the way I'd come, but on the way to the door leading to the basement, I lift the LED penlight just enough to find the door knob. The bluish glow splays out across the space exposing a library of books running along the back wall of the entire north side of the living room, the bookshelves covering the windows so that more space could be given to shelf the hundreds of books there. I'm not sure how I've missed this. Evidently I took these shelves in the darkened room for a bare wall like all the other rooms had.

I walk through the dining room to the living room and stand before this enormous library. As I swing the light across the rows and rows of books, I note that they are ordered by author—fiction and non-fiction, biography and memoir, essay and poetry are all shelved together. I also note that a good share of Francis's books have library identifications on their spines, that when opened are identified as library-stamped discards which he probably acquired in the twice-a-year books sales in town. Could be he was given them in exchange for some of his odd jobs that the director-librarian had mentioned. But there were enough books here for Francis to have scouted around the entire county and beyond.

The first book among all of these that I notice is one at the far left end of the shelf at eye level. The enormously thick book has been laid on the shelf horizontally as it is too large to be placed vertically with the others. My first impression is that it's one of those antique dictionaries from the Webster-Merriam series published during the 1800s through the turn of the century, but when I turn it around and pull it toward me, I discover it is much smaller than I originally took it to be. It's a family Bible, one which has faded gold print on the spine and front, in Old English Letters, *The Holy Bible*.

I carry it to the kitchen table and open it to its title page. It's a King James Version, published in 1867. On the Family Registry page, at the top, the elaborately decorated oval for Birth and Marriage of the Ancestral Parents is empty but under it, in the two-paged columns for subsequent Births and Marriages, are lines on which ballpoint pen and pencil scribblings have been written, barely legible, in modern-day cursive: *"father died, 1988. brother deceased on,*

Jan. 3, 1991, 'suicide,' shot in head. mother living in Ridgerton, Ohio." So this was a Bible that Francis had probably purchased or been given at some book sale which he had filled out for himself. He had not dated his mother entry, and he had not indicated if his mother was still living or not. If so, she hasn't come forward yet to claim or identify her son's dead body. And Francis had not added more siblings, living or deceased. Here again, guessing my way along, I'd say he had only the one brother, since he had mentioned him and his father as deceased and his mother as living at that time and even given her location. At least, I knew now he did have a family that he had been connected to in some way as recently as 1991—which actually wasn't so recent when I thought about it.

After examining most of the pages, I carry the Bible back and push it into its place and begin fingering the books along the same eye-level shelf when I stop abruptly at the "H's," at "Hemingway" in particular. Protruding a half-inch from the others, all aligned with intentional precision, is a thick-spined book of Hemingway's short stories. I pull out *The Complete Short Stories of Ernest Hemingway*. At the bottom of the plastic-protected cover, half-obscured by a bar code, is Finca Vigía Edition with a foreword by three members of the Hemingway family. I had owned an edition of Hemingway's short stories, though not this one, when I'd begun my teaching career, giving my hardback copy to a student with literary promise, meaning to replace it, which I never did. I do know that Finca Vigía—translating literally to "Look-out Estate"—was Hemingway's home in Cuba, where he began writing *For Whom the Bells Tolls*, based on his experiences of the Spanish Civil War during the years leading to World War II. For whatever reason, scattered parts of history and literature classes stick with me.

I open the edition in my hand, slightly less than center, to a story entitled, "Today is Friday," which has a large pencil check at the top. Since I note that it is only three pages long, I begin reading, holding the open book with one hand and scooting the penlight along the lines with the other.

Hemingway has written the story in the style of a stage play. It is an everyday dialogue between three soldiers who have just participated in Jesus's crucifixion. They are in a Hebrew wine cellar at eleven o'clock at night. The banter is between soldiers who have stopped at a local bar to have drinks at the end of their work on a Friday night. They have their say about the lingering women at the foot of the cross, and one soldier is very much taken with the way Jesus carried himself through the whole ordeal, though he isn't directly named except as a modern day swear word and an accusation made to the charitable soldier as being a "christer." After their talk and their drinks, the soldiers walk out onto the street and into the night, still complaining about having been out there at work too long, and the wine having gone sour in one of the soldier's stomach. It's pure Hemingway, who was openly anti-religious and anti-Semitic as well, though just as openly gladiatorial in his approach to life. He was the supreme representative of the soldier and his "afterlife."

I turn the page and see the next story is also checked and is only one and a-half pages long, so I begin reading "Banal Story." I remember well that my admiration for Hemingway, when I read him at university, was not for his novels, filled as they were, to me then, with ultra-macho overtones of combat, safari hunting, ocean fishing and sexual inequality, too often with a strained and mysterious veneer of repressed longing and fatalistic inevitability. I admired the terse, focused concentration of his short stories which, seemed to me, to have a wider range of subjects and approaches to them.

This story is about a booklet called *The Forum* which is being read by a young man I take to be a student or planning to become one. The booklet itself seems to be the main character as it is being digested—the young student is eating an orange while he's reading— the booklet's content given to the reader by the mouthfuls. He is impressed with the intelligent, well—very smartly—written message concerning the potentially bright futures for bright young people if they look up to bright—and the right—mentors and guides for the direction of their lives. All of this is great Hemingway tongue-in-cheek. Several names are mentioned in *The Forum* text as possible mentors, especially for young women of the age of eighteen—possibly as potential conquests for the young man reading the magazine?—and then, suddenly, there it is, what I've been looking for, the answer to Francis's clues, including the sewing machine! Hemingway mentions Betsy Ross along with Joan of Arc and Bernard Shaw's plays, known for their strong-willed women with independent aims in their lives. I whisper, *Dum, dee, dum, dum, dum, dum.* "Oh, say can you see, by the dawn's early light...."

gave proof through the night that our flag was still there." *The Star-Spangled Banner* by Francis Scott Key! Inanely, I wonder if I can sing all the right words, but I don't try.

The point is that so many dangling strings are now tied together in my Francis hide-and-seek: Betsy Ross's sewing the first American flag, Francis Scott Key's writing what would become the National Anthem—possibly Francis's namesake and F. Scott Fitzgerald's, friend to Hemingway during his Paris years—even the reference to the nation's Western Expansion and Manifest Destiny as well as the whole film industry's history of Western movies, cowboys and Indians—including *Dead Man* and *The Lone Ranger*—plus Francis's seemingly off-center reference to Beethoven, *the* Ludwig van Beethoven, who was so troubled by Bonaparte's abandonment of the Republic when he crowned himself emperor that the composer tore up the first page of the *Eroica* that he'd originally dedicated to Bonaparte.

Francis had known exactly what he was doing with his chosen words to me, well, at least most of the time. The zig-zagging connections had an element of chance about them, but handing me the *key* to a sewing machine? And muttering "Hemingway" as he left me the last time I saw him? It had to be this, all of this, and possibly more. I had put some of it together but not with Hemingway, and even yet, it is foggy and not complete, but I know now, just *know*, it is here—the pieces needing to be *sewn together* even though I know I'm pounding the metaphor to death.

I can't help but see Francis standing in front of me, hiding his grin in his beard, anxiously slapping his leg and asking me if I knew any good musicals worth watching. There's always *1776*, isn't there? For a guy who didn't get around, Francis got around plenty. I'm not sure where the poet William Blake figures in this, but I'm beginning to think that he's going to show up somewhere, sometime soon and let me know—maybe as a statue staring at me from across one of the Finger Lakes!

A kind of thrill overtakes me such that I make an on-the-spot decision. Moving all the closely fitted books so that they are flush along their spines again, taking the time to fill the gap left by the retrieval of Hemingway's book, I begin shifting and moving authors catalogued as H, I, J and L for some nine, ten minutes until all of them are closely aligned. When satisfied that the shelves look as though I'd never touched them, I walk through the basement door with Hemingway's book of stories under my arm and an armful of information I didn't have before this break-in.

As I'm crawling out of the foundation window, a thought trickles through my mind. *What were the wedding vows doing in the middle of my follow-up on Francis's clue about Hemingway?* He had said, "To Have and to Hold," hadn't he, when he dropped the sewing machine key in my hand? Hemingway had been married four times, and as I remember now from literature classes where I'd studied his fiction, he was fixated on relationships. But what does that have to do with Francis? The Bible's registry hadn't indicated any marriage of Francis Keyton, and it would be very likely that if he had married, Francis would've noted it, especially since he hadn't hesitated to declare the status of the members of his family. Was there nobody to come home to? Was he estranged from his mother? Was his mother now gone as well?

Despite my knowing some of the answers, these questions bring a new uneasiness. I can't even be certain that what was written in the Bible was by Francis's hand. But everything in the house, including the photographs on the refrigerator, is claustrophobically him, him alone. There isn't even a second chair at the table, only a twin mattress on the floor of the bedroom and single towels on the racks in the bathroom. This is Francis, all Francis. I'm more certain of it than ever.

"To Have and to Hold," he had said. I've assumed it's the wedding vows only because…well, *why*? The next thing he'd clued me to was, "Hemingway." Why haven't I realized that the chances are good for Francis to have done one of his slippery associations again, as he'd done with Beethoven and Rossini and with Johnny Depp as William Blake and Tonto? Simple slips, which I have just realized moments ago may not have been so oblique at all, fitting nicely into the whole red-white-and-blue scheme he had outlined and was posthumously coloring in for me.

In the car, with my key in the ignition, I looked down at the ring holding my house keys, jangling them with my fingers, and remembering I had seen a good-sized box of keys in the bins in the kitchen near the ones with locks, latches, hooks, knobs and internal door and window hardware parts. Why "To have and to hold"? Maybe he thought I'd find what he held dear, what he was "holding onto" as I'd just tried to do, had done. But why would he think that, unless he knew he was going to die or was close to it? Surely he didn't *intend* for me to break into his house, for godssakes.

I sit in the dark and silence. There is no way I can examine all the keys in the box in his house to see if they unlock some treasured answers to his life, answers hiding in the unexamined drawers of his constructed shelter. *Hemingway*. I'm more and more certain that Hemingway is the key. I have to smile at my metaphor. Could Francis have meant Hemingway's *To Have and Have Not?*" and I am inventing a convoluted storyline out of a mistake, another slip of his? There does seem to be a thread running through the cloth he's woven, though, with some frayed strings left dangling. I play with several possibilities before turning over the engine and driving home.

———

After a thrown-together pizza out of naan bread, instant pizza sauce, onion, garlic, zucchini, mushroom, a baked chicken thigh sautéed in butter, and topped off with shredded mozzarella and parmesan, I sit drumming my fingers at the kitchen table while it bakes in the convection oven. Laptop before me, I Google search, "To Have and To Have Not," read both the novel's and film's plot summary, scoot my chair back and grab the pizza out of the oven just short of too thin and crispy. I'm laughing a little while I do this, because I've retrieved two little tidbits from my search that indicate I'm pointing in the right direction, even if I'm not getting all of what I need to bring the bird down into the frying pan—I have dinner on my mind.

In the analysis of the film plot, the articles state that Hoagy Carmichael plays piano in a club, singing some of his made-exclusively-for-this-movie songs. His character's name is Cricket. The writer and director had to've had some fun writing the line for Bacall that audiences would delighted in for years, the one where she tells Bogey that if he needs her, all he has to do is whistle, and she'll come running. So Francis knew his films, inside and out. *Pinocchio*, the film in which Jiminy Cricket first sings, "Give a Little Whistle," was released in 1940. And *To Have and Have Not*, the movie based on the Hemingway book, in 1944. It was reported in entertainment news that audiences would whistle when Bacall uttered those lines during reruns for years after the film's release.

Even though there were these little connections, there was something in the "having and holding" business that I just wasn't getting. I could feel it. So I googled the obvious: "To Have and To Hold." And amazingly found a book written in 1899 by Mary Johnston about the establishment of Jamestown, a Virginia Colony settlement that, I remembered from high school history, had been founded a decade earlier than the widely-acclaimed Plymouth Colony of Massachusetts. Why I haven't searched this directly earlier, who knows? But the real question for me now is: Had Francis made one of his intentional reference-slips between Johnston's *To Have and To Hold* and Hemingway's *To Have and Have Not*? It's unnerving. And if he had, what had he meant to tell me? Again, I wonder if I'm hunting for clues and grabbing onto the smallest strings to tie Francis's given references to some kind of theme or storyline I'm inventing. And even if I am, how much concern had he really put into this, any of it, actually? Was it just his sleight-of-mind kind of game with people, playing with me as he did with everyone? Was that what the librarian was alluding to when she said that he sort of drove them all crazy in the library with his pride-in-learning?

—

I lie far into the night reflecting on what I've put together as missing or odd bits of information that don't fit in the story I'm building. What does Jamestown have to do with what I've gathered? Or Tonto? Is there more to them than just book and movie asides or Francis errors? In the case of Tonto, was Francis's mentioning the Indian only a reference to the American West or was he tying in the whole "God Bless America" theme? And although I've made connections between the Hemingway film version of his book and Jiminy Cricket, including the song Francis had alluded to, what does all this add up to, for chrissakes? Actually just about everything I've put together is like this. I've begun calling it a red-white-and-blue theme in my head, but even so, so what if Francis was patriotic, caught up in America's early history? What is the sum total of this, in meaningful terms, especially to me?

Perhaps my friend was a lover of Clue, the mystery board game, though I'd seen no evidence of games of any kind in his house, but who knows what lay hidden in all those bins and drawers? Some corpse? I literally shudder at the thought. That would be hardly funny. The thought of my roaming around in a house with an unclaimed hidden body in Francis's knowledge was a double dose of irony—an unclaimed body holding an unclaimed body. *Lord Jesus Christ of America!*

And then continuing with the dangling untied strings on the level of actuality, who had cleaned out Francis's refrigerator? Carried out the trash? Who had selectively rearranged his cabinets and his medicine cabinet? If he had a heart condition, medicines would have been somewhere—given Francis's tendencies, I would think, in his medicine cabinet. Was this cleaning-and-clearing of perishables and chemical substances part of the work of the crew that secured the house after death, while the medical examiner's office, together with the state's Public Health and Safety Department, attempted to locate the family of the deceased? Or did he have somebody looking out for him in the community, and if that were true, why hadn't they come forward, identified the body, written an obituary, organized some sort of memorial service? From these unsolved clues as I know them, and others I'm not bringing at present to mind, I have to concede, I may never know the answers. I may have to reconcile myself to knowing what I'd found and be done with it.

—

Several days pass in which I give myself to my writing and put Francis aside, though never quite out of mind. Hints, clues, questions, potential answers and solutions hum under my more creative thoughts, annoyingly distracting at times.

One evening, close to a couple of weeks after I'd been through Francis's house, I pick up the book of Hemingway's short stories that I'd taken from his library intending to read before bedtime. I haven't opened it since I'd read the two stories while standing in the darkness of Francis's living room, following my penlight across its pages. Everything I'd gleaned from it has sort of fallen like sediment to the bottom of a pond. I simply don't have the energy to wade back in and begin searching among the grit and grime for more than I already know about Francis.

I've received his ashes by direct delivery from the funeral home, in a wooden box, that now sits on my mantel over the living room fireplace. For years I've had a large ornately framed mirror above this shelf, at a height—short as I am--to reflect only my face. The day I placed Francis on the mantel, it was disconcerting to see how grim and utterly strange I appeared to myself, especially cut off in that way, as though the familiarity of my person reflected there was lacking identity as a whole "me." It was even stranger to see Francis sitting next to my cut-off head, both, as we were, staring back at me. I had become, Edgar Allen Poe-like, the head that was reflecting on Francis-as-boxed-and-kept ashes, ashes that I was holding, waiting for the right time to throw them to the wind.

In bed this evening, though, I leaf through the pages to select a story in Hemingway's book, when I feel a small scratch on my leg. I look down to find a corner of what appears to be an envelope hanging slightly out from the back of the book. I turn to the end pages and discover an envelope has fallen out of the laminated flap-over of the back cover. It is a letter that is now hanging diagonally from its designated slot. I carefully pull it free and turn it over. The envelope is still in good shape, though it has been cut off to fit the length of the book and taped to size. On the front, a logo is clearly visible as **OMHCAS** printed across the upper left corner. The words, Ohio Mental Health Center and Addiction Service, form a circle around the logo on the letterhead inside. The letter is one of release from a psychiatric hospital in Ridgerton, Francis's mother's hometown, and, I'm taking it from this letter, evidently his at the time as well. The letter is addressed to him at a Ridgerton address and is a formal statement dismissing him from the hospital under his own management and care.

It suggests strongly that he pay visits to a physician at the Ridgerton

Mental Health Center, Dr. Jay Singh, beginning June 2nd. The release date of the letter is May 5, 2000, nine years after the Gulf War. Another thin letter, folded carefully to fit, is inside the envelope, dated 31 March, 1991. It has the seal of the United States Marines on its letterhead and is a formal statement of honorable discharge from the service due to injuries incurred during The Battle of Khafji, Saudi Arabia, in late January of that same year.

A final inclusion is a three-by-five photograph of Francis and a friend who are pictured in what appears to be a desert extending behind them to the horizon. They are side-by-side in a shoulder-locked embrace, heads touching, both grinning shyly at the camera. To the side and back of them is a Humvee camouflaged such that it is almost invisible in the stark light. They are boys in their early twenties, I'm guessing, bandanas around their heads, and outfitted in desert camouflage. They each hold a helmet. On the back in pencil is the faded and smeared words, "Lee and me before the rescue mission in Khafji, January 30, 1991." On another line, in the same hand that appears to be written from another day, "Lee gone forever, one of only 35 killed by friendly fire." Then under this with a downward slash leading from it, "Che mala fortuna." Italian, which I didn't know, but could figure out easily enough. *But in Italian? Why? Was his friend Italian, but with the name 'Lee'? Could 'Lee' be a stand-in for something else?*

I know that photos were strictly controlled during wars after Vietnam, with requirements that journalists be accompanied by military-assigned personnel during Desert Shield and Desert Storm. And combatants could be discharged for taking photographs even during the Vietnam conflict. Of course, photos were always sneaked through. And it could be that the man behind the camera was a photojournalist. Perhaps the shot was one of many passing approval which were never used in stories, so this one was given to Francis with his dead friend. But I thought it was more likely a sneak shot by a fellow Marine primarily because of its size.

I lay my head back on the pillow and suddenly find myself crying, from sadness and strain, but also from relief. I feel I can now put, at least, some sort of a final scene to the scattered staging of the life I knew as Francis.

How many clues do we need to fill in a person's life? What life story can I give from what I know that can claim with reasonable accuracy who Francis Keyton was? Several years ago, I had been a volunteer for hospice in town, part of a team that recorded the life reviews of dying patients for their families. I was struck during those interviews by what the patients chose to tell about their lives, what they left their families and friends as their recorded history. In many cases, I knew after these interviews about as much as I knew about Francis, despite all my efforts. It isn't just memory that fails or our weak perception of the events in our lives, but when confronted with the whole of our history, who we think we are through time, it is very difficult to retrieve those milestones or pivotal events that we believe defines who we are to ourselves. Our life stories resemble a mosaic more than any sequential storyline. But it is the storylines that we believe in, and therefore, who we become, despite everything. We are those stories we tell others and those they tell about us. We are especially the personal stories that we tell nobody but ourselves.

So what of Francis, then? Who was he—from what he told me indirectly, and what others revealed about him, and what I found out through my own searching?

What I've put together has taken some extrapolation, but here it is.

Francis lost his father about the time he graduated from high school. He joined the Marines shortly afterward, with or without his mother's approval. After basic training, he was airlifted to Saudi Arabia in the late fall of 1990 where he became a driver for transport of ammunition, cargo and/or personnel—I was to learn that this was the major function of the Humvee during Desert Shield and Desert Storm. Somewhere during this tour of duty, Francis had gone on a rescue mission, probably to retrieve an injured soldier or soldiers on the front in Saudi Arabia where he was stationed at the time. From the inscription on the back of the photograph, he had lost his buddy through friendly fire, later to find out that Lee was one of only thirty-five such recorded accidental deaths during the Gulf War.

Whether he had been given this mission as a regularly assigned ambulance driver or he had been ordered to a sudden emergency, whether his buddy had been on this assignment with him or had been hit while on another assignment apart from him, I'll never know. I take it to be the former, because he had noted that the photo was taken just before they left for Khafji. He received word of his brother's suicide while he was still on tour, and if this came at the same time as his buddy's accidental death, as it seems to have, it may have been the trigger that sent him over the edge.

I knew he was hospitalized—perhaps more than once and in different hospitals— between the time he was stationed in Saudi Arabia and when he was released from an Ohio Psychiatric Hospital on April 25, 2000. Since the Battle of Khafji had been at the beginning of 1991, and the war ended on the last day of February of that year, it wasn't likely that Francis's injuries kept him in hospital for nine years. He had been hospitalized in Ohio for reasons *after* the recovery of his combat wounds, which may have been both physical and mental, and took place in a VA facility. The Ohio psychiatric hospital specialized in addiction, so the drinking problem the librarian alluded to as having been cured, may have happened before Francis moved to New York. He had a lot to carry—the death of his father shortly before he enlisted, the death of his brother by suicide, as well as the death of his close friend from friendly fire, together with a mother who seems to have either died or abandoned him. She may have had a hand in his admission to hospitalization because of alcohol addiction, just as Hemingway's mother had been intrusive in his life such that Hemingway moved away from her.

If all this were true, it would explain Francis's overly obsessive character concerning his tasks, his home and his dress. He sought to control what had been uncontrollable before.

As to his family, he makes no mention of anyone other than his father, mother and brother. If his mother was still alive, there was no evidence he had any connection with her. I found no letters, no pictures, nothing connecting him with *anybody*, let alone any family members, in his house, other than Lee in the photograph. And though I hadn't done a thorough examination of every drawer and bin in the centers of each of the rooms of his home, I had gone through all the lower drawers in his bedroom and living room where such items would be most likely found, if he meant to look at them from time to time. There were no albums, no scrapbooks, no archival boxes anywhere. Francis seemed to have chosen to be a maverick, intentionally answerable to as few people as possible. He didn't trust. I was going to say others, but from what information I had gleaned, Francis simply didn't trust, not just people, but life. He gathered his most immediate and significant tools for living and held them close. *To Have and to Hold*. He had meant it literally. He needed to belong so he sought out community, but he never brought that community into his private space. His shelter, trench or foxhole, if you like, was his very own. He didn't intend to make it vulnerable to loss of any kind—theft, destruction, extinction.

He was not just into obsessional possession. He was holding onto his soul in the only way he knew and could.

What happens when a person loses everything? To accept it as caprice is just too impossibly difficult. Many who cannot do otherwise, kill themselves. But to choose to live—or to simply choose not to die—a means has to be found to carry one's self daily and that means is usually consigned to a First Cause, to God or some equally transcendent justification. As a soldier, it makes perfect sense to consign it to Country, to what "Country" means to Everyman. First Cause, in Francis's view, was what he was literally living *for* on the battlefield and later, *from* in the life after the battle was over. It's the only way he and others in his world can get through the terrors of war without going insane and in their "afterlife," to live sanely in a normalized world. In the end, there is little mystery in this, after all. Francis was saving himself from madness by ordering his world such that he could find what he needed as quickly as possible, to reach for it and know it was there when he did. And whether he had intentionally decided it or whether it had come upon him intuitively, he had given me, as fiduciary keeper of his estate, an obligation to bring his life's story to closure in the manner of his own having and holding. My hope is that I've done him justice. But then, all of this might be my need to romanticize. Perhaps he, sensing death near, only wished to be singularly remembered by the nearest person at hand which happened to be me.

—

Using his sewing machine I create a thirteen, five-pointed star flag. I contact the local VFW and discover that I can properly burn an American flag, then bury it. So I follow the procedure given to me, putting the flag-ashes in with Francis's.

I've decided not to throw him to the wind. I buy a small plot on the edge of the cemetery at Shelville and pay to have him buried without ceremony and with only a small stone marker inscribed with "Francis "Scott" Keyton, January 16, 1971 – August 16, 2016." I obtain his birth date from his expired driver's license when his belongings were given to me with his ashes. There is symmetry in the numbers, though hardly complete closure.

I did find out who had cleaned his house, though the receptionist at the Medical Examiner's Office who informed me, did so reluctantly. A crew was hired by the county to dispose of immediate waste and medical substances in houses of the unclaimed deceased. Francis's household goods went on sale a couple of months after I received his ashes, handled by an agency that manages estate tag sales for a percentage of the gross profit. I didn't attend this auction so I don't know what happened to his books. I never asked the librarian if she took them as donations, and she didn't offer the information. It was odd, but we hadn't exchange information about Francis after that day several weeks ago when we had had our quietly intimate conversation about him. Of course, she wasn't often in the library when I was. But this silence between us, intended or not, reminded me of the inevitability of the drift into obscurity that we all will ultimately make.

A brief belated memorial statement appeared in *The Finger Lakes Sentinel* and *The Local Press* with a hazy black-and-white portrait of Francis obviously cropped from some snapshot taken at a local event of the attending crowd. I had given strict instructions and served notarized legal statements to both the Medical Examiner's Office and the Shelville Funeral Home to not mention my name in connection with Francis's interment. And this must have done the job because nobody ever indicated they knew of my connection to Francis outside what others in town had had with him.

And I never learned the answers to many clues left dangling without answers, and I couldn't be certain, of course, if my storyline accurately fit the facts. But

I did know Francis had been liked, if not loved, and had found his own way to reach out and connect after his broken life was patchworked together again. How he found his way to our town in upstate New York, who knew? And why he didn't remain in Ohio after being released from the hospital, I could only guess may have been his mother. I pretty much stopped calling, googling and searching after I found his papers in the back of Hemingway's book.

Francis's mother never came forward and claimed his body. I did follow up on her to this degree. I attempted to locate somebody associated with him through the address given on the envelope that held Francis's hospital and U.S. Marine release letters without success. It was entirely possible that Francis's mother had a different last name through a second marriage, if she hadn't kept her maiden name to begin with. But the envelope did dispel my doubts as to whether Francis Keyton was his real name. It was there all right, with its unconventional spelling. In all probability, I dreamily surmised, he was named after the father of our National Anthem, and there may have been a middle name of "Scott" that Francis chose to drop, though, it would have been unlike him to do this, unless he wanted to be "lost," as it appeared that he did. 'Francis Scott' together with his surname would have stimulated discussion with others, but perhaps over time it had become too much attention for him, so he dropped it when he came to our town. It's even possible a relative became overwrought with the name "Key" and changed the family name to Keyton to bypass any connections with his famous ancestor, or by accident, it was altered when the family entered this country. Very strange, seemingly impossible alterations did occur, especially in those overly jammed nineteenth-century immigration days.

―

The first year, I went to Francis's gravesite once a month, a ritual I kept sacred and honest, finding in the steadfastness of it a kind of honor he was never given in life, one that perhaps he wouldn't be happiest about himself, since he had desired anonymity. And, if so, ultimately, he did get his wish, because life's monotonous rhythms carried me month by month further from his site. Initially, I missed the designated day I'd assigned each month for my

Francis visitation, then started sliding into the following month without making up the last, then drifting into a three, then six month visit routine, and finally once a year. In the end, I left him to the elements and to the call of birds and scavengers of decay.

There was some posthumous residue. One evening while re-reading several of the stories in Francis's copy of Hemingway's book, I decided to Google Ernest's biography and happened upon the fact that Hemingway's hatred of his mother began in his early childhood when she dressed him in little girls' clothing, including dresses, and let his hair grow long, while his sister was dressed like a boy. According to the article, this bizarre practice continued until Ernest was six. So perhaps his difficulties with women, especially his mother, was far more complicated than I could have dreamed back in my college days when I thought the macho bias in his writings was simply a feminist issue.

I also discovered years later, when revisiting Hemingway's *The Sun Also Rises*, that one of his characters empathizes with Jake Barnes's impotency through injury by using the phrase, "Che mala fortuna," an American English equivalent of "What a pity," but which translates more literally as "That bad luck," the Italian phrase Francis had scribbled on the back of the photo of him in Saudi Arabia with his friend who died so many years ago.

So Francis was heavily steeped in the Hemingway mystique. I did think considerably on why Francis placed his important letters in Hemingway's book of short stories. I think he identified with the author-man primarily because both had suffered tremendous losses—through suicide, through hospitalization because of combat wounds, mental illness and addiction, through service to the First Cause of a soldier, especially through Hemingway's long, distinguished writings on war. Hemingway had met with near-death experiences over and over—in several car crashes, two airplane crashes, one in which he almost did not escape through a back door of the plane, and had reportedly had two hundred pieces of shrapnel removed from his legs when wounded in a World War I combat zone. He had been involved in an ammunition site explosion, as an ambulance driver, having helped collect body parts—this when he was only in his teens. He had physically carried the wounded out of harm's way. In the war's aftermath—and he had served in World War II as a reporter as well—he had drunk heavily and had, in the end, lost his mind to depression and paranoia, and finally to suicide.

To Francis, perhaps, it was a bit like the dying looking up at the crucified Christ. He had pencil checked Hemingway's story of the Roman soldiers and their reaction to their participation in Christ's death. In his writings and interviews, Hemingway had demonstrated concern about his soul "being lost," although, not quite in the religious sense, but in connection with his war wounds. In "Now I Lay Me," a story which Francis had pencil-checked in the Finca Vigía collection as well, Hemingway speaks through the narrator of the story as being afraid to fall asleep lest in the dark his soul leaves his body, because after the narrator was blown up—as Hemingway had been—his soul left his body but then came back. It was as though he feared once it had left him, it might be irretrievable.

Hemingway had told one of his biographers that he believed in the immortality of his soul and was afraid of losing it because of the hurt and injury he had caused his first wife for leaving her as he did, for loving two women at the same time. He said he had offended his soul, had "blackened it." He spoke about needing to have a light on in darkness because he was afraid his soul could leave him during the night and not return. He sought ways for the rest of his life for his soul to not condemn him.

It was obvious that Francis had read all of Hemingway's books as they were there on the shelf when I discovered his library, and he had chosen to store his most treasured letters in Hemingway's collection of stories. He must have felt kinship with both of their inabilities to integrate well into society after war.

And there was also the details. They both had been ambulance drivers—Francis of a sort—and both had poor relationships with their mothers. One of Hemingway's friends, John Dos Passos, would write that Hemingway truly hated his mother, who after the publication of *The Sun Also Rises* had told her son that it was one of the filthiest books of the year. He had spoken about longing to leave Oak Park, Illinois, where he was born and raised, enlisting in military service to get away, and after the war, when returning to his hometown with his war injuries, desiring and finally getting away again from his bible-totting, constantly nagging mother. Could Francis have left Ohio to rid himself of his mother? Francis had returned to his hometown, where his mother was, after his discharge from injuries after the Gulf War. And both Francis and Ernest had suicide in their families, Hemingway taking his own life, as had four other members of his family. I'm sure it occurred to Francis about himself, probably the desire living with him daily.

I'd often wondered why Francis didn't identify in the same way with F. Scott Fitzgerald who was his namesake, and, also, had an overwhelming alcohol addiction. Scott Fitzgerald was even related to the Early American patriot. I'd come to the conclusion that the primary reason for Francis's choice of Hemingway was one of war. Fitzgerald didn't belong in this. He enlisted and was a second lieutenant during WWI, but the war ended before he was deployed. He was a privileged boy, who'd gone to Princeton, even though he wasn't a good student and had dropped out to enlist. Hemingway, to Francis, must have seemed a working stiff. He had chosen a reporter's career over higher education, while Keyton hadn't gone beyond high school and had become a Marine. But there was this: Fitzgerald died at the age of 44 and Francis at 45.

Whether Francis intended for me to find out "who he was" in all of his clueing to me, will remain a mystery. I've come to believe, in my storyline of him, that he wanted somebody to know of his sacrifice to his Country and what it meant to him, because in that long line of cars he saw moving down Main Street each morning while he drank his coffee, he knew he was lost to those behind-the-wheel, without a chance of ever being noticed, let alone acknowledged for what he'd done for the Country that they took so for granted.

The most interesting bit of knowledge I'd gathered in the years I'd come to think of as "After Francis," was that there is no statue of William Blake across the lake in the movie, *Dead Man*. I have watched this movie innumerable times and simply cannot find what Francis was alluding to. The only extant three-dimensional portrait of the poet that I could find after a quite exhaustive online and offline search was a larger-than-life-sized bronze bust now located in Westminster Abby.

However, in keeping with Francis's inimitable slippery information-style, I did notice one of the early scenes in the movie in which Johnny Depp a.k.a. William Blake is reading a journal on his long ride to Machine, the town to which he is headed, at the end of his line. That journal was called "Illustrated Bee Journal," and after turning the initial page with various advertisements, William Blake stares at an illustration of a man standing in a conquering position on a small pedestal, looking much like a statue, which is entitled, "Triumph of the Bee Hive." William Blake gives this picture a double take—*as though he spots his own name there?* I was curious about the scene, and after seeing the movie several times, decided to Google, "William Blake and bees."

One site took me to Volume 22 of *The American Bee Journal*, page 509. In the left column was a small advertisement for Honey and Bees For Sale. The name of the seller was William Blake. The date of the journal was 1886 and the English poet had died in 1867, perhaps film director Jarmusch's inside reference to the death waiting Johnny Depp's character as he later received a spiritual passage from this life to the next by Nobody, his Indian guide, at the end of the movie.

And if that wasn't sufficient, at the very beginning of the film, *The Lone Ranger*, Tonto says to Kemosabe, his trusted friend and lost brother, "*Dead man strike fear in heart of enemy.*" Well, Tonto meet William Blake. But whether the director of *The Lone Ranger*, Gore Verbinski, meant to refer back to the earlier Depp film, who knows? "Dead man" is a common enough phrase, but, then, by now, I'm seeing Francis's clues in everything.

REVIVAL

I hear them all the way across the highway to the veranda of Grandma's house where I sit on the swing, waiting for the evening shower to give way to the night and the stars. I still call this house "Grandma's house" even though it, the whole farm, fell to my mother almost thirty years ago when Grandma died, and is the place where I was born and raised. When Mama dies, my family inheritance will amount to a few photographs, some of tin, and Grandma's house. The barn's been gone for a long time, the boards sold when my parents could still get out of them what it cost to tear the whole thing down.

Grandma lived most of her life on this farm, once not even on the outskirts of town, but out in the country, where she and Grandpa milked cows, raised chickens, grew gardens and hoisted enough well water to carry them through droughts, the Great Depression and near foreclosure twice. When my mother inherited it in the seventies, she and Dad put in running water, electricity and got on city sewage. They kept the wheat farming going until Dad died ten years ago. It didn't break my Dad's heart that I didn't want their way of life when I returned from Vietnam, but he was disappointed. Mama told me, when she still could talk, that she weathered it all to see herself die of old age and cancer in the family bed. Lessie, her hired woman now, has placed her near a window where she thinks Mama can still see the traffic speed past. Mama was right about it all except the cancer, which was a lie her doctor decided on telling her.

"It's not going to help her any, knowing she's losing her mind, Steven," Karl Childress had said. "This way she can enjoy what little time's she got without looking over her shoulder, feeling God's constantly stealing her thoughts away. I'll tell her that her befuddlement is the painkillers. By the time she catches on she'll be far enough along for it not to matter much." Good Baptist man, I think. In her better days, Mama would have appreciated more of the truth, but what the hell.

"They holler day and night!" Lessie calls from the phone, not saying but wanting me to come a night early so she can leave. "They's here in cars and trucks off the highway in a big tent to keep us awake until all hours of the night. Why don't you come see for yourself! Nothing can be done, they's telling me from the courthouse. It's country, they's asayin', the other side of the highway. They can make all the noise they like without any stopping to it. Some damn farmer's rentin 'em that part of the pasture. He don't live 'round here, whadda he care?" She's full of complaint, her voice weary from lack of sleep. "Course you can wait till tomorrow as usual, no pressure you," she says this as she lowers the receiver to its cradle. She knows I'll come. There's no other obligation to worry my weekends. No wife, no kids, not a dog or stray cat. There's not even a plant in my apartment, which is fine with me. There's enough worry with my machinist job and its odd hours, Mama's care and the newspapers.

"Holy Rollers," she calls out to me as I enter the room. "Can't do nothing about them neither." She yells as though I'm still coming into the house. "They's here to stay, your guess as any for how long, praising God whether the neighbors want to or not." Before I can respond, Lessie meets me at the bedroom door, pocketbook over an elbow, her hand reaching out to receive the weekly check. This was her idea, this pay every visit arrangement. "Best we do it as we go. She's not in this world too long, Mist' Clarridge. But I'm here till she's gone, that's a promise you." Lessie still calls me Mister despite the fact that she came to work for our family when I was only a toddler, when my mother became overwhelmed with the financial distress and her depression so deep it took years to root it out.

Jamaican-born, Louisiana-raised and Oklahoma settled-through-marriage, Lessie's tongue has always delighted and fascinated us. She was and is the family general, standing above, hollering out orders, drawing out the battle lines, moving us around to save us from losing each other. It's like her to work for the best, but be prepared for the worst. She's just eager to quit working, I think—after all, she's almost eighty as well. But my mother's dementia has lasted seven years and doesn't show any signs of change. Her progress toward incontinence and cognitive deterioration was rapid, then after two years seemed to suddenly halt, as though by the hand of God. She lies now, unchanging, in this clean house, in daily laundered clothes and linens, waiting for death that's hiding behind the glaze of her eyes. "Give a greeting to Seb," I say to Lessie as the screen door closes gently.

"Hello, Mama," I say, going to her bed, taking her hand, this gesture too unchanged these years. I sit and listen for her breathing which I never hear, searching for life in a vein running down her neck. "I'm here," I say to the ticking clock, moving back in my chair. "Just you and me until Monday morning." I sigh, then smile as though she can see, understand, me. "Well, and those shouting fools across the street."

I hear the music rising. If they go at this until dawn, Lessie's right to leave. I glance toward the living room where I've left my mystery and spiral notebook. I'll read or write without a problem. I've turned a deaf ear to believers for a long time. "We don't abide churchgoing stereotypes in this house," Grandma, and Mama after her, used to chant as their neighbors sped past the farm on their way to church Sunday mornings. So it seems unfair, even untidy, that fundamentalists are grouping just outside Mama's door at the last of her life. The family practiced asceticism, the purity and simplicity of daily sacrifice, on this farm for over sixty years. It seems only right that she die as unfettered as possible.

The porch swing is hard and I look in the living room for a couch pillow as the preacher invites the audience to bow their heads in prayer. They're settling into the preacher's rhythm as I fall into my softer seat on the swing, pushing out and in with my heels. They're praying out loud after him, a mesmerizing effect, as they catch his pleas on echo. "Restore," he shouts into the microphone. He is using a microphone though the audience numbers no more than two, three dozen people, bending and swaying amid a host of folding chairs. "Restore us, Jesus, to Thy graces. Lord, restore us to Thy fold."

Then his voice and head drop. "Believe," he whispers, voice trembling. Believe, believe, believe, the audience calls back. "Jesus," he hisses, barely audible. Jesus, Jesus, Jesus. The music begins to swell from an electric keyboard on spindly legs positioned dead center to the crowd with two powerful speakers. A pudgy teen with bleached hair and in a pair of baggy overalls and a designer jersey shouting U2 plays with rising and falling arms, in broad, overly dramatic gestures, flinging his wrist out before he hits each chord. I wonder what kind of teen would be playing for such a crowd on Friday night. A closeted MTV watcher, an outsider who dresses like everybody else but can't be part of everybody else, I reason, noticing my contempt. My God, I don't know this kid from Adam. Why should it matter to me?

"Come," the preacher intones. Somewhere between the time I spent with my mother in the bedroom and the eating of the homemade microwavable supper Lessie had left me in the kitchen, this preacher has made his way to the altar call, or is it to be a healing line? In either case, I know the service is just beginning. "Hear us, Jesus," the preacher pleads. Jesus, Jesus, Jesus. A small ball of anger begins to flare in my duodenum, acid spreading in my stomach and gut. Wonderful! A welcomed evening shower turned sour by a raving loony. Is this revival tent and everything within it, an American phenomenon? Remembering a drunken night in the Philippines, on an unexpected layover en route to Vietnam I stunned myself as well as fellow soldiers, the locals and bar whores by doing an altar call much like this one, on one of the tables, with a microphone borrowed from the band, announcing Jesus's saving powers as though on the air from Del Rio, Texas. I earned a lot of whiskey that night. It seemed to me then, as it does now, that on some level this, like jazz, is a universal language. It gets inside.

Suddenly, as though orchestrated for my flagging attention, a man in the middle row stands, raises his hands upward, throws his head back as though shot and yells, "Come!" Come, Jesus, Jesus, Jesus, the audience echoes the preacher's microphonic voice. "Come on down to Jesus," he proclaims as though he's MC for *The Price Is Right*. It's the altar call, then, I think. Who among these few would step forward, who in this small crowd didn't believe? "Come to Jesus and be healed," the preacher adds. Ah, so it is to be the healing line. Or perhaps both. Believe and be healed, yes, that's how it works. Come to Jesus, believe, and then be healed.

I stand to make my way to the refrigerator and a cold beer. "You," the preacher shouts, and I stop and search the crowd to find the member of the audience he has fixed on this time. His arm, the one not holding the microphone, is outstretched toward the night, across the highway, finger pointing, just like Uncle Sam, at me. "You come now!" he says, as the recruiting poster would shout, if it could speak, as it did speak, as I answered and went. I am stunned, riveted to the porch, my feet won't move. "Yes, you, son," he coos softly, "come on home to Jesus."

His arm moves in an arch back to the audience, and I realize he isn't speaking to me after all. He's used some intimate generalization, some metaphoric reference that deftly implies himself to be God, or at the very least, God's messenger, which in turn implies others to whom he is pointing and speaking to be God's own, like Jesus, all of us, his children, only bringing with us our human sin. But knowing all this doesn't help me. I still can't move away. He has spoken directly to me. I'm sure of it. I can feel it. "Nobody looking around," he admonishes the audience, his finger and arm moving back and forth as though whipping the crowd down to knee-size. "Everybody praying in his heart for this sinner to come home to Jesus. He knows he's a sinner. God knows he's a sinner. Everyone praying for this sinner to restore himself to Jesus." He bows his head and begins his prayer in the microphone. "Oh, Jesus." He moans, the audience moans, over and over, Jesus, Jesus, Jesus. So that's it: I'm the designated sinner, the errant child, the one needing to make my way back home. What home? I never belonged to his family.

Go to hell, I think, and I plan on turning to the front screen door, to the refrigerator, to the beer. But my feet turn in the opposite direction and begin descending the front porch steps. Even as the taste of beer fades from my mind, I follow the swinging of my arms, the stiff movement of my hips, of this skeleton, this whole interior person of me, both hard and fragile. I watch and follow my moving across the highway to the microphone held by this preacher in this tent in front of this crowd of swaying believers. The teen's music is trilling now, gone crazy with excitement and approaching climax.

"That's right!" the preacher bends down now to take my hand as I walk up the steps. I pass the hand, his hand, on my way to the platform, the stage, where he has been pacing and panting, performing. "Come on up to Jesus," he whispers, but upon seeing my face, in his voice a small doubt seeps through the mike as to what might be actually coming next. "Give in to Jesus," he instructs me. I hold out my hand for the microphone, but he keeps it from me, smoothly swinging the long cord out and around like a tail, while he places a claw on my shoulder pressing down hard with his nails. I fall to my knees and think, what the hell, as he begins to pray. "Oh sweet, merciful Jesus, restore this Thy sinner to Thy side..." Oh sweet Jesus. Oh sweet Jesus.

The crowd is on its feet clapping and swaying and chanting. The teen behind me beats out magnified chords. The tent is alive, filled with blood pulse and thunder. I gaze at the makeshift, plywood floor. I look out over the crowd. The tent seems light and heavy, full and empty, strange and familiar. My hands reach for my belt, and I begin unzipping my pants, snapping open my shirt. The preacher attempts to hold me fast, but I'm not to be held down. I am standing, my legs out of my trousers, my shirt in a heap at my feet before he fully grasps what is happening. He is whispering in the mike, oh no, no, no, which the audience overrides as oh yes, yes, yes. The clapping and stomping are mad, a sprinkle of laughter rising to a full-house rollick by the time I stand nude in front of them. I am jumping up and down, running back and forth on stage, my legs, arms, head, penis jerking, waving, rising, falling in uncontrolled spasms. I am bucking wild. The preacher attempts to catch me as I pass, but his grabs and lunges throw him off balance, thrusting him into the keyboard that comes crashing down on the teen, leaving both of them splaying into wires and each other.

I grab the mike that's rolled to a stop next to the pulpit and yell into it, "Jesus be unpraised." I know instantly that this off, unbearably stupid and ungratifying. I stand transfixed by my verbal offering, waiting stiff-bodied and numb-brained for some enlightened comment to sprout full-blown from my forehead. I open my mouth to speak, to clarify in some way, any way, what has gone impossibly beyond me. The audience zooms closer, like objects appearing in the side-mirror of a car when a crash from behind is imminent.

They are in front of me, still behind, surrounding me in a space heightened by an approaching reality I have no means to understand. The preacher is scrabbling to his feet as I grab my clothes and run out the back tent flaps toward the adjacent cornfield.

I cross the highway fully clothed a quarter of a mile down from Grandma's house, circle around through the alleys, and have a change of clothing on when two patrol cars arrive at the tent. I'm shaken but calm, standing on the porch watching, a beer in hand.

Well into the conversation with the preacher, who points vigorously at Grandma's house and at me on the porch swing, while he dabs at his bruised forehead with a large white handkerchief, one of the policemen starts walking through the field, over the fence and through the ditch before crossing the highway. It takes a while and I've plenty of time to gather myself before he comes greeting me up the porch steps. I'm not surprised at his approach, though I figured they'd come in the patrol car. To tell the truth, I fully expected the preacher himself to be standing on my porch when I showed up from the fields. I'm as curious about why he didn't come across to confront me as anything this cop might say or do. The preacher's probably terrified. He thinks I'm capable of about anything, no doubt. The thought has not passed me.

"Good evening," the copper says to me cheerfully. "How are you this evening?" He sounds like a telemarketer.

"Hello," I say as cheerfully. "Can I help you?"

"Well, yes, perhaps you can. The preacher over there is pretty upset about an incident that he claims you initiated during his revival meeting." He waits and when I don't say anything, he says, "He claims you disturbed his service by running across his stage naked."

I smile at the cop slowly. "Well, now, I don't think that's possible," I say. "My mother is sick with dementia in her bed just inside the house. It would be irresponsible to leave her alone to come to a revival meeting, let alone one where I'd show up naked. You ask me, he's the one making the disturbance! Who is this preacher, this whole group over there, anyhow? He's been keeping us up nightly with his raving and antics. I think I'd like to talk to him about his accusation." I shift my weight, setting the empty can down on the swing arm, fully visible to the cop. Then I stand still again. I feel a little odd inside my body, a good deal like Clint Eastwood appears in his movies, like he's shifting inside a heavy overcoat, which he actually wears in his westerns.

"Well, that might be a good idea, but I think the best way to go about this, is for you both to come down to the station to iron this out," the cop says just like on *NYPD Blue.*

"I don't think I can do that," I begin. "You see I'm the only one here. There's no one to attend…"

"You don't have to worry about your mother," he cuts me off evenly as he reaches for his cell phone. "We can send an officer to stay with her until you return."

"Is this really necessary? I don't see…"

"The problem I'm having, I guess," the cop says, looking at me squarely now, "is that I don't hear you exactly denying what the preacher says is so. He's described what happened in pretty convincing detail." He looks down grinning, then meeting my gaze again, says, "And at least one of his followers has filled in what he's left out, so you can see the dilemma I'm in." He eyes me cautiously, no doubt studying my willingness to go peacefully with him. Lord, I hope he doesn't deliver that well-worn line. He shrugs as though all this is no big deal, squinting down the highway in the direction I took to get back to the house. "And we got a call from one of your, well, one of the neighbors down the road. Seems somebody, some *male* somebody, about your height and weight was seen dancing unclothed on stage, confirming pretty much what the others are telling us. And there's the description of the beard." He looks back at my shaggy face and breaks a small smile. "To be truthful, if it was up to me, I'd say good riddance, but we have to follow up on any charges."

"Charges?"

"He's filing charges. He claims you disrupted his revival so that he won't be able to do his ministry here as he's planned."

"Okay," I say reluctantly, still with good nature. "Let me talk to my mother, just let her know I'm leaving. She won't understand, but…" My voice trails off. "How long you expect it to be before the unit arrives?"

"Be here any minute," the cop says. His cell phone rings, and as he listens, he casually points a finger at me, waving the air in a gesture for me to wait. It's the second time this finger pointing has happened tonight. I glance at the sky. The shower that had misted the air a few minutes before has lifted and stars fan out across the night hovering over the preacher walking to his van, the teen carrying his audio equipment to a beat-up truck, and two others nodding and glancing toward Grandma's house, as they work at folding up the chairs and pulling out the stakes to the tent. I see now the pickup and van both have the same handmade sign: Melvin Marvin's Ministries for Jesus. I wonder why he didn't put "the Messiah" in place of Jesus and have complete alliteration. The teen's the preacher's son, I think, with surprising sadness. "Run," I want to call out, "before you inherit the family business."

The cop smiles and flicks the cell phone cover down, slipping it back in its case on his belt. "Seems Brother Marvin's dropped the charges," he says lightly. "Background check wasn't in his favor. We have computers in our units these days. Sometimes they can shorten the process." He adjusts the plastic on his hat and snaps closed his see-through slicker, as though it could start raining again any minute. He turns on his flashlight. "Well, goodnight," he says and I watch him walk across the highway, get in his black and white, fill out the paperwork for a good while, before clicking off the reading light and leaving the scene. And now it's all over, just like that, I think.

I go inside and get another beer, take a long pull and return to the swing. And then the memory hits me: a time in Tacoma while I was in college, just before I enlisted in the army. It seemed that once, twice a month, on Saturday mornings, when it was best for sleeping in, the Jehovah Witnesses—or was it the Mormons?—would knock on my apartment door at ten, eleven o'clock in the morning, waking me out of a haze from the after effects of the late night before with friends. The first few times it happened, I attempted to tell these messengers that I wasn't interested, ask them not to call again, saying all the things one tries to think of to be, if not kind, at least polite, to be fair, respectful of the other guy. But after the insistent ringing of the bell had disturbed my sleep several times, I opened the door in my robe and slippers one morning, to ask them yet again as nicely as I knew how, to please leave—there was always two of them, two men all in black except for their white shirts, Bibles under their arms, never the same ones, always different fellows. They didn't listen to my request, of course, but this time when they started their pitch, something very different took over me inside. It wasn't a thought-out idea, my body just responded to its need for them to be gone, for it to resume its sleep, so I let my robe fall and stood before them unencumbered, totally unadorned, while I opened the door and invited them in to discuss whatever they liked. I discovered then that there is nothing like a naked bodily urge to throw people's whole religious order out of whack.

WHITE HORSES OF THE APOCALYPSE

MAGIC WORDS

~Nalungiaq

In the very earliest time,
when both people and animals lived on earth,
a person could become an animal if he wanted to
and an animal could become a human being.
Sometimes they were people
and sometimes animals
and there was no difference.
All spoke the same language.
That was the time when words were like magic.
The human mind had mysterious powers.
A word spoken by chance
might have strange consequences.
It would suddenly come alive
and what people wanted to happen could happen—
all you had to do was say it.
Nobody can explain this:
That's the way it was.

(translated and edited by Edward Field)

The quad is empty. I sit staring at Doyle Hall Tower where my final exam for my final course toward my undergraduate degree in philosophy will be given within the hour. Symbolic Logic. I'd finished my Latin proficiency exam two hours earlier for entrance into advanced classes in the fall. Now I sit staring at a barren patch of earth where my sandals scoot back and forth causing small puffs of dust to rise in the early morning sun. I watch my feet in my sandals swinging side-to-side as though they belong to themselves, quite apart from anything I have to do with them. I wonder for a nanosecond who will be writing the answers to the Symbolic Logic problems in that packed room in Doyle Hall Tower—my fingers and arm or me. As clichéd as it sounds, even to my dog-eared brain, what I need is to stop the world and watch the grass grow. My eyes jump two feet to where well-watered, buzz-clipped grass stares back at me. As soon as Logic is done, the blue book dropped in the basket on the monitor's desk, I will go—I promise myself through gritted teeth—from this insane world of over-cultivation to the open country, a territory, I long to believe, is still wildly unschooled and principally ungovernable, a world filled with the hissing of insects, the call and song of birds, the distance moan of machinery on the land that may or may not yield to its owner. I fix my eyes on the small sliver of blue sky hanging between bricked dormitories on the other side of campus before draining my Styrofoam cup of coffee, and stepping to the trash basket where I deposit the cup and soiled napkin that I slide past my sugary lips one more time. With a sigh, I begin the slow walk toward the future I've created from the university brochures sent to me four years earlier. At minimum, I have two like years ahead—possibly six if I decide on a college-over-public-school job—before I can teach the questions of life with labels and definitions but few answers.

—

It is an unusual, soakingly hot day of early summer, close to ninety, by the time I motor my way past the city limit sign, out on Highway Nine to the small diner in Clover where I fill my tank with gas and my belly with overly butter-slathered French toast and leathery eggs drowning in syrup and catsup.

As my father used say, with a wink behind my mother's back, while he mixed everything on his plate—pancakes, eggs and bacon— "It all ends up churning around inside anyhow."

Once out of the lot and into the open air—I have no air conditioning in my disheveled, rusted-out Dodge Dart so all windows are open to the max—Johnny Cash fills the interior of the sedan with "I Walk the Line" and "Ghost Riders in the Sky" which is hardly my fare. My normal tilt is toward Callas over Cline, but today's an exception. It's country I need, pure and simple, so when the D.J. begins his squawk, I turn the knob down and listen to the whine of the wheels against the asphalt. I have no idea where I'm going, but I know beyond doubt it will be as far from anything accessible to mind as possible.

When a road appears without a county sign, I turn onto a two-rutted, graveled lane, wondering if it's a driveway to somebody's homeplace, but there isn't a "no-trespassing" sign, and I find out soon enough the path leads to a gated pasture where cows huddle underneath the shade of a cluster of trees. An abandoned windmill and galvanized watering tank round out the postcard picture. Now, here's the Oklahoma where I was born and raised and was meant to find again today. I grin when I note that scraggly blackjack oaks make up the good share of the grove lining the far end of the field. It's against the law to open the gate or go over the fence without the owner's permission, but I look around for signs of a farmhouse where I might inquire. All I can see in any direction are barbed fences, posts and grazing land bordering a long line of indigenous oaks, American elms, with a smattering of yellow pines, red cedars and two startling tall cottonwoods near the northern end of the property. They clap loudly as I slam the car door and walk toward the gate.

It's an easy trespass. Only a wire loop holds the gate closed. But on the walk across the packed grassed field, I've underestimated the distance to the far end of the grove to the cottonwoods. As a kid, I'd run such pastures with my boy cousins to their pond where we seined for tadpoles and stick fished for catfish, where Leon and I raced through Mexican sandburs for Tommy Don's old issues of comics—the least amount of stickers, the greater the prize—and where we sat and watched cumulus clouds float in and out of the shapes our imaginations pictured from the shifting wind in and around them. In that same heat this afternoon, my memories swell. I smell the ripe sweat on my arms, neck and in my hair and heard the rise and fall of cicadas that carried us over the uneven earth toward our play, our carefully constructed plans. It was in such pastures that Uncle Clifford and his hired hands branded cattle, carried hay to feeders for the livestock, and exercised and trained horses and ponies for the county fair. It was in such fields I learned the life and death rhythms of the ranch and the farm.

I saw my first pig slaughtered and rendered, watched the harvesting, storing and preserving of alfalfa, wheat and fruit from orchards, and went sand plum picking along the farm roads leading to and from my cousins' homeplace. During summers, Leon and I sat for hours by a hand-made orange crate stand, trying to sell lilacs from the bushes that lined the road from which we were selling them. The mailman stopped one afternoon, gave us a nickel, but told us that it was all right to just go ahead and keep the bunch we had stuffed in a milk bottle with well water.

I knew the difference between horses by color and type—chestnuts, bays, appaloosa, palomino, pinto, quarter horses and thoroughbreds, light and dark, spotted, dappled, paints and even flea-bitten—by the time I was able to hang on a fence without help. Not that Uncle Clifford had all of these horses, not by a long shot. But they were an important part of my summertime stays at the Ratzlaff homestead through the feed company calendars, farm and ranch magazines and constant table talk about "the life."

My uncle owned four horses, one for us kids to ride, a near-black Chestnut he called "Darkie"—such were the times and my uncle's proclivities—and around eight milking cows, give or take one or two—all milked by hand before he gave in to electric milking machines that cost him more than he and his bank wanted to pay but did anyway. He bred both horses and cows through intervention, using vets and hired hands. I was never allowed to watch this process, though I knew what was involved, because when I asked questions about sex and reproduction, my mother always answered me as directly as she felt I was able to understand at the time I asked.

I remember well when I was nine, sitting with her at the kitchen table, watching her draw the appropriate parts of the human and animal anatomy, while she explained to me "how babies are conceived and born." It took about ninety minutes in lecture time, complete with several drawings on a lined Big Chief tablet, and my father's being barred from the room.

Uncle Clifford never allowed his farm to become a bona fide ranch, which is to say, he never exceeded his capacity to barn and properly care for his horses and cattle. He had a quarter section of land, but four horses were his limit because he used most of the field for grain and feed. So when dust bowl drought almost took them and the cows, he sold all but one. Darkie was put down in his old age just before my aunt, uncle and cousins moved to town, giving up "the life" forever. Uncle Clifford became a carpenter and swore he never looked back. When I asked him why, he shrugged, grinning at me. "Wasn't right for any man to have that much fun."

But I did look back, despite the urge to make a different life from that of my childhood. And today, sick of mind and tired at heart, I'm wondering why I ever left, but then I know. It was the call of the larger world and the promise of more than what I took to be, back then, the narrow perspective of small town and country living.

When I reach the cottonwoods, I'm out of breath and longing for a deep drink of water. I remembered to bring a bandana but forgot the water thermos. Then I hear the small stream passing behind the trees and understand fully why the cows have chosen their spot. But even more than the longed-for shade, the tank water is undoubtedly warm and scummy, that's if there is any. I won't be drinking from the stream, of course, but I can soak my head, arms, legs and feet. I'd challenged myself to walk the pasture barefooted and my soles were tender. Downstream, I notice several cows standing just as I am, on the slippery rocked bottom, all of us allowing the water to course past our ankles, a flowing water still smelling of algae and moss. Lichen and shelf-mushrooms collect on the bark of trees nearby.

The cottonwoods continue to clatter, the one with the wedged trunk is no longer in the shade of its own branches, the sun having reached under and around them, magically transforming leafy shadows into dappled light. After lying in the stream, getting my shirt and shorts thoroughly soaked, I climb up the slight embankment and lie on my spread-out clothing under the trees, letting my thoughts drift into their noisy, rustling leaves. Some of the cottonwoods' fluffy seeds still cling to the field and wild grasses, a thin layer of snow powdering the pasture under and around its trunk. The bustling branches sway before my eyes, the lazy wind breathes upon my skin, the brittle grass crunches under my weight.

Soon, I fall into sleep.

I awaken to the earth trembling in heavy, even rhythms beneath me. *Earthquake*, I think, but I instinctively know otherwise. *My heart*, I think then, it's simply objectifying my fatigue. I feel I'm coming out of a grave as I raise myself up on elbows and squint past legs and feet to the far horizon. I'm holding fast to some inner sense that whatever danger is advancing toward me, I can seize what it is before it overtakes me. But its momentum is greater than the time I need to comprehend it. A line shoots across memory suddenly set loose from *Macbeth*, that this image, this hallucination, is emanating from my heat-oppress'd brain, that what I see before me is an illusion, a hypnopompic paralysis fastening me to my dreams.

But my better sense perceives through the sun-soaked haze, something real, *very real*, and just before I fully recognize it, I grasp three pale horses running with strangely metered regularity, necks and legs moving up-and-down, up-and-down, much like the carved wooden horses on a carousel, only these are merry-go-round equines gone mad, accelerating at breakneck speed directly toward me. Closer, I see them as white stallions, with blanched manes and tails rising and falling in the wind they are creating around them. They are encapsulated in an aura of light, and I recognize their breed instantly. They are Whites, from their pure coloration, I'd guess, dominant Whites, undoubtedly with pinkish-colored skin and hooves, because pigment cells are lacking. Their eyes will be glassy and dark with pronounced pink skin around their eyelids and muzzles. I do not want them close enough to verify this as fact.

Along a line as clearly drawn as an arrow on a page, I am racing from where I lie to the wedged cottonwood's trunk. I am propelled by some interior force far beyond calculation, to run, outrun the horses, to the trunk for safety. A trumpet blast fills the air and thunder mounts from the racing hooves and from some unknown source on the other side of the stream. The air grows abruptly dark. Rain begins to fall as I crouch inside the trunk and wait for the horses to pass.

As they do, I hold out my hand. Hair, sweat and heat slide into my palm from the horse nearest me. This is no illusion, no hallucination. This is the feel of life both concrete and transcendent, the knowledge of flesh and blood, energy and endurance incomprehensible. The animal smell smothers me in its reality—the overwhelming odors of breath, mucus and saliva, of cud, sweat, piss and feces, of blood, breath and gas, of skin, hair, nails and hooves and all that enters and falls away from sentient life as it is lived. The sky clears. The horses now slow to a trot at the northern most end of the pasture. They gather, stomp and wait, snorting and baying, heads bobbing in triumph, in their power and majesty.

As I step down from the cusp of the tree, a white, shiny pick-up flies past on the other side of the stream with a man in a cowboy hat and light shirt hanging out of the window waving his arms and yelling in my direction with exaggerated get-out-of-here gestures. He is honking his horn in jerky intervals. From the wave of his arms and hands, I know he wants me off his property instantly, out of his pasture and as far from what has just happened as possible. The last thing I want is for him to drive his truck around to where I am. I see he has a back load of hay for a feeder that I'd missed seeing near the fence at the end of the copse where the Whites now stand.

Taking the time to study the horses carefully before walking back under the trees, I see I've misread them. They are Cremello Quarter Horses with light to white manes and tails, one with a creamy sheen over its pale coat and an almost sorrel-colored tail. Any or all of them could have blue eyes. I chide myself for not looking as they passed. It was all I could risk to reach out to touch the one nearest me. I turn my hand over and smell. He is a ghostly trace still in the palm of my hand.

I glance up at the skies. The thin over-drifting of dark clouds that brought the sudden shower is floating away leaving scattered cirrus behind. I feel naked in my underwear so I walk quickly to pick up and examine my shorts and shirt, now a ripped wad under the trees. I put them on. At least they can cover me enough to get across the pasture, should the cowboy be looking. I won't throw them away. I'll keep them in a bottom drawer as a reminder of a sign for which I do not yet know the meaning.

But the meaning haunts. After all, I'm a philosopher, a young and eager one, despite moments of exhaustion and doubt, but, nonetheless, still a thinker about such experiences as the one that I've just had. After supper and after long and steady ruminations while attempting to read into the night without any concentrated success, I step-ladder to my mother's inherited Bible on an unreachable shelf in my study. I flip to *The Revelation of St. John the Divine*, the last book of *The Holy Bible*, and search for the chapter on the Four Horsemen of the Apocalypse. As I remember, there are four riders and two of them are on pale and white horses. I've forgotten what they signify and want to know. I flip until I find it, the sixth chapter, the chapter of The Seven Seals. It is in the opening of the first seal that the white horse and its rider appear. The rider is carrying a bow and is given a crown and he goes forth "conquering, and to conquer." The pale horse shows up when the fourth seal is opened. Its rider is Death who is followed by Hades and together they are given power to kill a quarter of the earth by sword, famine and plague and by wild beasts. I close the Bible and place it back on the shelf and climb down the ladder.

I walk to the living room and fall into the recliner where I sit without light, in silence.

—

So here I am as I sit, hours later, caught in the betrayal of ordinary life, after having been transported only hours earlier into some metaphysical realm by a dream, an illusion, an actual event, call it what I will. What strange beings we all are, all of us who breath and die, who soar and sink into our sentience, attempting to define, describe, divide, distinguish everything, absolutely everything, when in reality we are all who we are in this world of light and darkness together and no amount of mental constructs can really distinguish one of us from the other, even though I tell myself, and live, otherwise. We are not just *in* but *of* the world, and all the stories and definitions I invent around what happened to me today cannot disconnect me from the white horses that passed me in the afternoon under the cottonwood where I woke from my sleep. I again smell my hand, and despite all the actions and washings from that time to this, he is still there.

—

I accept my Bachelor of Philosophy degree through the mail, forfeiting the graduation ceremony to my parents' consternation. I glean from the degree what I can for electives toward my Masters of Fine Arts, in studio, having applied, shown my portfolio and been accepted for the program late summer. I did this without too much agonizing reflection but with great determination that an important change is necessary in my life. I need a closer relationship with the earth, with other living beings, with my impulse, intuition, foreknowledge. I have studied nature through drawing and poetry from the time I've been "knee-high to a grasshopper," as my father used to say, relying on my hand to guide me toward some understanding that I haven't grasped until its creative conclusion. I've decided to trust that guidance with my future.

THE SIGN

Sarah. She changed her name to Sarah. From Sally. It came in a memo without explanation. From the principal. The school secretary would now be called Sarah.

When I saw her I told her it was a beautiful name. From the Bible. An old name with dignity. Then I asked her if she was pregnant and I thought she would laugh. She just looked at me, her grey head motionless. Sarah, I explained, was one of the oldest women known to get pregnant, and it came with a name change—somehow. From the Bible. She just continued to look at me, her mouth a bit twisted. I thought I knew her well enough. When she continued to look at me unmoving, expressing nothing, I simply left.

I didn't see her much for the next weeks, except in passing. I came into the office, got my mail and left, not looking in her direction. It seemed to me when I did glance her way, she still had that twisted look on her face as she sat there typing. She never really looked at me or at least she didn't seem to see me when she did.

One day about a month after the first memo, we got another note from the principal. Sarah had taken a leave of absence. I didn't know secretaries took leaves of absence but Sarah did.

After a winter she returned. She looked at me straight away now, her mouth tightened, eyes ablaze. She was angry, but she never said anything. I didn't either. It had been a long time since I had seen her, it seemed. I had grown accustomed to the woman who replaced her and I hadn't thought about Sarah anymore. As I went to the office every day, I would see her at her typewriter, back stiff, her attention on her work. Then she would look up, stop what she was doing and stare at me, her mouth set. I felt I didn't know her at all now. I didn't know what to say to her so I didn't say anything.

One morning when another secretary was at her desk, I asked the principal about Sarah but she was vague. Sarah had not been traumatically ill or anything like that. She had requested another leave of absence and it had been granted. I listened to her, but I didn't learn anything more than what I already knew. Sarah was away for a time. She would return hopefully sometime soon.

But she didn't. She was granted a longer absence and then another and finally, it was announced that she would not return, at least not to our school. Time passed and I didn't think about her anymore.

Shortly before my retirement, one day at the supermarket, I saw her, and she caught my eye, looked away and tended to her buying. I turned my cart down another aisle and disappeared.

When I left teaching, I worked part-time at a library nearby. She came one day, saw I was at the desk and walked away before she had opened the door. I walked outside as though to catch up with her, but I only stood on the steps watching her retreat.

—

"Have you accepted Jesus?" Mother asked, her breath uneven, the words coming out in spurts. The nursing home smelled distant, like somebody else's things, somebody else's place.

"Momma," I said. "I…"

"You must tell me now, so I know if I can see you or not."

"Momma," I whispered. We had to go through this each visit. I wasn't sure why I couldn't lie to her to give her peace, but I couldn't. It seemed wrong on such a visceral level that after all these years I just let the words flow without much thought. "How can I tell you…"

"You must say it because I am dying and I want to feel where you are. I can't know you if you don't know Jesus." She raised an arm toward me as though either reaching for me or to give a benediction in my direction. "Have you gone away or are you still here with me?"

"Momma, try to understand. My way isn't your way…"

"The way to and from Jesus is always the same."

"Momma, I want to be near you now. I want to be close to you."

She looked at me not saying anything. Then she took a baby that wasn't there into her arms and began to sing. I always thought when she did this that she was rocking me, her only child, from a long time ago. Who else could it be?

"Rock-a-bye baby, away from the storm,
I will protect you; I'll keep you warm,
If you don't go, then I will stay,
Sweet baby Jesus, keep us we pray."

She suddenly bolted upright, flinging the baby aside, which was startling as she'd never done this before. "You aren't mine," she screamed. "You aren't mine and you never have been. I don't know you." She knocked over the water on her side table. "Get out of here." She made a lunge for me as the nurse came running in the door. I retreated several steps back, out of the way. Mother had been upset with me before but this viciousness was new. She'd never ordered me out of the room. It sounded like she was consigning me to eternal darkness.

"Oh my dear, why do you torture yourself so?" the nurse said to her. "There, there," and she held her like the baby Momma had just cradled in her arms. "I have to ask you to go," the nurse said to me. "I'm so sorry. But she must calm herself now."

I stood and looked at my mother, finally bending over the bed as though to kiss her. Her face twisted away from me, her mouth clamped in a tight line. The nurse touched my arm and nodded gently toward the door. My hand on the knob, I stopped to see her again. She dropped her head, her breath falling over unmoving lips.

Shortly after the visit with mother, I called my doctor for a checkup. I felt tired from work that I no longer did.

When I went in for a follow-up on the blood work and tests, my doctor said, "You need a vacation. There's a little anemia but mostly you need a break. Just put this responsibility aside and go somewhere. Somewhere entirely different."

"It's good advice, of course. But I can't just leave mother. Not now. Not like she is."

"Of course you can. She's been this way for years. She's well taken care of and I strongly suggest that you go."

"But why? I mean why leave?"

"Because you need to leave. For just a little while."

"A vacation."

"Yes. You need to go away. You need a change."

"A change."

"Yes."

"Okay then, maybe I will."

"There, that's the idea. Now, go and do it."

On the shore, I watched the sand and the long horizon that lingered beyond my view. I studied the small objects around my chair, moving them with my feet. And then I suddenly saw her. A dim figure at first but clearly recognizable as she came closer. She seemed to shimmer against the morning sun.

"Sarah!" I said, standing to greet her.

But she didn't stop walking, only looked at me with a stony grin. "No, I don't think so," she said as she passed. "You have me confused with somebody else."

Within a week of my return home, Mother was gone and I never saw Sarah again.

HOW TO DEFROST THE REFRIGERATOR

During my time with Darcy, I got very good at defrosting the refrigerator. So this story was a little like that old story about telling everyone on the committee at work you can type. You get all the typing jobs from then on. And so it was with Darcy, my lover-roommate, when she found out that I came up with a special strategy for defrosting the refrigerator. She never lifted a finger to help me again—forget about her doing it on her own. And that was for five years! I did this *and* mopped the floors *and* carried out the garbage *and* drained the water out of the radiator of the car every night during January and February so the thing wouldn't freeze and burst the already cracked radiator to smithereens. We were fortunate that we were living in the South where solid winters were short. Anyway, these were my jobs, well, among other things. I hadn't learned yet about fair labor laws in relationships.

The car business was another one of those you-do-it-well-you-do-it-alone jobs. Through it, I learned loads about how to keep a car from freezing up when you can't put Freezone in it. Darcy's brother, Curly, had loaned us his new yellow '57 Mercury when he joined the army and went to boot camp in West Virginia—anyway, it was new to him and brand new to us. It actually was only a little over a year old, but Curly had bought it from a used car salesman who knew another used car salesman who knew a friend of…well, you get the idea. Curly said we could have it for the years he was gone if we'd get the radiator fixed and put new tires on it. Of course, we said we would. Hell, we would've promised anything to get some wheels. We were in our twenties and broke all the time. We both had jobs, just not high paying ones. Darcy used most of her salary buying clothes anyway. And I was to learn from the Texaco man up the block on Clinton Street that radiator damage isn't easy to find or repair. And when the cracks are finally found and fixed, they cost a bundle.

Curly left in the summertime, and we had a ball running around all over creation in his car. We had to add water like crazy, but we didn't mind as long as we could *go*. But we started having blowouts every other week so we'd have to take the bad tire down to the Texaco station and exchange it for a recap for which we paid less than ten dollars, usually nearer to five bucks. And away we'd go again until the next blowout. After three or five of these in the first month, we had new tires put on both axles, totally exhausting any extra bucks we'd put in the party jar in the pantry. But after the new Firestones, we thought we were set. And then it turned cold, and although the radiator would hold water all day while we were at work when the temperatures were warmer, we had to drain the thing at night because we learned early that if we didn't, most of it would be in our driveway in the morning, as wide and slick as a skating rink, having busted out the knob holding the water in.

Darcy and I rode together to work because our jobs were just a few blocks from each other, mine at the Langley and Moore Accounting Office as a file and claims clerk, and hers at Sturges Department Store as a saleswoman. I also thought of myself as a writer of sorts, though I'd not earned a penny from anything I'd written so far. But since I spent as much time tapping out stories on my old Smith-Corona as I did as a file clerk, stories that I'd submit from time to time to various journals I purchased from a nearby book store up the street from where I worked, I automatically assumed being an author would figure in my economic future somewhere down the line.

In my personal lexicon, "author" meant someone who had published, was publishing and would continue to publish for money, while "writer" meant someone, like me, who was hoping to become an author. I'd entitled my latest submission, "The Sex Life of the Fiddler Crab," which I sent to some high-brow university review and which had come back in a manila envelope with a full-page form letter, rejecting it for their publication. A handwritten note, however, had been attached that stated my writing showed promise but I needed to research the subject more carefully before tackling such a difficult subject. It was a note with just the right tone, but obviously the editor or reviewer had taken what I'd written to have come from some personal experience and had suggested that I might look into some therapy, which they added, with great sensitivity, could only help my writing about this particular subject. With the note now in hand, it did occur to me that my narrator's tale of the story of her incestuous sexual abuse could only have elicited this sort of response. It didn't stop me from continuing to write more stories with similar intense emotional content, but the rejection haunted, especially the handwritten note, the reviewer now sitting on my shoulder as I tapped away, whispering in my ear that I had a long way to go before achieving any realizable authorship.

As to my real life and livelihood, I'd let Darcy off on my way to the Bass Buildings where the accounting firm was located, which we called the Brass Buildings because we thought it was funny—we were young, remember; and it was the fifties— and because the Brass Buildings were two phallically vertical, round at-the-top towers that shown bright as the ancient pyramids with their brick-and-limestone façade in the early morning sunlight. It was hard to believe that the architects didn't have some devious scheme in mind with their design and the CEOs hadn't caught it, or, more likely, they had seen the design's intention completely and decided to go for it fully aware of what the effect would be. "Here we are, all you other guys, the two big boys in town!"

The first thing I did when I got off work was to look under the car to see how bad the leaking had been that day—that's if it wasn't apparent on sight—and anything short of a river, I'd ignore and make the trek over to pick up Darcy after which we'd hightail it home as fast as I could drive without getting caught.

After supper, I'd crawl under the car and unscrew the knob that let the remaining water out, and when the radiator was dry, I'd get back under there and screw the knob back on, not too tight to keep me from being unable to unscrewing it the next morning. I'd learned the hard way that freezing-up is a tricky state-of-affairs. The slightest bit of moisture can make such a simple task frustratingly difficult when you are late for work and need to have water in the radiator to even start the car. Sometimes I'd do the water-letting as late as midnight, because I'd procrastinate while I looked longingly at Darcy in the living room who kept snacking on the couch while reading one of her romance novels, mostly of the western variety which should have been a clue right there—her taste in literature was as abysmal as it was in everything else—except for her choice of me, of course. She never acknowledged my entreaties, so I'd go do the thing that needed to be done before bedtime.

In the morning, I'd get up early enough to bring the garden hose in from the breezeway, hook it up to the kitchen faucet, run it through the hall to the bedroom window and then out into the carport where I'd stick the rubber hose in the radiator hole, race back into the kitchen, turn on the water, race back to the car to watch until it was full and then race back again to the kitchen to turn the water off, undo the hose, march back through the house, holding it up over my head like some snake charmer in a circus act until all the water drained out of it onto the carport concrete. Then from the bedroom window I'd carefully push it out into the breezeway so none of the left over water would run over the carpets or bed. Our landlady, Paula Boucher, would've loved keeping our deposit when we moved out, which was a month's full rent, and I was bent on making sure she didn't get her satisfaction. After the watering or dewatering of the Mercury was completed, I'd coil the hose up, leaving it like the dead thing it was, in the breezeway until the next morning when I'd start this ritual all over again. The routine was preordained as there was no outside faucet.

But after I'd done this for the first couple of months, I told Darcy we had to do something. This garden hose-radiator thing was wearing me out. So she gave the Clinton Street Texaco man—'Dale' by now—a call and asked what the exact cost would be to fix a crack in a radiator. He gave a long explanation about the procedure in locating such a problem, followed by some astronomical figure neither one of us thought we'd heard right. But then he said, "There are some sealants you could try. I can't guarantee they'll work. It all depends on how large the crack is, but we could give it a go, if you want." And so we did the sealant thing that shot several evenings at Furr's Cafeteria right out the window, and as it turned out several more as well.

Three sealants later, we gave in to the fact that this strategy of Dale's wasn't going to work, and I went back to the garden hose trek. I did this for two more months. And when I finally demanded some relief from Darcy, things got worse. She simply could not do the easiest part of the procedure, like waiting in the kitchen until I yelled from the carport for her to turn the water on in the kitchen. I couldn't yell too loud because it was early in the morning and Paula's bedroom window was right next to our carport—on the other side, actually, so she always knew our comings and goings, which I detested no end. I'd have to step into the bedroom to call out to Darcy, and, of course, she couldn't hear me—anyway, that was her claim—because the long hall to where she stood prevented my voice from carrying, especially around the corner into the kitchen. I figured that by the time I came down the hall, close enough to be heard, which in her case would seem to be yelling in her ear, I might as well do it myself. So it became a habit. I did it alone and with resignation every single day like I took my shower, brushed my teeth and made my breakfast. And that's how it got to be with the refrigerator as well. I just seemed to know instinctively how to take care of these hard-to-do jobs so, alas, they were "mine."

The refrigerator business was one of those situations where I thought a good defrosting would make an old, very old, Coldspot start acting like an operational refrigerator again. I should have known better because while it very quickly collected massive amounts of ice around the freezer unit, it barely kept the items frozen inside. Darcy's mother, Margaret, came to visit only occasionally but once she showed up while I was defrosting the refrig. She said she knew this woman who'd craved the ice around the freezer unit while she was pregnant. But when Margaret took a close look at my freezer unit, she told me that Dollie could've had herself an endless nine-month supply.

Owning a garage apartment on Spelling Avenue as Darcy's mom did, she suggested that we not bother our landlady with complains about buying us a new refrigerator which Paula Boucher wasn't likely to do and complaining would only "turn her against us" so that anything else we might really need badly in the future, like heat or water, we weren't likely to get right away because of our attitude. Margaret's advice was to defrost the old Coldspot often enough so that the build-up wouldn't get so out of control. And if we did that together with not opening the door any more than we absolutely had to, she thought that would take care of the problem or at least make the refrigerator "manageable"—whatever in the heck that meant. There was no point in informing her that defrosting the refrigerator as often in the summer as it needed it, would have meant, every other week. In other words, 'manageable' wasn't manageable.

But I should have listened to Margaret's advice. Because after several attempts to catch Paula when she wasn't on the run to explain, as politely as I could, that something really had to be done, her response was pretty much as Margaret had said it would be. I finally cornered Paula on her front porch one late Saturday afternoon telling her that the Coldspot was breathing its last, and we really would appreciate something that would keep our food from spoiling. She responded that she'd had the refrigerator inspected thoroughly by an appliance repairman—as she always did when she had a change in tenants—and he said that the unit was completely workable for anybody who wasn't going to use it "like a chest freezer." After this definitive statement, she simply turned her back to me, unlocked her front door and walked inside as though I was no longer there.

In the summer when it would get to be a whopping 100 degrees or more for days on end, our refrigerator would begin to complain with loud wheezing sounds much like an overweight human with high blood pressure and would refuse to keep anything inside much below lukewarm. When the center of the ice cubes refused to freeze, I knew it was time for a thorough thaw.

The first time this happened, I came back from the grocery store to find Darcy jabbing away at the freezer unit with a butcher knife. And although I was thrilled she'd taken an interest in housekeeping, I went crazy, dropping the groceries and running up to her screaming so fast and hard, she went into a hysterical fit in response and dropped the knife on her bare foot, leaving a good-sized slice on her big toe. After all the anger and bleeding subsided, I told her, "Don't you know that you can ruin the freezer that way because if you poke a hole in the unit, the ammonia escapes and it blows the whole refrigerator? You wanna buy a new one that we can't take with us when we leave?" She sat on the living room couch, holding her toe, while—I'll never forget this—she said through gritted teeth, "Then don't let me near that friggin' thing again if you want a running ice box in this house!"

So I got very good at defrosting the refrigerator, especially from June until September when the amount of ice-build-up was the greatest. Every two weeks or so, I'd drag the fan to the kitchen, put it in front of the open refrig that I'd turned off a half an hour earlier and let the blades whirl at top speed while I put scalding hot trays of water in the freezer unit until the ice began to loosen from the sides, top and bottom. Sounds easy but it wasn't. These trays had to be emptied every five, seven minutes because the water would get cold and the melting would slow down, if not stop altogether. After an hour or more of this tray exchange business, the entire slabs would finally fall like an avalanche so that the total contents of the refrigerator had to be removed before I even started this procedure or I'd find leftovers swimming in a lake of destruction with the produce. You can forget about crisper bins. This refrigerator had lost those years ago, taken, no doubt, by some renters who needed extra containers for their possessions in their hasty getaway. So the ritual here was this: after disposing of the ice—which had its own challenges—sopping up the flood on the bottom of the refrig, and mopping up the floor from the leakage, I'd put the food back, close the door, turn on the electricity and sit on the couch while I turned the fan on me, and drank a lukewarm beer.

But both of these domestic challenges paled compared to the one Darcy introduced to me one evening when she walked through the front door holding a small kitten in her arms. We should have called him Ash or Smut. Lord knows he looked like a charcoal stick left over from the remains of a burned-out grill. But Darcy insisted we call him Algernon Moncrieff after a recent production of Oscar Wilde's *The Importance of Being Earnest* that we'd seen in the high school auditorium because a friend with whom she worked had a son playing the part of Algy. But before I begin with the life with *our* Algy, I probably should tell you a bit about Darcy and how she became my live-in lover. It will explain loads about our domestic chores problems and about the kitten in particular.

Darcy was a product of divorce, as the trite saying goes, but in her case it wasn't only her parents' divorce but also her own. Let's just say that through it all her mother hadn't made a positive imprint on her daughter about how to handle the men in one's life. Darcy's mom, Margaret Kahn, had married young and was pregnant with Curly before her fifteenth birthday. Margaret's alcoholic mother, Elsa, had given permission for her daughter's civil marriage without so much as a glance at the man she was marrying, a man over twice her age and without a job or promise of finding one. Elsa was quite glad to have her daughter out of her hair and house so she could continue to enjoy, or detest, her live-in boyfriends as they came and went without worrying about her daughter in the mix.

After Curly's father left Margaret hugely pregnant, he returned three years later to knock her up again—this time with Darcy—only to retreat once more, this time for good. Margaret filed for divorce after several years of his not returning and the state granted her one. She did this, she told Darcy years later, so that her snake-of-a-husband couldn't sneak back into her life and try to take her kids from her when they were old enough for him to entrap them into earning him a living.

In the meantime, Margaret made her living in the only way open to her, menial domestic work. She worked long hours, including week-ends and took in washing and ironing on the side. But in time, Margaret Kahn quickly gained a sizable reputation and clientele for her fast, honest and reliable work. Within three years, she was working for the young wives of local affluent businessmen, women who spent their days shopping, playing canasta or bridge and gossiping in and out of rows and love-making with their own and each others' husbands. Margaret knew enough insider secrets of the rich and well-recognized in the local community by the time Curly was three to procure job security with supplementary income through substantial tips. However, it was a tenable position, she knew, because, more than once, she'd walked inadvertently—and sometimes not so accidentally—into danger zones, ones which could've gotten her either fired or killed, probably the latter since firing her would've been riskier than removing her permanently from the scene. She knew too much about her employers' corruptions and betrayals and she had become far too complicit and accommodating under pressure so that she often lay awake late in the night in her bed at home with her children sleeping nearby, shuddering to think what could happen if she took a careless step this way or that. She was watchful, but with high-strung, affluent people who drank too much, one never knew. And she'd done what they asked, even if it crossed personal and sexual boundaries.

When Elsa died in a state-run facility as Curly had just turned eleven and Darcy eight, Margaret surprisingly discovered her mother had left a sizable sum in a savings account at a regional bank. And even more amazingly, her mother had backed up the account with a living will. Since Margaret was Elsa's only child, she inherited the entire sum which was enough for her to purchase her Spelling Avenue house with a garage apartment for income. And in another stroke of good fortune, after both Curly and Darcy had grown old enough to care for themselves, she met a cook at a local diner she frequented for lunch in between cleaning jobs, who invited her first to his house, and then to his bed, and not long after, asked her to live with him permanently. Darcy watched her mother's growing involvement with this man with great confusion and trepidation but when, over time, she saw that it gave her mother stability and happiness, she gave Margaret her belated approval.

Darcy's own story followed a somewhat parallel path. She was married at sixteen to Dwight Fugate, with her mother's consent, much as it had been given by Elsa to Margaret. In less than a year Darcy'd had a miscarriage from which she recovered quickly, as though fate had taken care of a burden she wasn't likely to bear well under her circumstances, but it did leave emotional scars. She wanted a child, but didn't know how she could care for it without getting her mother tied to her life. She wanted and needed her independence and Margaret would be, to her mind, an overbearing influence in the baby's future. Her marriage was uneventful while her hubby was in the service overseas, but it suddenly became terrifyingly frightening to her when he returned from his active duty full of alcohol, meanness toward anything that didn't suit him, and physically, but primarily, psychologically, abusive.

Darcy lived with her mother and on her own salary while Dwight was in the service, because he never sent any money home to her. And when he returned, he purchased a dilapidated acreage far enough from town to keep himself and his wife away from everybody, while close enough to the bus line for Darcy to get to work. He spent most of his time at home, tending his broods of chickens—for the sale of fresh eggs and roasters, he told her.

One afternoon when Dwight suspected Darcy of leaving the house to see somebody—he wasn't sure who, only that she'd left without his permission—he chased a chicken across the yard, caught it, and brought it over close to her face. In a rush, he slashed its throat with one swat of a knife, spraying her dress with its blood, and told her that if she ever attempted to leave him—by this she knew he meant permanently taking off from their marriage—her mother would look just like this chicken when they finally found her body.

One year later, she divorced him, suing for extreme mental cruelty and under the protection of a lawyer and a hidey-hole provided by a hooker girlfriend her husband didn't know she knew, Darcy managed to remain safe until his papers were served. Her mother was living by then with her cook, so, to Darcy's way of thinking, Margaret was under the protection of a man in her life. At first Dwight refused to sign but after restraining orders and warrants from a judge to search his property for drugs, he gave in to the court's pressure. A couple of years of leeway from his threats and entrapment—despite the fact that she had a secure job that paid well enough to support her—she started on a relentless pursuit of finding a man to marry, one whom she envisioned would protect her from the likes of the one from whom she'd just claimed her freedom.

But Darcy had no powers of vision when it came to men. She consistently sought out those who were married, having affairs with them in the hopes of luring them from their spouses. To her mind, their marriages had to be sour or why else would they be sleeping with her? She never succeeded in finding what she was looking for, or rather she found exactly what she was looking for, but couldn't picture anything outside the frame handed to her by Elsa and the younger Margaret. Unfortunately the older Margaret, the one who found happiness with her cook, was not one that could any longer influence the likes of Darcy. The last man Darcy'd been with before she met me was a flyboy stationed at the nearby training field for pilots, was German and spoke English through a thick accent she found charming. He took her to his bed in a fine motel on the first date and continued doing so every leave he got from the base, wowing her with gifts, very fine gifts, after spending each night with her. After a couple of months of courting, he asked her to marry him but it was under the condition that she leave the United States, obtain German citizenship and live with him forever-and-ever in his hometown outside Cologne for the rest of her days. He stressed the importance of family, their family, the one he wanted with her. This was in the late fifties and, as she told me later, her lover had visions of his country rebuilding itself after the war. The new Luftwaffe needed competent pilots and Wolfgang Becker had been trained in America to fill that gap.

She was in a quandary for several months because "Wolf," as she called him, was coming to the end of his mission at the local air base. Darcy didn't seem to recognize the same claustrophobic signs in this lover as her husband, though there seemed to be some tiny hesitation that warned her that something wasn't quite right in all this. Wolf was becoming very demanding about her going back home with him, saying he couldn't wait, wouldn't wait, as he couldn't and wouldn't return to the States to get her once he'd gone nor did he want to sit at home in Germany, wondering and waiting for her to come to him. Wolf was only four years younger than Darcy, but she saw him as still barely past teething at twenty-three. She was both smitten and hesitant with his demands.

But she needn't have worried as fate took all of her future possibilities with Lieutenant Becker out of her hands. He was burned alive on his last solo flight during a botched landing. Darcy found out about Wolf's death and deception when she read his obituary in the Landing Field section of our hometown newspaper. The surviving wife back in Bad Münstereifel had not only been suing him for divorce while he was in the States but was also fighting for custody of their infant daughter. She undoubtedly would've succeeded as she was doing so on the grounds that Wolf had another marriage in France. When Darcy met him, she'd been impressed that he'd known four languages, so, to her mind now, there was a great possibility that he also had some marital connection in Spain that just hadn't been discovered yet. How he'd pulled all this off at his age while in the military was far too convoluted a script to doubt, though she'd never read such unreasonable storylines in fiction, and she was a prolific reader of popular romance.

Being Darcy, she didn't waste time either pursuing more information concerning the matter nor grieving for what she could have seen as extreme loss. She simply told herself she was relieved to learn of his lying nature before she or he purchased her ticket to Germany. Here at home she could at least tell me loudly and clearly in her native tongue what she thought of the bastard. I knew from the start that attempting to scrutinize with her about why Wolf would've done such a thing, a thing which he seemed to have a compulsion to do, would only have been viewed by her as interrogation. She wanted to distance herself as far from her disgrace as possible. And this suited me with my own hopes and purposes just fine in light of her statements about never getting involved with another man as long as she lived.

I met Darcy immediately following her Wolfgang Becker ordeal. We met at a bar, where she was self-medicating her way through feelings of self-deprecation from her having been so easily taken in. It did not take us three or four evenings of drink and talk to fall into a mangled mess of sheets and surprise—her surprise more than mine, as she'd never considered a female lover. Actually, it didn't even take us two evenings. We went directly from the bar after our initial meeting to my apartment where Darcy continued to spill her tale of woe, and I comforted her throughout the night. It was the one and only time she spent grieving over Becker with me. But from the night of our wake and burial of her indiscretion, she began a bond which tightened through drink and talk, but talk with a change of subject from Wolfgang Becker to men in general. I didn't have much to say on the more generalized topic, because I wasn't a man-hating lesbian. I simply loved women, and I saw Darcy as gorgeous, sexy and having fallen into my lap. If she wanted to hate men, even for a little while, I was game.

She seemed to like my bed, which pleased me no end. I had a few questions about why she was still living with her Mother while expressing a desire to have a place of her own—after all she had a steady job—but also explaining she hadn't found one to her liking as yet. In time, I began to wonder if the bed that I offered her, the one she seemed to love so much, wasn't because I paid the rent and wasn't asking her for her share while she had the added advantage of being out from under her mother's contentious nature. But I had put all that aside at the time, satisfied as I was with our un-conjugal bliss, and now here we were five years later with me playing house with her, far too close to the role of her mother, as I did all of the housekeeping and most of the cooking, and perhaps in the role of her older brother as well, as I took care of the car.

So I knew the cat that Darcy carried in her arms that late afternoon she walked into our apartment was more than just a hope for diversion and preoccupation, a little plaything while away from work. She was literally holding her entire world in her arms—her child who hadn't live, her marriage that was abusive and unfair, her dead and deceptive lover who almost ensnared her in a legal mess in Germany, her fatherless childhood and her memory of the countless men rising and falling in and out of her mother and her grandmother's lives.

It struck me that she wanted to set all this right through the perfect parenting of an unaltered, un-vaccinated, taken-out-of-box of newborns from a flea market, domestic Siamese kitten. It was written all over her face. A hole began to form in my chest so deep and vast I wasn't sure I could speak. But I didn't need to. She told me everything I needed to know in the first utterance out of her mouth: "We can keep it, can't we?" I simply nodded my consent and decided to wait to talk about the added responsibilities of food and other amenities, as well as vet and safety concerns. I was encouraged by her immediate attention to the cat's fundamental needs. She'd stopped by the grocery and drug stores, bringing home dry and canned cat food and a litter box and the filler.

From day one, Darcy showed an over-protective interest in Algy's whereabouts. She needed to know where the cat was every minute she was at home and she queried me relentlessly about my care for Algy when she wasn't around. She put warning prompts on the doors and windows throughout the apartment—the doors included the cabinets in the kitchen and bathroom. *He is to be visible at all times* was message on the large carefully printed signs. I attempted to address her fears about his possible "disappearance," but she simply shrugged and said, "He's so small and needy, he's utterly dependent on us. If we don't pay attention, he could get lost without our ever knowing it."

Through the first couple of weeks with Algy, I felt a growing resentment building over Darcy's concentration on the kitten's every need while disregarding any of mine. Her involvement in any domestic responsibilities had always been minimal, but now her negligence had grown into an assumption that I would simply tend to what needed to be done in and around the house while she'd take care of the cat. She did launder her own finest clothing. In fact, I dare not touch those. Everything else, her underwear and ordinary jeans and shirts she wore at home, she seemed to view as part of the household chores which were my job since I'd have to be doing all this anyway if I were living on my own. Over time, I began to see that the division of labor fell along the lines established in her home with her mother and her and her brother. She'd never lived on her own, so I reasoned she was simply transferring the roles and routines from her original family to ours.

When I reflected on my resentment and its increasing intensity, I realized that I was feeling upset more about Darcy's behavior with the cat than with anything else. It struck me at one point that this was a bit like the parallel resentment a husband must feel when the first child is born and he takes a back seat to the demands and attention given by the mother to the newborn. But my gut was telling me that there was something I wasn't grasping in all this, something underneath that was harder for me to discern, some deep wound from the relationships in her life before this one with me.

It wasn't only the amount of time that she was devoting to this kitten's care. It was that she appeared incapable of viewing his behavior realistically. It was as though he simply did what he did, and we found ways to deal with it. It never seemed to occur to her that a change had to be made, that something had to happen that would make his disruptive and destructive actions come to an end.

From the day he entered our house, Algy had a fixation with our curtains. Paula Boucher had installed heavy burgundy corduroy drapes complete with cornices outlined in gold piping with a fringe of tassels that matched exactly the burgundy and gold patterned carpets she'd installed throughout the house. These were obviously what she viewed as her defining marks in offering an apartment of distinction in a neighborhood on the cusp of being on the lower end of the class spectrum. To hell with the outmoded refrigerator. The interior decoration was the selling point. But Algy didn't even bother to give these draperies a cursory glance before he made his virginal leap from floor-to-mid-curtain. It was as though he had energy to jump and the drapes seemed the most obvious place to land or climb, simply because they were before him, because they were *there*. But once that first jump had been made, a flyboy was born, one that could've made the pilots out at the Landing Field blush.

Algernon Moncrieff was a feline raptor. From his first jump, Darcy stopped worrying about where her cat might be in the house because from his first leap to his last each day, she knew he'd be perched on one of the cornices, usually the longest one in the living room where he would pace back and forth at length before leaping mid-air like some trapeze artist, grab a pawful of corduroy and swing from it to the floor with the confidence and grace of a spider monkey. He flew over and on anything in sight. He even climbed up our skirts, clawing vertically through our sheer blouses, sinking his claws into our flesh as though we were stuffed couches. We clipped his claws down to his bleeding quicks, and he still was able to gain leverage enough to slash through skin, cloth, leather and even wood, leaving marks on the surface of Paula's tables that no amount of shoe polish, stain, furniture wax or Danish oil could hide.

In less than a month of Algy's having come into our lives, I had run out of ideas as to how we could curtail his feral flying. Darcy simply thought he was delightfully charming, shrugging when I mentioned our deposit.

But we both were at wits end when his crying began. The first time he expressed a sound beyond a simple, small meow, we thought he'd met with terminal disaster. It was loud, mournful and close enough to a human baby's cry to send shudders down our spines. Now Darcy's anxiety hit a new high mark. Her obsession became that Paula would hear his howling and investigate. Our renter's contract stated very clearly we were to have no pets with the exception of fish in a properly installed aquarium. The large print didn't allow so much as a hamster on a wheel. Suddenly, Darcy became once again obsessed with the possibility of his "disappearance," especially through the doors, because she was totally convinced that Paula Boucher would came into our apartment if she heard Algy's caterwauling and let him out.

"She's that kinda person," she groaned to me. "You think some little piece a paper she's signed gonna keep her out? And anyway, how we gonna prove she's nosing around in here? She doesn't exactly leave smashed cigarettes in ashtrays, for godssakes." Darcy asked me these questions contentiously, as though I was challenging her position on Paula Boucher and the woman's vengeful nature.

"Well," I retorted one day, "if she discovers Algy in here and hits us up for it, we can sue the crap outta *her* for breach of contract. It's against the law for her to come into our apartment without our permission. She's supposed to tell us when she's coming."

"That's if you can prove she's been in our apartment. How you gonna do that, let alone prove she's the one who's let Algy out? We can't accuse her of a thing about our cat without owning up to *our* breach of contract. We have him in here when the contract says positively no pets. Remember that agreement?" She glared at me and added a final zinger, "Anyway, she can come in, according to the contract, if she suspects some *safety* issue in here. That's vague enough to permit her to come in any time she feels like it. She can hear a faucet dripping and claim it's the advent of a flood."

I remained silent. The thought of her cat disappearing under *any* circumstances took Darcy to the edge of hysteria. And now that she'd come up with the script for the possibility of Paula Boucher's doing just that, and with malice of forethought, her imagination was carrying her straight into panic attacks. I'd noticed that she'd begun swallowing Librium tablets that she was getting from one of her co-workers, with her nightly beers. So far our letting Algy out accidently wasn't feasible because we had sure-safe procedures in place for leaving and entering the apartment. So our concern finally had come down to the fact that we had no control over Algy's behavior when we weren't at home and that might give Paula cause to discover he was with us. He flew noisily, thumping against walls as he swung from the curtains and leaped or fell to the floors with a thud. And his pacing along the cornices was done with an almost continuously murmur of cat-calling wails.

So Darcy's new obsession was no longer the condition of the curtains and furniture in the house—those were long-gone concerns—but with Algy's constant thumping, thudding and crying. And her blame for this circled around me. She complained that my incessant talking to him had created this stimulus response in him, and that we needed to provide an atmosphere at home of equanimity and restraint until he outgrew his kittyhood. She started looking for where Algy was the minute she entered the house and once he was found, falling into a catatonic state on the couch as soon as she shed her shoes. It was as though she was paralyzed by anything she could imagine beyond what was actually happening. I began wondering how this might be affecting her work.

Our first hope had been the advice our veterinarian had given us upon our visit for his physical exam and vaccinations. Algy would calm down after he was neutered, she told us confidently. She had estimated that he was two months old, so he could safely go through the surgery any time we decided to do it. We scheduled the procedure on the following Saturday. For this new financial addition to our budget, Darcy had gathered her courage and approached her mother for a small loan. In one of her rare moments of generosity, Margaret had handed Darcy the check with a laugh, saying that the money was a shower gift for her daughter's new baby. I wasn't there, so I don't know if Darcy smiled at this or not. I rather thought not.

But Algernon was neutered. Whether he would calm down or not, remained in the air, as it were, because, as things turned out, all of Darcy's concerns about his disappearance were warranted.

We came home one afternoon to find Algy was gone, absolutely nowhere to be found, inside or outside the apartment. When Darcy answered the rap on our front door after an hour of searching, she stared into the face of our sneering landlady who demanded that we leave the premises within thirty days with the forfeiture of our deposit plus a bill of one hundred and fifty dollars for the estimated cost of damage to the drapes and furniture. With one mighty swipe, she had erased us out of her life, and in one afternoon, had called her lawyer and a brother-in-law who refinished furniture who came immediately, making the damage estimates on the tables, cornices and headboard of the bed. She had the original invoice she told Darcy for the making of the curtains and cornices so she knew the cost on those. As to Algernon, she had no idea where he was. She had no part in his disappearance. He was hovering on a cornice when she left the apartment. Paula handed Darcy the paperwork all neatly bradded together in a black paper file which Darcy threw on the nearby couch without ever taking her eyes off of our landlady and slamming the door in her face.

That night Darcy was inconsolable. When I offered condolences and possible solutions to our dilemma, she simply turned her blank face toward me with a barely discernibly shaking of her head. Her response to all this was frightening because she sat in the recliner utterly expressionless and silent. I went to bed, slept fitfully, getting up every other hour to find her exactly as I'd left her when her withdrawal began.

In the morning, she called into work sick and before drinking a sip of coffee, telephoned the SPCA to discover that Algernon was not one of the newcomers brought in overnight. When she put the cradle down on the phone, she began to cry. When I say she was inconsolable, I mean exactly that. She didn't want to be touched, listened to or be near, so I left the room, filled the radiator of the Mercury from a watering can, enough to make it to the Texaco station where I had Dale finish the job, handing him a tip while swilling the station's sludgy black coffee out of a Styrofoam cup. We could have done this all along, I thought, if I'd had the money for daily tips. The water spout wasn't available without the key.

I attempted to reach Darcy from work during the day without luck. I was in a state of heightened anxiety when I entered the living room, found her just as I'd left her and asked if she was all right. She nodded her head and in a voice hoarse from crying, said that Curly had called from his base in West Virginia, telling her that he was to be stationed at Fort Hood but was coming home for a month's vacation before being flown there. He made light of the fact that he and Elvis both would be stationed there at the same time and might actually become friends since Curly said he played the guitar too and could gyrate his hips with the best of the boys. She said when she told him of our dilemma with Paula Boucher, even informing him that we had put new tires on the Mercury but couldn't afford to replace the radiator, he'd told her jovially, not to worry, that he'd managed to save most of his money while at camp, supplementing his income with some card playing on the side. He was certain he could save us from the clutches of "the Boucher bitch," restore the Mercury and even help us move.

Upon his suggestion, she called her mother who offered us her newly-vacated house on Spelling Avenue at a small discount, so our life had taken a decisive turn from down to up. I was so delighted with these new turn of events, it never occurred to me at the time that downhill travel can be easier than that on the uphill.

Curly did come home and save us, including tossing a few choice words at Paula Boucher before driving the van away with us in the front seat and our goods in the back—it was a small van as the apartment had come furnished and we owned only the clothing on our backs, a few wire hangers in the closets, a couple of waste paper cans, the garden hose we'd used for the Mercury, and such. It wasn't much. Curly handed Darcy the receipt from Paula for the money he paid for the damages. We were to pay him back as best as we could, as we could. He grinned as he said it as though he knew his payback would be a long time coming, if at all.

He spent two days of his leave helping us set up in our new digs, took us out to dinner a couple of times, hit on me without success after we'd stayed up late drinking too much wine one night with Darcy snoring in the back bedroom. During his stay on his leave with his mother and her boyfriend, he did take the Mercury down to Dale's and got it fixed while he hitched rides around town with his old friends, at least from the two or three who were still in town, joining them at the bars they used to haunt before he went into the army. Darcy had to admit the service had done her brother a world of good.

But something close to what I'd call sinister had happened to Darcy with the loss of Algernon. She began coming home at all hours, sometimes not at all, showing up the following evening as though she'd been home after work all along. When I asked her where she'd been, she shrugged, and said she'd drunk too much and went to stay with her mother. I felt certain she was lying but also knew that no amount of inquiry was going to get me anywhere. I was on the edge of confronting her about where she saw our relationship going, when one evening after work, I drove past our old apartment for what reason I couldn't say. Perhaps sheer nostalgia drew me back to where Darcy and I'd had our initial live-in together. And I had to admit I wasn't sure what that time really was but despite all the money, chores and car troubles, it felt, in memory at least, better than what was going on at present.

As I turned the corner onto the street where Paula Boucher's car was still parked in its usual spot in front of her house, I noted a faded blue Chevy sedan in the carport attached to our old apartment. I looked up the street to catch a glimpse of a group of children playing with a cat, which was running around them, jumping back and forth toward one, then another. In an instant, I knew I was looking at Algernon. I'd know that jump anywhere, even if I hadn't recognized the dark thin veneer of Siamese fur. Driving up slowly along the curb, I stopped just short of the intersection where these kids were.

I walked slowly up to them and dropping to my knees, I called for Algernon, who turned and looked at me straightforwardly, seeming to blink several times, before miraculously running toward me. I picked him up and looked him over. He appeared much as he had before, perhaps a bit more disheveled and thinner but there was no doubt, it was Algernon who had a dark black stripe up his nose and a right ear darker than the left. He reached a sharp claw out rapidly, grazing my cheek. I stood up and started turning toward the Mercury.

"Hey," a boy of about twelve yelled at me, walking my way. "Give us back our cat."

"Sorry, kid." I turned back to face him. "But this here little bugger is *my* cat that got out and away from us when we lived in the Boucher apartment up the street." I nodded my head back toward Paula's house. "You wanna complain to somebody about it, just go right ahead." I stared right at him taking some steps toward him, where he'd stopped with a screwed up look on his face. "And you know something," I added for emphasis, "I'm bigger and a helluva lot smarter than you are. In fact, I'm smarter than all of you put together, and I'm tougher as well. So get this. I'll make chicken shit out of the first one who attempts to take this cat away from me. You doubt that, just try it. Don't let my high heels fool you, lads. Because if you do, you'll get the surprise of your life, I promise you that."

I knew it was a crappy thing to say, but I was oddly thrilled, feeling in some twisted way that I was getting even with Paula Boucher for her unspeakable offense to us. I never looked back as I walked toward my car parked at the curb, but I felt the whiz of a rock just missing my leg as I opened the door to the yellow Mercury and set Algy down in the passenger seat. Closing and locking my door as quickly as possible, I started the engine, glancing into the rearview mirror. The boy I'd verbally assaulted stood exactly as he'd been standing when I walked away from him. It occurred to me that he could be memorizing my license number and that this might not be the last I'd hear about my kidnapping. But it was doubtful. The interaction between the cat and the kids struck me as a chance encounter, not one based on ownership. And even if it was, he didn't strike me as caring enough to follow through on a call to the police or the SPCA.

As I turned the car around and drove away, I looked down at Algernon who had placed himself along the back of the seat, stretching out as though he was going to nap, and lying there relaxed as he was, he suddenly raised all his legs and paws up into the air and hung that way, upside down, staring at me. As though fixing me in his world once again, he let out a deep Siamese cry. On the way home, I fully expected him at any moment, to fling himself around, jump onto the back of the seat and start flying all over the interior. But he stayed as he was, continuing to stare at me with the nearest thing I could read as kitty contentment. I couldn't help wondering where he'd been, if the kids or one of the kids on the street had claimed him as an outdoor cat, or if he had become feral, running this way and that, from house to house. Perhaps he was called who knows how many names by the different people he'd encountered while away from us. How long had it been? Months. At least six, seven months since he went missing. It was hard to imagine Algy staying with anybody too long with his bizarre behaviors. But it was harder still to imagine that he was lying in the seat next to me after all this time. It felt oddly predestined. What were the odds of these kids being on the street with Algernon on this day I'd chosen to drive past in the early, still chilly, days of spring?

When Darcy came in late that night, I was on the couch with Algernon in my lap. I hadn't turned on the radio or put music on the player. I was enjoying simply listening to our lost-and-found kitty purr and feel him knead my leg gently after he'd eaten his fill of Cat Chow. Upon seeing him, Darcy dropped everything in her arms, running to us on the couch. Throwing herself against me, she pulled Algy to her, asking, "What? Where? When? How?"

Algy cried out as she kissed and hugged him from head to toe. She shocked me by handing him back to me abruptly, then breaking down uncontrollably. I put Algy on the floor where he laid down immediately and began calmly and uncharacteristically licking himself clean, finishing his interrupted after-dinner preen. I gathered Darcy into my arms, holding her close until her crying subsided. She looked up at me with swollen eyes and asked pathetically, "Will he stay?"

"I believe he will." And he did, but how was I to know when I told Darcy this, that Algy would stay only so long as he could, and when he did go again, I would go with him? I'd based my answer to Darcy's question on a belief I'd observed about his present behavior. He no longer seemed to have any desire to jump and fly. In fact, as time passed, I began noticing that he clung tentatively to the edge of any surface he was considering jumping from, and more often than not, before catapulting himself forward, which he would have done before without hesitation, he'd sit back down and stare at the landing place ahead without conviction. When he did decide to jump, he always missed, landing just shy of where he was aiming to go. He was a sport. I had to give him that. He'd pick himself up, wobble for several steps before gaining his footing and half-running away as though he never intended to go anywhere other than the floor.

One evening when I caught Darcy staring at Algy after he'd fallen down from missing a pulled-out dining room chair, I suggested that we take him to the vet's for an evaluation. She looked at me with concern for a moment, but finally nodded her agreement.

"Without x-rays," the vet told us, "I can't make a definitive diagnosis, of course, but my informed guess from seeing this syndrome in other animals is that Algy has suffered some trauma to his spine. It's left his back legs incapacitated when it comes to jumping. He's able to walk well enough, but if you observe him closely, you'll see he moves his hind legs jerkily and slowly which is indicative of some sort of neurological difficulty."

Darcy gave a little moan and stroked his back. "Is he in pain?"

"No, there's no indication of that at all. I can take him through a series of tests if you like, but if it's the injury I'm expecting, the solution is a very difficult surgery with a long recovery period, and I can't guarantee that it will solve the problem."

"Would it be costly?" Darcy asked in a voice very near a whisper.

"It would." The vet informed her with a sympathetic tilt to her head. "You know, other than needing to adjust a little to his new disability, he seems to be doing just fine." She picked up Algernon's head and looked him directly in the eyes, "I'd take him and love him just as he is, if it were me."

I asked her what could have caused this sort of spinal injury.

"There are a number of possibilities. He could have been struck hard on the back, could have taken a serious fall, been attacked by a dog, could even had had a tendency toward some weakness in a vertebrae that became inflamed with a traumatic event. He wasn't sensitive to my manual examination, so I don't think this is anything you should be alarmed about."

She told us that she simply couldn't know a more precise answer to my question without more information.

Darcy didn't need to give the situation any more thought. In fact, she couldn't get out of the office fast enough. She found the notion of probing around on Algy's spine terrifying, and so we took the vet's advice, carried him home and loved him as he was—now without his most original defining feature—his ability to fly.

In a few following months, though, he became deeply apathetic. He still talked to us from time to time, but seemed content, too content, it seemed to me, to stay in his basket in the bay window sleeping, getting up only to eat, drink water and use the litter box. We both became concerned that Algy's use of the litter box was increasing as well as the amount of water he was drinking. When I found him in his box one Saturday afternoon unable to get up on his own, we knew something was very wrong. He was still a young cat, and he was acting like he was in his elder years.

This time we came home from the vet's with bags of saline solution and an IV after a half hour's demonstration from the technician on how to give Algy fluids daily for his renal failure. Of course, Darcy couldn't bring herself to inject the needle into his thin skin, so I was left with this task. Instead, she took to making him foods which took a great deal of effort and time—

baked or poached fish and chicken with mashed whole grains, boiled egg and tuna sprinkled with dill, or egg, tuna and bacon with a sprinkling of grated cheddar cheese. She also bought him several lap blankets with different soft textures—fleece and fake velvet surfaces which Algy either soiled or scratched at frantically in an attempt to find the worn quilted blankets we'd initially put down in the bottom of his basket.

As Algernon grew steadily stronger from the fluids, Darcy came home regularly from work, looking for any signs of change, especially seeking those of renewed life in him. She noted he was walking faster or more steadily, perceived that he was gaining weight and urinating less, or pointed out that he was playing with us more like he had before he went missing or before he "got sick."

But then toward the end of winter, he took a sudden downward turn. The morning I found him dead in his basket, Darcy left the house early and didn't return until the following morning. We were in a deep winter freeze, despite the approaching spring, temperatures plummeting to four, then ten below zero, the ground hard as a rock. There were only two choices that I could see for the disposal of his body—we could either take him to the vet to be cremated or wait to bury him in the backyard. When I put it to Darcy, she said she couldn't in her wildest dreams imagine cremating him. It would be an image that would haunt her for the rest of her days, she said, so she sat in the living room on the couch, lighting a candle on the coffee table, while I wrapped him in a thin hand towel and plastic, finally laying him in a cardboard shoe box, which I placed in a cleared-out spot in the back left of the freezer unit in our refrigerator. The plan was to have a quiet ceremony for him when the ground thawed enough for a proper burial.

Darcy began coming home hung over and exhausted, falling into bed for days at a time. I say days, but it really was only over the weekends because though she continued to work, she no longer lived at home during the week. Finally she came home only randomly, continuing to restore herself with sleep when she did, getting up on work mornings and leaving without any indication when she would return. She took taxis when she left. I had no idea how she was affording any of this—the cabs, where she was staying, eating. I made every attempt to communicate with her, but she had little to say to me other than refusing anything I offered and asking me to allow her the time and space she needed to adjust. Adjustment was her major explanation and excuse for her comings and goings. It seemed to me that I had no choice, so I let it ride.

Finally, after a couple of long weeks of her not returning home at all, I called Margaret.

"Darcy's always had an independent streak in her. Don't be overly concerned, my dear. She's probably found some man to keep her company, but eventually, she always returns or lets us know where she is."

To me, Margaret didn't quite understand my concern since she didn't know that her daughter and I were more than roommates and friends.

"Oh," she said in that dismissive way of hers, "I don't think we've told you, but Walter and I are moving to Edmond, you know, renting out his acreage, because he's found a sponsor in Oklahoma City for the wooden toys he's been making, and he's certain the market for his product will increase there over time."

"So he's no longer cooking?" Last I heard Walter was still working full-time at the restaurant-bakery where Margaret met him.

"Oh, heaven's no. Didn't Darcy tell you? She can get like this when she's upset, but don't let it worry you. It'll pass." She stopped long enough for me to hear an intake of breath. "We were married in a civil ceremony, intentionally not informing his two boys or you, Darcy and Curly so we could keep everything quiet—without a lot of hullabaloo, you know." She informed me that they wanted to get relocated before the announcement, away from the place their kids called home which she and Walter felt would only raise all sort of objections and turmoil.

"Now that everything's settled, everybody will simply have to adjust."

There was that word again. It did occur to me that this is where Darcy had probably learned to use it.

My call to Curly wasn't much more reassuring.

"Naw," he said lazily over the line. "She hasn't contacted me either, but she does these disappearing acts every now and then, especially over something like Algy. But I wouldn't get too concerned yet. I'm surprised you don't know this about her by now. Hell, all of us in her family do." He made it sound like Darcy had a vastly extended family, instead of only himself and Margaret.

And it seemed that Curly's recent life had taken much the same arc as his mother's.

"I've signed up for another tour in the army, if you can believe this." He was all excitement about what he called his 'new life.' "I've met this wonderful woman in Texas who's moving with me to Germany, of all places, well, that's if my orders grant it, but my commanding officer doesn't foresee a problem. We're planning to stay in Stuttgart, at least until my tour ends in four years."

If his new wife wasn't able to accompany him, he said, he'd return home on leave as often as he could. He would be working to help American troops establish themselves on bases as they were being shipped into the country. Martina, this new wife, was pregnant with their first child, and he couldn't be happier. So here was another significant change in Darcy's family that she'd failed to tell me about. Curly went on without inquiring into my life or my concerns about Darcy.

"I'll letcha know if Darcy gives me a call, but knowing her, the way she is at times like this, I really doubt that she will. You know, I think if I were you, I'd turn over a new leaf and start living without her. She isn't the kind of person who's going to remain in one place very long. She just doesn't attach herself to anybody for any length of time—except for Mother and me, of course."

I hung up realizing how very far removed I was from him, despite Curly's involvement in Darcy and my life before he left for his return to Fort Hood. I suddenly wanted to take his advice and turn that new page—to call Margaret and tell her that I'd decided to give up the house on Spelling and seek another place, cheaper place, one of my own, perhaps just a room. But every time I started to lift the telephone to call, I put the receiver back in the cradle wondering if it was possible for me to end a relationship this way. It wasn't in my nature. If I walked out with things hanging in the air, it felt as though the whole time with Darcy lacked meaning with no definitive answer as to what had actually taken place or what was happening now. It felt as though Darcy had gone suddenly missing in a way that made it seem I'd made her up and our living together had been created from my imagination, as though she hadn't actually happened. I had heard people explain the end of a relationship as sometimes not having closure. Perhaps what I was feeling was what this meant. Whether it was right or wrong, best for me or not, I found I simply could not leave without knowing what had happened to her, to us.

So I began a restless pursuit to find her.

I started my search by going to her work place at Sturges Department Store where I received the first in a series of shocks I was to experience in the days ahead. Darcy had resigned her position three weeks earlier, receiving her last check thirteen days ago. The customer service department told me they could not give me her forwarding address even if they had it, which they did not. I stumbled down Main Street and around the corner to the nearest bar, where I had a double scotch on the rocks and asked the bartender if—this purely on a whim—he knew Darcy. I held out a picture of her I pulled from my wallet, much like detectives do in crime shows on television. He did know "this woman," he said, handing the photo back to me, but he hadn't seen her in a couple of weeks.

"Unusual, real unusual," he said, "because she often stopped for a drink after work, not staying more than an hour or so, but Darcy was a regular, steady customer. And then all at once two, three weeks ago, she stopped showing up."

He gave me other possible lounges, his name for bars like the one we were in, where she might have gone, but he doubted that she would be found in any of them, because, he didn't think she would suddenly prefer other places to what she called her "home away from home," by which I took he meant his bar. I curtailed my drinking after a couple of the other places where I went to look for her, because I knew if I didn't, I'd never have made it home standing upright. After no known sightings of Darcy in any of the seven lounges I trudged in and out of, I went home and fell into bed, not bothering to undress.

Over the next several days, after work, I exhausted the possibilities of where she might be. I even went to see one of the commanders of personnel at the Air Force base where Wolfgang Becker had been stationed and died, but I embarrassed myself by not knowing exactly what to ask.

When I finally found somebody who knew what I was talking about, I simply told the officer I was trying to locate a friend who had dated several pilots at the base, one in particular, and wondered if he knew how I might go about finding who any of these men might be in order to talk to them. I gave him Darcy's name and Wolfgang Becker's.

He looked at me with blinking, but clear blue eyes. "There's no way I can really help you, ma'am. Over three hundred pilots are at the field, and most of them dated girls from town at one time or another. To search down this Wolfgang Becker, I could do that, but if he's been killed in an accident, as you say, I'd have to have permission for information concerning him to be released, you understand? Information to anyone outside the military about individual servicemen is for the family only. And to be frank, even if permission could be procured, I simply don't have the resources right now or the time."

I walked out of his office, not only feeling like an idiot, but ashamed that I'd given him Darcy's name. He had to have wondered why I was concerned to the degree I was, especially with such little information. Girlfriends don't ordinarily keep track of girlfriends with this much interest.

"Do you have any reason to suspect foul play of any kind?" he'd asked me.

"Well, no. Not really."

"Did she leave a note telling you of any reportable incident having to do with a pilot at this base?"

Again, I had to answer no. His questions only indicated to me how weak my rationale for attempting to find Darcy was, not only with him, but everywhere I'd gone. The commander had been kind, even condescendingly polite, but I knew he was covering his own behind just in case something was amiss as much as attempting to help me out.

So I gave up the search.

Each evening I came home to an empty house, and so it went, until the weather changed to warmer, steady temperatures, sometimes ushering in storms which brought hail, lightning and chaos which was the usual transition to spring in these parts of the country and what I now viewed as the perfect atmosphere for my meaningless, despairing situation. Our hometown was not hit directly by a severe storm or tornado but Edmond was. It was an excuse to check in with Margaret, who told me the storm had been a frightening experience, but they were fine as they weren't hit directly so didn't have much property damage and went on to inform me that Walter's business was booming.

"I've not heard a thing, you know," she informed me concerning Darcy before I asked. "But she'll call one day, outta the blue, like she does, and then I'll call you, of course." How Margaret and I would communicate this, I wasn't sure, as she didn't say, but I didn't push for more.

And then, in a sudden rush of insight, I told her I hadn't called just to check on her and Walter's safety, I'd also wanted to let her know that I was leaving her house-apartment within the next thirty days—the required time to inform her of my leaving according to contract. She took it in surprising stride.

"Well, if you leave, my dear, I'll simply sell the place. Now, if you change your mind, about leaving, I mean, I could sell it to you at a very fair price."

"Thanks, Margaret, but I need to move on."

"Well, in light of what's happening, with Darcy's leaving as she has and all, I certainly understand that."

"I'm not sure what to do about the Mercury, though. Darcy's pretty much left it to me by default, so I don't feel it's truly mine to take."

"Well, I don't know, dear…"

"Tell you what. I'll leave it in the drive, so when you come to get the property ready for sale, you can take it with you to Edmond."

"Oh, I don't know about this, really. It's Curly's, by rights, so why don't you give him a call? He's the one to decide, I would think." I thanked her and hung up.

I wasn't sure about keeping the Mercury, should Curly offer it to me. It seemed somewhat central in the whole Darcy drama which I was beginning to realize now I wanted to get as far away from as possible. But I gave Curly one more call, and we settled on a price that I couldn't refuse, telegraphing him the money in exchange for the title to the car which arrived in less than two weeks.

In the meantime, I began packing my belongings in boxes I got from the grocery store around the corner and up the street. I took my time as I really didn't need to rush since I had a month of paid rent. I didn't look for a place in town. I decided to go into free fall and see where I landed or see if I landed on my feet at all. Perhaps, like Algernon, I'd wobble out of town on not-so-sure footing without looking to see if I cared or not. Packing was a snap as I'd brought little to the affair and so there wasn't much to take with me.

When the weather seemed to have settled, I took Algernon from the freezer one Saturday morning, dug a hole at the end of the property line and placed him deep inside. I couldn't bring myself to look into the box. I didn't want to remember him from the freezer, his stiff-as-a-board cindered body desiccated over time, his fur probably clinging to him like a waterlogged rat. I covered the hole without ceremony, standing still for a moment, bending over the shovel as though a figure in Millet's *The Angelus,* then without a word, turned and walked out of Darcy's life. She got her way in the end, I thought. No statement on any of it anymore, really. I certainly wasn't going to subject Algy to any more response than necessary. He lived enough in my head as it was.

One evening I came home to find the door unlocked and a strange car in the drive. With caution, I entered the apartment to find Darcy seated at the table with a cup of coffee in hand, smiling as though she had been there every evening from work all along. I simply walked to the other side of the table and took a seat. She waited, perhaps expecting me to ask where she'd been. I didn't say a word. She was as gorgeous and sexy as ever. Nothing like the bedraggled woman I thought I'd finally see, if that ever came to pass. It was as though we were in that booth in that bar back when we'd first met, beginning all over again. She shook her head and her red hair moved softly in the kitchen light. She looked at me directly with those clear green, hazel eyes, the ones I'd fallen into that night five, six long years ago.

"Aren't you going to get a cup of coffee and be friendly?"

"I can be friendly without the cup of coffee, Darcy."

"I owe you an apology, I know. I've come to pick up what things I've left behind..." she paused at her mismanagement of words.

"I'm not a thing," I said, working to keep contentiousness out of my voice. "But, I doubt that you've come back to pick me up." I paused, watching, as she pulled her lips over her teeth in a grim imitation of a smile and looked down. I decided to let her off easy, why not? I had nothing to lose anymore. She, our life together, was gone. "But I know what you mean, I think. I'm gathering my things as well, so nothing will be left behind."

"Well said." She cleared her throat. "I've met a man. It's where I've been all these nights away from...." She stumbled over the word 'home,' and chose to substitute "you" instead, saying again that "being with him" is where she'd been, if I cared to know.

I informed her that I had attempted to locate her, to know not *where* she was so much as *how* she was. "It would have been the kind thing to do, at the very least, to let your Mother and Curly know that you were all right."

"I've called them. They know. They both are married, did you know this?" She smiled at me as though we were having a conversation as new acquaintances, just after I'd met her mother and brother. She had to know I'd talked with them, because she'd talked with them. God only knew when. And with this thought, I realized I no longer believed in any of these people.

I said nothing.

"Well," she said with finality, "so it is. I...well, I just couldn't continue to live with you anymore."

"Nothing could have been more obvious, Darcy," I replied matter-of-factly.

She was sorry, oh so very sorry, she said. But now that she was again with a man, she realized that she wasn't...well, whatever it was that we'd been together, she couldn't be *that*.

I wasn't too stunned by her sudden appearance and detached attitude to not be angry. I attempted to force her to say what she didn't want to admit. "And what was it exactly that you thought we'd been?"

"Well, you know...*that*."

"Oh, but you were *that* and very willingly and for a good long while." But I knew this was only partly true, because I'd known from the very first evening together that this time, as it was right now between us, was coming. I shook my head. "It doesn't matter, Darcy. Truly. Just get your things and go." I got up from the table, indicated where I'd put her things, and walked out of the room.

I heard her rummaging around in the closet where I'd put all of her belongings together and after listening to a couple of her walks up and down the stairs, I heard the slamming of a car door, the starting of the engine and the slow crawl of the car's tires along the drive and out onto the street. I spent the evening packing everything in the Mercury, unplugging the already defrosted refrigerator, throwing the leftovers in the kitchen trash can and then hoisting the entire can into the outdoor barrel. I slept deeply that night on clean sheets without so much as a squirm.

The morning sunlight streaking across the bed from the curtainless window awakened me, followed by a familiar cry of a Siamese cat stretched out on the bed no more than two feet in front of me. I closed my eyes and waited for reality to sink into my foggy brain. In the mornings, I never was much use until after my first cup of coffee. But the muted crying continued so I squinted, opened an eye and gave the feline presence on my bed another peek. Algernon Moncrieff was preening himself right next to me in the full light of day. I reached out tentatively and stroked his charcoal fur. He looked up at me, momentarily stopping his cleaning ritual, taking me in as though he was placing me in his world once again before he went back to his task of licking himself from head to toe.

I threw my legs over the side of the bed, stood, walked to the bedroom window and looked out across the yard to the lilac bush and maple tree where in a small niche I'd dug the hole for Algy and buried him only days before. The ground was smooth with newly grown grass, not one sign of the small mound of dirt and stone I'd placed on it to indicate Algy's final resting place. I turned around quickly, fully expecting him to have disappeared, but he was still very much there, leg in the air now, head into his inner thigh in that characteristic pose cats take when they intend to give themselves a complete saliva bath.

In my slippers and house coat, glancing back at the bed before leaving the room, I went downstairs, out the back door to the trash barrel I'd left by the side of the garage. Inside I found the kitchen trash can with leftovers from the refrigerator I'd thrown there the night before, nothing else.

I simply could not resist walking to the small niche at the edge of the lawn and scraping the grass with the heel of my foot. In the area where I'd dug the hole, or thought I'd dug the hole, there were no signs of anything other than grass having grown at the same rate and color as that everywhere else around it. I stared out across the yard, then walked around the periphery of the lot, wondering if I'd somehow confused where I'd dug Algy's burial place. At the far end of the property, I stood immobile as a statue for a long time, finally looking up at the bedroom window on the second floor. It felt as though I'd walked through some portal, some anomaly as described in so many science fiction novels, and entered another world and time from the one in which I'd fallen asleep only a few hours before. But nothing appeared or even felt eerie or strange about the environment around me. Everything in the yard and outside of the apartment was exactly as it had always been every single morning I'd arisen and gone to work. The Mercury stood exactly in the spot where I'd left it when I'd come home yesterday afternoon.

Once more, in the house, I walked through each room making sure I'd not left anything behind. Picking up Algernon, I stripped the bed of the sheets in one fast grab and pull, rolling them in a wad around him much like a mother would hold a baby in a blanket and walked with him out to the car. I opened the door to the yellow Mercury and set Algy down in the passenger seat. Closing and locking my door as quickly as possible, I glanced down at him as he stretched himself along the back of the seat, as though he was going to nap; and lying there relaxed as he was, he suddenly raised all his legs and paws up into the air and hung that way, upside down, staring at me. I started the engine, backed out of the drive and onto the street while he continued staring at me with utter kitty contentment.

On a sudden whim, I drove by the mailbox, open the lid and extracted one letter there. I had stopped the mail the day before, but it evidently took time for the notice to become effective. I glanced at the return address and then at the clear, plastic opening showing my name and address. It was from West Mountain Review and the paper looked interestingly like the light green shade and texture of a commercial check. In a gesture of great abandon, I threw it unopened over my shoulder onto the back seat. It couldn't be much, I reasoned. After all, it was only an obscure review and it figured so small in the jerky shift my life had taken forward.

"Okay then, buddy," I said aloud, as though Algy'd understand exactly what I was saying to him. "Let's see how our world spins itself out this time." He let out a not so soft, deep Siamese cry as I glanced in the rearview mirror watching the Spelling Avenue house grow smaller and smaller behind us.

THE FLIRTING

She is standing on the stoop, sneakers partly hanging over, like she's pedaling a bike. Her hands are fists in her pockets. She's hunkered down, protecting her neck from the cold. When I drive up, she drops her cigarette and smashes it with her sneaker. I notice she doesn't have her stocking cap on like usual.

I swirl the truck around like I'm casing the A and W and stop so that she can see me through the passenger's side window. "Are you open yet?" I mouth through the glass. My truck is so old it still has manual knobs for rolling down the windows. I'm thinking she's the woman who always pumps my gas, but then I'm not so sure, now that I'm closer and see her grey hair all in curls without the cap. She nods largely and grins.

I back up so I'm not blocking the door and jump out. I start to walk over to where she is, but she's coming my way, so I stop and wait. She's grinning at me, shyly, like I'm young, fresh and good looking. I know she's a dyke. She knows I know, but she's not so sure about me. We both know we aren't going to mention any of this outright.

"Good mornin'," I say, my Okie accent very thick. She nods and takes her hands a bit out of her pockets, hanging her thumbs over the edges, like her index fingers are the barrels of toy guns.

"I got my truck looked at yesterday at the Quick Lube," I say enthusiastically, talking as slow as I can, lifting my eyes a bit. What the hell am I doing, I wonder. I'm flirting with her, for godssakes. Well, why not, I'm thinking? I straighten my smile and soften my twang, trying to fit more comfortably into the stirrings deep inside. "They told me the transmission pan needs a new gasket or seal or some such and I may be leaking fluid." She nods seriously, looking right at me. I continue: "Uh, I have to drive to....make a trip, out of town." Now I'm utterly self-conscious. For chrissakes where else would a trip be but out of town? "I'm afraid I may be too low for that." I am solemn, grasping for composure. "I wonder if you'd mind taking a look." Her eyes don't move. They are sealed to my face.

"Oh sure," she says casually, not noticing that her positive answer makes her reply a negative. I swallow. Jesus Christ, what's the matter with me? "Just let me find a rag." She disappears on the run into the station. She comes back on the same run with a blue floppy something in her hand. She starts to put the hood up and I say, "I have the owner's manual inside. I think this might be the one." I point to a dip stick with a yellow ring on it.

"Nope." She leans over to pull out another stick on the other side of the engine. "This is the one." She looks the stick over carefully, then holds it shakily in front of me and as it bobs up and down, she says, "Really low."

"Yeah," I say, feeling silly. What is going on? I am perfectly happy in my situation at home. I have a partner who understands me, loves me and that's reciprocal. All at once with this grease monkey, I'm hormonal putty? "Do you have any transmission fluid? The manual says Dexron." I want to kick myself. Why the hell am I asking if they have transmission fluid? It's a car repair filling station. It's why I'm here. Jesus. She obviously knows what she's doing. I keep throwing information from the owner's manual at her, like I sit reading it every night at six.

"Sure do." She puts the stick on the hood. At least she didn't say, "Of course." She runs on short legs back inside. When she comes out, two cars are huffing and puffing at the pumps. A woman unrolls her window and glares at me. My mechanic comes running up with a black plastic bottle and funnel in her hand and begins to put a funnel in the hole where she took out the dip stick. But the funnel wobbles precariously each time she tries to insert it.

"It's okay if you catch those two." I take the funnel like I know what I'm doing. I wanna say, "It'll give me some time to collect myself." But of course, I fiddle with the funnel like it's malfunctioning and needs an expert hand.

"Thanks," she says without looking at me, and she's gone, to the window side of the Honda.

Ten minutes later she comes back, wiping her hands on the blue rag and apologizing. I hold up my hand. I am calm, cool. Of course, I've been watching her the whole time. "No need," I say like an executive in a tailored-for-success suit.

"Always busy when I got somethin' else to do." She takes the funnel I've managed to get in place and begins to pour the transmission fluid down the hole. Halfway through the job, the funnel moves and transmission fluid runs down the side of the engine. Smoke rises, and she groans. "Well, you're not gonna smell too good for a while." I laugh. She looks up and grins, then puts the cap on the empty bottle. Her eyes are grey, like her hair, with flecks of light in them. I can't see her body, her legs. Everything is hidden behind the Carhartt work overalls. "Sorry about that," she says as she gets ready to lower the hood.

"It's okay." I smile. "Really it is."

"I used to work on my truck." She snaps the hood and runs the blue rag over the finger prints she's left there. She takes her time cleaning the spot where she'd put the dip stick. "But ya can't do that anymore. You have to take five, six parts away before you can get to the one you need to change." She looks at my truck with something like affection. "This is a beaut."

"How much do I owe you?"

"Three dollars and forty-five cents," she says, then adds quickly, "for the fluid."

I hold out a five. "It's yours." I think, *Big spender.*

She says thanks and walks toward the station. As I snap my seat belt in and begin driving away, I see she's back on the stoop, rocking a bit on her heels there.

And that's the way she looks when I see her again. She's grinning at me, looking at me full face. I park my truck and walk up to her saying,

"Wow, what the hell is that?" I'm pointing at a huge tractor with magnum wheels parked under the billboard announcing "Charles Marsh's Sunoco Convenience Mart."

She laughs and takes her hands out of her pockets and waves one in the direction I'm pointing. "It's *my* truck, what else?"

I look back at the tractor, and suddenly we are in a barn behind the station I'd never noticed before. It's full of these tractors, the kind with wheels so big you have to have a ladder to get into them.

Several have drivers revving their engines. And then, just as suddenly, all of them begin to move, like giant ants or beetles, toward a starting line. The roar is enormous. I put my hands over my ears, and my mechanic is bent back laughing.

Then I feel my foot stepping on some soft gooey stuff and realize I am not able to move. She doesn't seem to notice that I can't move. She is walking toward a tractor parked to the side. I think, *She is going to race with them*. I am overcome by the feeling I am being left behind, that I could have gone along for the ride, but I am planted, unable to lift my feet to run with her.

I reach down to get my boot out of the smelly goo. I pull my leg up and with my hand I touch the stuff holding me in place. It peels off easily and when I look closer at it, I see that it is tire tread. I am holding the rubbery thing up when my clock's luminous dial reads 6:30. I snap off the button, just before the alarm goes off.

My first fully waking thought is to wonder why I didn't just tell her that my father worked as a mechanic for the Chrysler Corporation for forty years but none of that engine repair stuff rubbed off on me. At least she'd know I'm not a total doofus about her passion. But there's another less realizable feeling, an uneasiness that takes its place. I lay my hand palm down on the still warm spot where Madeleine spent the night by my side. I hear the sputtering of the coffeemaker and hear Maddie's singing in the kitchen. I fling the blankets back, turn in place and set my feet down on the carpeted floor. I'm floating, I think, between some knowledge that I don't quite understand yet and a curiosity that knows no bounds. My desire is to be awakened, to see and feel something that's hiding in the middle.

"Honey," Maddie calls up the stairs. "You better get a move on. You're running late."

I continue to sit, as immovable as in my dream. I reach down to feel the bottom of my foot and almost laugh out loud. I'm not as glued to my spot as I dreamed I was.

"I'm on the move," I yell down the stairs on my way to the beginning of another day.

ROBERTA

I've read a lot of fiction. I've read a lot of mysteries. I've read so many that sometimes I feel like I'm in them, you know, walking down sin-riddled streets, wearing a fedora, brim turned down, or a beret, hanging on the side of my head, or even a trench coat, collar turned up, with a hard-boiled scowl on my face and a cigarette, waiting for a light, dangling from my lips. I dream of being the savvy, sassy detective straight out of film noir or from the pages of the likes of Grafton, Scoppettone, Cornwell, Reichs, Tey and Sayers.

Truth is, I'm only an ordinary person absolutely terrified of bullets, guns and knives, but that doesn't mean I don't do my fair share of sleuthing. Maybe "sleuthing" isn't the right word since I'm not covertly observing people in the sense of sitting in a hotel lobby with a newspaper and sporadically peering around its edges attempting to find the person of interest, record what he or she does, and then consign this bit of observation to my mental file which I later retrieve for some case I'm trying to solve.

What I do is more like nosing around to satisfy my own curiosity. In my kind of detecting, I *stumble upon* people and interpret what I think their motives are for what they're doing and then decide how that fits into my life.

Now take for instance, the woman driving ahead of me in downtown traffic right now who's swatting at her kids in the backseat of their beat-up Chevy. I watch her, decide she's tired, is undoubtedly listening to hard rock, and desperately wishes she hadn't done her two boyfriends to make these kids happen. But that's an easy case. I lived in that one myself, my deadbeat parents doing the swatting and resenting, until I grew up to be seventeen, left them, taking one hundred fifty dollars I stole from their pockets, and then worked the rest of my way through college as a claims clerk in the registration office at a small college in Pennsylvania, tuition-free gratis for twenty-five hours a week. You talk about a place to do some real detective work. It's a wonder I had time for study! Working there had its advantages, though, because my kind of observing has quite naturally turned me into a writer about ordinary people and the ordinary stuff they do, which has led to some extraordinary plots, that's when I bother to follow the line of the story all the way through. This is one of those.

But the part of this story that's different is that I got caught in a circumstance in which I became the person I was observing, while I thought it was somebody else. In other words, I got caught in my own detecting game. And it was the chick on the bus who did it to me. What I'm trying to say is that what should have been the most ordinary of events—a bus trip from Long Island to Oklahoma City to visit my brother—turned out to be the most exceptional experience of my life.

So why was I on a thirty-five hour bus ride when I so easily could have flown in half the time, even with stopovers in terminals along the way? Okay, it's hard to admit but the night before I was scheduled to leave my local airport I received a premonition, a really hard-to-overlook message that I was going to die in an airplane crash. In what I took to be a prophetic dream, I went flying head first out of a Delta Airlines window, still strapped to my seat, and just before I hit a patch of pastureland somewhere in the Central Plains from an altitude of twenty-five thousand feet, I woke up.

So at the break of dawn, I called Trailways. Amtrak had started up by then, but with a whole lot of hitches, so I opted to go by bus, which had lots of hitches too, but I told myself it would be cheaper. In the long run it wasn't, with all those stops at diners and fast food places along the way. Some charged New York City prices for a plain sandwich. At others, I had to pay to pee. But looking back, I realize if I hadn't taken that Trailways bus, I never would've met Roberta, which brings up the whole issue of cosmic intervention and, therefore, raises more questions than any I got answered, and believe me, what I did get answered was quite enough.

She was sitting alone when I got on. I was expecting to find the bus filled by this time, because I'd left the house late, playing with Harley, my parakeet, before leaving him to the silence of the house broken only by the radio I'd set on a timer and by my friend Alice who was coming in daily to whisper to him and drop some seeds in one cup and pour water in the other. But from the time I got on that bus, I felt like I was a character in a conveyor-belt narrative leading me toward some teleological conclusion I knew not what. It certainly wasn't anything I could've planned, even thought up. I guess it's one of those gifts of life, a stone thrown in your path by the gods who make you take a side step that changes the direction of your life forever.

—

Here I stand on the last step on the inside of the bus, looking around and there she sits alone, holding a compact mirror in front of her, applying lipstick, twisting the tube down and snapping the lid back on with her thumb, and me staring at her while she runs a pinkie back and forth over her lower lip, then wiping her finger clean with a tissue. I never learned to do things like this, really feminine things, like putting on lipstick in one movement, then gritting my teeth in front of a mirror to look for smears, and checking my stockings for runs or sags while tugging my skirt down. I did these things when I was twenty like every other woman I knew, but I always felt like my mother was doing them inside me, like you felt when you were a little kid and got into her closet and played grown-up. This woman does this stuff for real—she's making quick little movements with her hands, fluffing her hair, slapping her cheeks, powder puffing her face, pulling down her t-shirt. Now she looks up as though she's expecting me, gives me a big smile and says, "Hi, I'm Roberta. Please don't sit over there where you're going. I'd love it if you'd sit with me." She snaps her compact closed and drops it in her purse that she closes with another snap, and finally ends it all by sliding the clutch between her thigh and the side of her seat.

Her voice is deep and throaty, and I have this odd sensation that I've just stepped through the cover of a Mickey Spillane paperback, one of those throwbacks from yesteryear hanging in plastic at the Now and Again Bookstore, stamped thirty-five cents but selling these days for six bucks.

"Are you talking to me?" I look around as though other people are everywhere, filling every cockeyed seat, me setting my duffel bag down where I was intending to sit, across the aisle and up a couple of rows from her. I never carry a hard suitcase since my Samsonite got badly bashed on a flight back from Cologne a long time ago. I attempt to disregard her invitation by reaching to move a pillow left on the seat by an earlier passenger.

Roberta bursts out laughing in that sensual no-laugh-at-all Lauren Bacall-ish way—little sound, all air—so that I stop and smile back at her inanely. "Looks like you and me are the only ones around." She pats the seat beside her. Before I can decline her offer, she says, "Look, it's going to be a long ride and hours before the next stop. We might as well keep each other company."

I shrug, pick up my bag and dump it on the seat across the aisle from her. She moves over to the window spot and clears the way for me to make an easy entrance next to her. Once I'm seated, she looks right at me and says, "There now!" She has impeccably shaped eyebrows, large warm eyes, perfectly Maybelline-d lashes and long red hair that's falling lightly across her shoulders. Her face is the spitting image of every actress I've ever seen on the silver screen. It's hard not to stare, but her eye-leveling gaze makes me uneasy so I look away. I'd look like an idiot if I attempted a gaze like that. Where does such self-assurance come from? Undoubtedly from the mirror and, well, the silver screen, whether she's really on it or not.

I try to hide my shuddering sigh. I'm not at all sure about what I've gotten myself into. It's one of the strangest situations, me sitting here next to this woman I don't know on this Trailways bus that seats no less than seventy people and nobody else showing up. It's a lot like those times at the matinees just before the feature begins when you're the only one in the theater and you're wondering if they're even going to show the movie for you alone, when this one person comes in at the last minute and sits down right in front of you. This has happened to me more than once, and I've wondered what causes that. Strange, at the very least. I didn't get up and move any of those times, that's even stranger when you think about it. My sitting there without moving must've had something to do with my worrying whether this person would think I thought they were offensive in some way or something. Why would I care? Just dumb crazy is my thought now.

So when the driver gets on and thanks us stiffly for traveling with Trailways, looking from side to side giving the company line as if the whole bus is filled with business men from a whisky convention, I have to stifle a laugh. I look over at Roberta who's taken out a small plastic bag that I see is filled with Ruffles potato chips, is opening the top with long red immaculately polished nails and finally shaking the bag, offers me some with a smile. I hear my voice squeak, "No thanks," attempting to get out my bestseller as I watch her crunch down, blood red lips over a wavy chip, without dropping a crumb. "Don't you just expect Roy and Dale to show up singing 'Happy Trails?'" she giggles deep down inside herself past the mouth of Ruffles.

The bus jerks out of its spot and turns with small grinding spurts. I hold onto my book like a grab strap on a subway and struggle to stabilize my attention in the direction of the flow of words and what the author is saying.

"Are you going the distance?" Roberta asks.

"Excuse me?" I respond, knowing I heard her clearly.

"You going to Portland? That's where the ride terminates."

I clear my throat as though I'm the one who's been eating the potato chips. I certainly feel like something's stuck in my throat. "Portland? Well, I suppose I could, that's where a friend I know from college lives, and I'd love to see her, but, no, I'm going to Oklahoma City. I'll be switching at Chicago, and then St. Louis. Long way around, but it's something about bus line trouble running through Indianapolis, some strike with the drivers' local union or the mechanics or some such. Don't ask me why it's only Indianapolis, I didn't ask." Why in god's name I'm taking the long way around in my explanation I'll never know. I'm being congenial, right? Not a rude bone in my body!

I start to ask her if she's in for the long haul herself—obviously she must be since she knows the bus route terminates in Portland—when I seem to pass into a time-space zone of my own, not hearing a thing she's saying, though it seems like she's talking to me, her lips moving in unison with the flowing landscape through the window over her shoulder. The bus is smoothing down the highway sending us swaying in an easy motion, while I'm sensing a gap between what had immediately taken place before and what's happening now. Am I in some kind of dream? Everything around me doesn't feel exactly real—the woman next to me, the empty bus with the driver seemingly a football field's length from us, the easy swaying of the ride down the road. But at the same time, if I'm dreaming, I'm definitely aware of it and that's not usual, is it? And I'm relatively comfortable, pretty much at ease, just moving along with Roberta by my side, watching the world swish by. Then as though to answer my concern, Roberta grabs my duffel bag that I've placed between my feet and pushes it under her seat. She doesn't say anything, just reaches over and does this, making one of these silent charade kind of signs that says, "I'll get it out of your way by putting it here." I don't stop her, though the idea flits in, then out, of my mind. It's at this moment that I see the bird tattoo, a parakeet, a good-sized yellow-and green-Harley, to the very feather, staring back at me from her upper arm.

"Do you ride motorcycles?" I ask—this coming from some hidden place I know not where.

"God, no." She gives me a luscious smile, patting the bird on her arm she undoubtedly caught me noticing. "I like to feel airborne. But I'm chicken. I never fly. Not by plane or bike! I always travel by bus." I watch her take another Ruffle out of her plastic bag and snap it between her teeth. She really has my attention now. I'm more or less mesmerized. Enthralled is more like it. "I have a twin brother," she continues as though I've asked her some important question about her life. "His tattoo is exactly like mine except it's an eagle."

She laughs throatily again. She laughs a lot, actually. "So I guess it's really totally different. His is a magnificent bird in flight, about to land—it's like mine that way, but his eagle's talons are spread ready for grasping this branch that runs down his bicep to his elbow, where it snakes its way around, running underneath until it becomes a vine wrapping around his wrist like a bracelet." Her red nail follows the trail of her brother's tattoo along her arm, not quite touching, as though her parakeet was on her finger taking a little stroll. "We got them at the same time, at this little shop called "Skin SM-Art," in Grand Junction, Colorado. That's 'smart' with a capital S and M and then a hyphen with a capital A, like S-M, Art." When I don't say anything—what's to say?—she goes on, "He had to go back quite a few times, of course, to finish it all—took, as I remember, over twenty hours—so we stayed in that town for a while. Beautiful area. God, the mountains are majestic."

Uneasiness begins in my chest and spreads to my breathing. My heartbeat picks up, but I attempt to stay calm. Now that I'm more or less committed to this seat and my duffel bag is under hers, I figure I might as well see if I can make some sense out of her drift. I try for a little normalizing conversation.

"I've been to Grand Junction once. My brother and I were coming back from California." She stops eating and holds a potato chip suspended in midair when I say this, and an odd queasy trembling begins inside. 'I, we, didn't have such a good time of it there. In California, I mean. I found work, but it was the recession, back in the early sixties. I had to pay a lot of money for my job that I got through an agency. My brother was young, a teenager, seventeen as I remember, and he didn't look for work, wanted to hang around doing nothing, so I shoved him off to a Navy recruiting office. When he got out of boot camp, we left and went back to Oklahoma together." I say all this in one big rush and when I get it out, Roberta chomps down on her Ruffles, still listening, her eyes glued on me. Incredibly, I continue to babble on. "We stopped at Grand Junction for an overnight. It turned out to be several days because I got sick. With stomach cramps so horrendous I thought I'd have to go to emergency. Probably food poisoning at some rest stop along the way. You aren't going to believe this, but I think I know the parlor you're talking about. I passed it on the way to the supermarket, on Main Street, when we stopped to stock up before leaving town. I don't think it was called 'Skin SM-Art' though. It was something else. So maybe it wasn't the same shop at all. It just hit me that… well, I remembered when you were talking that there were a number of bird tattoos all over this shop's front windows—a flying chickadee or maybe it was a canary, some small bird caught my attention…in particular."

Closing my eyes, I see the shop's window clearly and begin reporting what I'm seeing as my vision moves across the window. "And a blackbird with an olive branch shaped like a peace sign in its beak, an enormous white heron or egret opening its wings, and a pelican with a fish falling into its mouth...." I'm trying to see more when I come back to my senses, glancing around as though the movie I've been watching has ended, and I realize I'm not where the picture has taken me.

Embarrassed, I mumble to Roberta, "...well, that sorta thing." She doesn't say a word, still as a church mouse, watching me. I fill the silence. "I've always wanted one, a tattoo, but it seems so, oh I don't know, so unlike what I'd normally think of myself wearing, if wearing is the right word. I mean, you have it forever, don't you? It's not like a coat you can put on and then take off." Her eyes are on me unmoving, listening, that's if eyes that greenish gray can hear you. *She's so intense*, I'm thinking when she speaks again.

"Good God, I didn't think before I did this." She's grinning, breaking the mood, her head to the side a little, while she flips potato chip crumbs that aren't there from her lap. I look her over when she's busy with this. She wearing a baggy blue-grey t-shirt, same as that actress from *Flashdance*, Jennifer Beals, with a navy-blue tank top underneath, no bra, and tight-fitting jeans, and, I notice with a start, very high black heels. She's tall already—she's got to be from where her knees jut out from the edge of her seat—so this takes some real spunk. She fidgets with her seat's adjustments, pushing a button that makes a little pop, after which she falls back comfortably, gently squirming around.

"Robert and I passed the shop, and I just went in with him and did it. Robert's my twin brother's name, of course. Evidently our mother was not only irresponsible—she left us with her parents when we were babies and never came back—but not very inventive either, at least not in the names department. Robert and Roberta. Kinda cute though, especially since he calls me Robbie and I call him Bobby, but he doesn't like anybody else to. He's sensitive about his feminine side. We're both queer as two marbleized ducks."

Now I feel my breath in my mouth like a shallow pool. What she says hits me like a tidal wave, but I stay as calm as Laguna Beach on a sunny day, carefully closing my book, but bobbing up and down in water way over my head, sucking in air through my nose and mouth softly, like I'm about to drown and don't want the lifeguard to notice. I swallow and sit there for hours and hours waiting for my mouth to dry up and my breathing to be restored.

"Are you lesbian?" she asks in the next breath.

My mouth flies open, and it stays this way. Nothing comes out. I don't seem to be able to close it. I have lockjaw. And I can't look at her. I just sit there with my mouth half open staring at the seat in front of me. She reaches over and pushes my chin gently up until my lips meet. I sense her nails ever so lightly touching my throat. They feel like small machetes. I look at her, sort of, from the side.

"Oh, don't mind me." She gives my knee a little nudge. "I'm compulsively curious. It is forever getting me in trouble." She scrounges around in her huge pocketbook again and pulls out another plastic bag. This time it's Cheez-Its. She untwists the tie and shakes the bag toward me, and I reach in for two, automatically.

What am I doing?

"I just love being lesbian," she says as easily as you would drink a glass of rum punch, once the umbrella is gone. "It gives me incredible confidence with people. I've found most folks are terrified of who they have going in and out of their underwear most of the time—who am I kidding? All of the time. The people married the longest are the most terrified. In fact, they're so terrified, they find it hard," she stops here for emphasis and laughs lightly, "to even let somebody they've been married to for thirty years get in their pants! That's where I come in!"

She laughs lustily, nudging my leg a little again, assuming I'm enjoying her clowning around with me. "Being a lesbian is very liberating when you think about it. It's just like being a hooker because you're the ultimate secret that everybody knows but acts like they don't. That's why it's a crime when you come out of the closet with either one of these, because it's the supreme exposure. You are *'sex-you-all.'* You know, all at once everybody knows you do it and with whom, maybe everybody! That's what it means to have the label 'lesbian or hooker,' well, in my case, I should say 'and,' because I'm both. Double whammy, you see!" And she laughs at her own coming-out-of-the-closet joke. "We remind people that it's possible to do it with anybody you want to *and* in any way you want *and* as often as you like—that's just terrifying to them. And it doesn't matter if we really aren't doing any of these in actuality. We are the *possibilities* of any or all of them. It's why we're so despised. Sexual freedom, oh, my, oh, my, oh, my! It's sad, but I've found that far, far too many people do it in the dark and only as often as they dare."

She rubs her tattoo and grins. "I'm not out all the time with both of these—you know, being a lesbian and a hooker—and certainly not with everybody. I'm chicken sometimes, but then sometimes I'm not!" She slaps my leg easily. "Guess I'm not too different than anybody else, really, despite all the self-promotion I do."

Roberta leans over and looks up toward the driver. "I'll tell you this, though. It's a challenge waking up in bed with guys and knowing they'd be pissed to the gills if they knew I was the other one too. Gives me incredible distance. Loving women. One of these days I'm gonna quit all this and just tell me like I am, to everybody. Me and Raquel Welch, right?" She's grinning from ear to ear.

Now my mouth is welded shut. I can't open it. My teeth are so tight against each other I think my tongue will never get out. I feel my legs pressing together and my stomach pushing in on my backbone. I know my eyes are bugging out of my head. Or maybe not, because, god knows, I've got them permanently squeezed closed. I don't know if I'll ever open them again. Of course, I don't look at her for fear all this posturing will fall apart and tumble into the space between us.

"Look, kid, I can see you're nervous as a cat," she says. "Don't think about what I'm saying too much. It's just me and my silly curiosity. I do that to people sometimes. Who am I kidding? I do it, well, let's just say, it's what I do. I'm sorry, really I am. But think about this, will you? I'm with you on a bus to wherever." She snaps her fingers. "Oklahoma City, like you say. I'll never see you again. It's one of those incredibly marvelous opportunities, you know, even if it's a cliché. You can say anything to me and you will never feel the consequences of it in any way other than that you told somebody. Telling 'yourself' to somebody, that's how you can think about it." She looks at me and smiles. Her eyes are deepening. I see she is very sincere, down to the core. And she knows very well that I'm the apple she's just bitten into.

"Like a confessional," I say limply, without air.

"More like a fantasy." She smiles easily.

"Like hookers do," I say and feel immediately sorry I have.

"Like hookers do, exactly," she echoes with so much energy and pleasure a little shock run through me.

If speech is breath with sound, as they say, I've run out of words. But I sit there studying my open book I forgot I'm reading while my mind's racing a hundred miles an hour, leaving her hanging out there by herself. I know she isn't going to be gone when I look up, but I'm hoping this just the same. She's going to sit, I just know, right there by my side, all the way through this little bus-ride noir.

―

So just about now, Roberta reaches over and closes my book. Her hands are surprisingly large but soft. Her palm covers the whole face of Sandra Scoppettone on the back cover, her fingers falling over the sides of my book like she's picking up a brick and getting ready to hurl it away. And that's what she does. She picks up my book and tosses it in my duffel bag. Why am I not disturbed? I sit there, a lump, watching her do this. Mainly, I can't decide if what she's done is *to* me or not. I'm in that movie house, and she's waltzed right in and sat down in front of me. I'm paralyzed. When she starts talking again, I look at her and listen as though nothing's happened. First, she laughs, eating some more, points to things out the window, touches my arm and my leg, comments on what she sees as we go along. I hear her. Of course I hear her. She's irresistible. But under all the verve of my side comments and ooohs and ahhhhs, I stay back there on that talk about lesbians. I keep snatching glances at her lips, her chest, her straps-and-heels under the hem of her jeans, like a guy does. What the fuck is the matter with me? But that's exactly it, isn't it?

"How old are you?" she asks, looking at me again, with deep interest. It's as though this question might be some clue for her about how to go on.

Breaking out in a twisted smile, I shake my head back and forth in disbelief.

I don't say anything. Well, of course, I don't say anything. I just look down. She gets the message.

"Oh, I'm sorry. There I go being too pushy again." She flips her hand a little in the air as though she's shaking off the salt left on her fingers from the Cheez-Its. "Putting you off." She puckers her lips briefly as though disgusted with herself.

"No, no," I say, though I'm thinking "yes, yes." I mean, how pushy is too pushy? She took my book and threw it in my bag, what about that? And that's only the last thing she's done. Serious as can be, though, I say, "I always hesitate telling anybody my age, because people usually think I'm younger than I am, and I like that. The minute I tell someone how old I really am, especially anybody younger than me, I can be sure they're getting ready to ask when I'm going to get married and have kids, so I end up telling them I frost my hair *intentionally* to keep them from asking this." She laughs her throaty laugh, and when she offers me Cheez-Its from another plastic bag she pulls out of nowhere, I take a small handful. Is she a representative for the Sunshine Biscuit Company?

But unexplainably, I blather on. "I used to go to the carnival and walk right up to the booth where they guess your age for a stuffed animal. I did that without hesitation for five, six years, because I knew they'd miss, and the signs all say they have to guess within two or three. I've given teddy bears to my niece and nephew and half the neighbors' kids." And we giggle together as Roberta reaches over and lays her hand lightly on my knee, leaving it there while I stumble on idiotically. "But you know what? Since I started getting my hair frosted, they've been guessing my age right on target!" She nods and makes assuring noises in her throat. Her throat is a gift. I'm in love with it.

"The frosting." She takes her hand away in order to toss Cheez-Its in her mouth.

"Frosting?" I'm thinking of icing on cakes, such is the slippery-slide kind of mind I'm possessing by now.

"Yeah, something about trying to make over too naturally what should be done very *artificially*. No, now hear me out." She acts like I'm contesting what she's saying, when I haven't raised an eyebrow. I see her in hotel rooms having these conversations without another soul in the room, well, unless she has a client. She's going on, so I'm back in the flow of her words.

"The carnival guys, well, and everybody else can see the over-consciousness of your attempt to appear natural. You can get away with purple hair, hat and shoes—probably all at the same time—if you feel comfortable with them. I keep this red color in my hair that couldn't, not in a million years be real, but I've worn it so long and feel so totally at home with it that everybody thinks it's naturally me, as unnatural as it is. You see?"

She leans away from me and sizes me up. "I'd say you're, hmmm, thirty-five." She must see the dead-give-away on my face. "How good is that?" she asks, laughing. "Oh, don't get your knickers in a knot. You frosted your hair the minute you saw one gray strand, didntcha? Idea was to zap aging before it zapped you, am I right? I'm going to let you in on something, sweetheart. Rita Hayworth was your age when she made *Miss Sadie Thompson*, you see that movie? In order to get past the censors of the fifties, they had to show her as a steamy nightclub singer with a *past* who hooks—instead of hookers—Aldo Ray."

She laughs a little again. "Let me tell you, not a soul in the theater missed that she was a prostitute and 'steamy' *is* the operative word, woo, woo, woo. Every actor in that movie is dripping with sweat supposedly because of the tropical weather on Oahu or wherever in the heck they were, but for moviegoers, it was Rita Hayworth who was making everybody melt or should I say SM-elt!"

Why hadn't I noticed Roberta's resemblance to Hayworth before? How could I've overlooked the long, flowing red hair, with blond highlights, the pronounced chin, those large brown eyes? Didn't one of Hayworth's lovers say her eyes had green and gold flecks in them, like the ones hypnotizing me now? She's saying in that direct Hayworth way,

"And listen to this. Gloria Swanson and Joan Crawford were half a decade younger when they did their versions, and they look every bit half a decade older by comparison. But now, here's something you don't hear anything about. Francine Everett, the star of the African-American movie version of that story...you probably know it was based on Somerset Maugham's *Rain*." After I nod, and she pauses, she says, "Well, Everett was thirty-one and one sexy bombshell. Her movie came out in 1946, right after the war, so bombshell is the right word. Unfortunately you have to wait the whole damn film before you get to see her strip tease, and then her actor-boyfriend stops it, before she gets to take off more than her gloves—the Gypsy Rose Lee of racy films, I guess you could say!" Roberta raises her eyebrows, her mouth caught between a smile and sneer. She's no bigot. All women of her faith get her blessing.

"Well, all that to tell you, you can be sexy as you want to be at any age, but if you're feeling worried about it, hey, you really only have two choices with your hair, honey—bleach or color like mad. Never hang in the middle. Be Shirley MacLaine as Sweet Charity. Now there's a picture and a *real* sexy dame. It was made in 1969, when Shirley was, here we go again, thirty-five, bingo! Role model for you there." I start shrinking into my seat, pleading with the fabric to smother me whole. Roberta pats her tattoo. "Guess what, Luv! Sweet Charity had a heart tattoo with the letters, C-H-A-R-L-I-E, running on an inked ribbon over it. Uh-huh!" I think, but, of course, don't say aloud, Charlie rhymes with Harley!

"You're a writer, huh?" She changes tracks just like that, as though she's getting a little tired of herself. It almost derails me. Maybe she's tired of me too?

I feel uneasy again, hell, have I felt anything else since I laid eyes on this woman? It's uncanny the things she comes up with, hitting me right where I sink in. All at once, I'm overtaken by a flash of anger, and guess she sees it, because she motions to the leather-bound writing tablet I carry everywhere.

"I have one too," she says, pulling hers out where she's stuffed it by her leg against the other side of her seat. "Bought this after my first trick when I was sixteen. It keeps me sane most of the time. Holds all my thoughts together. I lost it once, but it came back to me. In the mail. I turned a trick in Oklahoma City." She points at me and winks. "Yeah, I've been there before, and he, whoever my trick was, sent it to me. Can you believe that? I had written the post office box number where an aunt of mine collects things for me when I need an address—my hometown. I say 'hometown,' tongue-in-cheek. It's where *she* lives, so it's a place I can point to on a map and tell people, you know, to send stuff there. I drop in on her and get it from time to time."

Does she ride the bus non-stop, I wonder? How and when does she decide to go to her tongue-in-cheek hometown? Tell me she's a rest-stop hooker! She's too fine for this. I'm feeling way, way too much like that preacher in Maugham's story who wants to save Sadie while he's dying to sleep with her. Roberta's found *me* on a bus, hasn't she? So what's my problem?

"I'm not a writer." Panic races through me. "I write. There's a difference. Well, okay, I write on my job, I guess you could say. I teach creative writing in high school along with composition and literature. I sponsor the student literary magazine and every now and then I write a review that makes it in a literary journal." I look at her and surprise myself by saying, "Read me something." And now it's Roberta's time to look uneasy, but she recovers quickly."

"I never get to read out loud to somebody else. This is special. What? Poem? Random thoughts? That's all there is. I mean, that's all I write." She begins to thumb through the pages.

"Your choice," I say.

"Well okay, but then you have to."

"Oh," I whisper, and she laughs again. "Well, okay," I agree, but begin worrying about what I might have in this leather-bound book I carry everywhere. "I don't finish much. I never sell."

"Doesn't matter. Read part of something you have. Here goes me."

Roberta clears her throat and begins, "Oh, this one I like. I read it sometimes out loud to myself like somebody else has written it." Her brown, green-and-gold flecked eyes look at me and she smiles. "Poems are the best when they're read out loud, don't you think? And, you know, we rarely hear them unless we go to a reading of somebody famous somewhere." She clears her throat again. "I call this *Song of Longing*." She pauses, begins:

"I enter now into this
hypnotic trance,
the dance of distant lovers
    lost to others and selves,
        as I sweat out their songs
I give my body
turnings,

    feeling torques, twists down
to wrench
    flight from me.
In this,
I am my own discovery
in shifting sheets,
outer fusion
joys of ritual
the praise of body's own delight.

Move me.
Come, move me now.
Enter into my secret parts and make me holy.
Give my song lifting,
place my soul to the mouth
    of your striving and set me free."

She closes her book as though I'm not there and says, "I lived several years with a woman once. Stayed put and didn't go anywhere, just living with her and loving it. But she had a hard time with our being together, you know, as women in love, so we parted ways, and I met up with Bobby. That's when I got the tattoo, on my travels with him, after living with her. Tattoo-bird's been my companion since Bobby found himself a mate." Roberta pats her upper arm. "She and I had a parakeet. She took Charlie when we separated." *Charlie?* I want to find out more, especially how many times she might have told the MacLaine-Charlie story during her travels, but her voice is shaky. I think she might cry, so I don't ask. She closes her writing book, red nails flashing. "That was one of the poems I wrote while I lived with her." Roberta runs her hand through her hair like that's the end of a scene, and smiles. "What do you think of it, kid?"

I hesitate long enough for her to look over at me, one eyebrow raised. I don't know quite what to tell her. I've critiqued so many poems, yes, even given them grades, my mark left on them like some barcode or sign of the beast!

THE MOST INTANGIBLE THING

I'd give this one a good passing mark. It's a poem in an older style. I can just about see it on the published page, regardless of how she's written it in her notebook. I wonder what poets she's been reading, if she does. What I'd pencil in red, if I were honest, would be that this poem is young, undernourished, self-conscious and brash. But it has the uneven rhythm of many of poets of the sixties, seventies, Robert Creeley comes to mind, the beat generation, the Black Mountain College poets, even a little of William Carlos Williams. But that's the teacher in me. What do I really know of her experience of love in my criticism of rhythm, syntax, line and structure? These academic criticisms haven't ruled her heart and pen as she's written her poem out on paper and read it to me.

"I like it. It was very..." I stumble on the honest word, so I say feebly, "Uh, it's very nice." I look at her and know immediately by the steely flicker in her eyes that she feels slighted. Truth is—I know what I've done all too well—the poem's quality is beside the point. I'm having a hard time dealing with its message, spoken so unabashedly to me by a stranger. The teacher's pencil is there for cover.

Roberta frowns. "Do you know what the word 'nice' means, kiddo? I looked it up after I heard it so often from people during my travels. It means 'dumb,' no, I mean, that literally is what it means. It comes from the Latin word *nescius* meaning 'ignorant' and the French word *nescire* meaning 'not to know.' And from this we've managed to transform this word into a filler expression of *approval*."

I feel my face redden, heat rising, and start to apologize, but she interrupts me. "Now, what did you really think of my poem?" Her voice is not angry but genuinely searching, insistent.

"It's," I begin and decide to give her the word that had initially come to mind when she asked me for my opinion. I stammer out, "highly *sexual*."

Roberta waits, the edge of her mouth curling up a little. That curl says "No kidding!"

Desperately, I add, sighing to myself, "The rhythm is uneven. I'd say almost like...quick sex." I have no idea how I've managed to spew this out, nor where in the dickens it came from. Looking over her shoulder, out the window, I watch the flowing Midwestern landscape as though the dashing phlox and

Indian grass can help me through what I'm about to say. "It begins with a slowly-paced declaration," I say in a subdued but nonetheless instructive tone. "Then it moves into a rapid description of the physical act of sex, followed by a stanza concerning the same thing, this time with lyrical grace, and surprisingly the poem ends in a prayer-like plead to the lover *during* this act of love..."

I have no idea for certain where I'm going with this, pulling it out of a void or my rear end as I go, so I rush on. "The last line pulls the poem together. You've taken what's normally thought to be the spiritual essence of human nature, 'soul,' and put it with what's usually thought to be very unspiritual, the body, especially as it is in sex, and united them." Putting tantric practices aside, I'm thinking this is the most overused idea in all of literary criticism, when she responds with great enthusiasm.

"I like that! That's exactly what I wanted to do. I wasn't consciously thinking to do this when I wrote it, of course, but that's right. Yes, I see now this's what I wanted this poem to do, make people feel. Don't you think our feelings are what drive the creative act? Certainly it's not our heads." She pats my hand, satisfied, rocking back and forth slightly, completely to herself. I wonder what kind of critique she thought I'd give. What I just told her was gloss—it came far too easily from years of analyzing poetry as a form—which is all in my head. I feel like a cad, a worm, in the slang of the movies she watches, a stinker. But it's best, I'm thinking, to let romance ride the trails for now. When she stops rocking, she says, "Your turn."

I am beyond, way beyond, nervous, but I shrug and leaf through the pages. There's more here than I thought, and that gives me a lift. I decide to stop randomly, telling myself that this way the choice is fate—wherever my eyes land, this is going to be the one I *should* read. After all, Roberta is right. She's a woman on a bus I'll never see again. What does it matter?

So I begin, and when I do, I remember how and when I wrote it. "I call this *Phantasmagoria*," I say and she nods. "It has 462 words. I wrote that down here in the margin." I point to the penciled notation as though she has bad eyesight and may need a guide.

Roberta roars. I don't know what's so funny, but after she settles down, I read.

"When she woke up, her skin was transparent. She held up her arm, looked through it to the sliding glass doors and beyond to the front yard and then to the garden. She flew past flesh and sinew to dahlia, heart of flower, to orgasmic *parfum*. She rushed on to where petal folds and pod emerges, where the womb waits until it swells. She arched her belly upward and from between her legs, the bodies and placenta of her four children sprang out onto the earth fully formed.

"She jerked her arm back, wiping her forehead dotted with sweat and dew. Very slowly and carefully she held her arm out in front of her again. She saw past it to the soiled graying carpet and beyond to the cellar steps and on to the ground and the hairy roots, in darkness, bending and twisting their way toward their own ends. Deeper still, she smelled the decay and fermentation of her body. She felt the drying up of her blood and the bread and wine she could no longer eat or drink.

"She brought her arm back, then up and around, swirling her life in circles before her eyes. She ran, pressing her arm, like a magnifying glass, down on her possessions as she leaped around the room, jumping on furniture, touching walls, pictures, the lamp. With each pressure she was carried into such richness of sensation and experience, she fell after several minutes in a swoon. I've died, she thought. I'm spirit, weightless, ethereal. But she wasn't. She was grounded like always, moving on legs and feet, dressed in her usual robe and slippers. When she put her arm next to her side, kept her eyes straight ahead, she saw everything as she had always seen it.

"Then, ever so slowly, she lifted her leg and looked through it to the stove, the fire, the center of its burning. Smoke lifted her up, out the chimney, over the scratching of trees and shriveled leaves, up, up, up in flight, to freedom. Contagion filled her nostrils, passion inflamed her mouth, hooves sped her toward apocalypse. But when she looked down she was seated on the couch, her legs pulled tightly together. Blinders pressed against her eyes, protecting her vision from wind and fire.

"She sat there, arms against her sides, eyes straight ahead, on guard, watching the clock, listening to its compliant regularity. Finally at noon, she stood and, not looking to the left or the right, she walked to the kitchen and made her lunch. Only when she bit down on the tomato and saw through her fingers to the blood flowing in her veins, spilling out over her lips, did she recognize the bitter taste of her life's revenge."

Looking down at my hands, I notice they are trembling. My voice is almost gone by the time I finish, my breath coming out in little gasps, as though I'm about to faint. I realize that I'm crying, in small spasms that become amplified by the steady hum of the engine of this bus rushing down the highway back toward the home of my childhood.

Roberta folds me in her arms, and I weep uncontrollably. She kisses my hair and presses her hands against my back and neck. I feel her nipples through her t-shirt and the fragrance of her hair and her mouth. She kisses me softly on the lips, but I pull away, use the tissue she hands me to rub my eyes.

I don't look at her when I say, "I wrote it when my grandmother died. It just seemed to me, while I watched her being lowered into the ground, that she'd never lived. She took a straight, narrow path, the one before I knew her, even before I was born, but the one that I saw her living throughout my childhood with my grandfather. She was a good woman, especially to me and my brother, but empty… no, that's not exactly right. She wasn't fulfilled, that's what it was. I remember her always in control, never taking any risks, never doing anything in service to herself. Always for others. It seemed to me when I grew old enough to understand that there was some kind of self-contempt in that, maybe. She gave herself away to us and Grandpapa. I often wondered what she thought when she was alone. I've wondered if she ever saw this, the horrible sacrifice, maybe just the awareness of it would be a kind of getting even or back, I'm not sure, though, at whom. Maybe just knowing what she'd done would've been a kind of payback on her own terms?"

Roberta watches me in silence as I wipe my eyes, blow my nose. "Her life was this little cocoon that became dry and brittle, like her body with cancer before she died. It's so sad. I can't bear to think about it, because I never acknowledged what she gave up for me, us, my brother and me, and Grandpapa, and god knows how many others. And I could have because she died when I was in high school. I knew by then. I should've at least told her I cared about her."

Roberta hands me another tissue. "She raised me, if there was any upbringing in it. I didn't live with her exactly, but I stayed with her and Grandpapa a lot, sometimes for weeks, along with my brother who was four years younger than I was. My parents didn't care. They drank themselves to oblivion, both died sick and crazy. And Grandpapa is in a nursing facility, beyond knowing any of us. There's only Dobson now and his family." I sigh, looking up to see the question on her face. "My brother, Dobbs. He played in the minor leagues, Midwest, so we have that together...." Trailing off, I then add sadly, "Baseball." She's looking at me intensely so I end with, "I miss her and wish she could've given herself another life through some desire, passion, or something beyond what she lived."

"You know something about her she probably didn't." Roberta's hand touches my arm. "She probably never told herself what you've just told me, and now that you have, you *have* given her life. If you asked a lot of people what the most intimate thing they can do is, most would say sex. I know, because I've asked. But, you know, it's not. It isn't that sex can't be. It can, of course. But what makes sex intimate or anything else, for that matter, is the sharing of some simple truths, sometimes the giving and taking of even just one significant, honest thing with somebody else. You and I've just done that. And you've done it not just with me but for and *with* your grandmother."

I hold her eyes. I'm too vulnerable, too oddly connected to her. Who is this woman? Anybody I've ever met? Irrationally, I begin searching through all the people I know when I catch myself, realizing the silly desperation of this. She's like me. Yet she's not like me at all—she's wonderfully somebody else. Am I wishful dreaming? Abruptly, a terrible jealousy invades me. Is this what the men tell her after she's given them sex, that she's that one intimate thing? Or, I wonder, does money take care of their intimacy with her?

"Oh look," she says with triumph, pointing out the window. "We're coming into our stop." She leans over close to me but without any great effort to lower her voice, "Do you have an extra ten dollars? I've just run out." Her eyes are on me now, watching my reaction, but before I can answer, she looks away and says, "Just a loan, of course."

"A loan?" It comes out sounding a shade on the side of sarcasm, like we both know better. But she acts like she doesn't hear this, or she really doesn't. I can't tell. So money must take care of it, I think.

"Yeah," she says finally, turning to look at me directly again, with a great smile. "I don't take hand-outs." I don't know if she means payment for the comfort she gave me a moment ago, or she's talking about repaying the loan. But her hand is open between us while she sort of looks out the window. Don't prostitutes usually ask for their money *before* their tricks? Is there more to come? I'm musing over this as I open my wallet. Thank god, I had the wherewithal to keep my purse out of my duffel bag, and I hand her a ten dollar bill from the thin bulge I have there.

"Thanks," she says in an airy whisper as she clamps her fingers around it, pushing it into her pocket. It is a small, automatic gesture that I will find later I can't forget. I will play it over and over in my mind, an instant replay of myself with her. Now, I have to look away, because as she takes it, she stops looking out the window, turns to face me and smiles so sincerely I'm filled with shame, an acute recognition of my needing to ask like this so often. An image forms of a hole that I want to fill, of deep darkness inside that I'm stuffing with all the things other people give. I feel like her fingers I see curling around the money that she's stuffing into her pocket in one stolen movement. I steal for myself like this over and over. I have to ask from others again and again, because I don't seem to know why I'm asking or even what I'm asking for. Was that what I was doing with her a few minutes ago in her arms, asking for one thing but really trying to get another? A chill goes through me. I shudder.

"Are you all right?" Roberta takes my hand in hers. Her touch is hot lead.

I shake myself past it, but I don't take my hand away. "Oh, oh sure. Tired, just tired."

Roberta slips her hand away, and I'm instantly tons lighter. "You can't be tired yet." She runs her hands through her hair, fluffing it out as she stands to walk through the bus to the diner. "Cause if you are, you're going to be dead by the time you get to Oklahoma City!" This is not what I needed to hear, and she must have seen my face, because she laughs with true abandon while she starts down the steps in front of me. The driver looks at us with distant eyes.

"Bus stop in Mentor for forty minutes." He says this over our heads to all the others who aren't there. Then he is gone.

In the Pork and Park Diner Roberta orders an "Xtra-hot" tamale plate with green rice and chili con carne on the side, overlooking altogether the list of BBQs filling the middle section of the menu. It's clear pork isn't the only meat being served up. I'm envisioning a slaughtered cow, half of it ground down to fit onto Roberta's plate!

"Cherry coke. Lots of ice," she says. The waitress doesn't look up but replies, "Well, I would guess!"

Roberta dismisses herself to the lady's room while I skim the heavy menu for something like the dieter's platter. I order a tuna salad on greens with cottage cheese and a Nutra-sweetened Sprite. It was the best I could do.

The waitress slips the pad into her pocket as she gathers up the dirty dishes from the booth next to us and yells at the table while she wipes it dry, "Tammy two with chili-con. Green tuna plate." *Green tuna?* I'm wanting to reorder when I notice the cook looks up long enough for me to see his bushy eyebrows and tiny narrowing eyes sitting close to a nose supporting small round glasses, a white navy cap on his head, brim down all around like there's a torrential rain in the kitchen. He looks like a chipmunk trained by Navy Seals on some island owned by the CIA, a nastier Mel Sharples from the TV show, *Alice*. I think he's disappointed when he doesn't see a man with a double chin sitting next to his skinny-as-a-rail wife. But he resumes his deliberate cooking movements under the window ledge where three dishes of steaming food sit waiting.

The waitress glares at a younger woman in a red-checkered uniform with white apron as she carries glasses through her fingers, water jiggling, toward the kitchen. Nodding at Miss Apron, she shouts, "Red coke with blue and Slim Sprite."

I'm decoding our order given to the cook and waitress when Roberta comes back, slides into the booth and says, "It's so great to find a real john every now and then." She grins. I think ruefully that she could just as well be talking about some trick she's turned, but she clarifies. "The bathroom is cleaner than the kitchen. You ought to use it while you have the chance."

"Thanks, Roberta," I say. But I stay put. "How do you do it?"

"What's that?" she asks cheerfully.

"How do you eat this and not die? I'd be in hell."

"Oh." She laughs. "I blow out the plumbing sometimes, but I must have guts of steel. People say this to me all the time. I don't know. I don't gain weight either. I just stay the same, and I pretty much eat all the time."

"I noticed." I smile back and feel suddenly open and unguarded. She's so gorgeous. I'm wishing I were ten pounds lighter and twenty times smarter when the waitress jerks me out of my day dreaming by slapping down our plates and leaving without a word. She doesn't think either one of us is worth spending a second more of her time.

"Look." Roberta unrolls her napkin and forks out a huge bite of tamale pie. "Other than sex, eating is the one great sin for women, don't you know? We're supposed to eat like birds and do sex in much the same way, nervously and in very small amounts. The people who think like this just don't know very much about birds." She sets down one shovel and picks up another, taking an even bigger portion of the chili. Some oozes from her suspended spoon and plops without grace back into the bowl.

"Most birds," she says before she dips back down and her spoon jams the con carne into her mouth, "eat five times their weight in food every day. And I don't know if you've ever seen a bird or chicken do sex but there's enough flutter to go around for her, and the rooster, and anybody who might be watching." She eats with gusto. I haven't lifted my fork.

"Better pick away, kid." She points her utensil at my plate, then glances at her watch. "Thirty minutes to flight time."

Tasting the cottage cheese, I turn up my nose. While Roberta is laughing she lifts half her tamale pie in the air and puts it on my plate. "Tums-de-Tums-dum," she sings. She then turns her chili bowl over my half of her pie, leaving a trail between our plates that she tries to wipe up with her small napkin.

"Eat," she orders. "Now!" She signals the waitress for more napkins which is ignored, so she marches over to a table nearby, seizes those by four place settings, utensils clattering, and plops the napkins down on our table. "There. Bottoms up!"

The chili and tamale burn all the way down my throat, but the fragrance filling my nose and mouth is sheer joy. I inhale chili powder, cilantro, cumin and garlic before I grab the Sprite and gulp down half a glass. Roberta is beside herself. She claps and laughs and drops her head almost to her plate.

The waitress comes over and to my surprise begins to smile, hands on her hips, a female caricature complementing the cook. I wonder if she has an anchor tattooed on her bicep. Before she can say anything Roberta says, "We want another tamale and chili please, but you gotta hurry or we'll have to leave half of it behind." Surprisingly, the waitress spins on her heels and shouts toward the cook, "Another Tammy two with con." Am I the con sitting next to Tammy-Tell-Me-True? Might this be what the waitress is alluding to? What a strange retro experience this place is. The waitress still loves us, so I'm guessing she's decided to ignore the table Roberta has left in shambles while retrieving our napkins, at least for the present.

"Greta Garbo got her start in a film called *Our Daily Bread*," Roberta begins again as though she's been telling me a story about Hollywood that didn't get finished. "Do you know this?" I shake my head slowly to the left and right.

"Her latest biographer thinks it should've been called *How Not To Eat* because of the director of the film." Roberta takes another bite, chews and swallows, leaving an empty plate ready for her refill. She doesn't drink water. She continues as though I've asked her a test question on old-time films.

"Captain Ring was known for his funny advertising and promotional films that he made for stores and the like. Well, her first with him was called *How Not To Dress*. In it, Garbo's dressed up like she's going to take an automobile ride—you know, like they used to dress, because you could get covered with mud. The cars in those early stages were totally open and had wooden wheels rimmed with rubber. Anyway, her togs disintegrate in this film. She ends up being dressed in a riding habit through a series of dematerializations that Captain Ring was trying to work out on film. Does this sound like a thinly-disguised strip to you, like it does me? I've never seen it." Roberta shakes her head playfully and her hair moves like a tree top in the wind.

"Anyway, because he liked Garbo in that film, Ring used her in his next film for a bakery. She spends the two minutes she's on film eating pastries so fast that some of them fall out of her mouth which she picks up and stuffs right back in again. It was not a ladylike thing to do, but Captain Ring left it in the film, and everybody loved it." Roberta points her fork at me. "Now, there's a star. Oh, is she ever *beautiful*! I use the present tense because she's still alive, but nobody ever sees her. My greatest wish would be to sit for an afternoon and talk with Greta Garbo. She knew how to eat and laugh, right on film for everybody to see. These are the two very best traits in women, I think."

Roberta is staring intensely at me while she lowers her fork, but it's as though she doesn't see me. "Have you ever seen *Queen Christina* or *Grand Hotel*. Or *Ninotchka*? I see *Ninotchka* every chance I get. I went fifty miles out of my way once to go to an artsy-fartsy theater in New York City just to see it again. She's so marvelously alive in this film, despite her stern role as a comrade for the Reds. She laughs when she finally lets go in these great ringing bursts. She was a superior comedienne. When Garbo lights up, she's elegant *and* radiant." I sit there not saying anything, and not eating either, just looking at Roberta, so she asks, "Who's your favorite actress? No, no, don't answer now, you must eat, or you'll not finish before we have to leave."

"Katharine Hepburn," I say, ignoring her instructions to my surprise and surprising myself even more by digging into the leftover mess on my plate.

"Oh, she's a good one." Roberta wipes her mouth with her napkin. "She was a spitfire early in her career. In fact, she starred in a movie by that name, but you probably know that."

I shake my head.

"I guess she started out in Hollywood on the wrong foot altogether, mostly to let that totally male world know she was in charge of her own life and not the studios, like they all owned everybody back then. She came the first day to report to work at RKO in those '40s trousers she always wore off set, still does, even today, and in a rented Hispano-Suiza as a gag. But it turns out that the car she rented was Garbo's in *Grand Hotel*! Even when she wasn't meaning to, Hepburn made connections. That's how it works." When I don't ask 'How does what work?' like I think she's probably expecting me to, she continues. "The producers weren't stupid, but they didn't get what was really going on. They just picked up on it and used it. It's how most people do hookers, too. They don't get it, the real stuff going on. They sense something they don't understand is happening and usually decide to play it or fight against it, because they feel that otherwise they might somehow get taken."

I want to ask her what really is going on with hookers, but then she'd know I was one of the stupid ones. She's talking and eating faster than I can eat and listen.

"Hepburn," she says as though she's her biographer, "usually looked only like herself, but they shot her in those neck back poses from the side with light filtering over her face, exactly like promo shots of Garbo. At least they got that part right. Hepburn was as angular as Garbo, even down to her regular features and graceful walk. As independent, too. Garbo also wore men's clothes, and it didn't escape everybody that she enjoyed saying things movie stars just didn't say, like, 'I like being left alone,' which they misconstrued to mean 'I want to *be* alone.' And she also said that she was not going to marry. In a world where every woman is killing herself to find the right man, not to mention the endless movie scripts of this genre, what in god's name could Garbo be meaning by saying such a thing? Somebody as beautiful as Garbo simply couldn't be queer, heavens! She wrote in one of her letters to a man friend that when they drank together, they would have to have what she called 'bachelor evenings,' because she would always remain a bachelor. Those were her exact words, and she said she couldn't ever see herself as a wife.

"Hepburn was married only once and not for long, five, six years. She's always said she never particularly wanted to be married. Of course there was Spencer Tracy."

Roberta pauses while the waitress brings our second round, then picks up her fork and continues eating *and* talking. "So there were these two very independent women Hollywood didn't know what to do with. So they coupled them. And both of them almost got chewed alive with the bad scripts and press, before they 'found themselves' and outwitted them all. Garbo did it by leaving and dumbfounding everybody. Hepburn did it by leaving and then coming back to a career so great she was nominated for the Academy Award six times in her next ten films."

I don't know what to say. How does Roberta know all this stuff? Does she read while she's having sex? But then maybe she doesn't turn a lot of tricks, just gets paid well, buying books and spending her down time reading. My mind is a whirl. And I don't tell her the truth. Doris Day was my favorite actress when I was in high school. I see her on television these days and inside a feeling still leaps to life when I do. Roberta will think I'm a sap, lusting after the girl next door, so I told her something else.

We take turns eating everything we both ordered. And then she asks for three scoops of ice cream while the driver is drinking his coffee at the counter, talking with one of the waitresses he seems to know from regular stops here.

"Vanilla," she says, "because you gotta have at least one thing during a meal that's bland."

"The last time I ate this much food," I say to Roberta with a laugh, "is when I was a kid and Dobbs and I went to my grandparents' house for Thanksgiving. We stuffed ourselves like animals that were going into hibernation. And the food was incredibly delicious. Now I eat out two, three times a week, and I don't know how to taste something special anymore."

Roberta gets up and sighs. She throws my ten down on the table and I start to put more down for the rest of the check and tip, but note that Roberta's generosity has covered it.

"I never eat anywhere other than out." She smiles. "Listen, kid, you need to just eat and enjoy it regardless. There's no specialness in sacrifice." We both are undoubtedly thinking about my disastrous diet tuna plate. "Just love the food, you know? That's what makes it taste good. Food is good for you. We don't eat, we die. When I eat, I love it, because I'm taking in life."

She straightens her t-shirt and checks her jeans. I notice with amazement once again that her heels are very high. I think of Hayworth and Hepburn and Garbo, yes, and Doris following in tow. The cook watches us leave. I feel his eyes looking past me to Roberta's long flowing frame exiting the door.

The driver sits down and messes with knobs and levers on the dashboard, adjusts his outside mirrors. Once settled, he turns the ignition switch. The slow hum of the bus grows louder, and the air inside rushes through the vents. The cool, stale smell of the air conditioner flows over us as Roberta falls in beside me. I put my head back and Roberta reaches across my lap and pushes a button that lowers my seat.

I lean forward and look at her. She isn't paying much attention to me. She's adjusting her own seat now, falling back and closing her eyes. I still feel her arm across my lap. As the bus takes off into the acceleration lane, she reaches over again, this time taking my hand in hers. "It's okay," she says, "just relax for a minute."

All this touching, and I'm supposed to relax?

My hand rests in hers. I don't seem to be able to move it. I'm paralyzed. I can't simply move my arm and reclaim my own hand. It stays there, my palm resting on her palm, her fingers and thumb holding me in my own lap. My fingers fold around her hand, her lips curling into a faint smile.

"There now!" she whispers as she drifts off to sleep. So I simply sit, moving down the highway on a Trailways bus taking me the long way home while I'm holding hands with this lesbian hooker I just met a few hours ago.

My eyes are closed, but I can't sleep. So I watch Roberta's head sag a bit to one side, her mouth open slightly in a heavy in and out of breath, and I don't know what to do. I think that when she gets far enough into sleep, her hold on me will relax, and I'll be able to place my hand in my own lap, away from her. But as her fingers release me, I don't move. An unexplainable comfort overtakes me, and I realize I don't want to be alone anymore. A rush of conversation fills me up when I close my eyes again. I have this talk with Roberta right there beside me that she can't hear.

"Well, here you are. In my head like always. Oh, yes, I know you, even when I'm lying to us both that I don't. You are the woman who is that bright red blur that burns when I pinch my eyes from that too, too hot image of myself, the one I can't look at in the daytime, the picture of me I carry into dreams so that I don't have to resist it anymore. And there you are the woman in my night who wears black, in the shadows, who lies dark and mysterious under my eyelids while I sleep my life away." I wait and wonder if Roberta will wake up and ask me what I'm thinking, but she doesn't.

"I lived with a woman once too," I tell her silently while she sleeps on. "For seven years. Every weekend she'd go out, and she'd make love with the boys who lived in our home town. She'd come home, sometimes a mess, and I'd gather her up and hold her all night long. We never made love. I lay beside her for seven years under the white knuckles of desire. And I never acknowledged any of my feelings for her to myself. I just did it, because I had to. I couldn't stop myself. In the end, I went out on double dates with her and her boys just so I could be into the hot grasp of her sex, watch her make love while I did, all the while keeping my secret.

One morning she got up and told me she knew what I was doing. She knew what I was. And she didn't want to be around me anymore. She packed in less than a day and was out of my life forever.

"I'm going to wake up after a while, Roberta, and find you gone. I'm going to sleep and in my dream I'm going to watch you disappear into reality." I open my eyes and watch her sleep, feeling this wanting I've known for ever so long.

I close my eyes, once again, and melt into the road and my dreams of her sitting there beside me. When I awaken, my hand is resting in my lap. She is gone just like I thought she would be. The driver is calling me from the front of the bus, telling me I'm at the terminal in Chicago. I throw myself over to search for my duffel bag. It's still there, under Roberta's seat. Everything has been left undisturbed inside, including my book.

—

It was a long ride to Oklahoma City that summer. The bus was filled up with passengers from my connection in Chicago. Somewhere between St. Louis and Tulsa a different driver told us, along with a few other news tidbits, that Zsa Zsa Gabor started her three-day jail sentence in a rented El Segundo jail for slapping a cop. I sighed, then realized with a start that Gabor is an anagram for Garbo. So Roberta lingered still.

After an uneventful visit with my brother and his family, I took an air flight back to Long Island.

When I was going through the mail Alice had left me on my table and Harley was squawking his gladness to see me or his refusal to ever let me go again, I noticed a large faintly purple envelope addressed to me in an evenly spaced flourished hand. Inside was a crisp ten dollar bill. On it was written in indelible ink, "Always tell it like it is, kid, with a big Smile, a big Sigh, and on the big Screen. Roberta." All the "S"s were in capitals. Roberta must've found my address in my appointment book in my duffel bag. But when I searched for it, not remembering if I'd actually taken it with me, I found it in a desk drawer with my writing materials where I always keep it. Now, there was a mystery!

I took another ten dollar bill—I couldn't give up Roberta's—and quite a few others to pay the tattooist for the yellow canary I had inked on my upper left arm the day after I got her note. A ribbon ran under the bird, like Sweet Charity's, only mine had the letters R-O-B-E-R-T-A. I figured if I'm going to blow the whistle on myself, I might as well make it a full rite of passage, the one where I decide to be out there riding the trails, without disguise, enjoying good food, good company and playing my detecting game with everything I can put into it.

Author's Note:
"Magic Words" by Nalungiaq is from *Songs and Stories of the Netsilik Eskimos* by Edward Field. Used by permission of Edward Field.

Cly Boehs (pronounced Klī Bāz) was born and raised in Oklahoma. She taught art on Long Island and in upstate New York, where she has lived in the Finger Lakes area for over thirty years. She has been a member of Zee's writing circles in Ithaca, New York, and various regional writing and art groups including The Georges, T-burg Writer's Group and The 3pm Club and was a playwright, stage and costume designer and participating member of the original theater group, 3rd Floor Productions for nine years. She has exhibited her art and created ritual performances in Oklahoma, Pennsylvania, and New York. She has read her stories publicly for many years, including on television and radio.

She believes that we can be saved by deep conversations, books, and art, while our imagination and wonderment are what really keep us alive.

You can follow all of Cly's writing at *Mind At Play*, **www.cbfiction.blogspot.com**. She always enjoys hearing from readers. If you'd like to drop her a note, you can do so via **clyboehs@gmail.com**.

CPSIA information can be obtained
at www.ICGtesting.com
Printed in the USA
FFHW021203161019
55592180-61414FF